God of War
Ares

Brandon Chen

God of War
Ares

Researched and written by Brandon Chen

For permission requests, please contact:
brandonchen997@gmail.com

Table of Contents

I dedicate this book to my family, who have all had a giant impact on my life and have helped me become who I am today. Thank you for supporting me.

Prologue

On the sandy wasteland of the Lost Sands, three figures stood at the edge of a pitch-black chasm that tore through the center of the earth. The fiery sun beat down its mighty heat upon these immortals, who were unfazed by the Lost Sands' extreme temperatures. The three figures gazed down into the darkness of the abyss before them as if transfixed by the depth of the fissure.

One of these figures was a man with a long, wispy, white beard and a wizened face. He wore a white, sleeveless chiton that revealed the right side of his chest and draped down to just barely above his knees. His blue eyes reflected the color of the sky. He grunted, running his left hand through curly white hair that was as fluffy as the clouds themselves. In his right hand, he gripped a live lightning bolt that cracked and snapped with energy, glowing with silver light. "Mithra, I believe that it was your duty to subdue Ahriman. Why was it that one of my own, Ares, was found slain on the battlefield? It couldn't possibly have been collateral damage."

Another man, wearing golden gleaming armor that glinted with the sun's shining light, stood beside the older immortal. He looked middle-aged, with horns protruding from his bright helmet. He had short, curly, brunette hair, and warm, orange eyes that would only be considered normal amongst deities. "Zeus, your fellow god fled Heaven with hopes that he would find a worthy opponent in the human realm. You and I both know what happens when gods leave Heaven."

"Their strength is reduced and they become mortal," Zeus murmured, understanding. Ares and Zeus were part of the same family of gods, worshipped by the humans in eastern Dastia, a continent on the planet Terrador. Zeus was hailed as the god of the sky and thunder amongst his family and worshippers, while Ares was recognized as the god of barbaric war. "So what happened here?"

"Ahriman tried to increase his own strength above that of any other gods by building an army in the Lost Sands in secret. I was sent as a representative of the Persian pantheon to halt him. But he did not heed my warnings and thus we began to battle. However, Ahriman's strength was far too much for me to handle alone. Ares arrived, hoping to be of some assistance, but even with the two of us, we were easily outdone by Ahriman's dark magic. If you had not struck him down with your thunderbolt, Zeus, I may also have been killed," Mithra said, bowing his head in thanks to the sky god.

Zeus looked at the giant fissure that stretched across the earth before him. It was at least a mile wide and two miles deep, caused by the single thunderbolt that he had thrown. Deep within this abyss laid Ahriman's corpse. If Ares and Mithra had not weakened the dark Persian deity, he might've survived Zeus's mighty thunderbolt. "What are we supposed to do about this now? A god's power never fades. If a human stumbles across Ahriman's corpse and drinks his blood, they will gain the immeasurable power of the fallen Persian god."

Mithra nodded. "I understand that. I will ask for each of the families of gods in Heaven to donate Guardians to help deter any power-hungry humans that come near Ahriman's body. He will be preserved and his strength will be locked away for eternity."

"And what about Ares?" Zeus asked. "Do you intend to do the same thing with him?"

"No," Mithra said, nodding to the third figure, standing behind him. "I believe that he will make the judgment regarding this matter."

Zeus frowned, eying the mysterious figure. He was a shirtless man with tanned skin, wearing a hat made of the carcass of a falcon. Long necklaces of multicolored gems dangled from his neck and rested on his bare chest. He was holding a staff that looked like an ordinary stick in his right hand, jamming it deep into the sand as he eyed Zeus with his mystifying golden eyes with thinly-slitted pupils, similar to those of an eagle. "Ra, I wasn't aware that your pantheon was a part of this quarrel."

"It isn't," Ra said in a deep voice. "However, I am the creator of the Lost Sands, and two corpses of great gods have ended up in my territory." He looked up at the sun and exhaled. "I do not believe it wise to use the same tactics on Ares' power."

"Why is that? If a human got his hands on Ares' strength then—"

"If," Ra interrupted Zeus, causing the god's face to turn red with fury. He was not used to such a lack of respect. "I control the Lost Sands. Those who give in to the temptations of the natural sins of man fall victim to the countless traps that I have fortified in this desert. The Lost Sands punishes those with weak will and ill intentions. I believe that passing on the power of Ares to an infallible human would be wise. After all, why waste Ares' power and leave it sitting there unused for millennia? Why not just pick a chosen hero who will claim his strength? One who is worthy."

"One needs responsibility when wielding the enormous strength of a god," Mithra murmured. "How do you intend to pick a human that has the capacity for such responsibility? How do you know that they won't abuse their strength and wreck havoc upon other humans?"

"I will judge them myself. And, of course, if my chosen champion misuses their magic, then you are free to slay them," Ra said with a small smile. "After all, Ares' strength can be contained. Ahriman's cannot."

Zeus scoffed, looking away. "Do what you want, solar deity. But if your little experiment fails, I will execute the new Ares myself and make sure his strength is locked away forever." He began to walk away from Mithra and Ra, not bothering to look at the other two gods any longer. There was a crackle of lightning as a thundering bolt ripped from the heavens and smashed into Zeus's body, sending surges of vibrant light flashing in the air. In an instant, the god was gone, with nothing but a crater of scorching-hot glass in his place.

Mithra turned to Ra. "I expect that you'll be testing candidates yourself to pass Ares' strength onto, correct?"

Ra smiled slyly. "Of course."

Prince Darien

A succulent slab of meat sizzled loudly on the black stone pan. Oils bubbled around the crispy brown beef, which gleamed with perfection. The king's personal chef, wearing a tall white hat embellished with a red crown insignia, tossed the sizzling pan forward and back. He hummed a small tune as he cooked the king's personal lunch. There were many chefs wearing aprons in the room that were preparing a feast for a casual meal for the royal family of Persia. Though, every single meal was a feast for them.

The head chef adjusted his hat as he took the pan off of the fire, which blazed upon a group of closely clustered stones. He gently scraped the slab of delicately cooked meat onto a glistening golden plate. The chef carefully picked up a silver creamer filled with gleaming hazel-brown sauce. The wonderful aroma of the peppered gravy drifted freely through the packed kitchen and the other cooks smiled at its exquisite scent. The head chef stroked his curly grey mustache as he was about to gently pour the sauce onto the delectable meat. It had to be perfectly done, otherwise the chef would have to toss the food and redo it from scratch.

Suddenly someone bumped into the chef, causing the creamer to fall forward and spill the thick sauce all over the plate and on the table, splattering it haphazardly on the meat. The head chef stared at his creation in absolute horror, his hands trembling with profound rage and frustration. He spun around to see who had bumped into him and frowned, seeing that there was no one there. The cook then heard a dissonance of screams and shrill screeches echoing from his fellow chefs. The head chef spotted two young boys sprinting through the kitchen, playing a friendly game of tag as they chased each other playfully, creating a trail of chaos to everything in their path. "Stop!" the head chef bellowed, his face turning bright red as he continued to yell at the two children, who didn't seem at all intent on stopping.

The boys burst through the door that exited the kitchen, out onto a stone pathway with a crimson-red carpet running along it. One boy tackled the other and they playfully rolled together on the ground, laughing hysterically.

One of the boys propped himself up into a sitting position, tossing his curly blonde hair, revealing cerulean blue eyes that reflected the same color as the open skies on a sunny day. He had full lips, and grinned a bright smile, filled with glistening white teeth. The boy wore expensive blue robes that were draped over his delicately woven white linens. His name was Darien, and he was prince and current heir to the throne of Persia, the most powerful empire in the continent of Dastia.

His friend, named Tetsu Hayashi, was a foreigner to the continent. He had black, spiky hair with sharp bangs that sliced down his forehead, and darkened eyes that gleamed with glee as he beamed at his friend. He wore a black, sleeveless shirt with long, baggy pants.

Normally, Darien wasn't allowed to interact with people like Tetsu. Anyone of a lesser status than nobles was usually not even able to come into contact with someone as important as the prince, unless they were serving him. However, Tetsu was an exception. The boys were only fifteen years old, and Tetsu was already widely renowned throughout the Persian Empire for his expertise with the sword.

Tetsu was born a member of the renowned Hayashi clan, a clan that many considered to be demons in disguise. Most didn't even consider them to be human because their superhuman reflexes and combat skills exceeded those of any other human. Tetsu's small village had been raided and obliterated by another empire when he was younger. His family was slain and he was taken as a slave. He won his freedom within several months by fighting in the arena against other gladiators. The boy was a prodigy with the sword, and had slain hundreds by the time he was in his teens. He then fled the empire as a free boy and came to Persia, offering his services as the king's protector. While it was a long process before Tetsu finally became a member of the Persian king's royal guard, he eventually was assigned to protect Darien. The two, coincidently being the same age, quickly became the best of friends.

"What are you two doing?" a high-pitched, wavering, voice hollered in the hallway.

Darien and Tetsu glanced in the direction of the shaky voice, expecting to get scolded and punished after sprinting straight through the royal kitchen. But they turned to find their other friend, Yuu, standing there. The boy was wearing fancy white linens with golden buttons running down his shirt's center. His black pants drooped down to his snake-hide leather sandals. His abnormally snow-white hair was flat on his head, and he had long bangs that flowed like a stream just above his eyes. His irises were turquoise blue, and tiny tears gleamed in the corners of his eyes.

"Having some fun, Yuu. You should try it sometime," Tetsu sneered.

"Shut up, Tetsu! You know that one step out of line will bring dishonor to my family. I cannot have an atrocity such as that happen! As for you, Darien! D-Don't you think that your father will be angry with you for interrupting the chefs' preparation of the meals? I-I mean, you know Hussan is just doing all of it for your family."

Hussan was the head chef, appointed by Darien's father himself. Darien shrugged. "I guess. But Tetsu dared me to do it."

"Did not!" Tetsu protested.

Suddenly Hussan burst through the door into the hallway, a vein bulging from his forehead as he confronted the three boys. The chef wasn't afraid to get furious around Darien; after all, Hussan had been around since the prince was born. The fact he hadn't been executed throughout his many years of service was a feat in itself. Those who didn't meet the king's expectations were immediately disposed of; that was how things worked in Persia. This meant that Hussan had yet to fail the royal family, and he definitely didn't intend to let them down anytime soon. The chef reached out and grabbed Tetsu and Yuu by their ears, ignoring their squirming. "Listen, you two, I was just about to have the damned meal finished for the king! But you troublemakers screwed it up, so now I have to start all over again!" he boomed at the two boys.

"Ow, ow, ow!" Tetsu yelped, wincing.

"It wasn't me! It wasn't me!" Yuu screeched.

Hussan glared at Darien and sighed. "Milord, what were you thinking?"

Darien shrugged. "Clearly I wasn't."

Hussan released Yuu's ear and used his other hand to smack Tetsu upside the head. "You kids better not come into my kitchen again or cause any more mischief! All I've been hearing is how Tetsu and Prince Darien have been messing around all about the castle. You two have been up to no good recently."

"We haven't been doing any harm to anyone!" Tetsu complained innocently, but Hussan raised an index finger, exhaling his rage from his nose.

"I ought to take a ladle and plug your damned mouth shut so you'll stop talking. You aren't a noble so no one will be able to protect you from my wrath," Hussan growled, clearly showing his distaste toward Tetsu.

"Try it, old man!" Tetsu challenged the cook.

"My, my! Now, I almost thought that we'd get through a whole day without trouble!" A middle-aged man with a long, grizzly, black beard sauntered through the hallway. He wore a long, black robe that draped down to his tiger-hide boots, and a golden necklace rested on his chest. The man smiled through his thick beard. "Hussan, I do apologize for my nephew and his friend's misbehavior. I hope that you can come to forgive the two of them." Darien's uncle, Cambyses, bowed his head lightly to the chef.

Hussan's face paled as white as a ghost. Having a member of the royal family bow like that to him sent a tingling feeling shivering through his body. He swallowed the rock in his throat. "D-Don't worry about it, Lord Cambyses. I'll have the next meal ready as soon as I can. J-Just make sure that these two young boys don't disturb my work again. My job, serving the king the best food in the empire, is already difficult enough. Having interruptions and disturbances makes my profession much harder."

"Of course, Hussan." Cambyses smiled. "I'll make sure these boys are tame by tomorrow so they won't bother you again."

Hussan nodded and disappeared back into the kitchen.

Cambyses turned to Tetsu and Darien and sighed. "What were you two thinking?"

"That's what I asked!" Yuu exclaimed a little too rashly. He blinked, realizing the words he had been thinking had just slipped out of his mouth, and quickly covered his lips with both his hands. "S-Sorry! I didn't mean to answer without being spoken to, milord!"

Cambyses laughed heartily and patted Yuu on the head. "No worries, son. You are the one who maintains stability in this crazy trio. It's a wonder why you hang around these other two, huh?"

"Yuu is too much of a baby to do anything that we do," Tetsu teased.

"A-am not! You guys just do really dumb things that will only get you in trouble! They heed no benefits except thrill and that's not worth getting privileges revoked or a terrible scolding from Hassan and our king!" Yuu retorted.

Tetsu grunted, folding his arms and glancing away. "Stop using big words, you baby."

"You boys should follow Yuu's example. After all, he's widely respected by his peers and is getting top marks on all his tests. He's going to make his family proud of his accomplishments."

Yuu put his hands on his hips and beamed boldly, as if he were some type of a legendary hero. Tetsu quickly put an end to his fantasies by giving him a gentle shove, pushing him off balance.

Cambyses chuckled at the children as they bickered. "Now, now, you two. No fighting. Might you give my nephew and me a moment alone? I would like to speak to him in private. I'll take him to dinner with his Majesty and her Highness, but we will see you two later, yes?"

Tetsu and Yuu exchanged puzzled glances and shrugged. The two of them argued quietly as they walked down the hallway, leaving Cambyses and Darien in silence.

"What is it, uncle?" Darien asked curiously.

"You are the heir to a grand throne," Cambyses began, and saw the prince roll his eyes, prepared for the same annoying speech he knew his father would give him. "Oh, listen to me, my boy. I won't lecture you on how you should act, because I expect that at fifteen years old, you already know what's expected of you as the prince of the largest empire of Dastia. Our prosperous nation is flourishing. It is all thanks to your father's great leadership that our empire is in a better state than it has ever been. But even your father has flaws."

"Flaws, uncle?" Darien repeated, raising his eyebrows. His father was doing something wrong? But how could he be, if the nation was doing so well? The young prince walked beside his uncle down the hallway, past lines of statues that represented ancient Persian kings and ancestors who had long since passed away.

"Your father is greatly opposed to war and is against fighting altogether. However, our empire's military is by far the strongest and largest of all the empires in Dastia. With it, we could easily be consuming other nations and bringing them under our control. We could share our wealth with the rest of the continent by making them a part of us." Cambyses sighed. "I believe that an ideal dream would be to unite the entirety of the continent, so that everyone would be able to live in our wealthy nation and have the same opportunities that all of us do. However, such a dream would require several years, or perhaps decades, of sacrifice. My brother does not have the heart to sacrifice what is necessary for the better of our nation and all of Dastia. What do you think?"

Darien stared forward, thinking hard on the subject. "I believe that the whole idea of having one united, peaceful nation without conflict is great. Then people wouldn't have to suffer like Tetsu did. But the path that you're suggesting is going to bring about several decades of war where many would suffer. It would be causing the same pain that we're seeking to prevent. If I were to make a decision, I would search for a solution that results in a united continent without having to resort to war."

Cambyses sighed and smiled. "You truly are your father's son. The two of you do think alike. But it is that kindheartedness that might be your downfall one day. Make sure you keep your eyes open. You never know who might take advantage of your weaknesses, my boy." He placed his hand on Darien's shoulder, and nodded to two Persian soldiers that stood at the end of the hallway.

The guards, wearing black cloaks and sheathed scimitars,

elegantly pushed open the door at the end of the corridor for the two oncoming members of the royal family.

Darien walked through the large doors with his uncle following close behind, into a gigantic feasting room. There was a long table that ran through the center of the room, blanketed by a large white cloth. There were dozens of seats on both sides of the table but the only occupied seats were on the far side of the table where Darien's father and mother sat. The king sat at the head of the table with the queen on his right.

The king had curly brown hair, sapphire blue eyes, and a grizzly brown beard. A small golden crown sat upon his head. He wore rich robes of crimson that draped down to his ankles. Dangling from both his ears were large sapphire rings that jabbed through his tender lobes. Golden necklaces embedded with assorted colored gems shone around his neck, though most of them were hidden underneath his beard. His fingers all wielded rings that were made of gold and embedded with diamonds, making his hand gleam like starlight. He was middle-aged, and was a bit chunky from all the exotic foods that he stuffed himself with every day. But he could afford to. After all, the country was flourishing because of him. Why wouldn't he treat himself to the greatest delicacies in the continent?

The queen had long, blonde hair that draped down past her neck. She had a small golden crown as well, and wore a lengthy blue dress that touched the carpeted ground. A necklace of shining pearls curled around her neck and drooped near the top of her breasts. She pursed her thick lips together as she addressed Darien with a slight nod.

"Remember, not a word of our conversation to anyone but us," Cambyses whispered to Darien. The uncle walked over to his seat beside the queen, nodding to a servant who pulled out a chair for him.

Darien sat on his father's left, spreading a napkin gracefully over his lap.

"The food is taking a lot longer than usual," his father murmured. "I heard that there was some trouble in the kitchen. There's been a lot of mischief going around lately, hm, Darien?"

"Y-Yes, father."

"And would you happen to know anything about why Hassan is delaying the meal by several minutes today?" His father's unwavering stare bore straight into Darien's soul. The prince refused to meet the king's eyes as he spoke.

"No."

"I don't like when you lie to me, son." His father sighed. "When it is finally my time, Darien, you will need to gain the peoples' trust. For this country to prosper, the people are going to need to be able to believe you. They'll look to you to solve their problems, and will revolt and protest when you don't. You need to be ready to make the right decisions when it's finally your time to take the throne and…."

"I understand," Darien murmured, looking to see Hassan and several other chefs come out of the kitchen with platters of steaming hot food in their hands. They set down several superb dishes that gave off delicious aromas that made Darien's mouth water.

"I apologize for my son's disturbance in your kitchen, Hassan." The king gave his favorite chef a friendly nod.

"It's alright, milord. It only took a moment longer to make another meal for you. I do hope you enjoy it," Hassan said, bowing with his entire body.

The king smiled warmly. "You prepared delicious beef with your infamous sauce. Why, it's my favorite. Of course, I'll enjoy it."

Hassan stood up and beamed proudly before promptly returning to the kitchen with his staff.

Darien and his family enjoyed a silent dinner. The prince could tell that his father wasn't so much annoyed by Darien's mischievous behavior as he was irritated by the prince's blatant lie. The king burned Darien with a few powerful glares that made him tremble, but thankfully, there was no other punishment. It felt like lengthy hours before he was finally released from the torturous confinement that was the dinner table. In reality, it was probably less than thirty minutes.

Patting his bloated, full belly, the prince stormed through the castle's many hallways. An amalgam of thoughts exploded through his head, but one emotion stood out from the various thoughts that conquered his mind. Anger. Why was it that he had to worry so much about being king? Was a single lie going to set the entire Persian Empire crumbling? *Trust. The people need to trust me, huh?* Darien narrowed his eyes as he trudged forward through the hallway, past several servants who were dusting the windows. His father was still relatively young for a king, and would rule for many decades before it was finally his time. So why did they keep saying that Darien was going to have to prepare himself so soon? He was only fifteen. He didn't even want to *think* about having such a responsibility. In fact, he didn't even want to be king.

Being king meant that all the freedom he currently had would vanish in an instant. His free time would be replaced with work, analysis, and deep thinking on how to better the nation. Darien knew from watching his father work day and night to solve the empire's issues that there was never a moment of rest for a good king. He even noticed that the king had begun to grow a few grey hairs as a result of the immeasurable amount of stress that he endured every day. Darien didn't want to endure such hardship, and he knew that he would never live up to the incredible legacy that his father was leaving behind.

Leaning up against the sandy brick walls of the castle, Darien sighed heavily as he looked through one of the tinted windows. He moved to the window and pushed it open, the view becoming clear as the glass panes vanished from his line of sight. The prince gazed through the opening at the grand city of Persepolis, the capital of the Persian Empire. The king's castle sat upon a hill that overlooked the rest of the city, letting everyone know that they were of lesser status than those who lived in the castle. The king also kept his close advisors, friends, fellow nobles, and important workers living in the castle with the royal family, for he believed in keeping close to his allies.

Stretching across the city were thousands of homes made of brick, stone, solidified mud, and marble, creating a vast variety of buildings and architecture in the city. Some buildings had flat roofs, while others had dome shaped ones made of smelted bronze that gleamed in the descending sun's light. Torches were being lit, preparing for the oncoming night, and Darien watched as the sun begin to vanish over the horizon, releasing its last dazzling surges of warm light into the sky.

Staring past Persepolis and the city's grand, towering walls, Darien saw the endless wasteland in the distance, just outside of the city. Those were the Lost Sands, a forsaken desert. There was no information regarding what the Lost Sands was like, because no one had ever entered it and come out alive. Supposedly, the desert spanned three hundred miles wide and three hundred miles long, but that was only an estimate. It was said that creatures of ancient lore and mythology, that would slaughter any intruder, existed within those dangerous lands. There were also rumors that said that the desert itself was alive and could deceive any journeyers that ventured into the Lost Sands. Darien was almost positive that within that perilous desert, there were priceless treasures. That was why explorers kept disappearing into the Lost Sands, never to return.

Darien sighed. No one had ever seen any of the creatures from the Lost Sands so no one actually knew if they existed. Now, sending criminals to the Lost Sands had become a form of execution. Rather, the king claimed that it was merely "banishment." But the exiles that were forced out of Persia were tossed in the Lost Sands, doomed to their ultimate demise. The prince, however, was interested in seeing some of the creatures that he had read about in tales. Pharaohs, Sphinxes, Core-Diggers, undead mummies, and many more were rumored to plague those lands. If they did exist, the prince hoped that he would be able to see them someday. Without dying, that is.

"And here we have a royal prince, dramatically staring in deep thought at the grand empire that he will soon rule!" Tetsu mocked in a deep tone, surprising Darien by jumping from behind and wrapping his arm around the prince's shoulder with a friendly grin. "What's got you in such a grim mood, Darien?"

"Yeah, is everything alright?" Yuu asked, stepping to Darien's side.

"Of course everything's alright," Darien murmured. "It's just, you know, all this talk about becoming king and preparing to rule the empire already. My father isn't going anywhere soon so I don't know why everyone's hyping me up for the throne. I don't know the first thing about leading a country, and no matter how much I study the economics of the empire, the agriculture, and the military strategies that I'll need to know when I'm a leader, I don't think I'll ever be ready. That type of responsibility … it's way too much for me to handle." He ran a hand through his hair and exhaled. "Man, look at me. I'm a mess."

Tetsu gave Darien's shoulder a good squeeze. "Hey, man. Don't sweat it. If there's ever a problem, I'll always be here to steer you in the right direction. And I'm sure the nerd, Yuu, will be here to toss you some advice too, right?" he called to the noble.

Yuu's face reddened. "I-I'm not a nerd!"

"You're a nerd."

"Then you're a brute!"

Tetsu laughed. "And I don't mind that at all!"

"Seriously, Darien. There's nothing for you to worry about. We're going to be here to help you out when you need it." Yuu smiled reassuringly. "I mean, we're your best friends. Obviously we're not going to let you shoulder the throne's responsibilities by yourself! We'll do whatever we can to help. But that'll probably be really far in the future anyway. I'm sure your father is just preparing you to give you a head start. I mean, if you have the whole ruler mindset early on, in a decade you'll be more than ready for the throne. Right?"

"I guess…."

"Man, what's with all this depressing talk! Let's go do something fun! Want to go pull a prank on Yuu's older brother?" Tetsu guffawed.

"N-No! Don't do that!"

Darien looked between his two good friends and laughed. *Man, I wish things could just stay like this forever. With the three of us, happy, together, and free.*

Betrayal

The next day, Darien adventured through the streets of Persepolis with several guards escorting him, along with Tetsu, Yuu, and Cambyses. The three boys walked through the prosperous streets, marveling at how populated the city was. There were people walking everywhere, and exotic animals that Darien found fascinating were being led throughout the city. Creatures like giraffes and monkeys were scampering about underneath the supervision of their owners.

Darien had a ruby-red scarf tightly curled around his neck, and he wore a golden, short-sleeved shirt of fine linen along with silver shorts. A civilian showed Darien his camel, which was the goofiest animal that the prince had ever seen. The prince personally found the camel's humps outstandingly amusing, though he wasn't sure why. He patted the animal's snout but the creature returned his ecstatic gaze with an apathetic stare.

"Hey, Darien! Look at this!" Yuu exclaimed, pointing to a street performer who was tossing flaming torches through the air. At the same time, he was somehow spewing a jet of fire from his mouth like a dragon. Groups of lower-class civilians, wearing slightly tattered clothing, were cheering in awe at the performer's rare talents.

Darien's attention diverted from the exotic camel to the gifted street performer. "Say, uncle, how does he shoot fire from his mouth like that? Surely that can't be real."

"Oh, but it is," Cambyses said. "It's magic."

"Magic, such a thing must be myth. It's told in stories for children, nothing more," Darien said, unconvinced.

"Nope," Tetsu said. "You'd actually be surprised at how many people have somehow obtained magical powers. Don't ask me how they do it, but there are plenty of people who have it. You can tell that this guy has magic. The way he breathes fire out, it's being conjured from inside his throat. He's creating the flames. I mean, that's impressive enough but people don't seem to really notice. They just see his juggling and how he's spitting out fire like a circus act. He should be using that magic to serve a better purpose."

Cambyses nodded. "You should already know that your father has a mage who answers directly to him. Powerful mages who have absolute control over their magic are known to work for kings of nations. They're called Magi. Your father has a personal Magus that fulfills his wishes. And that mage will work for you when you take the throne."

"Huh," Darien muttered, watching the fire performer for a moment longer before moving onward. He had heard of Magi, but he had always thought that they were just religious leaders, not sorcerers. He couldn't believe that magic actually existed.

His party eventually stumbled across a group of lower-class civilians who were bowing and praying to a stone statue of one of the Persian gods. The statue had the head of a dog and the body of a man. Hundreds of copper coins were tossed into a fountain underneath the statue as tribute. The currency gleamed from underneath the calm fountain waters. Darien looked at the supposed deity with an emotionless gaze. He pitifully watched as several citizens bowed to the statue, pressing their foreheads to the ground. *Groveling in the dirt before a statue. How foolish.*

Darien's face twisted into an annoyed scowl. Personally, he didn't believe in gods. He thought that it was absurd that there was even the idea of a powerful deity floating somewhere in the universe amongst the stars. The gods never showed themselves and nothing proved that they existed, so what reason did Darien have to believe in their existence? And here these people were, humiliating themselves for the sake of praying to something that they didn't even know existed. Darien just didn't understand how people could put all of their faith, all of their hope, in something they'd never seen.

The prince suddenly spotted several tanned slaves, all collaborating to carry a large plank of wood, trudging past the statue. It was clear that they were drained of energy from the way they dragged their feet across the dirt. They were so skinny that it looked their stomachs were actually caving into their bodies and their ribcages were clearly visible. Darien stared at the starved men with shock as they slowly dragged themselves past the prince and his party. "Why are they so starved? Do their overseers not feed them?" the prince asked his uncle.

"Slaves are not treated as human in our empire. Surely you know that," Cambyses said, almost frowning at Darien. "They are the same as working animals."

Darien watched as one of the slaves tripped and fell over, causing the wooden plank to clatter to the ground. Several of the well-clothed civilians that walked by glanced at the struggling slaves in disgust. The prince could see the distaste in their eyes, which were dark as a blackened void.

A shirtless man stormed forward in annoyance, dragging a whip across the sandy earth. The man's body was tanned to a crispy brown after so many days in the hot sun and his lack of shirt exposed his rippling muscles, which bulged so much that he looked like a walking hunk of meat. This was clearly the overseer, one of the men who watched over the slaves. The overseer raised his whip and snapped it down on one of the weak slaves, flaying the man's flesh with a relentless crack. Blood splattered onto the ground as the sharp whip rent deep into the slave's back. The laborer cried out in agony as he collapsed forward onto his hands and knees, his jaw clenched tight as tears streamed down his dirt-caked cheeks.

"Please, spare me! I-I'm tired! It's hot and I just need some water! Please!" the slave pleaded, but the whip slapped down onto his back once more, creating yet another slash mark ripping across his scarred back. More screaming. More pain. Yet civilians just walked past as if nothing was happening. This was just another common occurrence to them.

Darien was about to step forward and order the man to stop harming the slave, but Cambyses held out his hand, halting the prince. "This is the natural order of things in our empire, Darien. In order to maintain prosperity, we must sacrifice the freedoms of a few to benefit the majority. That is how it has been and always will be. You should not interfere in such traditions."

There was a grunt and Cambyses turned to see that the overseer had been knocked back to the ground. Standing over him was Tetsu, and he was absolutely furious. The boy gripped the limp whip in his hand and gazed down on the overseer, who was now unarmed. "I don't think you know what it's like to be in their shoes," the boy snarled, raising the weapon into the air. "Do you know what it's like? To feel the hissing whip crack across your flesh and scar you so bad that it marks you up just like a bloody painting. I don't think you know what it's like, otherwise I think you'd be more merciful. Maybe I should teach you a lesson, huh?"

"No! I'm just doing my job! Please! I work for Master Shazir! Don't harm me!" the overseer pleaded, cringing in fear before the whip. "I beg of you!"

Tetsu swung the weapon downward, the whip slapping against the sand inches away from the overseer's face. He rolled his eyes and dropped the weapon onto the dirt, ambling away from the powerless man. "Next time you decide to punish someone, make sure that you put yourself in their shoes first and decide if it's fair."

The overseer gripped the hilt of his whip, pushing himself onto his feet. The color had returned to his face and he smiled nefariously. "Life ain't fair, kid."

Tetsu spun around, his eyes bulging with rage, and was about to tear the man apart when several of Darien's soldiers rushed forward and yanked the boy back.

"Tetsu must control his temper when he witnesses mistreatment of slaves," Cambyses said. "I can understand where his frustration originates. It is unfair and unfortunate, my prince. But, as the overseer said, many things in life aren't fair. At least we are able to make many happy with the services that servants and slaves provide us."

Darien watched as Yuu comforted Tetsu by patting the boy on the shoulder and agreeing that the overseer was a prick. The prince sighed. Despite the logical reasoning his uncle had given him, he did not agree with slavery or the horrific mistreatment of the workers. After all, it already seemed like they were being worked to death and their vigorous labor came with absolutely no compensation except pain and misery. "I want to go home," the prince said.

***

The next day, Tetsu mindlessly roamed through the halls of the grand castle of Persepolis. Usually he didn't get terribly upset over something that was out of his control, such as slavery. But for some reason, he couldn't get the image of the permanent scars on those slaves out of his mind. The memories of his own enslavement clung to him as tightly as his own skin. No matter how much he wanted to shake away those torturous memories, they relentlessly haunted him and it was impossible to get rid of them. Seeing those slaves get mistreated the day before only brought back the recollection of his harsh past.

Yuu had tried to convince him that there was nothing wrong with slavery and that social hierarchy was natural in flourishing nations. But Tetsu didn't like the idea that people were being treated like animals and burdened with the hardships of a nation while a group of rich nobles gobbled away at delicious foods and enjoyed their endless sea of fancy treasures.

Tetsu wondered what Darien thought of slavery. He lowered his eyes and suddenly heard a bumping sound. He halted in the middle of a silent corridor and turned his head. The noise had come from a small doorway where a pair of stone stairs led down to the Royal Jail of Persepolis. The boy reached to his side, skimming the tip of his index finger along the rough grip of the hilt of his sheathed sword. Narrowing his eyes, he began to slowly creep towards the Royal Jail's entrance.

Ordinarily there were three guards stationed at this entrance, making sure that no one entered the Royal Jail without authorization. But right now there was no one. The ominous silence that lingered in the jail made Tetsu uneasy, and the thumping sound that he had heard only put him more on edge. It had sounded like something hitting the ground.

Discarding his previous thoughts of slavery, Tetsu descended the stone stairway into the Royal Jail, darkness curling around him and locking him in a world of blackness. After several seconds of diving through oblivion, Tetsu spotted tiny flickers of light from lit sconces illuminating the darkness. Shadows receded from a moving light and Tetsu immediately knew that someone was moving there. Freezing completely, he curled his hand around the hilt of his sword, perfectly prepared to strike out at whoever was intruding.

"This scepter really is something." The voice shattered the silence and echoed through the entire room. Cambyses? "Where did you get it?"

Tetsu exhaled, relieved. There was no intruder. This was only Darien's uncle, the king's royal advisor. He began to descend the last final steps and saw that Cambyses was indeed standing in a long hallway, with his back to Tetsu. He held a lit torch in his hands, with his red cape cascading down his back and onto the floor.

The floor was made of coarse, stone tiles. They looked loose and beaten, as if someone had taken a hammer and bashed each individual tile in the hallway. On both sides of the corridor were iron doors that led into individual empty cells, filled with nothing but darkness so thick that Tetsu's eyes couldn't penetrate the cloudy mist of blackness that surrounded the silent rooms. Tetsu looked down at the ground and his eyes widened, noticing that a ghostly-white hand was limp on the stone floor, smeared with blood. A body.

Tetsu's throat tightened and he hastily slunk back up the stairs, away from Cambyses's possible line-of-sight. His heart was pounding rapidly against his chest, so hard that he swore that he could hear his own heartbeat. Sweat had formed on his brow as heat surged through every inch of his body, making him feel as though it was a hundred degrees. He tugged at the collar of his shirt and gulped silently. Why was there a dead body down there? Cambyses clearly seemed to disregard it. Could he be responsible for the corpse?

"The scepter is an artifact from Ahriman himself," a mysterious voice spoke suddenly and Tetsu frowned. He recognized this voice from somewhere. It was Zahir, the Magus who worked for the king. This was the strongest mage in all of Persia! "It was knocked out of his hands when the great god of darkness was defeated. This argonaut had it in his possession," he said. There was a shivering whimper that crept from the lips of yet another person, someone who was clearly terrified. "He's the first person to have survived a journey across the Lost Sands."

"So he's from eastern Dastia? Why, a journey there would take us months. If we even survived that long," Cambyses said. "So then, adventurer, tell us. What's it like over there?"

"C-Completely different, sir," a man's shaky voice croaked out. He clearly was scared for his life and the strain in his voice seemed to indicate that Zahir and Cambyses had already harmed him. "We have different gods, different cultures, different architectures, and technologies; everything is different."

"Different gods, huh?" Cambyses said, amused. "If so many cultures each believe in a different pantheon then how is it possible for them all to exist? This scepter is proof that our gods are real. Ahriman, the Persian god of darkness, wielded this scepter in our ancient texts that span centuries." There was a choking sound. "Your gods are not real."

"B-But they are! I saw them! In the Lost Sands … they were with your gods as well…!"

"Our gods?" Cambyses frowned. "What do you mean?"

"Ahriman … he battled another god in the Lost Sands. He killed one of the gods that we worship in eastern Dastia; his name is Ares. He was slain in the desert but another Persian god defeated Ahriman, who was weakened. He … he called himself Mithra."

Zahir burst out laughing, his guffawing echoing off the silent walls of the Royal Jail. "One of your gods battled against our Persian god of darkness. Then out of nowhere, our god of war, sun, and justice appears miraculously to defeat Ahriman. Yet you, an inept weakling, managed to survive their legendary battle and flit away with this powerful scepter. Now that is indeed a tale, adventurer." There was a snap and a body crumpled loudly to the ground. Tetsu placed a hand over his mouth, wincing. He exhaled slowly from his nose.

"We could've gotten more information on what's out there in the Lost Sands. Why the hell would you just kill him?" Cambyses boomed, shaking his head in annoyance. "The adventurer must've had secrets regarding how he journeyed across the wasteland and survived."

"Who cares?" Zahir smirked. "After all, we have Ahriman's scepter. With this almighty power I can make anyone bend to my will. Its legendary strength is mine to control now." He spoke now in a lower tone, dropping to barely even a whisper. "Now we can bring an end to this foolish king's reign and bring about the Persian Empire that you've always envisioned."

Tetsu's eyes widened and he began to retreat several steps backward. They were planning on getting rid of the king? With this new weapon that they had obtained, surely they would use its power to assassinate the Persian lord. *I have to get the hell out of here.* He staggered up the stone stairway and tripped suddenly, cursing as he hit the hard stairs. *Now's not the time to be clumsy!*

Cambyses and Zahir stopped talking, turning their attention to the stairway. "It seems that we have an eavesdropper," Cambyses murmured. "Kill him."

Tetsu saw a bright light reflect off of the stone walls of the stairway, vanquishing the shadows. The boy grunted, scrambling up the stairs as fast as he could, throwing himself out into the corridor. From the stairway behind him came a burst of fire that surged out into the hallway before flickering away. Tetsu clambered to his feet and sprinted down the corridor, his breath heavy. He heard someone dashing up the stairs behind him but he had already thrown himself around the corner, hoping that Zahir and Cambyses hadn't seen his face.

Tetsu pumped his arms as he raced through the hallways of the castle, his heart racing rapidly. His eyes darted left and right, completely alert and ready for any magic that Zahir might cast in order to catch him. But nothing came. He bit his lower lip, knowing exactly what he had to do. He had to warn someone. But who? He couldn't just go to the king without being summoned. He had to tell Darien first. Yes, Darien would believe him.

***

Cambyses climbed slowly up the singed stairway of the Royal Jail and out into the silent hallway of the castle. His bloodied hands were tucked into the long sleeves of his expensive garment. He turned his head and saw that Zahir was standing there at the end of the hallway, gripping Ahriman's scepter in his hands. "Did you see who our intruder was?"

"It was the young prince's little minion. The tiny bodyguard," Zahir muttered. The man had long strings of dark hair that reached down the back of his head to the base of his neck. His bangs were messy and came down over his eyes, which glowed an ominous purple. His ears were hidden behind the layers of his stringy hair and he wore a black cloak that was wrapped tightly around his body, buttoned up at the front. The whole outfit looked like a hooded dress for males.

"Then dispatch him."

"No," Zahir said with a sly smile. "I have a better idea. Allow for us to blame this entire conversation on Tetsu. We'll say that he's the one who's after the king's head. After all, who would the king believe? An ex-slave, or his brother?"

***

"What do you mean you don't believe me?" Tetsu exclaimed, pulling his spiky hair in frustration as he argued with Darien, who was folding his arms.

The two were standing in the Royal Library, where there were thousands of texts written on scrolls. These scrolls were rolled up and organized upon hundreds of shelves. Each shelf had a different category that was defined by the type of wood the shelf was made of. Overall, the library was just confusing, which was why Tetsu never came in here. The reason Darien was here, however, was because he had to read a certain amount of scrolls a day and absorb all the information that he read. It was said that by the time the prince became king, he would have to retain all of the information in the Royal Library. Or at least try.

"You know that I don't believe in the gods," Darien murmured, looking at Tetsu with a worried look. "So what if my father's Magus has some sort of scepter that he claims is from a god? They say that about plenty of treasures. And how am I supposed to believe that Cambyses is out to get my dad? The two of them are brothers for heaven's sake! Why would a man kill his brother?"

"Power," Yuu said, sitting in a wooden chair, reading a scroll while listening to his two friends bicker. When the two boys looked at the noble, he glanced up at them. "Well, it's been seen through history that some humans would do anything to obtain power.

Whether it's condemning an entire nation to oblivion, slaughtering a family member, initiating genocide, it doesn't matter. Power corrupts. Tetsu is suggesting that your uncle is misled."

Darien put his hands on his hips, irritated as he looked at Yuu. "And? Do you agree with Tetsu?"

"I wasn't there. I don't know if it's true," Yuu said silently. "B-But I don't know why Tetsu would lie about something as important as this."

Darien didn't respond. Yuu was right. This was big, and if Tetsu was lying about something messed up like this, it could result in his execution. But why would Cambyses let something like power get to his head like that?

The door of the library suddenly swung open and a dozen soldiers swept into the gigantic room, their weapons brandished as they stormed towards Tetsu. They halted before the boy, pointing their swords at him. "By order of the king, Tetsu has been condemned to death for treason. Come quietly and your execution will be swift."

"Treason?" Tetsu exclaimed. "That makes no sense! I've done nothing!"

Darien stepped between Tetsu and the soldiers, causing the Persian guards to flinch. The sight of their prince made them lower their swords, but they kept their hostile gazes trained on Tetsu. "It would seem that you were at the wrong place at the wrong time, Tetsu. I believe you." He held out his hands and all of the guards dropped to their knees, bowing before their prince. "Disregard my father's words! Tetsu is under my protection. If you want to execute him, you'll have to get through me first!"

Tetsu relaxed, looking at Darien with twinkling eyes. The prince was willing to put his own life on the line to protect him? One from the slums, an ex-slave. His life wasn't worth nearly as much as Darien's. But the prince didn't seem to care. For him, there was no price on a life. Tetsu smiled. If only everyone in this world was like Darien.

"D-Darien!" Yuu exclaimed, sitting up from the table. His eyes were wide and he pointed to a man who was across the room, standing next to a shelf of scrolls. The man was drawing back the string on a wooden bow, a nocked arrow aimed straight for the defenseless prince. "Watch out!"

Tetsu tore his sword from his sheath, the blade hissing as it whistled into the air. The arrow shot from the archer's bow with a muffled twang and the projectile pierced the air, moving towards Persia's beloved prince. The innocent boy stood with his gaping mouth and wide eyes as the spiraling arrow raced for his heart. Tetsu suddenly shoved Darien to the side and took the prince's place, using his incredible reflexes to smash his sword against the shaft of the arrow. It exploded into a hundred pieces of wood, the metallic head and fletching clattering to the ground.

The soldiers seemed to have expected the arrow to dispatch the prince immediately. But sly smiles spread across the warriors' lips and they all unsheathed their weapons, wildly charging straight for Tetsu and Darien like a pack of hungry hyenas.

Tetsu grunted, clenching his teeth tightly. These guys were in on the whole operation, weren't they? He gripped the hilt of his sword tightly and whipped his blade in perfect slashes, hacking the men apart by the dozens. The soldiers were in a complete frenzy. They lacked grace and were utterly brutal with their offensive strikes. Tetsu expected more from the Persian guard. They were acting very oddly, as if all of their training had been sapped away and replaced with maniacal survival instinct. It didn't take very long before the soldiers that had entered the library now lay in bloody heaps around Tetsu. Little did he notice the small wisps of black magic streaming from the lips of the fallen warriors.

The boy panted, perspiration pouring down his face. His black shirt was sopping wet from the heat of battle, yet his expression was cold as ice. He looked down at the corpses that stacked up around him and the puddles of blood that were forming rivers through the library. He reached into his pocket and pulled out a white, clean cloth. Tetsu wiped the crimson-red blood from the sharp blade of his sword, staring at his weapon so he wouldn't have to gaze upon the corpses of the men he had just slain.

"T-T-This is insane!" Yuu stammered, grabbing his head as he stared at the cadavers that were scattered all around him. He was hiding underneath the wooden table, his lips quivering with fear. His hands trembled and he was shivering as if he were in frozen tundra. "Y-You just killed all of those soldiers...."

"What else was I supposed to do?" Tetsu barked, turning to face Yuu. He threw his bloody cloth onto the ground in frustration and jammed his sword back into its sheath. Sorrow was reflected in his dark eyes. "They tried to assassinate Darien! These guys are the real traitors. Something crazy is going on right now and we need to get the prince to safety. Then I'll confront Cambyses and handle things."

"No, I'll go with you," Darien said.

"It's dangerous, Darien. You guys shouldn't get involved."

"Shut up," Darien murmured, reaching to pull a dagger from his belt. He twirled the small weapon in his hand and exhaled. "We'll do whatever we can to help. I'm not letting you go through this alone."

"Don't be an idiot. What are you going to do with that toothpick of yours?" Tetsu grumbled and turned to Yuu. "Hey, coward! You need to get up; we've got to get out of here before more guards come."

"W-Where are we going to go?" Yuu whimpered, rocking forward and backward with his knees drawn close to his chest. He was squeezing his skull and his face was so red that it looked like his head was going to pop like a balloon. "I-I … I don't want to die!"

Tetsu stormed over to Yuu and smacked the table over, grabbing the coward by the collar of his shirt, yanking him to his feet. "Open your eyes, already! If you stay here then you *will* die!" He turned, and his eyes locked onto a dead librarian wearing a long, white robe, slain in the battle. "Plenty of innocent people are getting caught up in this craziness, I'm sure. I'll get the two of you somewhere safe. We need to check on the king first, though." He released Yuu and began to step over the dead Persians as he rushed to the exit of the library.

Darien shuddered as he hesitantly stepped over the bodies. He had never seen a dead person before and he'd never witnessed murder. The images of Tetsu slashing his sword relentlessly across a human's flesh flashed before his eyes. He knew that he wouldn't forget such a horrific sight. Turning, he saw that Yuu was closing his eyes as he inched his way over the corpses in a slow attempt to follow Tetsu and Darien.

"Hurry up!" Tetsu called impatiently from the hallway of the castle. "Reinforcements are going to be here soon."

Within several minutes, the trio was sprinting through the empty, silent hallways of Persepolis's castle. Darien bit his lower lip as he ran with his two friends, his mind elsewhere. Someone had tried to assassinate him? He would surely have been dead if Tetsu had not been there to save him. What was going on? Who wanted him dead? Could it really be Cambyses, his beloved uncle?

Darien found himself stumbling into the throne room behind Tetsu and Yuu and saw that the king and queen were sitting upon their thrones. Squads of guards that had been standing around the perimeter of the room were now advancing forward, brandishing their scimitars at the sight of the falsely accused traitor, Tetsu.

"It has come to my attention, Tetsu, that you have been plotting against me. You wish to have me executed, when I bring hope, prosperity, and peace to Persia?" The king raised his eyebrows as he thrummed his fingers on the golden arm of his throne. The lord waved his hand to his guards, giving them the signal that they could strike freely. "Just don't harm my son."

Darien pulled out his dagger and held it with the blade pointing downward, gripping the small weapon in front of him. The guards halted, unsure of what to do. They definitely didn't want to battle the prince. If they accidently killed Darien they would surely suffer the king's wrath. However, they knew that they had to eliminate the threat, Tetsu. So the guards stood there with their weapons brandished freely, puzzled by their conflicted situation.

Tetsu shattered the confusion by impatiently rushing forward with his long sword gripped tightly in his hands. Whipping the blade in a sideways slash, the boy ripped a Persian's torso practically in half with a single blow. Blood spurted like a fountain into the air and poured onto the ground as Tetsu continued onward to the rest of his opponents. Tetsu was a perfected warrior, able to read the movements and actions of every oncoming soldier that rushed at him. He easily dispatched seven soldiers with seven fluent strikes, all of which tore the men apart with ease. However, in the chaos, one man approached Tetsu from behind, swinging his curved scimitar in a downwards swing at the boy's blind-spot.

Yuu suddenly leapt in between Tetsu and the man, shielding his friend from harm's way. The blade tore across the young noble's back, and the boy screamed in agony as his clothes were soaked with his gushing blood. He collapsed forward, his face smacking hard against the ground. His eyes were closed and he lay unmoving, his face blanching.

Darien's eyes widened as Yuu collapsed. His hands began to tingle, tightening his hold on the hilt of his dagger. *How dare you…?* Bloodlust usurped his mind, causing him to sprint forward and jam his sharpened dagger into the side of the assaulter's throat. Crimson-red liquid hemorrhaged from the fatal wound but Darien kept stabbing, driving the tiny blade into the man over and over again. For some reason that Darien couldn't describe, it felt good. All of the burning rage that he felt boiling inside of him was being released in the action of stabbing. Tears were flowing freely from his eyes as he pushed the man onto his back and continued ripping him full of holes, blood now spraying onto his expensive clothing.

Silence filled the room and Tetsu stared at Darien with shock as he mercilessly defiled the Persian soldier's corpse. After several moments, the prince lowered his bloodied dagger to his side and allowed the weapon to clank loudly to the ground. He was breathing hard and was exhausted. The prince stared at the lifeless corpse beneath him, his stomach churning and heaving, and he leaned forward, retching all over the floor beside the man he had murdered.

He had killed someone. The man's blank gaze penetrated his soul with its powerful, unwavering stare. And the blood. Darien was covered in it; the unforgettable miasma of the corpse filled his nostrils, making him want to vomit again.

"Yuu! Are you alright?" Tetsu was kneeling at the noble's side and Darien turned to find that Yuu's entire back had been practically torn open by the vicious slash of the scimitar. He had thrown himself in front of Tetsu to save the boy's life. Tetsu was trembling, unable to believe that his friend was dying. He touched Yuu's pulse, feeling that it was weak, but existent. "Hey man, I'm sorry for everything. For making fun of you, for wrestling you, and for this," he whispered, lifting Yuu's unconscious body into his arms. "Darien! We need to get Yuu help. Let's get out of here…."

But Darien was stagnant, his body completely paralyzed. His eyes had wandered to his parents and suddenly his mouth dropped open in shock. The king and queen had both been slain, their royal robes drenched with their own blood. Their eyes were still wide open, for their assassination occurred in a swift moment. "F-Father! Mother!" Darien screamed, rushing forward towards his parents. He halted at the foot of the thrones, an electrifying sensation stopping his body from getting any closer to his dying parents. Tears began to stream freely down his cheeks as he collapsed to his knees, his head bowing to the ground. *How was this possible? Tetsu and I didn't get remotely close to the throne! Someone else must've done this! But who? None of the soldiers were even near my parents!*

"Mage…." Darien's head shot up when his father wheezed out a few words, sputtering blood all over his cloak. "Betrayed … Darien … live … on…." His head went limp, his eyes fixated on the floor with a final word dying upon his rosy-red lips. *Run.*

Cambyses and several other soldiers burst into the room from behind Darien and Tetsu. The uncle stared at his brother's corpse, clamping his hand over his mouth with disbelief. "D-Darien, what have you done?"

Darien spun around to face his uncle. "It wasn't me! I swear that it wasn't…." He couldn't have murdered his parents. *I didn't do this…!*

"You two are the only ones alive in this room and you're both covered in blood," Cambyses said, clenching his teeth. "Magus!" he bellowed.

A mysterious man in a black cloak sauntered past Cambyses into the throne room, his eyes coruscating a flashing violet color. His cloak was unbuttoned, revealing a fine white cloth shirt underneath. In his hand he gripped a golden scepter that radiated a brilliant light from a shining ruby at the scepter's tip. "Yes, yes. I'm on it," the Magus said casually as he raised his scepter to Tetsu and Darien. "Forgive me, little prince. But you must be punished for your sins."

A red shockwave of magical energy pulsed outwards from the Magus's scepter, filling the room with a wave of mystical power that knocked Darien and Tetsu clean off of their feet. Yuu's body flew from Tetsu's arms and slammed heavily against the marble floor, rolling uncontrollably. Darien and Tetsu were launched backwards into the back wall of the throne room. The breath left Darien's lungs as his vision became unfocused. He collapsed forward, landing harshly on his cheek. His head was pounding and his ears were ringing. He weakly reached up, pressing his palm against the cold, hard floor. The muscles in his right arm cried out in agony, obviously too weak to support his body. Nevertheless, he tried to push himself up. *Stop this! It wasn't me!*

"Huh? We've got a fighter over here!" The Magus cackled as he sauntered across the room and pointed the tip of his scepter at Darien's struggling body. "Your uncle told me that you didn't believe in magic and gods. Little boy, you have to open your eyes to the world around you. After all, the existence of magic and gods has been right under your nose the entire time. Take your nose out of those books of yours and start being more curious, child. Cambyses, I must advise that you banish these two pampered boys."

Cambyses looked at Darien pitifully. "I agree."

"Then it's settled!" The Magus grinned widely, a wicked smile that stretched from ear to ear. "To the Lost Sands you go." There was a flash of red light and Darien felt himself falling backwards into an endless, dark abyss.

Find Yourself

Darien grunted, his body striking the hot, sandy ground of the desert. He stuck out his tongue, spitting bits of sand from his mouth as he turned to find that several men on horses had dropped him off in a random location in the arid desert. Tied up on the back of one of the steeds was Tetsu, who was still unconscious. The prince touched his temple with his palm, feeling a throbbing headache pounding inside his skull.

"We'll be leaving you here in the mouth of the Lost Sands. You are to travel east," a Persian soldier stated, pointing to the far-off distance where there were only endless mountains of sand. "If we see that you are coming back towards Persepolis you will be executed immediately. Do you understand?"

Darien squinted through the beating sun's powerful glare. "What about Tetsu?"

"He will be given the same treatment as you. A chance at life through trial in the Lost Sands. If you come out on the other side alive then you've made it to freedom. But there is no chance of that." The Persian soldiers laughed. "We will split the two of you up. But who knows, perhaps you'll meet each other once again in the desert. By then, both of you will have lost your minds so don't look forward to your reunion, prince." The Persian tossed a canteen of water through the air towards Darien and grinned. "Take it, boy. You'll need it more than me."

Darien caught the canteen and frowned, realizing that it was empty. He heard the Persians laugh hysterically as they began to gallop off into the distance, hauling Tetsu along with them. The prince gritted his teeth in frustration, hurling the canteen at the ground as he screamed into the sky.

Walking into the Lost Sands began with few obstacles. Besides the dunes of sand that seemed to stretch out in every direction and the scorching sun, there were no monsters to leap out and swallow Darien, as the rumors claimed. Not yet, at least. Hours of endless walking seemed to drag by and Darien wasn't sure if he was making any progress through the wasteland. In fact, his sense of direction was completely off. He didn't even know which way he was traveling because everything looked the same.

Darien smacked his chapped lips, hoping that at some point he would come across some mystical river that appeared out of nowhere. He raised his head to the skies and exhaled, perspiration streaking down his face. The prince now understood why it was that people believed in gods. To believe in the gods was to believe in miracles. It allowed humans to grasp onto hope even when there was none. He clenched his teeth as tears began to trickle down his cheeks. *Why is this happening to me? All I wanted to do was help my friend. Now Yuu's probably dead, and Tetsu and I are going to perish out here in this barren wasteland. Is this what I get for not believing in the gods? Is this my punishment?*

The existence of magic and gods has been right under your nose the entire time.

More hours seemed to flash by and Darien had taken off his

shirt, wrapping it around his head as the sun's unbearable heat burned on his back, roasting him alive. He felt like he was Hussan's meat, tossed brusquely onto a frying pan to cook. Darien staggered, his arms drooping lethargically at his side as his eyes fought to stay open. He tried to wet his parched, cracked lips but soon realized that even his tongue was as dry as sandpaper. He felt like a desiccated zombie, alive with no reason to continue onward besides purposeless existence. He had no destination, he had no plan, he had nothing. As he gazed blankly at the desert, Darien realized that he was not getting anywhere. He might as well have been walking in place because the never-ending dunes of sand still stretched on in all directions.

Darien fell to his knees, his eyes squinted from the crusty sand that was covering his face. The blustering breeze that blew through the desert did not comfort him and merely sliced his skin with the whipping sand. The bottoms of his feet were red, raw, and blistered from walking for hours on the scorching sand. Giddiness overwhelmed him and he collapsed onto his back, submitting to his ultimate fate. Staring up at the cerulean skies, his father's face suddenly appeared in his view and he blinked. He had witnessed his father's demise. Was he hallucinating?

"I am disappointed in you, son," the king said. "A boy born of royal blood, pampered with the best resources available, and the first time you've stepped outside of the empire you're giving up already. Is hope that far out of reach?"

"It is," Darien murmured. "There is nowhere for me to go. This is as far as I dare travel and I doubt I've even made twenty miles into the desert yet. I've lost my home, my birthright, my friends, everything! All in a single hour."

"A boy destined to be king…."

"Is that all you ever talk about, father?" Darien attempted to shout, his voice coming out as a raspy gasp. "How I'm supposed to succeed you and do a perfect job overlooking this rich country at the age of fifteen? Oh, but now you won't have to worry about it. You won't have to stress out in the afterlife about whether or not I'm fulfilling your legacy because all of that is gone now. I am forsaken and betrayed. Someone murdered you and mother, but I do not know who."

"What if it was your friend?"

"Tetsu? He wouldn't do such a thing," Darien said and then frowned. Would he? It was possible that Tetsu could've felt so angry about the announcement of his betrayal that he felt obligated to murder the king and queen. There had been no one else in the room. But the Tetsu that Darien knew never would've committed such an atrocity.

"Facts, facts, facts. Are you letting your beliefs cloud your judgment again, Darien?" Yuu's voice echoed in his mind and Darien turned to find his noble friend standing there beside him as well. "Think about the facts. Who should you blame for your misfortune? You must find out. After all, how are you going to get revenge if you are just sitting here baking alive in the sand?"

"I do not intend to get revenge," Darien murmured.

"But aren't you curious to find out who betrayed you?" Yuu asked. "Look at who the facts point to."

"Why would I have any reason to kill the rulers of Persia?"

Tetsu had appeared out of nowhere as well to defend himself in the argument. "Killing them would not have solved anything. Besides, they had provided for and protected me for many years. I am grateful to them."

"But I betrayed you!" the king shouted.

"And is that your fault?" Tetsu retorted.

Silence. Darien found that he was once again alone with the howling wind smacking against his reddened cheeks. Hallucinations? Dreams? Had he been asleep or was he just losing his mind? The boy ran a hand through his sandy hair. But the manifestations that his mind had created of Yuu, Tetsu, and his father were absolutely correct. He wanted to find out who had murdered his parents, and he did want revenge.

Newfound energy surged through his veins, and the prince forced himself onto his feet with great fervor, swaying slightly as sand rained off of his body. He turned and suddenly saw that there was a stranger standing there beside him.

It was a young girl with gleaming blonde hair that blazed as brightly as the sun. She had a white cloak wrapped tightly around her body and an orange scarf that came around her neck, to protect her from the pounding heat of the sun. Small beads of sweat rolled down her tanned cheeks. Her glistening blue eyes reflected the same color as the infinite skies of this sweltering-hot day. Strapped to her back was a long, gigantic orange shield, with a symbol of the sun engraved into the front of it. A broadsword was sheathed at her side, and she stood staring at Darien. She smiled at him. "So, you've finally come to. You look like you've still got some energy, huh?" She reached to her belt and pulled out a canteen of water, thrusting it out towards Darien. "Go on, drink. You look thirsty."

Darien blinked, frowning at the girl. How on earth had she just appeared beside him out of nowhere? And why was she being so kind to a complete stranger? What was even more puzzling was that this girl was out in the Lost Sands. Was she another hallucination?

The boy frowned, hesitating, before taking the canteen without saying anything. He trickled water into his mouth, which didn't seem to satisfy his unquenchable thirst. He lowered the canteen, thankful that it hadn't been empty. Darien handed it back to the girl and exhaled. "Thank you."

"So what's a prince doing out here in the middle of nowhere?" the girl asked, putting the canteen back on her belt.

Darien knitted his eyebrows. "You know who I am?"

"Who doesn't? You're the prince of one of the greatest nations in all of Dastia." The girl giggled. "Well, it's no use to stand around here all day. I suggest we move; being stagnant in the Lost Sands in unwise. We can talk as we go, yes?"

Darien told the girl of his life in the empire and how he had eventually been betrayed as they walked. He told her of how he didn't know who murdered his parents but he was determined to find out. The girl seemed interested in his story. He found out that her name was Ra, and he felt that he had heard that name somewhere before, though he couldn't quite place where.

Hours along in their journey, Darien snapped back to his senses when he heard Ra cry out in excitement. He turned and looked to see where the girl was pointing. The two of them were standing upon a mountain of sand, and she was pointing down to a giant city in the distance filled with tall, glistening, white buildings. Darien's eyes twinkled with hope and he grinned. Maybe he wasn't doomed to perish after all!

Darien and Ra broke into a brisk run, eager to reach the city in the distance. They raced across the sands, disregarding how weak they were feeling underneath the burning hot sun. The strong winds whipped sand at their faces, but Darien didn't falter and continued to dash towards the mysterious oasis. Staggering down the steep hill of sand, Darien ended up tripping and falling down a good portion of it. But he didn't let his fall crush his hopes and he quickly picked himself up at the bottom of the dune of sand, breaking into a jog towards the entrance of the city. Ra was right beside him.

The prince grinned. He was almost there! Civilization! He could escape this treacherous wasteland! Even if it was only temporary solace, that was better than staying out in the searing sun. *Wait, a civilization in the Lost Sands? What—*

Suddenly a fissure ripped through the earth, and sand spewed into the air like a geyser as a gigantic creature tore its way from underground to the surface. A massive hand made entirely of sculpted rock smashed down onto the ground, sending sand spurting out in all directions. A giant golem composed of rock had torn its way from the earth. Its body was similar to that of a humanoid, for it had limbs, a torso, and a head. This golem was taller than every building in the city, practically the size of a small mountain. How such a massive being had forced itself from the ground was something that Darien didn't understand. An enormous chasm that led into a dark abyss lay underneath the monstrosity. Enormous boulders and rocks were clamped together to forge this colossal elemental, whose eyes were two gleaming rubies. The monster opened its mouth, a pitch-black void, and released a bellowing roar that sent tremors through the desert.

Darien's eyes widened with fear and he staggered backward, his hands jittering.

Ra unsheathed her sword and pulled out her shield, which glowed with the insignia of the sun. She pointed the sharpened tip of her weapon at the gargantuan golem, her face fearless. "Darien, I'll draw its attention away for a brief moment! In that time, I need you to run for the city. I'll distract the golem long enough for you to get away."

Darien stared at Ra with disbelief. She was going to sacrifice herself for him? This person she just met? He remembered how Yuu had sacrificed himself for Tetsu. The prince clenched his jaw. He was sick of losing people that he cared about. Already he had lost everything. And now he was going to lose this girl that had saved him. *I'm not going to let you perish.*

The golem raised his massive fist and brought it crashing downwards on Ra's position. The girl didn't falter; her mind was made up. She raised her shield as if the tiny thing would be enough to block the colossal punch that was about to squash her.

Darien sprinted forward and tackled Ra out of the way, tossing the girl to the sand. The two grunted as they struck the ground roughly. "What are you doing? Get up and run!" Ra shouted as sand rained around them.

The prince mashed his teeth together and grabbed Ra's sword, prying the weapon from her hands as he turned to face the giant elemental alone. "You run. I'll buy you some time!"

"Stop this! You've got an empire that you have to return to, a life to live so that you can find out who killed your parents!" Ra exclaimed, staring at Darien in shock. "You have to find your friend, Tetsu, and save him! You've got a lot to live for, prince. Don't throw it all away now!"

"It's already all gone." Darien grinned as the golem brought its fist upward and swung downwards at the boy. The prince's gaze was powerful and resolute. His feet were planted into the ground and he squeezed the hilt of Ra's sword until his knuckles turned white. "Besides … I'm done letting people fight my battles for me."

Ra smiled.

Darien yelled as he swung his sword upwards at the elemental that was about to crush him. However, the monstrosity stopped his punch and halted his fist several feet away from the prince, who whipped his sword through the open air. The weapon was far too heavy for him, and he yelped as he fell sideways and hit the ground clumsily. Rubbing his aching head, Darien groaned while dragging the sword at his side. He blinked, realizing he wasn't dead. That was surprising. He looked up and saw that the rock giant had stopped its attack and was now standing tall, letting out a low grumble that sounded somewhat like snickering. "Uh…." Darien was perplexed.

"This is Amon, the Guardian of the Forgotten Oasis, Zerzura. He is also the Guardian of a god named Ares." Ra explained, standing up, grinning. "And you, my friend, are worthy."

"Worthy?" Darien frowned. "Worthy of what? Ra, what's going on?"

"Come with me," Ra said, walking forward past Darien and the gigantic golem.

Completely puzzled by the situation, Darien followed her. Amon gave a slight nod, making Darien feel a little uneasy for some reason. The prince stumbled through the front entrance of the white city and noticed that there was no one in sight. In fact, these buildings didn't even have any doors. The city looked like it was a setup created for a stage play. "Where are we?"

"I told you already. This is the Forgotten Oasis known as Zerzura. Surely you've heard the tales," Ra said.

"Zerzura was a lost civilization in the desert that had wealth beyond imagining. Its treasures supposedly were limitless, which was why the Lost Sands concealed it from those who greedily sought its fortunes." Darien looked around, looking at the blank white buildings and the numerous torches that lit a path for them. It was sunny; there was no need for this extra light. "But all that I see is nothing. No civilization, no treasures, and these buildings aren't even real buildings. Is all of this a hallucination? Have I gone insane?"

"Perhaps," Ra spoke, pointing down the pathway that led through the city. It eventually led to a giant pool of glistening, clear water that shone with ethereal beauty. The water was calm and unmoving, glowing from the reflection of the dazzling sunlight. Behind the pool was a towering statue of a warrior, a muscular man wielding a spear and shield. He seemed courageous and wore a determined expression upon his frozen face. "I suppose it depends on your definition of fortune and treasure."

Darien walked to the pool, stopping right before its edge. He stared into the stagnant waters, seeing his own reflection with clarity. It was as if he were looking right into a mirror. "This is what the legendary lost city has to offer? Water?" He smiled. "I guess I am pretty lucky for this oasis offers me life, more time to live on this blasted earth."

"Do you not want to drink from the waters?"

"If I drink I would save myself from dehydration temporarily, so that I could suffer in this perilous desert for a few days longer before I starve," Darien said and a weary smile cracked across his face. "But I'd rather try and live than just accept a meaningless death." He leaned down and cupped his hands together, lifting the water to his lips and sipped. His eyes widened. It was unlike any fluid he had drunk before. The purity of the water gave it a sweet taste, different from ordinary water. His thirst forced him to lean forward and drink larger sips from the pool, enjoying the treasure of the oasis.

Ra grinned as she watched him. "You answered correctly, Darien. However, you were wrong about one thing. The treasure of this oasis is not life. While this water does quench your thirst and gives you more time on this earth, that isn't its purpose."

Darien drew his head back, his face drenched with the pure waters of the oasis. He glanced over his shoulder at the girl and frowned. "Then what is its purpose?"

"To grant you immeasurable power," Ra said, and the prince stared at her with surprise. "This pure water that you see is the blood of the god, Ares. It was placed in this oasis to give those who are worthy a chance to claim Zerzura's treasure, becoming a new god. The Lost Sands torments every human that enters the forbidden wasteland. However, it tests each individual and chooses one person to be the one to find Zerzura. And that was you.

"The hallucinations that you had when you had given up were there to grant you hope. Their purpose was to prove that you had fortitude and were willing to persevere through any pain if you had a powerful enough resolve. The rock golem, Amon, was meant to test your courage. Your journey to this city displayed kindness, determination, bravery, persistence, and selflessness. And now by drinking this water, you will become a god amongst the human world and Amon will become your Guardian. Congratulations on claiming Zerzura's legendary treasure."

"What? A god?" Darien exclaimed. "How could I become...." He glanced down at his hands and suddenly saw that they were covered in red blood. He shook furiously, his eyes widening with disbelief as he realized that the pool he had drunk from was filled with the crimson-red liquid of a god. The once-pure well of glistening water was gone. The statue was replaced with a corpse, the same heroic figure with blood spewing from a wound in his chest into the pool. The mirage of an oasis had faded. It was replaced with the grotesque reality.

Blood? I drank ... blood? His mouth gaped open with shock and he felt a raging surge of agonizing pain ripping through his chest and pulsing through the rest of his body, creating seven seconds of absolute hell. He grabbed at his breast, feeling his heart exploding against his chest as scorching heat spread through every inch of his body, making him feel like a burning sun. Toppling to his knees, Darien bit down hard on his lower lip and gasped, his irises transforming into a beastly dark-red color. A fog of blackness arose around the corners of his vision, blurring his sight. The mist of darkness in his vision expanded until he saw nothing but black. *This … this can't be happening!* And then he collapsed.

Newly Born God

Darien opened his eyes and blinked, finding himself in the middle of nowhere once again. He was still stuck in the Lost Sands. Sitting on a flat plain of sweltering hot sand, the boy looked around him and saw that he was no longer in Zerzura. And the girl, Ra, was gone. He exhaled. A dream, so that was what that was. What a relief. None of that made any sense anyway.

He felt the ground rumble and turned to his right to find that Amon, the humungous rock golem, had plopped himself in a sitting position right next to Darien. The two stared at each other for a moment and Darien blinked rapidly, unsure of whether or not he should be surprised, shocked, or terrified.

"S-So, it wasn't a dream?" Darien whispered, gaping at Amon. He remembered that Ra had explained that this golem was to become his Guardian. What was that supposed to mean? Did that mean this giant monster was just going to follow him around everywhere? It didn't seem to mean any harm; otherwise Darien would probably be crushed into little bits already. The boy sighed, scratching his head as he reluctantly waved to the elemental. "Uh, h-hey there, Amon. My name is Darien."

Amon cocked his head to the side and grumbled. *Your name is Ares.*

Darien frowned, realizing that the golem hadn't actually talked.

But the words that the creature had meant to speak had just formed in his head somehow. What a unique form of communication. Was it magic? "Uh, no. My name is Darien."

Amon grunted. Your new name is Ares. You are a god now. Gods cannot have human names.

"A god?" Darien frowned. "I don't feel like a god. I mean, aren't gods supposed to be like able to fly around and stuff? Don't they get supernatural powers and watch over the humans from the heavens? And how can a mortal get transformed from a human to a god just by sipping some water from a random oasis?" He hoped that the blood was a mirage.

Amon reached up and tapped his giant chest with his rock-hand. *You were chosen.*

"Oh, lucky me. So you're going to follow me around then and make sure that I don't die in this blasted place?" Darien smirked.

The elemental nodded. I am your Guardian and will protect you from any harm. I will also teach you how to survive in the Lost Sands. Finding water and food is easy if you know how to do it. I'll also oversee your developing control over your new powers.

"New powers?" Darien exclaimed. "So what, I can shoot fire from my mouth or fly?"

Amon snorted with amusement, releasing a gust of hot air from two holes in his face that were supposed to be his nostrils. *Something like that.*

The prince scowled, disbelieving the words that the golem echoed in his head. He folded his arms and looked away. "I don't believe in gods!"

The golem grunted. You didn't believe in magic either until Persia's Magus used it to knock you unconscious. Just because you don't see it doesn't mean that it doesn't exist. You are a very small boy in a very large world, Ares. There is much that you don't know or understand yet.

"Fine! Show it to me then! How do I demonstrate my powers so that I can see that I actually am a god? Prove to me that this isn't just some crazy dream or a hallucination," Darien said.

The golem nodded. *As you wish.* Amon swung his rock arm at full force and smashed it into Darien, which should've easily splattered his body into slush. Instead, the boy went flipping wildly through the air, spinning uncontrollably into the sky.

Darien screamed in absolute terror as he found himself thousands of feet above the surface, practically flying. He crashed down into the ground, slapping across the sandy plains like a skipping stone. He finally landed a mile away with his face buried deep in the hot sand. He groaned, pulling his head from the earth. Shaking grains off his face, the prince turned to find that Amon was storming in his direction, leaping across the desert with ease. "What the hell do you think you're doing? You could've killed me!" Darien barked, his face red after such a terrifying experience.

But the fact that you're alive proves that something has changed, no? Amon halted before Darien and plopped down in front of the boy. An ordinary human would be in tiny pieces right now.

Darien stared at the golem. He looked down at his hands, which trembled before his shocked face. A small smile spread across his lips when he realized that he had somehow become superhuman. "Pinch me, I must be dreaming…!"

Amon flicked him in the face instead, sending him sliding onto his back. The flick was equivalent to a direct strike from a battering ram. *I flicked you instead.*

"It's just an expression!" the boy yelped, leaning forward, rubbing his nose. There was pain, though miniscule. That meant that this wasn't a dream. His body was somehow hardened to withstand stronger blows. He wasn't bleeding and there were no signs of bruises. Darien leaned forward, eying the golem curiously. "What else can I do?"

Amon cracked a tiny smile, opening his gigantic mouth. *Run and find out.*

The prince raised an eyebrow and pushed himself to his feet. *Fine, I'll do it.* He looked at the stretching sands that extended for as far as he could see. He broke into a sprint and the sides of his mouth curved into an excited grin as he propelled forward, faster than any horse could ever travel. He flashed across the desert sands in an instant, the pounding wind rushing against his face. He hooted as he jumped, flying hundreds of feet into the air, pumped with energy and excitement.

Every physical aspect of himself had been enhanced drastically, turning him into a powerful superhuman. He beamed. He wasn't powerless anymore! With this newfound strength, he could become more than just an ordinary human. More than just a banished prince. He was a god. And with this power he could change anything he wanted.

Descending back to earth, the boy smashed into the ground,

sending sand spraying into the air. He arose, running a hand through his blonde hair. He had created a crater in the sand with his landing, proof of his tremendous power. The prince turned to Amon, who lagged behind him slightly. *Is that proof enough, Ares?*

"Yes," Ares replied.

Thief

Tetsu wandered the Lost Sands for his third day in this hell. He had hydrated himself from the juices of a cactus, which had made him hallucinate for several hours. But it had kept him alive and that was enough. In terms of food, he regained his strength by crushing scorpions and eating their meat. He knew that he couldn't just survive on hallucinogenic fluid and tiny scorpion carcasses, though. He had to find a way out of this desert.

But everywhere that he looked, the endless plains of sand appeared to stretch beyond the horizon. The boy squinted his eyes, spotting something in the far-off distance. There was a cave in the middle of nowhere, just carving deep into a rock. It was rather ominous, but Tetsu knew that he had no other leads. There was really nowhere else to go but there. If it didn't provide any resources, at least Tetsu could shield himself from the punishing sun for a bit.

It took an hour to arrive at the cave, and he raised an eyebrow when he saw that the inside was actually filled with mountains of glittering gold and flashy jewels. All sorts of treasures filled the stone walls and climbed up to the cave ceiling. A clear pathway led straight through the sea of treasures and Tetsu reluctantly walked in. This looked too good to be true for any adventurers who happened to stumble across this cave. Then again, it could potentially be a trap. Tetsu had heard rumors of tricks that the Lost Sands had set up to deceive adventurers. It was as if the desert were alive, dooming any intruders that journeyed into its land.

Tetsu continued forward slowly and cautiously. His eyes flickered everywhere, making sure to take in his surroundings meticulously. He inched down the pathway silently and suddenly locked his eyes onto a single treasure that gleamed even brighter than anything he saw in the mountains of gold around him. It was an hourglass made of diamonds. But it wasn't the diamond part that interested him. The sand itself that trickled from the upper-half of the hourglass to the bottom was gold. However, the sand wasn't tinted, it was naturally gold. He had never seen anything like it before. Such a luxurious color made Tetsu's eyes twinkle and he inched towards the hourglass, mesmerized by its beauty.

He stopped in front of the hourglass and picked it up without thinking. Holding the brilliant object in his hands, somehow he immediately knew the name of the treasure. The Sands of Time. He frowned; he had heard stories of this object's incredible power. But what was such a rarity doing in a place like this cave?

Suddenly the entire cave began to quake furiously and Tetsu grunted, struggling to keep his balance. The boy felt the ground beginning to lift upwards. He glanced over his shoulder and saw that the entrance of the cave was now gazing up at the sky as the structure was torn from the earth. The cave was being lifted up somehow! Tetsu gritted his teeth and kicked off his back foot, bursting towards the exit of the cave. As he reached the edge, he gasped, slowing to a stop. He was already thousands of meters into the air; a fall from this high would kill him easily.

"*WHO DARES TAKE MY TREASURES?*" a loud voice boomed, shaking the cave.

Tetsu suddenly felt the entire cave tilting forward and he watched with horror as the floor began to slant, attempting to force the boy into the open air. He grunted, desperately trying to scramble back into the grotto. However, all of the mountains of gold began to roll out of the cave in a stream, cascading like a waterfall down towards the sandy ground below. The boy clenched his teeth, fighting against the relentless current of golden fortunes that smashed against him. But soon he lost his foothold and his eyes widened with terror as he was swept off his feet by the falling gold and was sent tumbling into the open air, plunging freely to his doom.

What had come over him? How had he been so stupid as to let something so elegant seduce him like that? Taking the hourglass had awoken something, and whatever that was had killed him. Tetsu's eyes flitted through the thousands of gold treasures that rained down around him. Gold, gold, gold. All of the golden treasures must belong to the owner of the voice that had spoken to him. But weren't there more valuable things in these piles than just gold? There had been the Sands of Time, surely there could be something in there that could save his life.

The final grain of sand in the diamond hourglass dropped to the bottom of the hourglass and suddenly time slowed drastically. Tetsu's eyebrows went up in surprise, finding that he was falling at an incredibly slow rate. And it wasn't just him. Everything was raining downward much slower than it should've been. He tried to move his arms but he felt as if he were moving through thick, mucky water.

His movement had been restricted significantly. Was it that time had slowed and his consciousness was somehow still active in this frozen zone?

Tetsu smiled. The stories of the Sands of Time spoke of how its wielder could utilize the object to control time. It was a tool and a weapon. And right now the Sands of Time had reacted to his call. He was falling much slower, but that didn't mean he was out of danger yet. He had to find something that would save his life otherwise he would still perish the moment he struck the ground. His eyes shot to something colorful that descended through the sea of golden treasures. It was a fine carpet made of purple and blue linens.

A carpet? The boy frowned. What on earth was something like that doing in a stash of golden treasures? Tetsu looked around and saw nothing else that caught his eye. He turned back to the carpet and sighed. This was definitely a gamble, but surely that carpet had something unique to offer. Otherwise it wouldn't be in this group of treasures. He definitely had nothing to lose.

Time reverted back to its normal state and the carpet shot past Tetsu. The boy grunted, turning around and bringing his arms and legs close together. He became as aerodynamic as an arrow and pierced downwards, ripping through the air as he plummeted towards the falling carpet. The ground was coming to meet him just as quickly. He grunted, grabbing the end of the carpet with one hand, holding the Sands of Time with the other. "Come on," he murmured. "Do something!" he yelled as the ground rushed to meet him.

The carpet snapped to life and yanked him, dragging him through the air as it soared up into the sky. "WHOAAA!" Tetsu screamed with glee, relief, and absolute horror. Sure, he didn't die from the fall. But now he was dangling off a carpet from over a hundred feet in the air. He blinked, looking up at the carpet. "Wait, you can fly?" He burst out laughing. "No way! That's extraordinary!"

The boy climbed up onto the carpet. Tetsu exhaled, wiping sweat from his brow. He looked at the Sands of Time and whistled. "Man, I just went through hell for you." He patted the flying carpet gently and laughed. "But I guess it was worth it, huh? Now I can get out of his cursed desert."

"*MORTAL! YOU DARE STEAL FROM ME?*" a voice exploded, sending a gust of warm wind rushing into Tetsu's face.

Tetsu turned and saw that the cave he had entered was actually the ear of a gigantic mountain giant. The creature was completely made of rock and towered so high into the air that its head was near the clouds. It was a humanoid, made entirely of boulders that were clumped together to form a gigantic beast. Its eyes were huge emeralds that gave off a green glow. Golden treasures continued to sprinkle out of his huge ears, deep holes that bit deep into the side of the titanic creature's head, creating carved tunnels of rock. Essentially, caves. How deceiving.

The mountain giant raised one of its large hands and brought it tearing downwards towards Tetsu. The movement was rather slow, but the hand was so large that it didn't matter.

"Let's get out of here!" Tetsu yelped, yanking on the front of the carpet. Immediately, the carpet responded to the boy's touch and burst forward at the exact speed that he wanted: fast. He flew away as the giant's hand smashed down into the ground, creating a tsunami of sand that swept outwards in all directions. The boy glanced over his shoulder and saw all the gleaming treasures poking out of the sand. He definitely had no intention of going back there to retrieve any of those.

Tetsu sighed, relieved. "I'm not going to die here. As long as I've got you two," he said, speaking to his treasures. His stomach grumbled and he smacked his chapped lips, groaning as he flew off into the desert. "Man, I've got to get something to eat. It's been a long day."

***

Hours passed as Tetsu flew at full speed across the Lost Sands. How many miles had he traveled? Fifty? A hundred? A thousand? He had expected to have flown across the entire desert by now with this carpet. Nevertheless, the sea of sand continued to flow underneath him, and he sighed. There was no way that Darien would survive in a place like this. The prince had always had things handed to him and never once had to fend for himself.

Tetsu felt his body growing weak and the carpet descended to the ground, dropping him gently onto the sand. The carpet rested beside him as he lay on the desert floor, tightening his jaw. He felt all of his energy sapped from his bones and he groaned, tears twinkling in the corners of his eyes. There were no signs of water after hours of flying. There were no animals. There was simply nothing for miles and miles; it was an endless wasteland of nothingness. Why did such a forsaken place exist? He gritted his teeth, grabbing a handful of sand in frustration. "Damn it … I can't go out like this…," he growled. Suddenly he felt a shadow looming over him.

The boy glanced up to find a young girl with blonde hair, wearing a white cloak that shielded her from the powerful sun. She had a silver scarf that was curled around her neck and a sheathed broadsword at her side. Strapped to her back was a gleaming shield that had an insignia of a sun inscribed into it. She was one of the most beautiful girls that Tetsu had ever seen.

The girl looked at him for a moment and smiled. That was the last thing that Tetsu saw before he lost consciousness.

***

Ares sat upon Amon's shoulders as they trudged through the endless Lost Sands. The boy gazed up at the sky and sighed. "So? What do we do now? We just live in this desert?"

This desert is the harshest environment in all of Dastia. In it, you will learn many things. You will find your power and yourself. Amon's voice echoed in his mind. This is where you will train. And this is where you will develop your powers as a god, Ares.

"What kind of a god am I?" Ares murmured.

The last Ares was a god of war. But I believe you always have the choice to choose your own path.

"I want to be a god of wisdom. You know, really smart." Ares exclaimed, throwing his arms into the air with a laugh. "Kidding, kidding. I don't know yet. This is pretty exciting, though. Transcending ordinary humans, I mean. Becoming a god means that I can do anything I want, right?"

Your limitless power does come with responsibility, Ares. After all, that is why the Lost Sands chose you. The last Ares perished and his power must be passed on to another. The Lost Sands wanted to pass the power to someone who would use its power only when it's meant to be wielded. Amon grunted. You must control your emotions and tame your power if you ever want to walk amongst the world of the humans again. Humans fear that which they do not understand.

"Responsibility, huh?" Ares said, lying back on Amon's thick, rocky shoulders. "I understand. Say, Amon, you're a pretty smart guy. Why didn't they just give the power to you?"

I have been around for several thousand years as one of the many Guardians of Ares. Amon snorted. I was created for the purpose of protecting my master.

"Master?" Ares' eyebrows knitted together. "That's a terrible name for me. Just call me your friend, alright?"

Friend?

"Yeah, you know, someone you see as a good companion. Uh, I don't really know how to explain a friend. I thought that the term was common knowledge." Ares scratched the back of his neck. "I could use more friends anyway. So, Amon? You'll be my friend, right? I mean, this desert is pretty lonely."

Of course, Ares.

Ares beamed and leaned forward, looking to see that Amon had stopped in front of a gigantic pyramid that towered even higher than the elemental did. The boy whistled at the majestic structure. "Whoa, that's pretty huge! What is it?"

It's a pyramid. A god must have a god's weapon. Call to it. Your weapon will respond to your beckoning call. Amon grumbled.

The new god frowned, standing tall upon Amon's giant

shoulders. Call to it? What did that mean? He extended his hand outward towards the pyramid, expecting the weapon to just appear in his hand. Nope. He flicked his wrist. Still nothing. "Come!" he shouted with authority and suddenly there was an explosion that sent the entire pyramid crumbling from the top to bottom. An avalanche of dust and debris rolled down the structure and swept down, engulfing the massive building in destruction. Emerging from the cloud of dust was a golden spear that whistled through the air and flew gracefully into Ares' hand.

Ares' fingers curled around the long shaft of the spear, and he stared at the weapon in absolute awe. The tip of the spear was made of a metal that reflected such a delicate color of silver that it looked as pure as the stars. Protruding from the bottom of the spear was also another sharpened tip made of some mysterious blue metal. The shaft of the weapon, made of shining gold, was easily grasped. The spear felt as light as a feather and he tossed it from hand to hand experimentally. "Wow! A magic spear! See, I didn't know that you could enchant weapons like that!"

You have a lot to learn, Ares. Amon chuckled. And I will teach you. We will live in this desert. If you can survive the hardships of the Lost Sands then you can survive anything. Any opponent that crosses you will be seen as tiny as an ant. You will reach new heights that no human will ever dream of achieving. I will train you to become a truly powerful god.

Ares twirled the spear in his hands and grinned, wearing a look filled with determination. "I'm ready." He was no longer Darien, the weak and powerless prince that had been afraid of something as miniscule as the responsibility of the throne. Now he was Ares, the legendary god, with all of the power of the world in the palm of his hand. He was ready to train with his new friend, Amon. He was ready to accept this new role as a god and work hard to obtain new heights. Most of all, he was ready to accept the perilous adventure that was offered to him. And he knew that he would not miss his old life.

Revenant

Five Years Later...

Aleysha sat on the wooden floor of a metal cage. She was confined with several other mercenaries that were like her, captured after failing a contract. She sighed, letting her long blonde hair roll down over her shoulders. The female mercenary wore an orange scarf with a black sleeveless shirt that revealed her tanned, muscular arms. She had baggy, ripped, white pants that had previously been equipped with an array of weapons. Unfortunately, her captors had frisked her and removed her weapons, leaving her unarmed in this cage filled with barbaric idiots.

As a mercenary, her job was to accept contracts from foreigners that came into her small city, Yuusus, and complete them. In exchange for completing them, she was paid a reasonable sum. Aleysha was known as one of the best mercenaries around for working on solo contracts. Her mistake had been accepting a contract that involved working with multiple mercenaries. On the mission, they had gotten in each other's way and were captured. Typical. She knew that she couldn't depend on anyone other than herself. Now she was probably being dragged off to Persia to be sold off to some pudgy, wealthy merchant that wanted some extra slaves. The very thought of serving one of those filthy bastards made her sick to her stomach.

Aleysha gazed through the cage's metal bars and saw one of the soldiers toying with her orange shield, which had an inscribed sun carved into the metal. She'd had that legendary shield for many years now and she definitely didn't intend to part with it yet. She reached out and grabbed the bars of her cage, pulling on them. Obviously they didn't budge. What was she thinking? "Hey! You better not touch that with your filthy hands, Persian!"

The Persian, wearing a black cloak, raised his eyebrows in amusement at Aleysha's threat. His skin was tanned from many years of working out in the scorching sun of Dastia. He lowered Aleysha's shield and guffawed. "You think you're in any position to make threats, woman? Sit down, otherwise I'll come in there myself and silence you."

Aleysha scoffed. "What are a couple of Persians like you doing so far from home? You're taking the path around the Lost Sands. Still afraid of going in there, huh?" "No human should ever set foot in that desert! It's already treacherous enough. But now you won't even last a day in there without perishing by the hand of the God of War!" the Persian growled.

Aleysha frowned. "The God of War? I haven't heard of such a god."

"Then you must be living under a rock," one of the mercenaries called from the cage. "Ever since King Cambyses claimed the throne, the Persian Empire has been expanding drastically. They've been dominating every nation in sight. Now that they've conquered most of the western side of the continent, they've attempted to set their sights on the eastern side. But the Lost Sands proves as a formidable obstacle in their path. To go around the Lost Sands takes ten times longer than going straight through the desert. The clueless king believed that if he sent a powerful army stocked with supplies into the Lost Sands, they would be safe from the dangers that plague those unholy lands."

"And what? He was wrong?"

"Not only are there hundreds of thousands of dangerous creatures that wander the Lost Sands, a new guardian of the desert appeared several years ago. He goes by the name of Ares. He single-handedly slaughtered the entire Persian army that Cambyses sent into the Lost Sands. Rumor has it that he's bound to the desert and can't actually leave. But no human can enter the desert without being slain," the mercenary said. "A god, that's what they call him. It's the only explanation for how a single man could obliterate a force of over a hundred thousand soldiers, leaving only a handful of survivors. Even the Magi cannot complete such an impossible task."

The Persian nodded. "You should listen to your friend there. He's right. Some unknown guardian has been haunting the Lost Sands, making it even more dangerous than it was before. It's not even worth going near it anymore."

"So instead you guys just go and conquer as much land as you can around the perimeter of the Lost Sands. Your king will be long gone by the time you finally end up getting to the eastern side of Dastia," Aleysha sneered. "He won't even get to see the united empire that he claims he wants."

"He's already dominated many nations, and he's accomplished

more than any ruler ever could using the powerful force of the Persian army," the Persian snarled.

"And millions have died because of it."

"They're not of Persian blood. That's none of my concern," the Persian retorted. "Do you want to get lashed? Because that's the direction that you're headed right now," he growled. Several other Persians had been drawn to the conversation and were now eying Aleysha curiously.

The mercenary knew better than to continue pushing these soldiers' buttons and retreated to the back of the cage, plopping back down on the wooden floor. At one point in time she had respected the Persians. But after Prince Darien murdered his parents and was banished to the Lost Sands, Cambyses claimed the throne as his own with no other members of the royal family to challenge him. The man was much different than his brother and abused Persia's incredible military arsenal. They swept across the western side of Dastia and conquered every nation in sight. Any country that opposed Persia was obliterated. The numbers of slaves captured from conquered nations had increased drastically as a result of Persia's relentless conquest.

Aleysha had been on a mission to escort a mysterious package to a small city in northern Dastia. However, it seemed that the Persians were now contesting that area. She sighed. The Persians weren't particularly skilled individually. But their numbers were so large that no one could stand against them. And with every conquered nation, their numbers only grew as they recruited foreign warriors. Aleysha just wished that there was hope for someone to stand up against these lowbrows. Suddenly there was a rumbling sound and the caravan came to an abrupt stop. Aleysha's cage, which was being pulled by several horses, also halted. The Persians were looking up at the sky as they unsheathed their swords, spotting a tiny dot speeding through the air. The dot descended and crashed into the ground at blinding speed, sending hot sand spraying in all directions.

The Persians yelped, staggering backwards as a mysterious figure exploded from the screen of sand. The figure drove a single punch into a Persian and the man was rocketed backwards as if he had been hit by cannonball, his body practically in pieces by the time he landed several hundred meters away.

Aleysha rushed forward and grasped the metal bars that confined her. What was going on? Was it a threat to her? Because if it was, she wanted to get the hell out of here! She tried pulling on the bars, her arms straining, but groaned when she realized she wasn't getting anything done. The young woman glanced forward and frowned when she saw that the figure that had descended from the sky was actually just a young boy.

The boy had flowing blonde hair that looked so fragile that it seemed as if it would shatter if one so much as poked it. His skin was slightly tan from the unbearable heat of the desert and he wore a black shroud around his buttoned white shirt and glistening gold pants, connected by a colorful blue sash that was tied tightly around his waist. A golden necklace dangled from his neck and rested on his collarbone. In his hand he was holding a double-bladed spear that was made of gold. The boy exhaled and smiled, revealing a set of perfect white teeth. "Well, well! What are you Persians doing here so far from home?"

"What's it to you, kid? Who the hell are you?" a Persian snarled, pointing his curved scimitar at the stranger.

"My name is Ares, Guardian of the Lost Sands!" the boy announced boldly.

The Persians all looked at each other, puzzled. How could such a little boy, who looked no older than fifteen years old, be this rumored God of War? This had to be some kind of a joke. Then again, the boy had just fallen straight out of the sky and emerged completely unscathed. "What is the God of War doing so far away from the Lost Sands?"

"God of War?" Ares said, tilting his head to the side. He chortled, holding his stomach as he laughed. "Oh, man! Is that what they're calling me? Hey, that's a pretty snazzy title! It has a nice ring to it. Actually, surprisingly enough, I haven't come here to halt your parade. I'm just here for that girl," he said, nodding to Aleysha.

Aleysha raised her eyebrows. This boy came here for her? What for? They had never met before. But the very chance of being saved from these damned Persians was enough to bring her hopes up.

"We won't listen to your demands, god," a Persian barked. "Go back to the Lost Sands where you're bound!"

"Is that another rumor of yours?" Ares smirked. "That I can't leave the desert and wander the world as I please? I must say, *sir*." He flicked his wrist and his spear left his hand and shot forward on its own, jamming through the Persian's stomach. The weapon tore out his back, splattering blood onto the sand. "You're completely wrong."

"Attack the boy!" another Persian yelled, and all of the soldiers surrounding the caravan rushed forward to assault the petite deity.

The mercenaries in Aleysha's cage all roared to life and cheered as Ares confronted their captors. Aleysha simply gazed with incredulity as the small boy smiled as the dozens of Persian soldiers converged on him. Hopelessly outnumbered, an ordinary person wouldn't have a chance. This was the boy's opportunity to prove that he lived up to his name as a god.

Ares twirled his wrist, motioning for the spear. The weapon whistled to life and tore itself from the Persian corpse that it was lodged in. It whipped through the air on its own, as if it were alive, and struck out at the Persian soldiers. The warriors screamed in terror, unsure of what to do. The boy controlled his spear by swinging his right hand about, as if he were conducting an orchestra. Ares' spear struck down the warriors with ease, and the Persians soon saw that victory was out of their grasp. Survivors attempted to flee, dashing for the rocky mountains in the distance.

The boy extended his hand and his spear threw itself into his grip. He spun the weapon and jammed it into the sand, reaching up to touch his golden medallion. "*Awaken, Amon.*" The moment the god said those words a fissure erupted in the desert and a gigantic rock golem exploded from the ground, sending the fleeing Persians flying through the air.

Ares turned his attention from the Persians to the cage, prying the metal bars apart with his bare hands. The captured mercenaries all stood there, quavering like frightened children. They seemed unsure of what to do in the presence of this young deity. "Hey, aren't you going to come out? I won't hurt you." He offered his hand out to one of the mercenaries but they simply leapt past him without a word, scrambling away as quickly as they could.

The boy watched the terrified men as they fled and bit his lower lip. He sighed and shrugged. It was clear that those men didn't trust him. And what reason did they have to trust him? After all, everyone believed he was a mass-murderer. He turned and spotted Aleysha from the corner of his eye, still sitting in the cage, unmoving. "You aren't going to run like the rest of them?"

"Why did you save us?" Aleysha demanded, her body paralyzed.

"I have a personal grudge against the Persians," Ares said. "More importantly I hate when they take people to be slaves. The main reason I'm here, though, was because I saw that you were captured."

"But you don't even know me."

"You're right. I don't," Ares murmured, the corners of his lips curving into a small smile. "But you remind me of a girl named Ra that I met five years ago. You look exactly like her actually." He chuckled, scratching the back of his neck. "She did me a huge favor back in the day. She saved my life and changed who I am."

Aleysha's eyes widened. Ra? The sun deity and creator of Dastia?

The mercenary glanced up in awe at the enormous rock golem that had ripped itself from the earth. She had never seen such a colossal creature before. She had read stories of ancient elementals that existed but she never imagined that she would ever stumble across one. And it seemed subordinate to Ares.

"Anyway," Ares said, scratching the back of his neck. "I'd better get going back to the Lost Sands. I just didn't want to see someone who reminded me of an old friend get captured, that's all."

"You saw me all the way from the Lost Sands?"

"I didn't," Ares said, pointing to the giant golem. "Amon did."

"Amon?"

"That's his name. He's a friend of mine."

Friend. Aleysha giggled at the absurdity of everything that was happening. So this teenage boy was a god and now he had summoned his friend, a huge earth elemental, to stop the Persians from enslaving a girl that looked like someone the god used to know. How simple. On top of that, the boy was wielding a magical spear. Even better!

Aleysha wondered if this was all just a reverie. "I must be dreaming," she said aloud.

Amon began to trudge over but Ares held up a hand, giving the golem a reproachful glare. "Don't even think about flicking her."

The elemental huffed, lowering its arms to its side.

Aleysha turned and saw that the other mercenaries had stolen the Persian horses and were galloping off into the distance in the direction of their homes. She winced, realizing that all the horses had been stolen and not a single one was left for her. "You've got to be kidding me."

Ares whistled. "Looks like your friends left you for dead, huh?"

"They're not my friends," Aleysha insisted, folding her arms.

"So you're the solo type."

"You've got it."

Ares laughed. "Well, Amon and I can give you a lift to wherever you live. It shouldn't take that long to get there." He turned and saw that some of the Persians were still alive, just lying on the ground at Amon's feet, cowering in terror. The god's expression hardened as he saw them alive. "Amon, crush them."

The rock golem nodded swiftly and raised a giant foot, covering the tiny men in a dark shadow. He roared, perfectly ready to squash these men like bugs. "W-Wait!" Aleysha shouted suddenly and the rock golem froze. The mercenary winced. *Oh boy, why did I just do that?*

Ares looked at Aleysha, perplexed. "Yes?"

"Don't kill them."

Amon and Ares both looked at the girl with puzzlement fixed on their faces. "You want to spare the lives of these men who had captured you and wanted to sell you off as slaves in the Persian Empire. Do you even know what they do to slaves in Persia?" Ares asked, his eyebrow knit together.

"No, but…."

"They work them until their bones are rickety and broken. They become so accustomed to the sight of their own blood that being lashed a few times is a daily routine. Their scars are cut so deep into their body that even if they were to ever regain freedom they would still never escape the nightmarish reality that they had experienced. They are driven mad. The overseers of the Persian slaves beat them if they don't meet their impossible quotas. Sometimes they slaughter slaves just because they feel like it. These men," Ares pointed to the terrified Persian soldiers, "will pillage more villages along the northern coast of Dastia and eventually will work their way to eastern

Dastia. When they do, they'll kill more innocent people and take home more slaves. Is that what you want?"

"No, of course not!" Aleysha exclaimed. "But they spared my life and captured me instead when I surrendered. They're clearly surrendering right now, there's no need to just execute them."

Ares rolled his eyes. "Death would've been a better path than slavery, lady."

"My name is Aleysha." the mercenary said.

"Right." Ares sighed and shook his head. He walked to the corpses of several dead Persian soldiers. The boy ripped off some of their black cloth and took some thick rope from their belts. He tossed the rope to Aleysha. "Alright, Aleysha. We'll do things your way then. Bind their hands behind their backs."

Aleysha did as she was told. Surely this would be better than just killing them off. She bound the surviving Persians' hands behind their backs and watched as Ares began to blindfold the men with black cloths. It wasn't so much the idea of killing that troubled Aleysha as it was being dishonorable by murdering people who had clearly surrendered. As a mercenary, Aleysha had dispatched plenty of enemies before, so bloodshed and cruelty wasn't new to her. However, she always upheld her honor when people submitted to her.

The Persian survivors had their hands bound behind their backs and were tied together in a line. Blindfolds made of torn black cloth covered their eyes, wrapped tightly around their heads. Ares then ordered the Persians to begin walking in the direction of Persia. If luck was on their side, they would run into someone who would save their worthless lives before they perished in Dastia's wasteland. Aleysha sighed. This was not much better than just squashing the soldiers underneath Amon's giant foot. But at least they had a chance at life. However slim.

"So, you still want a ride home?" Ares asked, turning to Aleysha.

"Uh, I live quite far from here," Aleysha said, gathering her belongings. She strapped her shield to her back and looked up at Amon.

"It's no worries."

"I live in Yuusus."

"Ah! The northern crossroads between the western and eastern sections of the continent, the upper center of Dastia, a very prosperous and diverse place indeed! It's an independent city, isn't it?" Ares said in awe. "I mean, I've only heard of the place. I've never been there."

Aleysha beamed proudly. "Yeah, it's not a part of any nation. It's just a neutral city where people from all nations gather together to trade. It's right next to the ocean too, so there's a lot of great resources there."

Ares' eyes twinkled and he grinned. "The ocean! Wow, I've always wanted to see that." He extended his hand to Aleysha. "Alright, it's settled then! Amon and I will take you home. It's been a while since I've left the Lost Sands."

Aleysha took the young boy's hand and screamed as she was suddenly whisked upwards, yanked through the air, landing gently on Amon's thick, rocky, shoulders. She panted, her heart racing from the rush. She glanced over the side of the ledge that she stood upon, which was the edge of Amon's right shoulder, and saw that the ground was frighteningly far away. She winced, shaking her head as she began to feel slightly dizzy. She absolutely despised heights.

"Hey, just don't look down," Ares advised, sitting down calmly.

Aleysha yelped, almost losing her balance as Amon began to storm forward. A single step from the rock golem dragged them half a mile across the earth. While it was a rather slow step, it was infinitely faster than traveling by horseback. They would surely make it to Yuusus in no time. The female warrior plopped onto the hard floor beside Ares. "You don't intend to bring Amon into the village, do you? I mean, I know that the villagers will be scared to death if they…."

"I know. We'll stop a couple miles outside of Yuusus and will continue the rest of the journey on foot, if that's alright with you," Ares reassured, patting Amon's solid shoulder.

Aleysha leaned back and nodded. "I'm used to walking anyway. I'm a mercenary after all. I've done plenty of escort missions where I've had to walk across entire deserts and barren wastelands to get to my destination."

"Wow, a mercenary!" Ares exclaimed. "That's pretty exciting. Must be plenty of unique contracts for you to complete since you're in the middle of the crossroads of the continent."

"Yeah." Aleysha tilted her head to the side. "There's been less work recently, though, since Persia's been taking over a lot of the nations to the west of us. I expect that they'll attempt and take Yuusus soon."

Ares said nothing and gazed up at the sunny skies.

"You know there are rumors circulating around saying that you're a merciless slaughterer, right? The name, God of War, was clearly created out of fear. People fear you, Ares," Aleysha said. "The rumors also say that you live in the Lost Sands."

"I do."

"But no human dares walk into that deadly desert. How...."

"I wasn't aware that this was an interrogation," Ares teased and Aleysha reddened with embarrassment.

"N-No! I didn't mean to...!"

"It's fine." Ares laughed. "It's been a while since I've actually talked to someone other than Amon. Maybe I've been cooped up in that desert for far too long. It's nice to have someone else to converse with." He leaned forward and called out loudly so that Amon could hear. "Not that there's anything wrong with you, Amon!"

Amon snorted, letting out a gust of hot air from his nostrils.

"Well, how long have you lived there?" Aleysha asked curiously.

"Five years."

Aleysha's eyes widened with disbelief. "Five years! Voluntarily?"

"Yep!"

"Why would you voluntarily stay in one of the driest and most dangerous places in the world?" Aleysha almost laughed at how bizarre this boy was. "Five years without any human interaction would drive me insane."

Ares scratched the back of his neck. He knew why he had to stay in that desert for five years — in order to learn what it meant to be a god and how to control his unstoppable powers. He also had to assure that he had grasped responsibility well enough before venturing a voyage out into the world while wielding such frightening strength. But Aleysha was right. It had been so long since he had seen a sight other than horrific monstrosities and plain sand. He needed to get out and see the rest of the continent.

The boy chuckled. "I guess you're right. Well, meeting you is a start, isn't it?" He held out his hand, beaming, offering a formal handshake. "I'll strike a deal with you then. I'll take you home to your city and you'll show me around. I don't think I'll be able to handle walking around a chaotic city packed with so many people alone. What do you say?"

Aleysha shook his hand, laughing. "Of course! It'll be my pleasure to show a god around the city."

***

Sitting on a wooden stool at a bar in Yuusus, a man lifted a jug of fine wine to his lips. The sweet, yet burning taste made his lips tingle and the foreigner exhaled as he took a swig of the wine. Lowering the jug to the counter, the man smacked his lips. His long, black, spiky hair cascaded down his forehead and curved sideways near his brown eyes. The foreigner wore a black, unzipped cloak, which was wrapped around his black sleeveless shirt. A long crimson cape draped down from his back to the bottom of his stool. He had a large metal belt wrapped around his waist that held an array of daggers, throwing knives, bombs, and pouches containing miscellaneous materials.

Women were gathering around the bar to marvel at the handsome foreigner that had waltzed into the city, infatuated by the amount of wealth that he appeared to have as well as his dashingly good looks. The man seemed to be only in his twenties and he drank wine like it was water. He had chugged through five jugs within the hour and claimed that it "quenched his thirst."

The man laughed hysterically at something a dainty woman was saying to him and commented on how goofy a giraffe looked as a group of marketers led the exotic animal through the streets of Yuusus. The stranger's cheeks were a rosy red from his drunken state, and he hiccupped. Little did he know that one of the women to his left was reaching into the pocket of his jacket, preparing to take some of the valuable gold coins that he had.

Just as the woman was pulling her hand back with the coins secured, the foreigner's hand lashed out and grabbed the lady by the wrist forcefully. The beauty screamed at the brutish behavior but the stranger simply smiled slyly. "Oh, man. Did you seriously think that just because I'm piss-drunk that you can take advantage of me?" Despite the fact that he was intoxicated, his speech seemed quite normal. "I'm not an idiot, you know." He pried his golden coins from her hands and shoved the thief to the ground, where she sprawled across the dirt floor.

"What do you think you're doing?" the other woman that the man had been talking to yelled. Attention had been drawn to the bar and many bystanders began to watch the drama unfold. "That was a bit harsh, don't you think?"

"Harsh?" The man burst out in abrupt laughter, his loud voice silencing everyone around him. He slammed his jug down on the bar, shattering the bottom of the clay sculpture into hundreds of pieces.

The remainder of the dark violet wine dripped off of the counter and dribbled onto the dirt. The stranger held the sharp, broken jug and snickered. "See, if I slit that lady's throat then that would be harsh. But I'm in a great mood after drinking so much. I suppose I'll let her live," he murmured, lifting the broken jug over his mouth to let tiny droplets of wine drip onto his tongue.

The woman stared at him in disbelief and took a step back from the bar. "You brute!"

"Brute? Am I the one who's trying to steal from another person? It's pretty obvious that you two are in this whole scheme together. Get a rich foreigner drunk and then distract him by engaging in a somewhat interesting conversation while your sneaky friend snags whatever the wealthy guy has in his pockets. Yeah, that would've freaking worked, but I'm a better thief than either of you two will ever be." The man snapped his fingers, sending a diamond ring spinning into the air. He caught the ring in his hand and held it out for the woman to see. It was her ring. "Ta-da! Missing something?"

"Y-You give that back right now!" the woman demanded and pointed at the stranger. "T-Thief! He took my ring!"

"Oh, wow. You're really going to pull the blame-game on me, lady?" The man continued guffawing, hardly able to even contain himself. "Is stealing from a thief even a crime?" He stopped laughing and smiled when he saw that there were several mercenaries approaching from across the street, their weapons unsheathed. The stranger sighed, eying the men from the corner of his eye. "Hello, boys. I was just having a friendly conversation with this lady here. I wouldn't recommend that you interfere."

"You stole a ring from her, give it back!" a mercenary with an eye-patch snarled. He had dark, curly hair, rotten teeth, and a scruffy beard. He and all of his cronies were wearing black shirts and baggy pants. His name was Bator and he was the leader of the group of mercenaries in Yuusus.

"Alright, I totally get it. You had a bad day; someone called you Cyclops, right?" the man quipped, laughing at Bator's eye-patch. "No worries, I'm looking to blow off some steam anyway." He reached into his jacket and pulled out a large crystal hourglass that gleamed as brightly as stars at night, and slammed it down on the table. Inside was golden sand that trickled down to the bottom half of the glass hourglass. "*One minute*," the man commanded and suddenly the sand began to leak down the hourglass at an increased speed. "By the time the last grain of golden sand leaves the top half of the hourglass, our dispute will be settled."

Bator gritted his teeth, annoyed with this foreigner's cockiness. "You think so? There's so many of us and only—"

The stranger leapt off his chair and kicked his wooden stool across the street, smashing it into one of Bator's companions. The stool exploded into multiple pieces upon impact and the man fell hard on his back, gripping his bruised ribs in agony. The cloaked man's red cape flapped through the air as he shot forward at Bator's gang.

A mercenary slashed at the cloaked man but the stranger seemed to anticipate the movement, as if he knew that it was coming. He ducked low, sliding across the dirt floor, and came upward, driving a powerful uppercut into the mercenary's chin. There was a crack as Bator's thug landed heavily on his back.

But the mysterious man had no intention of stopping there and raced forward, reading all of the bandits' attacks with ease. He avoided every slash, blow, and strike that rushed his way. His movements were like a gentle river, flowing and fluent. The foreigner easily forced himself closer to each of his targets and simply used his hand to chop them once in the throat, rendering them incapacitated.

Bator watched in utter horror as the unarmed stranger easily struck down his comrades. The cloaked man leapt through the air and kicked an opponent three times rapidly in the chest, sending the mercenary sliding onto his back. Landing swiftly, the stranger rotated his body and drove an unstoppable back-kick into the stomach of a bandit behind him. The thug was sent soaring backward and slammed the back of his head against the edge of the bar on the far side of the street, collapsing in a heap on the ground.

The unknown warrior finally turned his attention to Bator, who stood with his sword shaking as his hand trembled uncontrollably. His defeated companions lay groaning on the ground around him. The bystanders who witnessed the beating now pitied Bator, who stood alone against this skilled individual.

"W-Who are you?" Bator stammered, lunging outward with his scimitar. Ripping his sword in a downward slash, Bator watched with dismay as the cloaked man spun around the attack, avoiding it easily.

The drunk performed a front flip, driving the heel of his foot down into the back of Bator's skull. The mercenary was forced down to the ground, slamming his face heavily into the dirt street. Blood streamed freely from Bator's nose as he groaned, trying to grab at his scimitar, but his weapon was kicked away by the stranger. Bator grunted, watching powerlessly as the foreigner rummaged through the pockets of his unconscious friends.

The man pulled out a piece of parchment and raised an eyebrow as he read it. "Mercenaries, huh? That's what you lot are. Ah! So you guys thought that I was going to come into the city and steal all your business, is that it?" The cloaked figure chuckled and ripped up the paper, letting the wind sweep the pieces away as he looked at Bator with an apathetic gaze. "I have no interest in completing pathetic contracts for mere copper coins. I've gotten past that; my goals are now much higher. Higher than anything any of you thugs can even dream to attain. Oh, look at that." He walked over to the counter and snatched his crystalline hourglass, sliding it back into his cloak. "Time's up."

Bator clenched his teeth, clawing at the ground as he began to push himself onto his knees. "How dare you talk down to us like that…?"

"How dare I?" the stranger kicked Bator in the chest, sending the man sprawling onto his back. "You're the one who picked a fight with me, remember? Don't be so irritated that you and your cronies got whooped so easily. After all, it isn't your fault that *you were born into my world.*" The color of his irises had changed from their ordinary brown color into a demonic red, glowing as brightly as the sun.

Bator lay on his back, holding his chest in pain. He gulped as he stared at the foreigner, in shock at the abnormal color of his eyes, fear surging through every inch of his body. The atmosphere around the man had changed to one of terror. The aura that this cloaked man radiated was dark and vicious, making Bator feel almost surprised that he hadn't been killed. "W-Who are you?"

"My name is Tetsu Hayashi, the Demon Mercenary."

Reunion

Yuusus was a large port city with a giant wall made of solidified, packed mud that ran around its entire perimeter. Its main entrance, a wooden gate, was left wide open for any journeying adventurers. Ares looked around in awe as he sauntered through the entrance to the city with Aleysha. The girl wiped some sweat off her brow and whistled, extending her hand to the grand city before her. "Here we are, Yuusus," she breathed out a sign of relief after their long walk from the desert. They had to stop several miles outside of Yuusus to drop Amon off and then walk the rest of the way to the city.

The buildings in Yuusus were sculpted from solidified mud, clay, and stone to create massive structures that mostly had flat rooftops. Many of the people here were rich nobles from faraway lands, mercenaries seeking work, merchants, slaves and laborers, or simply wanderers who happened to stumble across the neutral city. Many enjoyed how busy the city constantly was. And it really was busy. Merchants were brazenly shouting over each other in an attempt to grab citizens' attention. Meanwhile, people were walking about and dragging exotic animals that Ares hadn't seen since he was in Persepolis.

Donkeys, giraffes, camels, and even monkeys. These were creatures that Ares hadn't seen in years and he gawked in awe at them, as if it were the first time he'd ever seen them. It was nice, actually, seeing a living organism that didn't want to swallow him whole.

Armed mercenaries who loitered around wooden benches and buildings were eying Aleysha as she walked through the streets. Some whistled and hooted at her, but she kept her face calm and continued forward. Aleysha explained that some merely found her attractive while others saw her as a threat to their business since she hoarded many of the contracts for mercenary work.

While Yuusus was lively, it was also very dangerous. Some of the mercenaries were overly brutish and extremely violent. Since Yuusus was a neutral city and did not belong to any particular empire, its law enforcement was weaker than that of ordinary cities. Some considered Yuusus to be lawless. A few of the mercenaries who lived in the city therefore abused the lack of enforcement and committed crimes, making it one of the most dangerous cities that Aleysha had ever been to. But it was also one of the richest cities due to the large number of foreign exchanges that occurred within the city. Yuusus prospered, and therefore Aleysha found it to be a fitting place to settle.

Aleysha and Ares walked past dozens of miniature shops that were set up. Merchants screamed out prices, raising their voices as they tried to shout over each other in a futile attempt to win over the hundreds, maybe even thousands, of customers that wandered through the sandy streets. Many of the rich pedestrians that strolled through the city were wearing stylish, colorful silks. The mercenaries, lackeys, and workers wore short, torn clothing that revealed their crispy brown skin, tanned from the long days in the sun. Some laborers could afford cloaks or silks to cover themselves, but most just wore whatever cheap clothing they could put on their backs.

Aleysha ducked into a small home that was crammed between many other houses that all looked identical. She waited until Ares entered her home behind her and closed the wooden door, exhaling. "Well," she said, waving her hand through the air, "it isn't much but it's home. My mom's at work and my brother is probably out completing a contract."

"A contract, huh? He's a mercenary too, then?"

"Yeah," Aleysha said, placing her sword and shield up against the wall. The girl pulled a band from her pocket and reached up, bundling her long, flowing blonde hair into a ponytail. She then walked to her table and picked up a pitcher of water, turning to Ares. "Are you thirsty?"

Ares nodded. It had been so long since he had drunk actual clean water. "Thank you," he said, smiling thankfully. He found himself examining Aleysha meticulously. She was very tan, clearly from many years in the scorching Dastian sun. Her muscles were toned, clearly from vigorous training. She definitely had a warrior's body, which was impressive. He wondered what she was like on the battlefield and whether or not she had actually fought in a real war.

The boy blinked. He realized that he too had yet to fight a war, despite his title of God of War.

He accepted the cool pitcher from Aleysha, feeling chills creep up his fingers as a gentle tingle shivered through his body. He brought the pitcher to his lips and let the fresh water stream into his mouth, filling him with its purity.

Aleysha put her hands on her hips, watching with a raised eyebrow as the boy chugged down the entire pitcher with one, long, gulp. "You must be really thirsty, huh?"

"I live in the Lost Sands. Can you blame me? We don't really have a natural source of water there." Ares laughed, taking a breath after swallowing the jug of water. "Whoo! That hit the spot!" He thrust the pitcher at the surprised mercenary and smiled innocently. "More?"

***

Tetsu tucked the Sands of Time back into his cloak as he stormed away from the scene, annoyed. The first time that he had been home in months and no one recognized him. Maybe it was because he decided to shave the beard that he had tried growing out last year. He sighed, trudging through the busy streets of Yuusus.

Five years ago, he had collapsed just at the edge of the Lost Sands, and fortunately had been saved by a girl who had been walking nearby with her mother. He had been lucky enough that the family had adopted him as one of their own and took care of him. Since then, he had worked in Yuusus, making easy money as a mercenary. He was titled the best mercenary in the entire continent, known by all for his incredible swordsmanship. They all called him the Demon Mercenary because his eyes changed to red when he grew angry. He figured that it was genetics that made his eyes change such a way, or perhaps a mysterious form of magic that he had obtained while he was in the Forgotten Sands.

Tetsu had returned home to Yuusus to pay his adopted family a visit as well as share some of his limitless wealth with them. He felt obliged to pay them back for saving his life five years before. Finally reaching his home made of solidified mud and bricks, Tetsu rapped his knuckles gently against the wooden door. The roofs of most buildings in Yuusus were flat, and the lower-income families usually had houses made of wood, mud, brick, or a combination of the three.

The door creaked open and Tetsu smiled to find himself facing his sister, Aleysha. "Hey, Aleysha. You're home already? I thought you were completing a contract that took you west," he said, embracing his sister.

"Yeah, I was. But we ran into some Persians and got captured," Aleysha said, hugging her brother back.

Tetsu frowned, pulling back. "Really? Persians have already turned their attention east?"

"They already dominate the entirety of western Dastia according to some of the mercenaries that I was working with. Looks like they're coming east now," Aleysha murmured, reaching up and rubbing her temples to ease her stress.

Tetsu glanced past Aleysha and saw a young boy sitting on the floor of their home, chugging a cold metal pitcher of water. The man frowned, pushing past his sister and walking into the house. His eyes widened as he stared at the boy. He shook his head in disbelief. "It can't be…."

Aleysha stepped up from behind Tetsu. "What's wrong?"

"Darien?" Tetsu whispered.

The boy lowered the pitcher and tilted his head to the side. "Wow, it's been a while since anyone's called me that."

Aleysha frowned as she glanced between her brother and the

boy that she recognized as Ares. Darien? Wasn't that the name of the insane Persian prince who killed his parents? She remembered hearing that he had been exiled to the Lost Sands where … wait. The Lost Sands? She turned suddenly to Ares, her mouth wide. "Don't tell me…."

"Prince Darien of Persia," Tetsu exclaimed. "I-It's me! Tetsu, remember?"

Ares' eyes lit up and he jumped to his feet. "Whoa! Tetsu! I thought you were dead all these years, man!" He leapt up and hugged his old friend tightly. "Wow, you look so much older!"

"And you haven't aged a day," Tetsu said with a frown. "How is that possible?"

"We have a lot to talk about, don't we? Come, sit." Ares said, motioning for Tetsu and Aleysha to sit with him. "I'll share my story!"

The boy told Aleysha and Tetsu everything about what had happened after he had been banished as a prince. For some reason, his story seemed to just flow out naturally. It was the first time in many years that he had shared so many words at once and he was glad to share his adventures with his friends. He told them of his treacherous journey after he became a god and how he had wandered the Lost Sands slaying legendary beasts of myth to push the limitations of his strength. His training in the desert had honed his power to nearly reach its maximum potential. He explained to Tetsu that he had saved Aleysha merely because she looked exactly like Ra, who had saved him in the desert.

"Aleysha shares every physical aspect with Ra!" Ares exclaimed, pointing to the gleaming shield that Aleysha had leaned against the wall of the house. "Even that shield! I remember it from five years ago when I saw her. I mean, it could've easily been a hallucination, but isn't it a little odd that I saw a mirage of someone that I'd meet in the future?"

"I suppose…." Tetsu shrugged. "Maybe Ra did it so that Aleysha would lead you to me. I mean, we were separated in the Lost Sands so that would make the most sense."

"Perhaps," Ares said. Maybe he was over-thinking it. Either way, he was glad to see that his friend was healthy and alive.

During Ares' stay, Aleysha's mother came home and prepared dinner. She welcomed Ares as one of Tetsu's guests and didn't bother asking for the details. The feast that she prepared was enormous for four people, but Ares ate like a gluttonous deity.

Set on a table was an amalgam of different foods spanning from seasoned curry to exotic eastern soups. Ares' eyes twinkled at how much food there was at one place. Every time he had wanted to eat in the Lost Sands, he had to slay a ferocious beast. And even then it took forever to cook its meat, so he'd have to wait a while before he was finally able to eat it. Finding water was even harder. He either stumbled across some lucky oasis or had to dig holes deep enough to get some murky fluid that didn't even look drinkable. Eating food like this made him feel like a prince again and he indulged himself with plenty of servings.

Tetsu and Aleysha watched as the youthful boy inhaled entire dishes on his own. His stomach seemed bottomless. Every time Ares raised his cleaned bowl into the air and asked politely for another serving, Aleysha's mother smiled. She didn't seem to care that the guest was hoarding all of the food for himself; she actually seemed flattered that he took such enjoyment in eating her cooking.

"Geez, Ares. You're eating like a barbarian," Aleysha murmured.

Aleysha's mother tilted her head. "What did you say his name was?"

Aleysha's face paled. "Uh…."

"Darien," Tetsu said, shooting Aleysha a glare. "His name is Darien."

"Ah, like that old Persian prince. That's a cute name," her mother said.

Tetsu exhaled. That was close. Practically everyone knew of Ares, and most of those who heard of him believed the rumor that he was a bloodthirsty deity that killed for fun and abused his limitless power. Never in Tetsu's wildest imagination would he have believed that the renowned Ares was actually his old childhood friend.

After finishing practically every single dish that Aleysha's mother prepared, Ares leaned back, patting his bloated stomach. Aleysha giggled. "What?" Ares smiled, finding that Aleysha's laughter was contagious.

"You look like a pudgy little kid right now!"

"Once I digest this I'll look like a bony weakling again. No worries!"

"Darien," Tetsu harrumphed, and the boy turned to look at his friend. "Come on, let's go for a walk. I want to talk to you about something."

Ares blinked, looking at his friend for a moment before nodding. He grunted as he heaved himself to his feet and turned, giving Aleysha's mother a deep, respectful bow. "Thank you so much for dinner!"

"You better not show him the whole city, Tetsu!" Aleysha called as Ares and Tetsu walked towards the door. "I promised him that I'd show him part of it myself!"

Tetsu grinned over his shoulder. "I'm just taking him to the ocean. The two of us have to catch up."

Stepping outside of the small building, Ares saw that everything was dark. Tiny lights flickered on candles and torches held by sconces, which illuminated the still-active city streets. While there were not as many people walking about as Ares had seen earlier in the day, there were still a reasonable amount of civilians occupying the streets. Most of the merchants had begun to pack their belongings and were walking with camels, which carried the packaged weight.

Tetsu led Ares through the city to the docks, without speaking a word. He watched as the lights in Ares' eyes lit up like two tiny suns as a broad grin stretched across his face. The boy seemed infatuated with every aspect of the docks and the ocean. The wooden docks were mottled with moss and random discoloration. Several ships were still docked and Ares leapt onto the wood ecstatically, thudding loudly as he scrambled to get a closer look at the ships.

Tetsu watched his old friend, smiling. It was like watching a younger brother get excited over the perfect gift for his birthday. Perhaps this was a gift. After all, Darien had wanted to see the ocean since they were kids. Cambyses had read them stories of the incredible ocean, a body of water that extended as far as the skies. If mankind could cross the body of water, they could potentially discover new lands, with new people and cultures. The very thought had boggled the minds of the two children in their youth.

Ares was gripping a rail, gazing upon the flapping white sails of one of the ships as a brisk breeze blew against it. The edges of the docks were soaked in brine, giving the wood a dark-brown color. The salty smell that filled the air was foreign to the god, and he turned and gazed across the swaying ocean with twinkling eyes. It was mind-blowing how the water moved on its own to create gentle waves that crashed against the docks and the sandy beaches. The Lost Sands was so deprived of water, yet here there was plenty! It was like an oasis with an unlimited supply of water!

The boy squatted down onto his knees and cupped his hands, dipping them into the freezing-cold water. He lifted his hands to his lips. "Darien, you might not want to…," Tetsu began to warn the boy but sighed when he noticed it was too late.

Ares sucked in his cheeks and winced as the salty taste of ocean water filled his mouth. He spat it out immediately, coughing and sputtering. His eyes were bulging and he shook his head, turning to Tetsu. He looked completely bewildered. "W-What's wrong with the water? Is it poisonous or something?"

"N-No…." Tetsu laughed. "It's not drinkable. Ocean water is for the creatures of the sea to live in, not for us to drink."

Ares crossed his arms and pouted, annoyed. "Why can't it be both?"

"The gods just didn't make it that way, I suppose. After all, if we stole all the water for ourselves then the creatures that need the ocean to survive would never be able to live. You know how humans are. Always greedy," Tetsu said, leaning against the wooden railing of one of the decks. "I want to talk about what happened on that day, Darien. There wasn't time for us to talk. I know that you acted on impulse, trying to protect me."

Ares sat on the edge of the docks, dipping his bare feet in the chilling ocean water as he gazed at the sea of glistening stars that gleamed in the night sky. A full moon beamed among the tiny stars, illuminating the dark sky with its brilliance. Ares personally didn't like to think of the memories that he had as Darien. Those memories merely brought him feelings of regret or nostalgia, both of which he loathed. "You would've done the same for me, Tetsu."

"I know that," Tetsu said. "Yuu was slashed trying to protect me. The horrific guilt of that day, knowing that Yuu was cut down because of me, haunts me in nightmares every night. Sleep is hard, knowing that the boy that I teased everyday was killed because he tried to save me." He swallowed hard, looking down at the crashing waves. "Though, I'm grateful to have had two great friends that looked out for me. Both of you risked your lives to save someone of lesser worth like me."

"You know that I don't see any human as lesser."

"But that's not how this world works, Darien." Tetsu closed his eyes, knowing the harsh reality of social hierarchy. "You and Yuu were worth much more than I was. The two of you were educated, and prepared to enter the world of politics that could influence the lives of hundreds of thousands of people. I'm just a person who influences the lives of those that I kill and their families."

"And those that you save," Ares added.

Tetsu nodded, a tear forming in the corner of his eye. "I suppose. I just wanted to say thank you. I mean, I wouldn't be here today without you. So thanks."

Ares smiled, kicking his feet through the water gently, causing the salty liquid to slosh around. "Like I said, you would've done the same for me."

Tetsu bit his lip. "I also want you to know that I wasn't the one who killed your parents."

"I know."

"And I want to find out who it was that committed such an atrocity and framed the two of us. I want them punished for what they've done," the Demon Mercenary growled, squeezing the wooden railing tightly. "I'll bet it was Cambyses. After the king and queen were out of the picture, pointing fingers at you was easy, and cleared the path to the throne for him. After all, as soon as he took the throne, he began conquering every nation near Persia. They spared the lives of no one, and either shoved survivors into slavery or had them decapitated and cremated to create fear in those who oppose the Persians. I'm telling you, I caught him conspiring with a Magus, saying something about a god and eliminating the king. He's insane, that man is."

Ares remembered how Cambyses had talked to him several years ago about uniting the continent as one and how his father had been foolish to attempt to create an era of peace. He lowered his eyes. "Cambyses had much to gain from eliminating the royal family, yes. But it was not him that physically committed the murders. There had to be others involved. You and I were the only ones in the room, but neither of us did it. That means that magic must be somehow tied into this. I'd point fingers at the Magus, if anything."

"The question is how many Magi were involved in this plot."

"There's more than one?"

"I heard that Cambyses has ten Magi at his disposal. Each one is assigned to a Persian army, practically ensuring victory because of their overwhelming power. This new era of war calls for magic. Without it, victory is very much out of reach. And Persia conveniently has got most of the magicians in its pocket." Tetsu ran a hand through his spiky black hair and exhaled. "We know for a fact that the Magus who knocked us both out is involved, though. He was the one who was plotting to overthrow the king with Cambyses in the Royal Jail. His name is Zahir."

"Zahir, huh?" Ares echoed. "In the end, it doesn't matter. The past is the past. There's no changing it."

"Aren't you angry? Don't you want to make them pay for your parents' deaths?" Tetsu exclaimed, turning to face Ares. "Darien, Cambyses has your throne and no one is punishing him for it! I've waited patiently for years for an opportune moment that would give me a chance to exact revenge for the injustice done on that day. But you don't even seem to care."

Ares said nothing.

"You and I have both suffered emotionally and physically from that day. Our courageousness and strength were tested in the Lost

Sands. If we had not been worthy, the two of us would've perished. The desert gave us a chance to make things right."

"The desert gave us a chance at life," Ares snapped. "So why are you so eager to toss it away again? If we're so lucky to be alive, then why do you want to challenge the greatest military in the entire continent? You're rushing to your death, Tetsu. You can't combat the Persians."

"But you can," Tetsu said with a sly smile. "I've heard the stories and I know that they're true. You bested a hundred thousand foot soldiers on your own. Now imagine if you had an army with you. You could halt the legendary empire and bring judgment upon the murderers of your parents. You could reclaim your throne and become the ruler of Persia—"

"I don't want to become a ruler," Ares interrupted him. "I've never wanted that responsibility. I don't want to hold the lives of thousands in the palm of my hand, knowing that every decision I make decides their fate. Kings choose whether they want to sacrifice their own wealth to help the people. Or kings can decide to let them suffer. Kings even have the power to, apparently, have any minority group that they want eradicated from existence. I've heard tales of what Cambyses has done to your clan in Persia. I believe that the power of a king is much more terrifying than that of a small god."

Tetsu closed his eyes. A year after Cambyses became king, he announced the persecution of everyone in the Hayashi clan. There was no real reasoning behind the mandate. But soon people in Persia began to use the Hayashi clan as scapegoats for their problems. The people of the Hayashi clan were pried from their homes by the dozens and all hung. Their dangling bodies were cut down and burned, as if they were executed soldiers of war rather than innocent civilians who deserved proper burial. A single command from Persia's king did that. Darien was right; the power of the throne was immense and terrifying. Such power had to be wielded by someone trustworthy. Not a man as selfish and merciless as Cambyses. "We can't just sit back and let Cambyses destroy innocent lives. Doing nothing now would only make things worse. You heard Aleysha, the Persians are beginning to look east. That means that they'll be at our doorstep in no time!"

Ares sighed, rubbing the back of his neck. "I was given the responsibility to wield the power of a god. The Lost Sands deemed me worthy because the gods believed that I would use this strength for the right reasons. Interfering in mortal affairs is not what this power is for."

"By interfering in these 'mortal affairs' you'll be doing what is right. If that isn't what your power should be used for, then when should you use it? Why did you train vigorously in the harsh desert for so long if not to wield this mighty strength? If you should ever use it at all, it should be to bring order and justice to Dastia," Tetsu said.

Ares lowered his head, defeated. Tetsu was right. He had no idea when he should use this power. But if there were ever a reason to use it, justice would be the answer. "Let me think about it. What you're asking is a big commitment."

Tetsu nodded. "I understand." He walked over to Ares and took off his leather boots, rolling up his pants as he dipped his feet in the water beside his friend. A freezing chill exploded through his legs and he shivered, wincing. "C-Cold!"

The god laughed heartily. "After so many years in the scorching desert days of the Lost Sands and the freezing nights, temperatures don't really bother me much anymore."

Tetsu wrapped an arm around Ares' shoulder and grinned, rubbing his knuckles into the top of the boy's skull playfully. "Hey, man. I really missed you."

Ares yelped, chuckling at his friend's teasing. "I missed you too, Tetsu." After finding his friend, Ares felt a hole in his heart that had previously been empty become filled. "I have to show you to a friend of mine. His name is Amon and I met him in the Lost Sands. I'll introduce you tomorrow."

Tetsu grinned, pulling away from Ares as he placed his palms on the wooden docks and looked up into the night sky. "Sounds good, I can't wait to meet him."

***

In the far-off distance, upon a mountain of sand, stood two mysterious figures that watched Ares and another man at the docks of Yuusus. One of the figures was wearing a black cloak with a cowl that covered the features of his face in dark shadows. Dangling from his neck was a skull pendant that rested on his chest. They were miles away from Yuusus, yet the man was easily able to see the God of War with his eagle-like vision. "It would seem that those blindfolded soldiers were correct. He does look like the deceased banished prince, Darien." Beside him was a giant, bald, shirtless man with rippling muscles and a thick brown mustache. A giant tiger's hide was wrapped around his shoulder and its head clamped onto the skull of the man, making it look like the stranger was wearing the tiger as a hat. The furry hide of the striped beast draped down as a cape and cascaded down the man's back. The man wore torn, red shorts that were just above his knees in length. He was walking barefoot in the cold desert night. "Darien, huh? Do you suppose that he's the real prince, then?"

The cloaked man shrugged. "Who knows? The rumors said that this renowned boy was a god of war. If he's a god of war, then why did he spare those Persian soldiers?" he murmured. "I would've expected him to execute them slowly and painfully merely for the pleasure of it."

"Perhaps he's not a sadist as the rumors say."

"Well, we'll find out soon. If this boy truly is as powerful as everyone says then he'll be able to halt the Persian advance into eastern Dastia." The man frowned. "It seems that he's with a man as well. A member of the Hayashi clan. I can feel the dark atmosphere radiating from his very existence even from this far away."

"And what do you feel from the god?"

"Nothing," the man muttered. "I can't read him."

"Huh?" The shirtless man grinned, intrigued. "So even a Magus can't read the god's aura. Now that's interesting." The man turned and saw that the cloaked figure was walking off, in the opposite direction of Yuusus. "Eh? Where are you going?"

"We're done here. We'll assess just how powerful this supposed Ares is when the Persian army strikes this city. Surely there must be a reason that the god left the Lost Sands for the first time in years. And

I believe that reason is in this city. If we invade it, I believe he will show his true colors."

Noble Awakening

Cambyses snapped his eyes open and bolted forward. Sweat was rushing down his face, soaking his black beard. He had shaved the top of his head after he had claimed his throne, and now he reached up, rubbing his bald head. Another nightmare. He was sick of hearing the cries of his dead nephew, brother, and sister-in-law in his dreams.

His luxurious room was filled with glistening treasures. The walls were made of shining gold and had various elegant paintings covering a majority of it. The fine, silky, white curtains that led to his balcony were blowing in a gentle night breeze. It seemed his window had mysteriously opened. How odd.

Cambyses glanced to his side at his gorgeous consort, a young wife that he had met a year after he had claimed his throne. He heard a gentle cry and his eyes shot across the room to a man wearing a long white cloak that curled around his body, making him look like a ghost. His black hair spiked down over his head, curling sideways near his gleaming violet eyes. His sleeves were rolled up, revealing a tattoo of a dragon wrapping around his arm. The marking was the color of blood. Ostentatious ruby, sapphire, emerald, and gold bracelets were wrapped around his right wrist, making his hand glow luxuriously. The man cradled a white bundled cloth that held a crying baby. He was stroking the child slowly, trying to silence it.

"Zahir, what are you doing in my room this late at night?" the king demanded as he threw off his covers and stood tall, storming forward angrily. A vein bulged from his forehead, his chest puffing out when he saw that the Magus was holding the child. "Put down my son!"

"Milord, there is nothing to fear. I'm good with children," Zahir said with a wicked smile.

"Put him down, now! *I command you!*"

Zahir shrugged and placed the bundled child back in his crib. The baby continued to cry and the Magus scowled, turning his head to the little monster, holding up a finger. "*Silence.*" Immediately, the baby's cries became muffled and no sound could be heard.

"How dare you use magic on my child?" Cambyses snarled silently, trying not to wake up his wife.

"Ah, it's harmless magic, milord. There is nothing to fear."

"What is it that you want, Zahir?"

"The army led by General Shazir that is heading east stumbled across a small group of Persian soldiers that had been blindfolded and tied together in a line," Zahir said. "They claimed to have survived a confrontation against the God of War, Ares."

Cambyses straightened his back, wrinkles forming on his brow.

"They claim that the boy has incredible physical strength and is able to summon a gigantic rock elemental at will. He also has some type of enchanted spear that he can control without even having to wield it. Such magical strength and precision would require decades of training for an ordinary Magus to perfect such a skill. Perhaps even a lifetime," Zahir said. "There is another catch, though. They say that he looks identical to the prince, Darien, just before he was cast into the Lost Sands to perish."

"Darien?"

The queen yawned, drowsily cracking her eyes open. "Mm? Cambyses, what are you doing up?"

"Nothing, my love," Cambyses reassured her. "Go back to sleep."

Zahir clicked his fingers and immediately the queen fell into a deep slumber. "It is quite possible that the prince is still alive then. Though, I am not sure if that boy is him. After all, I examined Darien and saw that he didn't have any magical prowess at his young age. There was no potential for him to ever become a Magus. And yet this Ares has an incredible pool of magical power and destructive capabilities. Besides, it's impossible for Darien to look the exact same age as he was five years ago. He was a growing boy; he'd be a man by now."

Cambyses exhaled, relieved. "You're right."

"Ramses has also sighted Ares at Yuusus. If our army is going to push into eastern Dastia as planned, we're going to have to go through the God of War," Zahir said.

"What does Ramses believe is the best course of action?"

"He believes it best if we test this God of War to see just how strong he is."

Cambyses raised an eyebrow. "So use Shazir's army as bait, then?"

"Meanwhile, we can send in our armies into the Lost Sands to locate the lost artifact, as originally planned many years ago," Zahir said. "Without Ares guarding the Lost Sands we can push deeper into the desert and perhaps find it. Of course, the desert is very dangerous and we are bound to have heavy casualties. But we will manage much better with Ares out of the way."

Cambyses nodded. "I see. Then use Shazir's army as you see fit."

"I must speak against that, milord," a voice spoke from the shadows. A young man with flowing hair the color of pure snow stepped out from the darkness, wearing heavy metallic armor that clanked as he walked. His hands were covered by black gloves and his turquoise eyes flitted from Zahir to Cambyses. A white cloak wrapped itself around his armor but was left unbuttoned, revealing an iron chest plate inscribed with a red insignia of a lion. "Sacrificing the lives of that many men is not worth petty information on our target."

"My apprentice," Zahir said with an amused smile. "I was not aware that you had followed me. You are much stealthier than I thought. I've taught you well, Yuu."

Yuu said nothing, nor did his apathetic expression change.

"What is this Magus doing here?" Cambyses grumbled. "My family is sleeping! We will talk about this another time. Zahir, continue with the plans. Yuu, we have plenty of men to spare. If those soldiers can stall Ares long enough so that we can get troops into the Lost Sands to begin searching for the artifact, then it is worth it ten times over." He dismissed the two Magi with a wave and wearily returned to his bed, plopping himself into the soft mattress.

Ares. There were many gods worshipped by different cultures. But in all of western Dastia, Cambyses had never heard of a god named Ares before five years ago when he had proclaimed his name to the world. A god of war that had simply appeared out of nowhere and was one of the first to interact with the mortal world. But what culture worshipped this god? It was not Persia.

Cambyses sighed and closed his eyes, trying not to think of it too much. Soon enough he would have the power to bring down anyone, human or god.

***

Yuu walked on the dust-covered walkway outside of Persepolis's royal castle, overlooking the city as he followed his mentor, Zahir. He had heard that this God of War, Ares, looked similar, if not identical, to Darien. The old memories that he had of Darien made him tingle with nostalgia, but he could not forget the fact that he had gone mad and murdered his own parents in cold blood. When Yuu had been woken after being slashed across the back, five years before, he had awoken to shocking news of Tetsu and Darien's banishments. The two of them, he knew, would not last a week in the Lost Sands.

But when Cambyses had told him of Darien's betrayal of the kingdom, Yuu couldn't believe his ears. Unfortunately, the noble was forced to believe it. Just before Yuu had passed out from his injury, he recalled seeing Darien's expression reflecting bloodlust as he relentlessly stabbed the corpse of one of the Persians. The sadistic look in his eyes had made Yuu question whether or not he truly knew Darien. The irate prince had gone mad from his untamable rage.

Yuu had passed out afterward, and later found himself slowly believing what Cambyses had told him. Accepting that Darien and Tetsu were gone from his life, Yuu had continued his studies so that he could make his noble family proud by becoming a powerful figure in the Persian government. However, several months after the banishment of Darien and Tetsu, Zahir approached Yuu and offered the boy an apprenticeship. He offered to make Yuu a Magus.

Becoming a Magus would grant the young boy, who had always been powerless, newfound strength. Humans in Dastia were either born with hidden magic, or they were simply ordinary mortals. In order to unlock that sealed magic one had to inscribe an ancient symbol onto their body, similar to a tattoo. That marking was their proof of becoming a mage. But in order to become a Magus, the mage would have to train vigorously to unlock their maximum capabilities and utilize their magic to its full potential.

Each Magus specialized in a type of magic that was determined when they were born. Many people who were born with magic were never actually able to use their magic, though, because they never received an ancient marking. Thus their secret power lay dormant for their entire lives. When Yuu discovered that he had been born with suppressed magic, he leapt at the opportunity to become one of the Magi, frightened of constantly being powerless and leaving his magic dormant forever. He had wanted to make a difference to the empire through becoming a strong political figure. But now with magic, he could change the world with a different approach.

"Do you truly think that Ares could be Prince Darien?" Yuu asked his mentor as they walked along the stone pathway, overlooking the gigantic city of Persepolis. Could Darien really be alive?

"The chances are highly unlikely," Zahir admitted. "I'd say that the two of them crossed paths somewhere in the Lost Sands. While Ares is an unknown deity to us, he is still a god. Thus he can change his physical appearance to his liking and he must have chosen Darien for some mysterious reason. That's my theory. Though, that means that Prince Darien could still be very much alive, given the fact that he has some type of a connection with Ares. It will be up to us Persian Magi to exterminate his existence, do you understand?" The Magus looked at Yuu over his shoulder with his glowing purple eyes. "You cannot let your past with him jeopardize the safety of our empire."

"I won't," Yuu reassured his mentor. "I would never spare a traitor to Persia."

***

The morning air was crisp and still, typical of the weather in northern Dastia. In the afternoon it would grow hot and humid, but for now, Ares enjoyed the cool temperatures. The god had slept on the floor between Aleysha and Tetsu, on blue mats, while Aleysha's mother took the bed.

The sounds of shouting merchants and bargaining shoppers soon echoed through the silent household as Yuusus awoke from its daily slumber.

Ares groaned, cracking his eyes open, and saw that everyone was already awake and moving about the house. He figured that it was time he got up too.

Everyone in the household seemed to have to contribute in some way. Aleysha's mother asked if Aleysha and Ares could deliver a heavy chest to a buyer from across the city. Ares didn't mind doing some chores to help out Aleysha's family. After all, it was the least he could do after her mother had cooked such a gigantic meal.

Ares picked up the one-hundred-pound package with one hand easily, lifting it over his head. Aleysha and her mother stared at him with shock. The blonde mercenary jabbed Ares in the ribs with her elbow and whispered hotly, "At least make it look like you're struggling with that! You look like you're only fifteen years old, and even grown men can't lift packages like that over their head!"

"Oh, got it. Wow, this package is *really* heavy!" the boy exclaimed loud enough so Aleysha's mother could hear. Aleysha smacked her forehead. Ares would never be an actor, that was for sure. This was horrible.

Tetsu burst out laughing, unable to control himself anymore.

Ares turned to look at his friend and accidently tripped, landing on the ground face-first with the heavy package slamming down onto his back. Aleysha's mother screamed as she rushed forward. Aleysha and Tetsu heaved the chest off of the boy's body. Aleysha's mother helped Ares to his feet. "A-Are you okay?" She was talking frantically, brushing dust off of Ares and checking him all over to see if he had any injuries.

The boy stared at the woman as if she were an alien and then smiled, a warm feeling rising in his chest. It had been a while since he had felt this way. Even his mother hadn't been this worried and affectionate. But Aleysha's mother genuinely cared for her guests. She truly was a kind soul.

Ares and Aleysha said goodbye as they left the house, and carried the chest through Yuusus. As promised, Aleysha showed Ares around the city as they made their way across Yuusus to deliver the package. The city had tons of shops and its restaurants were culturally diverse, bringing together a variety of different foods to this one central hub of the continent. People from all over Dastia came to Yuusus to offer new styles for making food and it simply fascinated Ares. He had always just had Hussan to cook for him back when he was a prince, and in the Lost Sands he would eat whatever he could get his hands on. But in Yuusus it was all about the difference in style and taste. They weren't just eating to survive like Ares did in the Lost Sands.

Aleysha led the young god to a large neighborhood of mansions, all of which were massive and made of expensive materials, like marble and gold, which made them stand out from the homes made of stone, wood, and mud. The two companions stopped at one particular manor, the largest of them all. The front door was made of a fine wood that was a dark hue of brown and had a golden knocker that took the shape of a malicious demon's face. Giant marble pillars supported the building's slanted orange-tiled rooftop, and several acres of verdant grass surrounded the mansion, which was surprising. Ares didn't see much grass in western Dastia, but this house seemed to have plenty of it.

Aleysha grabbed the golden knocker and gently rapped it against the demon's face on the wooden door. It only took a second before the door swung open and the mercenary found herself face to face with a dainty young girl.

The stranger's long brunette hair was tied up in a ponytail that blew in the gentle breeze that gusted through the area. Her eyes were the color of emeralds, glistening with life. She looked as if she was twenty, and she was absolutely the definition of beauty, even Aleysha had to admit to that. She wore a long, dark blue skirt that went just past her thighs and long white stockings that covered most of her exposed legs. The girl wore a tight blue shirt with a line of buttons running through the center of her clothing. Her skirt and shirt came together with a thick leather belt that wrapped around her waist, secured by a golden buckle. In her hand she gripped a carved staff made of some type of rare wood that Ares and Aleysha didn't recognize. The light brown stick was curved at the end and almost looked more like a cane than a staff. A necklace hung down from her neck and rested a small, cerulean-blue, circular trinket on her chest. The girl had forgone shoes and was walking on bare feet.

"Oh, hey Aleysha!" The girl scanned the area around the mercenary as if she were looking for someone. "Is Tetsu here?"

"Hey, Kira. Uh, no. He's helping my mother do some errands."

"But he's in town!"

"Yeah, he is." Aleysha laughed. "It's quite rare to see the two of you here at the same time."

"It is! I really miss him," Kira exclaimed, her eyes lit up like fireworks when she found out that Tetsu was in Yuusus. She turned her attention to Ares and smiled. "And who are...." She frowned suddenly, tilting her head. "Huh? I don't feel anything from you."

"What do you mean?" Aleysha asked.

"Normally with any mortals I can see the aura that they give off. But with him I don't see anything. That's really strange." Kira frowned. "Aleysha, introduce us."

"Uh, right." Aleysha indicated to Kira. "Darien, this is Kira. She's the Magus of an eastern empire called Luxas. Kira, this is Darien." She cleared her throat. "Is your king here? I believe that he was the one who ordered this package."

"Yeah, he is," Kira said, not taking her eyes off of Ares for a moment. "I'll make sure that the package gets to him." She tapped her staff on the ground and the package levitated into the air and drifted slowly into the house. "Darien, right? Well, it is a pleasure to meet you."

"Likewise," Ares said and suddenly his eyes widened. He jerked his head around and watched as an ominous shadow blanketed over the land. He could feel bloodlust in the air and an unforgettable violent aura permeated through the area. The boy grunted, grabbing Aleysha and shoving her into Kira's arms, forcing the two girls into the house. "Get down!" he boomed and slammed the door shut behind him, looking up at the sky.

The shadows that had stretched across the land were caused by a tsunami of arrows that were raining from the sky, slamming down and digging into the earth. Ares extended his hand outward, a brisk wind conjuring his spear into his hand. "*Aegis*." A giant, oval, shield materialized in front of Ares, halting all of the projectiles that were coming down on the mansion. The arrows froze as they struck the blue magical barrier, and they hovered in the air, unmoving.

Ares snapped his fingers and the arrows exploded backwards, returning back to their origins with blinding speed. The god gritted his teeth, turning to the mansion. It looked as if thousands of pricks were poking out of the grass, though the building was untouched because of Ares' conjured shield. He walked to one of the arrows that was lodged deep into the dirt and grabbed the projectile by its shaft, pulling the bronze weapon from the earth. He recognized the arrow's texture and closed his eyes, distraught. These arrows were made by Persians. It was common for Persian armies to begin an incursion with a volley of deadly arrows. They had enough archers to make it rain death upon Yuusus. Surely there were going to be many casualties.

Aleysha threw the door of the mansion open and staggered outside. "What happened?" she panted, scanning the area.

"Persians," Ares said. "They've come to invade Yuusus."

"How did you stop all the arrows like that? Are you a Magus yourself?" Kira asked, surprised.

"Something like that," Ares said. "You're going to need to get your king to somewhere secure. This place is going to turn into a battlefield once those Persians start to advance. I'll try to make them turn back."

"Oh my gods, what about Mom?" Aleysha exclaimed, covering her mouth with shock.

Ares reached out and grabbed Aleysha, sweeping her off her feet, holding the mercenary in his arms. "Hold on!" He grunted and kicked off of the ground, propelling himself hundreds of feet into the air as he soared over Yuusus, his eyes scanning for Aleysha's home. The mercenary's fearful screams echoed in his ears but he ignored them as he descended towards the city. He smashed down onto the ground, squatting as the earth cracked beneath his feet. Ares lowered Aleysha, who was trembling, to the street and scanned the area around him.

Every living creature that had been in the streets during the time of the volley had been killed. Arrows protruded from the bloody wounds of corpses that lay sprawled across the city streets. Camels, monkeys, snakes, and other animals also lay dead, penetrated by the deadly projectiles. Ares bit his lip and heard Aleysha's shrill scream. He turned and rushed through the open doorway into her house.

Arrows had torn their way through the roof in their home and buried themselves into the dirt floor. The windows were shattered and glass was scattered all over the floor in a chaotic display. Beside a broken vase was a bloody, unmoving body. Aleysha's mother.

Ares stared, watching as Aleysha cradled her mother's corpse in her arms. He felt a chilling sensation shiver through his spine and he winced. The image of his slain parents flashed through his mind and he staggered sideways, leaning himself against the wall of Aleysha's home. He closed his eyes and shook his head, feeling dizzy. Aleysha's mother hadn't deserved this horrible fate. She'd done nothing wrong. Yet the unfairness of the universe brought her this brutal end.

The Persians had attacked without warning. They released hell upon Yuusus with no care for the lives of the innocent people in this city. They were scum. No, they were worse than that. All of them deserved what was coming.

Boiling ire surged through Ares' veins as he mashed his teeth, storming out of the house. He couldn't listen to Aleysha's wailing cries anymore. He knew where he had to be. Ares jammed his feet hard into the ground and sent himself rocketing upwards into the air even higher than before. Flying through the sky from his incredible jump, the boy's arms flailed as he scanned his surroundings.

In the nearby distance, over the hills of sand outside of Yuusus, was a gigantic army of black-clothed Persians. The front line of soldiers had black turbans on their heads with scarves covering their mouths from the whipping wind. They had metallic chain vests that protected their upper bodies and wore white, thick pants. The front line was wielding sharpened scimitars and carrying a combination of spiral wooden shields that were coated with a layer of iron, making them gleam in the sunlight. The archers, however, were cowering behind the warriors and nocking their bows with bronze arrows. Clearly they were prepared to attack the defenseless city of Yuusus once more.

Ares plunged down towards the Persian army, the blistering wind rushing through his hair. *I'll make you pay for what you've done!*

***

General Shazir stood tall as he gazed over the prosperous city of Yuusus, clearly worthy of its title of one of the richest cities in Dastia. It had taken the Persian army months to travel around the Lost Sands to reach this city. The general was finally ready to seize the glory he had been promised and dominate this settlement. He was surprised, though. He had heard that this was a city of mercenaries, yet he saw absolutely no resistance. Then again, who could build up the courage to combat against a force over fifty thousand soldiers strong? After all, this was a small city. There were probably less than fifty thousand inhabitants in Yuusus. Only a percentage of that population could actually take up arms and fight. The general grinned, victory already in his sights. The riches of this land would become his and Cambyses would praise him for his effortless triumph.

"Milord, above!" a soldier yelled.

Shazir glanced up into the sky, and his eyes widened when he spotted a figure flying through the open air towards the Persian army. "How in the gods…?"

The figure smashed down into the front line of Persian warriors. An explosion of dust erupted into the air and swept outwards, sending soldiers scattering in all directions. A silhouette arose from the thick smokescreen, taking the dark shape of a young boy. As the cloud of dust dispersed, Shazir saw that a boy who looked identical to the deceased Persian prince, Darien, was standing there on top of a pile of corpses.

"Who are you?" Shazir demanded, the Persian troops all unsheathing their weapons and pointing them at the lone boy. "Do you know who you're standing against? We are warriors of the Persian Empire! And—"

"I don't care," the boy replied, brushing his blonde hair from his enraged eyes. "I'm Ares, and I've come to tell you that this city is underneath my protection. Turn back now or I won't be responsible for what happens next."

"A-Ares?" Words filled with terror began to radiate through the Persian ranks, causing some soldiers to tremble with fear. "The god who slays all in his path? How do we stand a chance against someone like that?"

"Under your protection?" Shazir scoffed. "I thought that gods were not allowed to meddle in mortal affairs. So how is it that you are unbound by the natural laws that control the gods?"

Ares gripped his spear in his hand and twirled it through the air, pointing the tip at the Persian army. "I guess I'm not an ordinary god then. You didn't offer quarter to the citizens of this city; instead, you attacked without warning. Why? That is a simple rule of war."

"A rule?" General Shazir guffawed, holding his belly. "Made by whom?"

"Me." Ares exploded forward, smashing through the Persian lines effortlessly as he soared towards Shazir, who stood in absolute shock. The boy had easily swatted aside the Persian warriors as if they were nothing. His spear was just about to strike Shazir's throat when a giant, meaty fist sank into Ares' stomach. The god flipped backwards wildly through the air, flying off of the hill, bouncing like a skipping stone until he landed at the bottom. Ares slowly pushed himself to his feet, spitting some sand from his mouth and glaring up at a burly man that now towered at the peak of the hill.

The shirtless man was wearing a tiger-skin cape and shorts. He was huge, a hulk of untamed muscle. He smacked his hardened fist against his palm and grinned brashly at Ares. "Why, if it isn't the infamous God of War himself!" The large man laughed, striking his bare chest with a hard fist. "I've been waiting years to test my limits against someone like you. I will show you why they call me the strongest man in the world! My name is Amam the Destroyer! Remember that name, boy!"

A black-cloaked man stepped up from beside the bulky man, his face covered by the cowl of his cloak. He reached up and pulled back his hood, revealing a young face. He had black, spiky hair that was pricked straight up. "We've been waiting to see how strong you are, God of War."

Ares clenched his teeth. So these guys had targeted Yuusus with that volley because they knew that he was there? He had jeopardized the lives of everyone in the city. He was the reason that Aleysha's mother was dead. But why were these people after him in the first place? "Who are you guys?"

"My name is Ramses," the cloaked man introduced himself. "We are Magi of Persia. We've come to put an end to your existence, god." He extended his hand and suddenly his palm began to glow an ominous golden color. A cannon of bright light burst from his hand and whistled towards Ares.

Ares grunted, leaping into the air as the energy bashed into the sand beneath him, sending the earth scattering in all directions. "*Awaken, Amon!*" he yelled and his giant friend tore itself from the ground beneath him. The god landed on Amon's head and exhaled as the rock golem towered to his full height over the Persian army, covering the soldiers in its gigantic shadow. "Sorry," Ares said, crossing his arms over his chest, "but I don't intend to die any time soon."

A New Resolve

Tetsu sprinted through the gruesome streets of Yuusus. The once-thriving city's roads and alleys were blanketed with corpses. Rivers of blood soaked into the dirt, creating an incredibly potent miasma that made the man feel like he were about to vomit. He slid into the street of his house, bolting for his home. But to his shock, he saw that Aleysha was kneeling outside their home. And she was kneeling right beside their deceased mother.

Tetsu's heart sank, and tears found their way down his cheeks as he staggered forward, feeling himself becoming dizzy. Earlier in the day he had left to go shopping at his mother's request. He had kissed her goodbye and promised that he would return promptly. He didn't expect that would be their last interaction.

His weakened hands dropped the groceries to the ground, causing the fruit that he had bought to roll around on the bloody streets. He lowered his head, clenching his teeth in unbelievable rage. *How dare these Persians…?* Tetsu suddenly felt Aleysha wrapping her arms around him in a tight embrace as she sobbed, trying to comfort him. But he shoved her back. His sister gave him a look of surprise, tears drying on her cheeks as she stared, shocked. Tetsu's fists were trembling at his side and he released his anger by bashing a hole directly through the wall of his own home. Pain exploded through his knuckles and he felt warm blood trickling down his hand as he slowly pulled his arm from the fractured wall. "Every time I get close to someone, something happens," he muttered as he reached into his cloak and pulled out a small blue cloth that looked like a handkerchief. He flapped the handkerchief and suddenly the cloth transformed into a long, expensive-looking, carpet. "Aleysha, take care of Mom," he said as he stepped onto the carpet.

The carpet whistled to life and took off into the air at Tetsu's command. Aleysha rushed forward, about to stop her brother, but saw that he was already out of reach. Her lips were trembling and she reached up and wiped the tears from her eyes. She turned and rested her weary eyes onto her sword and shield, which gleamed in the destroyed interior of her home.

Her mother was gone and there was nothing that she could do about that. Aleysha picked up her mother's body and walked into her house, gently placing her lifeless parent onto her bed. The sheets became soaked with her mother's blood but Aleysha paid it no attention as she walked away, snatching her sword and shield off of the wall. "Mom, I'm going out for a bit," Aleysha called, her blue eyes gleaming with fiery determination. "I'll be back, I promise."

***

Ares grunted as he battled against the two Magi on his own. Amon was holding off the Persian army, forcing the frightened men to flee as the enormous rock golem crushed their ranks. Bronze arrows glanced harmlessly off of Amon's tough armor-like body, and the Guardian roared, creating even more fear amongst the quivering Persian soldiers. It wouldn't be long before the whole army turned tail and began to flee for their lives.

However, Ares was having trouble with his battle. The brute, Amam, was slow but ridiculously powerful. Every punch that he struck Ares with sent agonizing pain exploding through his body. The god also had to keep his eye on Ramses, who was constantly hurling magical golden light at him. Fighting the two of them at the same time was near impossible. To eliminate the main threat, Ares would have to focus on Ramses. But he couldn't get close because Amam was applying so much pressure by constantly throwing punches that were strong enough to reduce a small mountain to a pile of rocks. He had no idea that Magi were this powerful.

"What's wrong, little boy?" Amam bellowed, striking Ares in the chin. The god's head snapped back as he flipped backwards and crashed hard onto his back, rolling back in the sand. "I thought gods were supposed to crush us mortals. But it looks like you're getting knocked around!"

"Back off," a voice snarled. A blurry figure flashed through the air and appeared behind Amam. The stranger had ripped his sword up along the Magus's forearm, down his chest, and finally across his torso, carving Amam's body with a lightning-fast, elegant stroke. Blood spurted from Amam's wounds and splattered onto the sand as a look of pain registered on the hulk's face.

"GAH!" Amam screamed in agony, grasping at his bleeding body as he crumpled to his knees. The action had happened so quickly and unexpectedly that the Magus had no time to react. He glanced at his assailant from the corner of his eye and saw that it was a black-cloaked figure with spiky hair riding upon a flying carpet. "You…!"

Ramses gritted his teeth. "Who are you? Another Magus?" There was no way that any ordinary human could've moved with such blinding speed. Even with that enchanted carpet that he was riding on, the two Magi should've seen him coming from a mile away. But the man had just appeared behind Amam as if he had teleported. This stranger couldn't have accomplished such a speedy assault without magic.

"My name is Tetsu Hayashi," the man announced angrily, swinging his long sword and splattering blood on the ground. "You Persians have really pissed me off." He was holding a diamond hourglass that glowed brightly in the sun. Ares couldn't help but marvel at the object's magnificence.

Ramses knitted his eyebrows. The Hayashi clan. Ah, yes, he remembered that this was the man who had been sitting beside Ares by the ocean last night. So this man has come to aid his friend. How gallant of him.

The Hayashi clan was widely renowned for their perfected swordsmanship and expertise in battle. Their unique ability to change the color of their eyes from their average dark brown to a gleaming red was what gave them an edge in battle. The visual prowess allowed them to act with heightened reflexes and enhanced vision. They were pronounced demons and were considered unfit to live amongst ordinary humans. All of the Hayashi clansmen were supposed to have been exterminated in the genocide five years ago. Persia had participated in the genocide and massacred dozens of members of the Hayashi clan.

Ramses pointed his index finger at Tetsu. "A demon from the

Hayashi clan, huh? It makes sense that a savage like you managed to injure Amam. I guess I'll just have to eradicate one more piece of garbage from the face of this earth."

"Don't talk to him like that!" Ares boomed, rushing at Ramses. The boy pounded the Magus's stomach with a heavy punch, sinking his fist into Ramses' flesh. The mage's eyes bulged as he lurched forward, the air choked from his lungs. He shot backwards with an explosion of speed, smashing hard against the sand. Ramses rolled several meters before staggering onto his feet, sputtering salty blood from his mouth as a sharp pain erupted from his aching diaphragm. "Keep your eyes on me."

Ramses coughed, grabbing his stomach in anguish. A forced smile cracked across his chapped lips. "So that's what a god's punch feels like...." He extended his other hand out to Ares and released a charged beam of golden light that roared through the air towards him. "God of War, Ares, show me more of your incredible power!"

Ares' expression suddenly became stern as he extended his hand to Ramses. His spear spurred to life, diving straight into the beam of light. The magic dispersed around the weapon's tip as the spear dove through the cannon of energy, until finally it buried itself into Ramses' shoulder. The Magus was forced backward and slammed hard onto his back, lying motionless in the bloody sand. Ares raised his arm and the spear tore itself from Ramses' body and returned to his hand. The god looked at the defeated Magi pitifully. "There you go."

Meanwhile Tetsu battled Amam, who was greatly wounded. The giant was suffering at least a dozen grievous wounds that were proving fatal. The hemorrhaging cuts in his body were spewing out blood like fountains, making the muscular man look like he had painted himself red. But the monster didn't seem to want to give up anytime soon, for he kept swinging punches wearily at Tetsu.

The Hayashi clansman could sense that victory against this Magus was approaching. His eyes, without his knowing, were glowing red. Immediately, he could feel his senses heightened tenfold. It was an odd feeling. He could see individual beads of sweat as they rolled down Amam's stressed face. He could see his opponent's bones moving and tendons contracting, allowing Tetsu to read Amam's actions before he moved. With the Sands of Time, Tetsu was able to slow down time, making the whole fight like battling Amam in slow motion, with a sign over the hulk's head saying what action he was going to perform next. This was too easy. Tetsu whipped his sword in a downward slash after toying with Amam and finally ended the Magus's life, tearing his blade across the man's heart. The giant groaned as he collapsed backward, smacking hard against the sand. His corpse began to slide down the slope of the hill, blood soaking into the dirt. The victorious mercenary was gasping for breath as he wiped his brow. He reached to his belt and pulled out a clean white handkerchief and used it to wipe the blood off of his steel sword.

As expected of the Persian army, after the loss of several hundred soldiers, they began to flee in terror. Amon stormed after them, raising his arms into the air to make him seem even larger than he already was. He roared loudly and the Persians replied with their frightened shrieks. When the army was clearly out of sight, Amon turned his head to Ares and snorted. *How was that?*

"Well done, Amon. You sure scared them." Ares grinned. "Did you capture the general like I wanted?"

Amon reached behind him and plucked a screaming man out of the sand, holding him by his head. It was General Shazir, who was kicking and screeching like a coward. The golem dropped the general at Ares' feet. Shazir stared at Ares and Tetsu, his body quavering. His gaze flickered from Ramses to Amam and he cried out in fear. "P-P-Please don't kill me! I'll give you anything you want! Women, money, jewels, anything!" He was on his knees and slapped his hands together, begging for mercy.

Tetsu's demonic eyes glared down at General Shazir. "I remember you from many years ago. You own a lot of slaves, don't you? I recall that I got into a fight with one of your hired overseers over the way he mistreated your lackeys." He reached down and squeezed the general's dirty face between his thumb and his other fingers. The mercenary pressed his cold steel blade to the throat of the man and growled, "So give me one reason I shouldn't slit your damned throat."

"B-Because I can give you all the treasures that—"

"*I don't want any of that!*" Tetsu bellowed, turning the general's head so that he was forced to look at Yuusus. Even from this far away they could see corpses scattered across the city's streets. The cries of mourning families echoed into the noon air. "Do you see that? Do you see what you've done, you sick bastard! Someone I cared for deeply is among those dead. You claim that you can give me treasures. Can you give her back to me then?"

"I-I…."

"Well, *CAN YOU?*" Tetsu roared, pressing his face up close to the general, who was now sobbing.

"P-Please…."

Tetsu grabbed the general by a bundle of his hair and stood tall, raising his blade, perfectly ready to hack the man's head clean off his body. "I have no mercy for men as guilty as you."

"Stop," Ares said, closing his eyes. "I can't do this."

"Can't do what?" Tetsu growled, glancing at the god. "You aren't doing anything. I'm the one lopping this mongrel's head off!"

"He's surrendered to us."

"And what the hell does that matter?" Tetsu yelled, lowering his sword as he turned to face Ares. He waved his sword as he shouted, pointing the tip at the general, who cringed. "This is justice. Killing this damned bastard will rid the world of one more scumbag that plagues this earth with his existence. The world is better off!"

"Do you know who you sound like?" Ares roared back, pointing to Ramses' body. "Him! You sound just like the Magus and everyone else who believed that the massacre of your clan was justified! The way you think of this man is how everyone on this planet thinks of you! And now, being a victim, don't you wish that if you were kneeling down after surrendering that your executioner would spare your life?"

"You're honestly comparing a slave-owning general of a merciless Persian army that is responsible for the deaths of thousands of lives and probably even more enslaved families, to a person who is guilty of no crime other than the surname they were born with?" Tetsu barked. "Perhaps the Lost Sands has made you lose your sense,

Darien."

"A life is a life," Ares retorted. "It was your sister who showed me that sparing the life of someone that has surrendered is honorable. I did not believe her until I did it myself. Killing a man who is trying to harm me does not haunt my sleep. But murdering one who has submitted themselves is as bad as slaying an innocent person. Release him; this is surely not what your mother would have wanted."

"Vengeance," Tetsu snapped, "you believe that my mother would be satisfied knowing that the man responsible for her death, and the murder of countless others, will just walk away scot-free so that he can commit the crimes again?"

"Mother would certainly not approve if you butchered this man after he surrendered." Aleysha's gentle voice said. Tetsu and Ares both turned to find the blonde warrior trudging up the desert sands. "If you believe that she expects you to avenge her, then you truly never knew her at all."

Tetsu winced at that comment and glanced away.

"I understand that you're angry and frustrated, Tetsu. I am too. But that doesn't mean that you can just execute him just because you feel that it will fill the hole in your heart. Killing can't fill that hole," Aleysha said and held out her arms to her brother. "Come here."

Tetsu hesitated but soon felt tears freely streaming down his cheeks and he staggered forward into his sister's arms, beginning to sob into her shoulder.

Ares sighed with relief as the two siblings hugged each other, relieved that Aleysha had come to calm Tetsu down. Without her,

Ares and Tetsu might've had to fight each other to settle the issue.

"Oh, how cute." There was an ominous cackle that split the silence as a black mist materialized in the air at the peak of the sandy hill. A black-cloaked man with dark hair and purple eyes emerged from the mysterious fog. "Two siblings hugging each other after the death of a family member. Now that just moves my heart."

"L-Lord Zahir! Please save me! These barbarians were discussing decapitating me!" Shazir cried out, scrambling away from Amon towards the mysterious new man.

Ares recognized this man as the Magus who had knocked him and Tetsu unconscious in the Persian throne room five years before. He squeezed the hard hilt of his spear and glared at the dauntless mage. What was this guy doing here?

Zahir's deadly gaze scanned over the entire area, taking in his surroundings. He spotted Ares and smiled. "So the rumors are true then; you do look like the old fallen prince, Darien. Is that truly you, banished prince? Or are you merely taking the boy's form for some inane reason? Ah, no matter." He turned his attention to Shazir and pointed his finger at the man. A surge of dark energy rippled through the air, leaving his index finger in the form of a concentrated beam that pierced the general. The magic tore straight out the man's back and dissipated.

Shazir, who had previously been wearing a smile at the sight of his savior, now stared in shock at the Magus. His mouth opened to say something but only a gurgling, choking sound crept out before he fell forward, burying his face into the sand. There was a giant, gaping hole in his chest from the mystical beam.

"Y-You killed him…!" Aleysha stammered, astounded. She glared at Zahir with such intensity that the Magus stepped backward. "He was your comrade, wasn't he? Why the hell would you do that?" she shouted.

"He is no longer useful. The scoundrel was clearly on his knees begging for his life. You could tell that he treasured his own life selfishly over his empire. He would've given away any information you children wanted as long as he could live another day," Zahir called, a sadistic smile creeping across his face as a dark shadow loomed over his eyes from his hair. "We don't need people like that alive. He's better off dead."

Ares exhaled shakily, trying to control the rage that coursed through his body. "You treat human lives as if they're nothing."

"As do you, God of War." Zahir grinned, revealing a set of sharp teeth that looked like they belonged to a shark. His violet eyes gleamed abnormally and he cackled manically. "You massacred a hundred thousand Persian soldiers in cold-blood in the Lost Sands years ago! And now, just look at how many soldiers you killed here today." He waved his hand, indicating to the hundreds of corpses that lay sprawled across the desert sands. "Your little golem may do the majority of your dirty work but it is by your command. You're still a murderer."

Amon growled. I'm about to squash this bug.

"Yeah, I guess I am," Ares said. "But at least I give my opponents a chance to run away. Those that I kill have already committed many atrocities, all of which must be judged."

"And you are a god that will bring judgment on those who have sinned?" Zahir guffawed, his bellowing laughter splitting the silence. "Then judge me, Ares! Judge me and show me what terrifying power you have! Surely an almighty god such as you should be able to squash a puny human such as I!"

Ares said nothing but Amon snorted. *Ares….*

"Maybe this will give you a little push," Zahir said, his eyes flashing maliciously. "*I am the one who assassinated the king and queen of Persia five years ago.*"

Ares' eyes narrowed and his heart slammed against his chest, thudding so hard that he could've sworn he could hear his own racing heartbeat. Small tears began to form in the corners of his eyes and he clenched his teeth, untamed rage surging through every inch of his body. He lowered his head, reaching up and grasping his throat, which felt as if it were burning. His chest felt as if there was a sun inserted where his heart was and scorching heat was incinerating him from the inside out. The god raised his head as ancient black markings appeared on his skin, curling around his body until he was coated in mysterious tattoos. His irises had changed to a blazing orange color, and he grinned, revealing a set of dagger-like teeth. "*Man, now you've done it.*"

Zahir's eyes widened at the boy's odd transformation. The aura that this boy radiated was ancient, dark, and filled with aggression. This was a completely different person from before. But Ares' reaction had confirmed Zahir's suspicions; Ares was Darien. The Magus clicked his fingers and a golden scepter materialized in his hand, pointing straight at the god. A swirling beam of red energy exploded from the tip of the scepter and streamed towards Ares.

Amon grabbed Aleysha and Tetsu, and leapt away from the area, getting them clear of the blast zone. An eruption rippled through the sandy desert, an outward pulse of force that sent gigantic waves of sand scattering in all directions. Gusts of powerful winds churned around the area, creating a dust storm that swept around Ares' position.

Tetsu grunted as a mighty force pounded against Amon's tough rock body. The blistering winds sliced at his skin, carrying tiny grains of sand that felt like they were daggers stabbing at his face. He held onto Aleysha tightly as she closed her eyes, hoping that the storm would subside quickly.

The smokescreen of dust separated with a single swing of Ares' spear and Zahir stared with incredulity at the god, who stood in a crater of glowing, purified glass. The scorching temperatures from Zahir's magic were powerful enough to smelt the burning sands into gleaming glass that blazed a hot-orange color, as if the delicate glass had just been dipped in lava.

Ares shattered the glass underneath his bare feet, his hardened skin not even scratched from the sharp, hot crystal. The god was completely unharmed and didn't have a single burn on his body from Zahir's magic. The boy sauntered forward, his eyes blazing as a sly smile split across his lips. Zahir stepped backward, not sure what to do. Ares' aura, his personality, his strength had all changed drastically. Zahir had been watching Ares battle Ramses and Amam earlier, and he had seemed almost weak in comparison to the mighty being that he was now. "Who are you?" the Magus demanded loudly, pointing his scepter at the god once more.

Ares exploded forward, his crazed eyes widening as he lashed out with his hand at Zahir's throat. "*Isn't it obvious? I'm the God of War!*" He halted suddenly and winced, the black marking receding from his skin. "*Darien … you idiot … what do you think you're doing? I'm about to kill this bastard…!*" The boy's eyes changed back into their sky-blue color and Ares collapsed to his knees, gasping for air.

Zahir stared at Ares, surprised. So it seemed that there was an alternate being in Ares' body that had taken temporarily taken control. Whoever that being was, he was much more powerful than Darien. But who was that? He pointed his scepter at the immobilized boy who was stuck on his knees. "I suppose I should question what that was … but I'd rather just get eradicate you now. Goodbye, Ares. Or should I say, Darien."

Tetsu shot through the air on his flying carpet and yelled as he leapt outwards, tackling the Magus clean off his feet. "Oh, no you don't!" he yelled, sending the two rolling across the ground.

Zahir grunted, flipping to his feet and pointing his scepter at Tetsu. A small ball of energy shot from the tip of his weapon and struck the man in the chest, immediately bursting into flames that razed through Tetsu's cloak. The mercenary screamed in agony as he collapsed onto his back, the fire eating at his skin.

"Tetsu!" Aleysha screamed, rushing to her brother's aid.

Zahir gritted his teeth, aiming his scepter at the two siblings. "My lucky day, I get to kill two birds with one stone!"

A bolt of electricity ripped through the air, smashing into Zahir's body, sending white tendrils of energy crackling everywhere. The mage staggered backward, his body trembling uncontrollably.

His arm was twitching and he nearly dropped his scepter. Cursing, the Magus glanced upward to see a young girl on a flying broom soaring through the air towards the scene.

"Kira!" Aleysha called, relieved at the mage's assistance.

"I'm here to help!" Kira called, twirling her staff as she descended towards the battlefield. She leapt from her broom and landed beside Ares, who was still frozen on his knees. "I managed to get the king to a secure location. But it looks like you guys managed to scare off the Persians just fine." She turned and looked at Ares, who was staring blankly at the ground. "Hey, are you okay?"

Zahir scoffed, taking several steps backward as he assessed his situation. He had no choice but to flee. "You pests just love getting in the way. No matter." His eyes flickered to Ares. "I've gathered more than enough information from this confrontation. Until next time, God of War." His body burst into a plume of smoke and just like that, he was gone.

Kira stared at the place where the Magus had been only a moment ago before she turned and sprinted to Tetsu, who was lying on his back, unconscious. His chest was red and raw from severe burns caused by Zahir's magic. "By the gods," she whispered, waving her staff, causing Tetsu's body to levitate into the air. "We need to get him back to the Luxas Mansion to get treated immediately! This burn is bad. Really bad."

"Alright, let's go quickly," Aleysha said with a nod, preparing for the long walk back to Yuusus. She turned to look at Ares. "Ares, are you coming or…." She bit her lip, realizing that the boy was still gazing at the ground as if he had just seen a ghost.

Amon stomped beside Aleysha and grunted. *I'll take care of him.*

Aleysha blinked. "Y-You can talk?"

If you call magically speaking in your mind talking, then yes.

Aleysha stared at Amon for a moment before nodding. She then turned to accompany Kira and Tetsu back to the city. "I'm counting on you, Amon. Thanks." She began to jog after the mage as they began their journey back to Yuusus.

****

Bloodlust, hatred, anger, aggression, and horrific thoughts of committing brutality. That was all that Ares had felt streaming through his body. When the other side of himself had taken control, he felt as if he were in a dream, watching a foggy nightmare unfold. The boy continued to stare at the ground, thinking about what would have happened if he had killed Zahir. Would he have turned around and attacked his friends as well? In that ancient form, Ares completely lost control over himself and fully embraced the dormant barbarian that slept within him, awakening whenever he sought to selfishly eradicate others without real purpose.

This was not the first time that Ares had lost control like this. The first and only other time had been when he had confronted one hundred thousand Persian soldiers in the Lost Sands. The enemy warriors had provoked him, angered him. And the more he fought, the more he lusted for their destruction. That was when he lost control and became the true God of War that the Persians came to know.

Amon thumped onto the ground beside Ares, sitting and playing with the glass on the ground, smashing it with his giant fist.

What is bothering you, Ares?

"A lot is bothering me right now. I lost control, just like last time."

That Magus provoked you by reminding you of the assassination of your old family. It brought forth rage and anger that was enough to awaken your inner warlord.

"Inner warlord?"

The previous Ares, before he perished, was defined by his strength, courage, and barbarism. He represents the untamed side of war and automatically assumes control of your body whenever you become bloodthirsty. In other words, whenever you want to murder someone for the sole purpose of killing, he will awaken. Most of the times when you've taken a life, there has been a justifiable reason. But when you went to battle those Persians in the Lost Sands and when you confronted Zahir, you had no real reason to want to slaughter them besides personal rage, Amon explained. Allowing your personal feelings to get involved is not something a god should do and therefore the ancient god of war will assume control over you whenever you lose sight of yourself.

"Why is this bastard dormant inside of me anyway?" Ares complained. "If he's dead, shouldn't he be gone completely?"

Gods never really die. He exists through the power that he's passed onto you. Amon grunted. You were chosen because you also have all the qualities that the ancient god of war did not have. Compassion, kindness, and selflessness. While you share many of the old Ares' qualities, you also complete him.

Ares sighed. "How can I control him? I don't want him taking over anymore."

If you want to control him, you can't lose sight of who you are. Expressing any of the barbaric emotions that the ancient Ares embraced could result in his awakening. Just stay true to yourself.

"Easier said than done," the boy huffed.

As are many things in life, young one.

Ares reached up and ran his hand through his blonde hair, exhausted. "Tetsu is injured and Aleysha's mother has been killed. It's my fault," he murmured. "I know that by getting involved with the Persians and my past that I'm heightening my chances of losing control to the ancient Ares. But I believe that what the Persians are doing is unjust, and they must be stopped."

Amon nodded. Merciless murder is frowned upon. However, this is not our fight, Ares.

"As Ares, a god of war, you're right. This doesn't concern me," Ares said. "But as Darien the Prince of Persia, it is my responsibility to stand up and bring Cambyses and Zahir to justice. Zahir admitted to murdering my parents and he was with Cambyses, my uncle, when they accused me of the crime. They blamed me and had me banished so that Cambyses could claim the throne as his own. He eliminated three obstacles with one swift move." The god lowered his eyes. "Many years ago while my father ruled, Cambyses told me often that he disapproved of how my father was ruling. He believed that Persia should be using its powerful military and limitless resources to conquer the rest of Dastia. Then, when the continent was united underneath one monarch, there would be peace."

But in order to achieve such peace he would have to instigate war first.

"Yes," Ares said. "That is what he's doing right now." The boy stood up. "I'll go back to Yuusus and gather some supplies for our journey. We'll head across the Lost Sands to Persia where we'll confront and stop Cambyses. He and Zahir will both pay for their heinous crimes and we will be the ones to judge their corrupted souls, Amon."

Amon nodded. I follow where you go, friend.

Ares smiled at the rock golem and held out his fist to the giant elemental. Amon reached out and bumped his hard knuckles gently against the god's. "Wait…," a raspy voice gasped.

Ares turned and saw that Ramses had spoken to him. The bleeding Magus was still alive and was lying on the ground, his eyes transfixed on the blue sky. The boy walked over to the injured mage and stood over his bloody body.

"I … I'll tell you what I know," Ramses let out, gulping. "Cambyses doesn't expect the other empires to merely surrender themselves to him without a fight. He … he has another plan that he's been working on with Zahir."

"What plan?" Ares asked.

"Zahir was promised by the king that he would obtain the power of Ahriman," Ramses said. Ares remembered that god. Of all the gods that Persians worshipped, people feared Ahriman the most. He was the god of darkness and everything that was evil. Why would Zahir seek such terrifying power? "He would become like you, Prince Darien. While you are indeed a deity, I believe that you are different from ordinary gods. After all, you understand what it is like to be human."

"Ordinary gods?"

"Yes," Ramses said. "Those are the ancient gods and there are many of them. So many that you could consider them an entire race of powerful beings. In order to come down to the mortal world and interact with humans, the gods must enter a weakened state in which they too become mortal. I believe that you are currently in that state."

"Mortal," Ares echoed. He already knew that he was mortal. He had to eat, sleep, drink, and he felt pain. The only thing that separated him from other humans was his special powers. "Should Zahir gain this ancient power, then what?"

"Then he will become Ahriman himself. He will become a god, like you," Ramses said. "With that power he could bring about death to all humans on Dastia, desolation to all lands, and decay to all plants. If a nation refuses Cambyses's demands to surrender, then Zahir would be able to obliterate the nation entirely on his own. He could bring about plagues, natural disasters, famine, and destruction. Many more innocent people will die. Persia's conquest has only just begun."

Ares gritted his teeth, a grave look looming over his face. Things were sounding worse and worse. "How is it that he will become Ahriman?"

"Zahir believes that deep inside of the Lost Sands, hidden away, is the body of the destroyed god. It is found deep inside of a fissure that is torn across the earth, digging thousands of meters deep into the earth. Many gods, not only the Persian ones, banded together to stop Ahriman during his prime. As a result, he was struck down from the heavens and buried deep in the ground. Surrounding his corpse are many Guardians, similar to your rock golem. Each pantheon of gods sent Guardians of their own to defend Ahriman's body from ordinary mortals."

"I would expect that is a lot of Guardians then."

"Correct."

Ares frowned. "So, if there are so many Guardians, how does Zahir expect to get remotely close to Ahriman's body?"

"He has several Magi accompanying him as well as the force of Persia, a great united army of all its conquered nations. They have hundreds of thousands of soldiers and plenty of mages to *distract* the Guardians while Zahir goes for the body. He will then harness Ahriman's power and be able to eradicate the remaining Guardians on his own."

"Thousands of men will die to get him there."

"In Zahir's eyes the sacrifice is worth it."

Ares closed his eyes and breathed through clenched teeth. "I'll stop him. Thank you, Ramses." He looked to the dying man with pitiful eyes. "Your name doesn't sound Persian. Where are you from? Why are you helping me?"

"I hail from a faraway land to the west. The Persians came and conquered our nation. I became one of the king's personal Magi because it would yield benefits such as the protection of my family. We had been told that you, Darien, were the one who murdered the old king and queen of Persia. As a result, many defeated nations not only blamed Cambyses for their misfortunes but they also blamed you for giving your uncle the throne," Ramses wheezed, closing his eyes hard as he felt a sharp pain rage through his shoulder. "When I heard Zahir claim that he was the real culprit behind the Persian rulers' deaths I knew that I had to help you, true Prince of Persia. It is Zahir and Cambyses's fault that my kingdom fell. I hope that you'll bring a stop to their madness so that the nations of eastern Dastia do not have to suffer as we of the west have."

Ares nodded, a gentle gust of wind blowing through his hair. "What does your name mean?"

"Son of Ra." Ares stiffened at the mention of the name. "That is one of the many gods of the sun. It is one in particular that my people worship for he has brought our crops fortunate weather and our people hope even in dark times."

Ares raised an eyebrow. *He? Ra is a male?* Then again, it was said that gods were allowed to change their appearances if they wanted. Ra had taken the form of Aleysha and had granted him this incredible power. He smiled at Ramses. Now the supposed "son" of Ra was helping him once more. *Ra, you're everywhere, aren't you?*

Ares turned around and began to walk away from Ramses' body. "Amon, grab Ramses and make sure you're careful with him. We're going to bring him to Yuusus to be treated," he called over his shoulder to the rock golem. Amon snorted in agreement and stomped over to Ramses, picking up the injured Magus in his hardened hands.

Ramses laughed, perplexed at his current situation. "I never would've imagined that one of the gods of war would've decided to spare my life after I meant to harm him. I was under the false impression that all of the gods who represented war were merciless. I'm surprised that you haven't left me to die, Lord Ares."

"Shush," Ares murmured, sliding his hands into his pockets as his spear exploded into a puff of smoke, vanishing from sight. "I'm not like the other gods that you've heard about," he said with a slight smile as he began the long trek back to Yuusus.

Taking a Final Leave

"How is it possible that we can't find ANY ancient texts of Ares? Are you trying to tell me that none of the civilizations of western Dastia worship this god? They haven't even *heard* of him? So, what is he? Just a random ghost that appeared out of nowhere?" Cambyses boomed, slamming his fist against the arm of his golden throne as he gazed upon dozens of frightened scholars from many different nations. These scholars had the sole job of searching through their nation's texts to find even the slightest mention of a god named Ares. There was nothing. In all of western Dastia, Ares was unknown and had no worshippers. "How many damned gods of war could there possibly be? Mithra? Anhur? Odin?"

"M-Milord," a scholar said quietly. "There are thousands of gods that exist. Just as there are many humans that exist, there are many gods as well. The nations of western Dastia might not worship this supposed Ares but he might be from a kingdom from the east or maybe even another human settlement from another unknown continent! Or even another world! Milord, we don't have enough information yet but…."

"Have this insolent fool killed," Cambyses ordered Zahir, who stood at his throne's side.

Zahir clicked his fingers and the scholar suddenly burst into hot flames that ate away at his deteriorating flesh. The Magus smiled sadistically and folded his arms again as the room listened in horror to the dying scholar's screams of anguish.

Cambyses slammed his palms against both arms of his chair as he stood up, bellowing loudly through the throne room so that all of the scholars could hear. "There is no information that is outside of our empire's grasp. Now find out Ares' origins or I'll have all of your heads! I want information on where his worshippers live and then I want them all killed!" he screamed, his face red with fury. He slumped back into his throne and waved the scholars off. The men all fled the room with haste, eager to get as far away from the Persian monarch as possible.

"You handled the news of the fall of General Shazir's army a lot better than I thought," Zahir admitted. "You've only killed one man so far. That's significantly better than the Hayashi clan genocide that ensued after you found out Ares slaughtered your army of one hundred thousand soldiers in the Lost Sands several years before."

"I didn't expect Shazir, Ramses, and Amam to fall so easily. Fifty thousand soldiers stormed towards Yuusus and they weren't even able to reach the city. How pathetic. Think about how that makes our empire look, how it makes *me* look! I would have Shazir executed for his poor leadership but he's already dead. You shouldn't have killed him so that I could have the satisfaction of decapitating him myself," Cambyses growled.

"Oh, milord, you know that would've only resulted in the leakage of classified information," Zahir said. "Our armies are searching the Lost Sands for Ahriman's body as we speak. We will be informed within a day of the discovery of the fault in which his body is buried."

"Good. Now, you said that you have information regarding Ares. Tell me what you know. It's clearly much more than whatever the damned scholars know so far. This god is apparently a ghost that no one of Dastia has heard about," Cambyses grumbled.

"Well, milord. It is still a possibility that the scholar, whom you blatantly had me execute, was correct. Perhaps Ares is of another nation to the east or even of another continent."

The Persian ruler rolled his eyes.

Zahir then explained everything that he witnessed during his confrontation with Ares, not leaving out a single detail. Cambyses's eyes were widened with surprise and disbelief as he heard the Magus's story.

"Ares is Darien? Then that must mean that he isn't a god at all! We know that Darien is an ordinary human."

"No, he is a god, and a powerful one at that," Zahir said. "I expect that he became Ares after being granted godly powers from the Lost Sands, similarly to how I will harness the power of Ahriman. That would explain how he managed to survive his exile."

Cambyses reached up and rubbed his temples. "So the original Ares must've been killed by some unknown means and Darien was lucky enough to stumble across the deity's corpse and harnessed Ares' power, huh? Interesting. How does one take the powers of a fallen god anyway, Zahir?"

"You must drink their blood."

"So Darien drank the blood of the dead god, Ares. I did not know that boy had it in him to submit to cannibalism in order to survive. He must've obtained the magic by accident," Cambyses insisted.

"Perhaps," Zahir murmured, the corners of his lips twitching into a sly smile. "Anyway, I've come to a recent conclusion that perhaps we should pull back a majority of our soldiers from the Lost Sands once we have discovered the fissure."

"And why is that?"

"Yuu and I will depart for the Lost Sands tomorrow morning. Once we find the fault, we'll only need a small force of soldiers to help harvest Ahriman's power."

"But what about all the Guardians that you were previously worried about?"

"I have disregarded them as a threat. Just trust me, milord. I will handle this. Have you ever had a reason to doubt me?"

He left, leaving Cambyses puzzled. The Magus walked out of the Persian castle into a lush, green courtyard, where he found his apprentice awaiting him. "Yuu, what are you doing here? I thought that you were to help the scholars in searching for the origins of Ares."

"He does not exist within our texts. The scholars are wasting their time," Yuu said. "No matter how much this king believes that the knowledge is within our grasp, it isn't. He is a worshipped god from somewhere else." He adjusted his metal gauntlets and looked at Zahir with his cold, turquoise eyes. "What of Ares? Did you come to a conclusion as to whether or not he is Darien after all?"

"He isn't," Zahir lied calmly.

"Is that so?" Yuu's eyes lowered and he sighed, as if

disappointed. "So then, what's our next move?"

"We will head to the Lost Sands tomorrow," Zahir said, walking past his apprentice, his eyes gazing across the prosperous city of Persepolis. "After battling Ares I have come to the realization that I'll need Ahriman's power in order to fully crush this unknown god of war."

Yuu raised an eyebrow at his mentor, surprised that Zahir was admitting to someone else's strength. "Was he that overwhelming?"

Zahir recalled the aggressive, beastly look in Ares' eyes when he had changed personalities. He nodded. "He was."

Yuu shrugged and turned to walk away back in the direction of the castle. "Fine, then. I'll head off to inform my family of my departure. Hopefully this venture will not be as treacherous as the rumors say. The Lost Sands is the pinnacle of danger in Terrador."

"But our hardships will be worth it in the end, Yuu," Zahir called to his apprentice. "Gaining the power of a god will enable new opportunities for the two of us, and will open doors that have always been closed to ordinary mortals. With the invincible strength of Ahriman, we can bring even the infamous Ares to his inevitable end."

***

Ares carried Ramses in his arms as if his weight were nothing, the man's blood dripping all over the ground as he was carried to the Luxas Mansion. The god walked through the large front yard of the estate, his eyes trained on the closed front door of the house. The sun's heat sizzled the boy's skin and the air was thick and humid. Ares expected his face to be soaked in sweat but, surprisingly, only a few trickles of perspiration rushed down his cheeks.

Amon stomped through the land behind Ares, being careful not to step on any of the corpses, people, or buildings as he slowly and carefully eased his way around the perimeter of Yuusus and around to the Luxas manor. The golem plopped down on the flat, open, yard of the mansion and sat, awaiting Ares' return.

Ramses saw many horrors as he was carried through Yuusus and he couldn't help but feel guilt ripping at his heart. At one point he had to close his eyes when he spotted a woman sobbing over her deceased child's body, cradling the corpse's head in her arms. Ramses wondered why he had even joined the Persians on their conquest when he knew what it was like to be a victim of their destruction. Was it that he wanted to be the one wielding the power for once? Maybe that was it. But in the end, there was no satisfaction to be obtained from being the dominator. The feeling was the same as being the dominated. Emptiness.

Kira opened the door of the mansion for Ares and frowned when she saw Ramses. "Why did you bring this man here? He's a Persian."

"A Persian who regrets his decisions," Ares said, walking into the home. "He's given me information and I believe he deserves a second chance."

The inside of the house was made of fine wood that one wouldn't find anywhere in western Dastia. A chandelier of glistening diamonds hung from the high ceiling, which had a circular window carved into the top. Sunlight flooded in through the window and refracted silver light off of the chandelier and onto the walls. There was a stairway several feet in front of the entrance that spiraled upward towards the second floor with a white mat cascading down the wooden stairs. Past the stairway was a living room where Tetsu lay on the floor on his back, his eyes closed.

Aleysha was kneeling at his side, pressing a soft, bloody, cloth to his burn wound. The mercenary dipped the white cloth into a wooden water basin, making the towel sopping wet with cool water. She grasped the cloth with both her hands and wrung it, squeezing water back into the water basin before pressing the towel back to Tetsu's injury.

Sitting in a leather chair before a blazing hearth was a man, with curly grey hair, wearing a golden crown. He glanced over his shoulder, which was tightly wrapped in a green robe, spotting Ares in the doorway. His wizened face was wrinkled from age and he wore a long grey beard that rested on his chest. His ears were bedecked with an amalgam of luxurious golden earrings.

The man smiled and stroked his wispy beard, turning back to face the flickering fire of the hearth. "So you are Ares. I've heard much about you. Rather, not so much about you yourself, but of your ancient tales."

Ares raised his eyebrows as he walked forward with Ramses still in his arms. "Ancient tales?"

"Several centuries ago, a foreigner from another continent in this world arrived to Dastia. He came with others who settled in eastern Dastia. He brought with him a pantheon of new gods that he worshipped in his old land. You were one of them. Ares, the god of untamed war. Yet you are not nearly as barbaric or manly as I had originally imagined you from your tales. You're a mere boy."

"A boy who can make this building crumble with a snap of my fingers," Ares growled.

"Calm yourself, Lord. I do not mean to insult you; I am merely puzzled, for you are not as the tales portray you." The man leaned deep into his leather chair, the fires of the hearth reflecting in his dark eyes. "I am the king of a faraway empire known as Luxas. I believe that you've met my Magus, Kira." The king rose to his feet from his chair.

"We are acquainted."

"In my empire, you are one of the many gods that we worship when we head off to war. You and Athena…."

"Look, I don't know who that is and—"

"Just hear me out, please," the lord said, facing Ares. "The Persians, as you saw today, threaten the existence of eastern Dastia. I offer you my army, Warlord Ares, so that you may protect eastern Dastia from the tyranny of Persia. All of my soldiers will be at your disposal."

"I am not interested," Ares murmured.

"Tetsu has spent the past several years forming diplomatic relations between the nations of eastern Dastia. After Persia demonstrated its aggression and attacked Yuusus without warning today, it wouldn't be hard to have the entire united army of the eastern nations at your command. You could battle the Persians and bring them to justice. All of the glory will be yours. My people and many other nations will worship you out of respect rather than fear and—"

"I am not interested in leading an army. I'm not interested in glory. And I don't care about how many worshippers I have," Ares snapped, silencing the king immediately. He placed Ramses down on the ground beside Tetsu and exhaled, standing tall. "I will be leaving for the Lost Sands with haste. I do not believe that the Persians will be returning for Yuusus anytime soon. Eastern Dastia will be safe for the meantime."

"Where will their troops be focused then?"

"The Persians are searching for a way to grant their head Magus, Zahir, the power of their Persian god, Ahriman. With that power, he'll be able to stomp out the nations of eastern Dastia with ease. It won't matter whether or not there's an army of you, because he'll slaughter you all." He turned around and began to walk towards the door of the mansion, ready to leave. "The Persians will be sending their men into the Lost Sands to search for Ahriman's power. I will go and stop them. No army of yours will help; you'll only slow me down. Though I encourage you to assemble yourselves anyway; you never know what's going to happen. But I will not be responsible for the lives of your men. I am no warlord."

The king of Luxas stared at Ares' back and sighed, an overwhelming feeling of powerlessness swooping over him. Leaving the fate of eastern Dastia to Ares was a hard thing to do. He watched as Aleysha got up from her brother's side and rushed after Ares.

"I'm coming with you!" the mercenary exclaimed, snatching her sword and shield off of the wall. She wrapped her orange scarf around her neck and dashed past Kira, who stood stunned. Staggering out onto the lush grass of the manor's yard, she watched as Ares continued to walk away with his hands jammed into his pockets.

"No," Ares said simply, without even bothering to turn around to face Aleysha. The god walked past Amon, who stood up with his giant eyes gazing at the female warrior who followed Ares.

"You'll need help where you're going! If you're going to face Zahir alone…."

"What are you going to do?" Ares declared harshly, looking at Aleysha from the corner of his eye. "Swing that silly sword at him and hope that it'll cut him down? Bash him with that flashy shield of yours? He'll incinerate you before you even get close to him. This is a fight that is out of your league, Aleysha. This isn't one of your childish mercenary contracts. I'm a deity, I'll be fine. But you won't. Turn back and tend to your brother. Let's go, Amon."

Amon groaned in a complaining tone.

"She's not coming with us," Ares murmured. "It's always been the two of us anyway. That's the way it should stay."

"You're the hero who saved my life!" Aleysha shouted, freezing Ares right in his tracks. "I haven't forgotten that you're the one who saved me from the Persians, Ares. I know that a lot of people fear you. There're a lot of rumors that are going around saying that you're merciless and brutal. Even your own worshippers believe the rumors. The king of Luxas confirmed it."

Ares narrowed his eyes. You're seriously not helping your argument.

"But I don't care what other people think because I know the real you, Ares. I know that you're compassionate, kind, selfless, and you're so determined to help others that you'll put your own life on the line. People misunderstand you. You showed me today that you'd sacrifice yourself for the sake of all the survivors in this city. And I'll show you that I'm willing to make the same sacrifice to help protect the people of eastern Dastia."

Ares breathed out a gust of hot air and cracked a tiny smile. He sighed and continued walking forward. "Go home. Man, you're annoying." he muttered through clenched teeth as tears found their way to his eyes. He couldn't bring her on this journey with him. As much as he wanted her to come, he knew that he would only be jeopardizing her life by letting her accompany him on this quest. *But … she understands me.*

***

A roaring storm of sand whipped through the Lost Sands, swallowing Amon and Ares in the windstorm. But they continued trudging forward, not allowing the fierce whirlwinds stop them. The powerful wind sliced at Ares' cheeks and nipped at his nose. The sand felt hard, almost like little pebbles were smacking against his red face. Nevertheless, this was nothing in the Lost Sands. In fact, out of all of the obstacles that the desert could've thrown at them this storm could be considered good fortune. Ares stopped and turned around to see that Aleysha was still following them into the Lost Sands. The mercenary had her scarf wrapped around her mouth and forehead, covering most of her face from the biting sand. Her eyes were squinted tightly as the roaring storm shoved her back with its mighty gusts but Aleysha held her hand out, forcing herself forward against the strong winds.

Ares raised his eyebrows as he watched Aleysha force herself forward through the storm. His hands were jammed into his pockets and he glanced up at Amon, who looked back at him in confusion. "What does she think she's doing?" the god murmured, looking back at the struggling adventurer. "Soon she'll be too far from Yuusus and it'll be impossible for her to return home. She'll die."

Amon released a low, yet loud, groan. Maybe it would be good to have her as a companion.

"Like hell it would be! I can't have a pretty girl like that around me; she'd shatter my concentration! She's just going to get in the way."

That's not really your reason, is it? Amon snorted. You were harsh to her back there, Ares.

Ares lowered his gaze and said nothing. This perilous venture was far too dangerous for someone like Aleysha. Sure, she was definitely tough, but that didn't mean that she was ready for the horrors that the Lost Sands had. Besides, what if Ares lost control and hurt her too? It was already his fault that Tetsu got injured and Aleysha's mother had perished. If another person that Ares cared for was hurt because of him he knew he would never forgive himself.

Amon grunted. She doesn't look like she's going to turn back. Are you just going to let her die?

"Of course I won't let her die." Ares pouted, folding his arms. "I'm a gallant warrior of justice! I would never let a friend of mine…." He turned and saw that Aleysha's face was planted in the sand and she was completely unconscious. Ares reached up and slapped his forehead in frustration. "And this is what happens when you don't think things through!"

With Amon carrying Aleysha's unconscious body, the three traveled to a stone cave that led underground. Meanwhile, the storm continued to churn, growing stronger by the minute. Ares was relieved that they had found refuge and had Amon stay outside of the cave, since he obviously couldn't fit in the grotto. He brought Aleysha inside and placed her on the cold cave floor.

Ares felt for her pulse and sighed with relief. She was just sleeping. He ran a hand through his blonde, tangled hair and undid Aleysha's scarf so that she could breathe easier. Ares took the pack off her back, rummaging through her things. The god wasn't surprised that she hadn't really brought any supplies. A full canteen of water that would only last a couple days and food that would probably last only two meals for one person. Traveling across the Lost Sands for an average person on foot would take months, if they could survive all of the dangers that the desert contained. Clearly, Aleysha hadn't thought very far ahead. Ares smiled. Then again, she didn't really seem like the planning type. Aleysha seemed to just do things that she thought was right without really stopping to consider the possible consequences.

"Why are you so desperate to help?" Ares murmured to no one in particular as he continued to fumble through Aleysha's stuff.

Ares took out a small silver necklace of a cross, letting the jewelry dangle from his hands. He stared at the cross for a moment and reached to his neck, touching a golden medallion that his mother had given him on his fifteenth birthday. Biting his lower lip, Ares tossed Aleysha's necklace back into her bag.

The boy leaned back against the hard wall of the small cave, the shadows sweeping across most of the area. He watched as Aleysha slept soundlessly, and he knitted his eyebrows together. *Gah! Why are you here? You're making things so much more complicated!* He reached up and began to mess up his hair, letting off some of his aggravation. *Why would you leave the safety of your home to embark on this hazardous journey with me? Revenge? Redemption? Justice?*

You're the hero who saved my life! Ares remembered that she had called out those words proudly as she marched after him and Amon earlier that day. The boy's cheeks turned a rosy red as Aleysha's words echoed through his mind. Ares quickly slapped his face with his hands, knowing that he was getting the wrong idea. "Gods," he murmured, tapping the back of his head back against the stone cave. "What do I do? This journey is just too dangerous for you. There's no way that you'll survive." He glanced out towards the dark night and noticed that morning was already approaching. Amon stayed outside with his gigantic rock legs crossed, guarding the cave.

Amon turned his head as Ares walked out of the cave onto the desert sand. A chilling breeze ran through the boy, causing him to shiver slightly. *What are you doing? You should be sleeping.*

"I can't decide what to do with Aleysha."

She seems to see a side of you that most don't recognize.

"I know."

Most people just see you as this bloodthirsty, barbaric, brutish….

"Make your point," Ares grumbled, wondering how many aggressive adjectives Amon could describe him with.

But she accepts you as you are and is willing to put her life on the line to stand beside you and protect you.

Ares folded his arms and pouted, his eyes narrowing. It was for that reason that he didn't want Aleysha getting hurt. He sighed, knowing how stubborn the mercenary was. No words would reach her, but at least she was strong-willed. "We're going to need to do our best to protect her then, Amon," he said. "It'll be difficult protecting her from the dangers of the Lost Sands and the Persian Magi. If I lose control as well, you'll have to stop me from hurting anyone. You better be prepared. This was your stupid idea."

Actually, it was Aleysha's. Amon clapped his hands together exuberantly, clearly gleeful that Ares had accepted Aleysha's company.

Ares squinted at Amon. "You seem overjoyed."

I've always wanted to see how the human emotion, love, develops between two individuals.

The boy's face turned bright red and he walked forward, kicking Amon's foot. Nothing happened. "S-Shut up! It's not like that!" he barked, folding his arms as he glanced away from the golem. "Stop being so stupid, Amon!"

Amon raised a giant hand to his rocky head and saluted Ares with a grumble. If you say so. You ought to go and get some sleep. Otherwise you're going to make me carry your heavy body again through the desert. We can't have that.

"Oh, quiet. I'm only one hundred and thirty pounds."

When was the last time you checked your weight? I could've sworn it was one hundred and thirty tons.

Aleysha lay awake inside of the cave, listening to the two arguing friends and smiled to herself as she gazed up at the dark cavern ceiling. She was relieved that Ares had accepted her but she couldn't help but be concerned by a particular thing that Ares had mentioned about losing control. She recalled that he had done so during his fight against Zahir. It was as if he had completely changed personalities. Should she ask about it? No, that probably wasn't wise. She should wait until Ares was ready to come out and tell her the truth himself. Right now, it seemed like even he was confused with everything that was going on.

The mercenary pulled her fluffy scarf tighter around her neck and closed her eyes. At least she could make her contribution to Dastia here and now. Ares was fighting to defend a faraway land that didn't even respect him. Everyone feared him, but despite that, he was still willing to fight to protect them. She recalled the memory of Ares saving her from being enslaved. The other mercenaries who had also been saved regarded Ares with terror and fled away as quickly as possible, thinking that the boy would slay them. Aleysha bit her lower lip gently. She refused to let Ares endure the burden of protecting eastern Dastia alone. Someone as selfless and kind as him deserved respect, not fear. He deserved companionship, not isolation. And Aleysha would do her best to make sure to let Ares know that, besides Amon, he was never alone.

***

Tetsu's eyes snapped open and he shot forward, his heart pounding rapidly against his chest. A sharp pain pierced his chest, as if a dagger had just been driven into him. He glanced down and saw a stretching wound that looked like raw meat had just been splattered across his chest. It was pink and fresh, a burn that surely would stay with him forever. He saw dozens of bloody cloths at his side and a water basin that was filled with red water. Sleeping soundlessly on the wooden floor beside him was Kira, who looked absolutely exhausted. Tetsu smiled wearily at the Magus. It had been a while since he had last seen her. After all, Kira lived across Dastia in the faraway country of Luxas.

"She's taken a liking to you over these past couple years, you know. She hasn't left your side once while you were unconscious. The reason you're alive is because of her medicines, magic, and persistence," the king of Luxas said, still sitting in his leather chair. He had a glass of dark wine in his hand. He swished the liquid around a bit before taking a small sip, letting the alcohol tickle his throat. The king smacked his lips, letting the sweetness of the wine settle on his tongue. "You should be grateful that you have someone like her in your life. Kira cares deeply for you."

Tetsu looked to the king. "Lord Alkaios, where has my sister gone?"

"She chased after Ares into the Lost Sands."

Tetsu closed his eyes in disbelief. That idiot. She had no idea of the dangers in that desert! "I need to go after—"

"You will not leave this mansion until you have healed," Lord Alkaios commanded, his back still to Tetsu. "My Magus has worked herself far too hard to have you get up and get injured again. There is no point in waltzing straight to your demise, Tetsu."

Tetsu's hands balled up into tight fists. "But…."

"Why is it that you think your sister went after Ares into that forsaken wasteland?" the king asked.

Tetsu said nothing, unsure himself.

"It's because she felt powerless just as you do now. Humans have a natural thirst for power. That drive only grows stronger when you realize that you are helpless in a situation. Aleysha was frustrated that she has done nothing but sit and watch everyone fight her battles for her. She scrambled after Ares, ready to make a stand for herself." The king took another gulp of his wine. "Because she lost her mother, she knows that she doesn't want anyone else to suffer like she is right now. In order to prevent the innocents of the east from enduring such agony, she must defeat the Persians."

"Then we must help her!" Tetsu exclaimed. "We can't just sit here and do nothing!"

"Yes, and we will." The king gazed into the burning fire that still blazed in the hearth before him. "I have already called for the lords of the United Eastern Nations to send whatever troops they are willing to spare to Yuusus to combat the Persians. You and I will lead the army to Persepolis and we will bring the fight to the enemy. We refuse to submit before the slave-drivers of Persia."

Tetsu grinned and exhaled, lying back on the ground. "That's more like it, old man!"

"Watch it, Tetsu. We aren't *that* friendly." The king chuckled. "I understand what it's like to feel powerless, like you're an ant in a world full of giants. But do not worry. We of eastern Dastia refuse to be pushed around by these Persian invaders. It's all thanks to you, Tetsu, for helping facilitate the alliances of all the eastern kingdoms over the previous years."

Tetsu gazed up at the ceiling, memories of Persia flashing through his mind. "I used to be one of them, you know. But they betrayed me and tried to have me killed. When I found myself waking up in Aleysha's home five years ago I had already made up my mind." The irises of the man's eyes morphed from their dark black into a glowing red. "I would do whatever it takes to bring about the collapse of the Persian Empire!"

***

Yuu galloped on his steed through the streets of Persepolis and halted at the front gates, which were giant solidified walls of metal that towered high into the air. His ebony horse whined and he reached forward, stroking the animal's snout gently, calming it. His eyes flickered up and he spotted Zahir on his hazel-colored mount, trotting about with several Persian horsemen accompanying him.

Crowds of people, who hailed the Magi as heroes, stood cheering for the departing party of Persians. They wore ragged, simple clothing in comparison to the nobles, but they seemed quite content despite their impoverished lifestyles.

Yuu remembered that at one time he had been among those crowds of people worshipping and applauding the Magi whenever they had left the city. No one really knew who the Magi were or what they actually did, which was all the king's dirty work. But the citizens simply adopted the idea that the Magi were role models and heroes who were respected throughout the empire, and didn't seek reasoning behind the belief.

The noble pulled on the reins of his horse as Zahir and the

other Persians began to file out of the gargantuan, open gates of Persepolis out towards the direction of the Lost Sands in the near distance. Yuu dug his heels into the sides of his horse and his steed bolted forward, galloping after its comrades. The chilly, yet calm, winds of the night blew into Yuu's face as he shot forward across the dirt in the direction of the desert. The earth was so flat that Yuu felt like he was riding off towards the giant moon that glowed in the distance and the glinting stars in the night sky.

Out there somewhere, Yuu believed that Darien was still alive after all of these years. It had taken him a whole year to move on from Darien and Tetsu's deaths. But upon hearing that there was a chance that one of his old friends was still alive, a slumbering spark of hope flared up in his chest and emotion cracked across his face for the first time in years. If this god was taking the form of Darien and if he was fighting to protect the defenseless citizens of Yuusus, could that mean that he possibly saved Darien when he was in the Lost Sands? The two surely had crossed paths in the desert. But what would Yuu do if he came to find Darien? The prince was a traitor to the empire and was to be punished, but Yuu knew that he didn't have it in his heart to go against Darien.

Yuu hardened his expression as he galloped forward. His mind was wandering; he had to focus. He was about to journey into the world's most dangerous desert; he should be worrying about his own wellbeing. Yuu had to make sure that he came out of this alive, no matter what happened. His eyes flitted to Zahir's back, the man's black cape flapping rapidly in the gentle night breeze. As long as he was with Zahir, things would be okay. The Magus had given him countless opportunities to better his life. The power that he now wielded was all because of Zahir. Without him, Yuu would still be that weak, shy, powerless child that he had been five years ago. Always letting others fight his battles was how Yuu had lived his life. But not anymore. *No matter what fears I battle in this desert, I'll conquer them and return home. I'll bring honor and pride to my family with my success on this quest. And Darien, I hope that I do get to see you again. Though, what will I do when I see you? Embrace you? Kill you? After all, Prince Darien, you are a traitor to Persia.*

The Deadliest Desert

"Just because I'm letting you tag along doesn't mean you can slack off!" Ares called over his shoulder at Aleysha as the girl jogged to keep up. He looked up at the beating sun that now gleamed in the morning day. It was a lot hotter than usual, even for the Lost Sands. This heat was so intense that it made the dry air feel heavy. It was almost like weights were attached to their bodies. He watched as Aleysha stumbled to his side, gasping for breath. Sweat poured down her face, creating a waterfall of perspiration streaming from her chin.

"Sorry, it's a lot hotter than I expected," Aleysha gasped, wiping her brow. She reached into her pack and pulled out a canteen of water and lifted it to her lips, letting some water trickle into her mouth to cure her thirst. Unfortunately, she didn't feel satisfied and continued to squeeze water into her mouth until Ares forcefully pulled the canteen away. "Hey!" Aleysha complained.

"The desert is playing games with you, Aleysha." Ares rolled his eyes, holding the canteen at his side. He nodded to Aleysha's feet.

Aleysha blinked and looked down, realizing that she had been pouring water onto the ground. That was why she didn't feel like her thirst was being quenched. She also realized that she wasn't sweating as profusely as she believed she was. Was that all an illusion? She closed her eyes and groaned. "I didn't know the desert could create illusions like that unless I was actually dehydrated, starving, or going insane."

"These are the Lost Sands," Ares said, tossing the canteen back to Aleysha. "Use your head. We've walked less than thirty minutes from the cave, do you honestly think you'd be sweating that much?" He scoffed. "You have to learn the tricks that this desert will play on you otherwise you'll die before we even make it a mile in." He looked at Amon over his shoulder. "Amon, have you managed to locate the general direction of Ahriman's body?"

Amon nodded his head, gazing out across the wasteland and pointing in a random direction that seemed to lead nowhere but sand. *There.*

"How can you possibly see that far?" Aleysha frowned.

"He's a Guardian. This desert is where he was born and he knows every inch of it. His eyes can also see over a hundred miles away with perfect accuracy," Ares said proudly with a smile and motioned for Aleysha to follow him. "Alright, let's get going."

The party of three began to walk through the scorching hot desert, feeling their skin being baked alive. During their several hours of traveling, Ares explained to Aleysha everything that Ramses had told him while they sat on Amon's giant shoulders, resting their aching feet.

"Become a god," Aleysha echoed. "So Zahir is trying to do what you've already accomplished?"

"Yeah," Ares said. "I expect that they're utilizing a lot of Persian soldiers to search for the fault. I'm not sure if they'll all perish in the Lost Sands either. The Lost Sands takes advantage of human nature and uses it to drive human invaders to their doom. But with the

Persians' massive pool of resources, some of the desert's tricks might not work." He leapt off of Amon's shoulders and onto the desert floor.

Aleysha blinked as Amon plucked her off his shoulders and put her on the ground beside Ares. "Why are we walking on foot? Isn't staying on Amon faster and less taxing?"

"Yeah, and it makes us lazy. The desert will take advantage of that and have us killed. We need to be alert as we travel," Ares said, beginning to walk across the endless hills of sand towards where Amon claimed was Ahriman's fissure.

It was only an hour before Aleysha felt herself growing heavy and exhausted once more. The baking heat made her feel sluggish. Dragging her feet across the sand, the mercenary winced as she saw that Ares was effortlessly trundling forward as if nothing were wrong. Aleysha knitted her eyebrows. She didn't want to seem like a burden to Ares because then that would only prove him right. She couldn't slow down. Aleysha narrowed her eyes and groaned. She wanted to just collapse so badly though!

The god noticed her lethargic behavior and sighed, pointing to a statue in the distance. "Just a little further, Aleysha. We'll take a break there."

Reaching the statue, Aleysha realized that the figure was positioned on top of a flat, marble platform that was unnaturally inserted into the sandy desert. A huge statue of a golden humanoid stood tall in the desert, wielding a powerful hammer with a long shaft. The head of the hammer itself was a rectangle shape and glowed mystically with purple arcane energy. The statue wore armor that was made of glittering gold and embedded with various jewels that made the figurine shine even brighter in the sunlight. The sculpture was that of a male human, standing completely straight with perfect posture, except it had the head of a dog. There were grey stones embedded in the eye sockets of the stone figure that suggested the life-like figurine was not animated.

Aleysha almost expected the statue to spring to life, but luckily for her it didn't. The effigy was placed in the middle of a flat, solid marble surface. The mercenary found it quite odd that the dog-man figurine had just been left out here randomly in the Lost Sands with all of these rich jewels embedded in it. She was surprised also that no one had stolen the gems off the statue; they were probably worth a fortune. More than she could've made in five years of working as a mercenary. Beside the statue was a naturally flowing fountain that seemed to constantly spew water up into the air, spraying it wastefully in the sand, where it soaked in and vanished.

Aleysha scrambled forward and put her mouth to the gushing fountain and allowed the cool liquid to satiate her thirst. She exhaled, splashing some of the water on her sweaty face before taking several steps backward. "What an oasis!"

"It's actually a trap," Ares observed, sipping sparingly from the fountain.

"A trap?" Aleysha blinked, eying the water precariously.

"Greed. There is a difference between what you need and what you want." Ares explained, stepping back from the fountain. "The water fountain has been conveniently placed next to this statue where there are beautiful gems of every sort embedded into its gleaming golden armor. If a single gem is taken out of place the Guardian will awaken. Those humans who seek to improve their wealth by stealing a gem from this statue will awaken the beast and be eradicated. This desert is a place for those who seek adventure, not for those who seek to fulfill their own selfish desires. This Guardian was created for the sole purpose of guarding the desert from the selfish humans that would plague the Lost Sands."

Aleysha gazed in awe at the statue. "T-That's a Guardian?"

"A slumbering one, yes."

"Well I wasn't even thinking about touching those gems anyway," Aleysha said, biting her lower lip. *I would probably be dead if Ares wasn't here.*

"Good. Wealth like that will do nothing for you in this desert." Ares stretched his arms. "Phew, if we didn't stumble across this place you probably would've been done for."

"Huh?"

"The desert was targeting you, making you a sloth," Ares explained. "That heavy feeling that you experienced while you were walking was making you feel defeated, right?"

"Yeah, why?"

"Well, eventually, the heat makes you give up hope. You collapse and most of the time, you become too lazy or apathetic to even care about getting up. You accept your death and succumb to yet another natural human sin, sloth. The desert takes advantage of such flaws and does its best to weigh you down. If you notice what the Lost Sands is trying to do, though, it makes it much easier to push through," Ares said and turned his head, his ears twitching.

"Something's nearby. Amon, do you feel that?"

Amon gently walked onto the platform, trying his best not to bump into the dog-man Guardian accidently. The golem had no intention of awakening a foe. Amon hesitated, listening to his surroundings and nodded, grunting. *Underneath us.*

"Underneath?" Aleysha exclaimed, looking at the ground. She didn't feel anything. "Uh, what's underneath us?" The moment she spoke, she felt it. The ground shook in a startling tremor, shaking the earth to its very foundation. Aleysha staggered backward, her heart beginning to race. "W-What's that?" She reached for the shield strapped to her back and pulled it out, brandishing her sword at the same time.

Ares' eyes darted around, absorbing their surroundings. The rumbling was coming from everywhere; he couldn't pinpoint where its origin was. He shut his eyes tight and exhaled through his nose, trying to calm himself. Clearing his mind, the boy felt his heartbeat slowing. Soon, he could hear everything. He could feel everything. Vibrations pulsed through the ground, rushing through the soles of his feet. He picked up on every movement the tremor created. His eyes fluttered open and he grunted, tackling Aleysha clean off her feet.

The earth suddenly erupted, sending a geyser of sand spewing up towards the sky. A massive worm exploded from the marble ground, sending pieces of the shattered platform splintering through the air. The gigantic worm had an oval-shaped orifice with hundreds of sharp dagger-like teeth that poked out of every inch of the creature's mouth. The worm's mouth opened up into a pitch-black abyss, and the creature itself was even larger than Amon.

"It's a core-digger!" Ares bellowed as the gigantic worm crashed back down, burrowing deep into the earth. The tremors started up again as Ares and Aleysha staggered back to their feet. "If that thing comes up to the surface from underneath us then we're as good as dead. It'll swallow us whole."

"What do we do?" Aleysha shouted over the roaring earth. "I doubt we can outrun that thing!"

Ares' eyes widened as a worm tore itself from the sand several hundred meters away, flying high through the air and descending upon their position. At the same time, he sensed movement right underneath Aleysha. He kicked off the ground and swept Aleysha clean off her feet again as another worm creature burst from the platform underneath her. Marble scattered through the air and Ares grunted as debris rained down around them. "There're two of them," he murmured, his eyes flickering to the first worm that was still falling down towards them with its mouth wide open. He pressed the soles of his feet into the ground and winced, knowing that he couldn't get out of the way of the descending core-digger. "Amon!"

Amon intercepted the worm and stepped between Ares and the creature, grabbing the top and bottom of the monstrosity's giant mouth. The elemental roared as he ripped the worm's jaw off, gripping the squirming creature by the nozzle. The rest of the monster's convulsing body fell down on the golem, who grabbed the elongated beast and hurled it through the air. The decapitated worm crashed into a sand dune a mile away, writhing around for several seconds before it finally went still.

The second core-digger smashed from the ground, seemingly enraged by the death of its companion, and dashed through the air at a lower angle than its partner. It flew horizontally towards Ares and Aleysha with its mouth snapping towards them, loose saliva splattering onto the cracked platform.

Aleysha leapt to the side, allowing the giant creature to fly past her. She brought her sword cutting upwards at the creature and blinked when her steel sword glanced harmlessly off of the worm's impenetrable hide. She staggered backward, realizing that an ordinary sword wouldn't leave a scratch on a beast this strong. The mercenary turned to Ares, who was still standing in the worm's path. "Ares!" she cried.

Ares extended his hand and his spear materialized at the tip of his fingers, levitating and pointing straight at the oncoming monster. The boy's face was calm as he breathed out, sending the spear whistling through the air towards its target. The weapon went into the worm's mouth and rapidly began to hack the creature from the inside-out, stabbing and jabbing the monster's innards. The god stepped to the side as the worm crashed down on the ground, sliding across the damaged platform until its body slithered off onto the desert sand. He turned to Aleysha and raised an eyebrow at the girl. "You've got guts," he called out, acknowledging her attempt to strike the beast. "Not bad!"

Aleysha beamed but still knew that she wasn't strong enough to defeat a creature of that caliber. Not with her ordinary strength. She squeezed the handle on her sun shield and sighed at the sweltering heat. The mercenary was about to go to the fountain in order to get another drink but realized that there was a cracking sound coming from that direction. She turned her attention to the statue and to her horror, the joints of the Guardian began to snap to life.

The mercenary stared in awe as bits of rubble and dust crumbled off the figure and soon the dog-man statue creaked to life, its limbs snapping as it stepped off its pedestal and down onto the hardened marble, gripping its hammer's long handle with both hands. A statue was coming to life? She supposed that she shouldn't be surprised by anything in the Lost Sands, but shock registered upon her face as the creature raised its hammer over its head. The grey stones in his eyes were now gleaming as brightly as pure rubies.

"Move!" Ares suddenly raced across the platform and tackled Aleysha clean off her feet as the dog-man brought its weapon crashing into the earth, shattering the ground like glass. The ground cracked as what remained of the solidified, marble platform exploded into the air, a gigantic cloud of dust swirling through the air around the area as the hammer tore through the floor.

Aleysha blinked, noticing that Ares was on top of her, protecting her from the falling debris that rained down around them. She opened her mouth to speak but the words died upon her lips. She was far too stunned by the bizarreness of this situation.

"Amon! How did the Guardian awaken?" Ares demanded, pushing himself off Aleysha and to his feet, turning to face the giant statue.

"The jewels…." Aleysha pointed at several jewels that had fallen out of the Guardian's armor and were lying on the ground. "They fell out!"

"So that's what triggered it, huh?" Ares murmured. It must've been all the rumbling from the worms and Amon.

Amon groaned an apology.

"It's alright, buddy. Let's take him out."

Amon released a bellowing roar as he stormed forward, his gigantic rock arms outstretched as he charged at the Guardian. The dog-man raised its hammer and smashed it into the side of Amon's torso, sending the golem staggering to the side several steps. But the colossal giant didn't let that stop him and tackled the statue, driving both titans into the ground, the earth quaking from their frightening power.

"What about me?" Aleysha yelled over the sound of the battle. "What do I do?"

"Stay here and don't die," Ares called over his shoulder, immediately vanishing into thin-air. He reappeared above Amon and the Guardian, who were on the ground wrestling for dominance. The dog-man had Amon pinned to the ground, pressing its hammer's long handle against the throat of the rock golem. Ares descended from the air and drove both of his legs into the back of the Guardian. Both of his hands were stuffed into his pockets as he shattered the spine of the statue with ease, the gleaming armor of the creature cracking beneath his heels.

Amon used his mighty strength to toss the injured Guardian off of himself, sending the dog-man tumbling across the ground. The golem groaned, pushing itself into a sitting position as it scratched its head. Ares landed on the ground before the giant, having leapt off the Guardian's back several seconds before. The god gave his best friend an approving smile.

"Hey! Dog-breath!" Aleysha yelled.

Ares turned suddenly and saw that the mercenary had taken out her sword and shield and was rushing directly at the Guardian, who had begun to push itself back onto its feet. He winced. *That idiot! She's going to get herself killed!*

Aleysha slowed to a stop in front of the giant dog-headed humanoid and held her orange shield up to the glowing sun. The light of the star shined down on the sun insignia engraved into her shield, and suddenly the entire shield began to evanescently glow with the warm colors of red, orange, and yellow.

Ares and Amon stood by with their mouths gaping, watching Aleysha with surprise. It seemed as if the shield was soaking in the sunlight, taking it in as energy. But what would that energy be used for and how was Aleysha doing this?

The dog-man creature didn't seem to be patient enough to find out. It gripped the hilt of its hammer tightly and lifted the gigantic weapon over its head and brought it crashing down upon Aleysha.

The mercenary continued to hold her shield confidently, sweat beginning to form on her brow. *Just a few more seconds! I can do this!*

Suddenly Ares appeared right in front of Aleysha, teleporting from his original position beside Amon. The god extended one hand outward, his other arm at his side, stopping the powerful hammer swing effortlessly. The earth beneath him cracked, absorbing the force of the blow and a cloud of dust swept outward from his position, swirling around him. Unharmed, Ares glanced over his shoulder at Aleysha and nodded at her.

Aleysha lifted her shield even higher now and a beam of bright orange light tore from the heavens and pierced through the sky, bashing down into the Guardian. There was a loud groan that sounded like a resounding horn as the incredible light sent glowing orange energy in all directions. The beam receded back into the sky, vanishing as quickly as it had come. A circle of black ashes surrounded the area where the Guardian had been struck, forming a symbol in the earth that looked like the sun. The statue had been completely incinerated. Nothing was left but ashes drifting in the desert wind.

Aleysha lowered her shield and exhaled, feeling slightly dizzy. She smiled wearily, glad that she had contributed to bringing down the colossal Guardian. "Got him…!" She was gasping for breath, her face slightly blanched.

Ares stared at the ashes of the obliterated Guardian. Aleysha had summoned that incredible surge of power that had roared from the heavens? The god, however, did not sense any magical presence radiating from the mercenary. He glanced at the shield, which had now stopped glowing. So it was that shield that had summoned such outstanding power. It must've been taxing for its wielder to call upon that powerful magic.

He flitted forward and caught Aleysha as she collapsed and slid into unconsciousness. The girl's shield clanked to the sand and Amon eyed it curiously, recognizing its unique design. Ares held the mercenary in his arms and looked to his best friend. "Amon, you recognize the shield as well?"

Yes.

"And you acknowledge that Ra disguised himself as Aleysha five years ago."

Yes.

"How is it possible that Ra knew what Aleysha would look like in five years? Do you know why Ra took that form?"

I do not know.

Ares looked at Aleysha's shield and frowned. "How do you think she got this shield? It can't be coincidence that our paths crossed and she happens to have this magical treasure. Clearly Aleysha knew of its incredible power."

Perhaps our interrogation may begin when she awakens, hm?

"Perhaps," Ares murmured, looking up at the glowing sun. "I just want to know who this god, Ra, really is. Is he on our side?"

Who knows?

Ares placed Aleysha in Amon's palm and sighed, letting the golem carry the unconscious girl. He looked at the sleeping mercenary and smiled at her. "You did well, Aleysha, and you've proven to me that you're more than ready to come on this journey with us." He kicked off of the ground, flying hundreds of feet into the air, and landed on Amon's shoulder swiftly. The boy brushed his blonde hair from his eyes and gazed out across the stretching desert. "Somewhere out there is the Persian army and Ahriman."

Amon grunted. They will be challenging opponents.

"Nothing that we can't handle, though," Ares said optimistically and pointed over the towering sand dunes in the distance. "Let's go, Amon. We don't have time to waste."

***

Ramses' eyes fluttered open, his blurry gaze wandering around the blank ceiling. He groaned, reaching up and running a coarse hand through his black hair. A throbbing headache pounded in his head and he blinked, realizing that he was lying on a soft, leather couch. A tight, bloody bandage was wrapped around the wound in his shoulder. The pain was mostly gone except for a slight ache. On a glass table beside him was a cup of still water. The man reached out and gulped down the water without hesitation. With his thirst slightly satisfied, his mind was cleared.

The Magus placed the cup down and scanned his surroundings, spotting a man sitting on a leather chair, gazing at a blazing fire. Ramses frowned, realizing that this man had not reacted at all to his awakening. The stranger simply stared emptily into the hearth, unmoving.

Ramses stood, and blinked when suddenly a man in a black cloak teleported in front of him, gripping a diamond hourglass. "Tetsu, was it?" Ramses muttered, his eyes on the gleaming artifact that the man held. The Sands of Time allowed the man to freeze or slow time, at the cost of physical energy. But judging from Tetsu's expert use of the relic, it seemed that he had had the object in his possession for quite some time now. Time was his to control. "I'm rather surprised that you haven't killed me yet."

"You should be," Tetsu said, his burning gaze piercing through the Magus, sending a disconcerting sensation shivering through Ramses. The Demon Mercenary placed the Sands of Time down on the glass table in front of Ramses and sighed, walking past the mage and casually sitting on the couch. "Ares, however, apparently insisted that you were to be given a second chance."

"Is that so?" Ramses said, his eyes not leaving the Sands of Time.

"I didn't hear the words myself," Tetsu said, observing the Magus. "But that was what Kira and Lord Alkaios told me."

There was a flash of movement as Ramses lunged for the Sands of Time but Tetsu kicked the table, sending the hourglass twirling through the air. The mercenary leapt forward and relentlessly tackled the mage, slamming him hard into the wooden ground. "But I knew that you were just another damned Persian!" he barked, raising a fist, ready to bash Ramses' face in.

"Stop it, you two," Kira called, walking into the room with a platter of grapes in one hand. She snapped her fingers with the other hand and the two men were both smacked by an invisible force and sent sliding to opposite sides of the room. "Be mature about the situation. Ramses, if you value your life then you won't try something as dumb as that again. I understand that you don't trust us, but you have to take our word that we won't hurt you." She pushed the glass table back into place and sighed, realizing that it had been cracked by Tetsu's kick. She put the plate of fruit on the table and pulled a chair over, plopping into the seat.

Ramses wiped his mouth, glaring at Tetsu. "I have no reason to trust Tetsu. Especially after the way that he talked about executing General Shazir. There's no doubt that you'll have me executed as well."

"Maybe I should have you executed then," Tetsu growled.

"Tetsu," Kira warned, "stop it!"

Tetsu walked over to the couch and sank into the cushions, folding his arms with a jaded sigh.

"Surely you've kept me alive for a reason other than just Ares' word," Ramses said, standing up tall. He put his hands on his waist as he turned his attention to Kira, who plopped a juicy grape into her mouth. "Tell me why."

"A war between eastern and western Dastia will break out soon," Kira explained. "Lord Alkaios has already called for the United Eastern Nations' army to arrive at Yuusus. They will be here in several weeks, fully ready to begin their march on Persia."

"And you want me to fight against Persia?"

"Correct," Kira said.

Ramses lowered his gaze. The Persian Empire was not a nation that he wanted to fight for. But he didn't want to battle against it either, not again. The last time that he had done so, he had almost lost everything. His friends, his home — all that he had left was his family, and the only reason they were still alive was because he had dedicated himself to the Persians. "My family is still in Persia. If Cambyses learns of my betrayal, he will have them executed."

"Then we'll save them," Kira said. "We have a couple weeks until the army arrives anyway. Tetsu and I needed something to do, right?"

"We have to go all the way to Persia for his family?" Tetsu winced at the very thought of such a venture.

"Yes, Tetsu." Kira shot him a fiery glare.

Tetsu sighed. Ramses was a Magus and would prove extremely useful, especially when the enemy was the Persian army. A Magus could defeat a thousand warriors alone if he was skilled. If they could save Ramses' family and secure the mage's allegiance without any losses, then the operation would definitely be worth it. But there was a potential risk. Tetsu knew that the families of the Magi, nobles, and higher officials in Persia all lived in the king's palace in Persepolis. Infiltrating such a fortified fortress without being spotted would be nearly impossible. Even if their little incursion succeeded, there was no guarantee that they would make it out alive.

The Hayashi clansman grabbed a fistful of his hair and exhaled through his nose. Sitting here doing nothing while Ares and Aleysha were out there trying to stop the revival of a god made Tetsu feel absolutely useless. Besides waiting for an army to arrive, there had to be something else that he could do to help. He supposed that this quest was it. "Alright," Tetsu murmured. "Lord Alkaios will be the Supreme General of the United Eastern Nations' army and will lead our soldiers to Persia in my stead, just in case we don't return in time. Ramses, do you know where your family is located?"

"Y-Yes," Ramses stammered, rather surprised that these two strangers were willing to go and save his family from the clutches of the Persian Empire.

Lord Alkaios turned his attention to the three guests in his living room and sighed. "So you're leaving me to manage the United Army, huh? What a drag that is." He smirked at Tetsu. "Always trying to squeeze out of the leadership role, aren't you?"

Tetsu shrugged. "I don't think I'd be a great leader."

"You don't know until you try," the king murmured. "At any rate, if you aren't home by the time the army arrives, we'll be storming across the deserts after you. You understand?"

"Loud and clear."

"Good," Lord Alkaios turned back to staring into the flickering flames of his hearth. "Now go and pack some food. I know how hungry you get when you go on long journeys."

***

Yuu's eyes were closed as he lay in a white tent beside Zahir, enjoying the little rest that he could snatch in the Lost Sands. Every second that they spent in this forsaken desert seemed to jeopardize their lives. A myriad of dangerous creatures of myth had leapt up and attacked them while traps, set by the desert itself, claimed the lives of countless Persians. Yet there was still no sign of Ahriman's fault. What if all of this was just superstition? What if the fall of the Persian god of darkness and death was just a tale? Persia was sacrificing a lot of resources in order to find this god's body. Thousands of lives had been claimed by the Lost Sands already. If there were nothing here then all of this would be an absolute waste.

A scream ripped through the silent morning and Yuu's eyes immediately snapped open. He flung his sheets off his body, grabbing his sword from next to him, and was on his feet without a single moment of hesitation. He brushed aside the flaps of his tent as he ventured out into the dry, hot desert. The noble was wearing a white cloak, leaving his suit of metal armor back in his tent. A red scarf curled around his neck and he pulled his hood over his head to block the sweltering heat of the blazing sun from cooking him. Brushing some white hair from his turquoise eyes, he gazed coldly over the dozens of tents that were set up in the campsite.

A gigantic scorpion, triple the size of the largest horse that Yuu had ever seen, ripped straight through one of the tents with a bleeding man caught between his pincers. Its massive tail skewered a second Persian who was running away, picking the man up and bashing him back into the desert sand. The shell of the creature was a pale golden color and its eyes were gleaming as red as rubies. The scorpion made a high-pitched screeching noise that echoed as it scampered across the earth towards Yuu, murderously ready to slaughter anything that moved.

The noble rolled up his sleeves, revealing that his hands were both covered in tightly wounded white bandages that hid every inch of his skin up to his forearms. Yuu broke into a sprint, bursting forward with speed, pumping his arms as he accelerated towards the barbaric beast. Kicking off of the ground, sending sand spraying backwards, the Magus leapt high into the air. He flew down at the scorpion with incredible speed, watching as the creature prepared to lunge out with its bloody stinger. Just as the scorpion was about to lash out at Yuu, the noble crashed down on the beast's head, squashing it like a watermelon.

Yellow liquids splattered all over the noble's boots and into the sand, looking like sticky honey. Unfortunately, it didn't have the same smell as honey and created a rancid miasma that made Yuu's nose twitch. The other Persian warriors were now awake, scrambling out of their tents at the sound of the ambush. It seemed that the creatures of the Lost Sands were eager to drive out the human intruders, because within moments of killing the scorpion, the Magus spotted dozens of enormous scorpions racing down a sand dune in the distance, skidding down the hill towards the Persian campsite.

Yuu's face didn't give off a single sign of emotion as he reached to his side towards his sheathed weapon. His relaxed touch drew his fingers slowly down the golden pommel at the end of his weapon to the grip of the hilt of his sword. He grasped the handle, yanking the weapon from its sheathe with a gentle motion, brandishing the beautiful steel into the air. His blade was golden and glowed in the beaming sunlight, cutting through the air elegantly. The mage exhaled and he pointed the tip of his sword at the oncoming scorpions that charged the Persians.

The Persian warriors didn't stand a chance against such monstrous beasts. They began to totter backwards, fearing for their lives. Turning around, they fled behind Yuu's tent for salvation for they knew that Zahir and Yuu would be able to protect them. Unfortunately for them, Zahir was somehow still sleeping through all of this commotion.

Yuu's cold gaze never faltered and he waited patiently until the scorpions were within a hundred meters of him. Suddenly the noble shot forward with a burst of speed. Adrenaline coursed through his body, giving him a newfound explosion of energy. He whipped his sword with one hand in a vicious uppercut that split a scorpion's face in two, sending yellow bodily fluids splattering across the sand. But Yuu's body continued to rotate, spinning around as he grabbed the hilt of his sword with both hands and forcefully wrenched the blade downwards, severing another scorpion's claw. The beast screeched as Yuu spun the opposite direction, bringing himself around to the creature's side. Ripping his sword backwards, he jammed his weapon back into the scorpion's ribs. All of this happened in such a fluent motion that it looked as if Yuu was performing a dance rather than mercilessly slaying these dangerous monsters.

The Magus tore his sword from the slain creature's body, spilling the yellow liquid onto the sand, filling the air with the pungent scent of the scorpion's blood. Yuu's eyes flickered between the remaining dozen of giant scorpions that raced towards him. They flitted with incredible speed but Yuu took every movement that they made into account. He calculated everything that these beasts would do and prepared his strategy. After all, he never made a mistake. He was the perfect warrior.

Yuu broke into a sprint as he rushed straight at one of the scorpions that snapped at him with one of its claws. The noble kicked off the ground and flipped through the air, gliding over the scorpion's body. He slammed his sword down into the creature's head and dragged it across the monster's body as he flew over it. Landing behind the slain scorpion, he continued to dash forward, slashing each beast down with ease. Each movement remained graceful and each step was just as he had practiced, not an inch out of place. Within a minute there were only three scorpions left, screeching at the corpses of their brethren that lay scattered across the sand.

"Go, Yuu!" a Persian cheered.

"He's saved us!" another cried.

Yuu looked at the surviving scorpions expressionlessly and exhaled. The creatures all scampered towards him in unison, their claws snapping loudly as their stingers all flexed, ready to skewer the noble. But the Magus unwrapped one of his bandages on his right hand, revealing a blue tattoo of a rabbit. The marking glowed for a brief moment and Yuu exhaled once more. But this time his breath was visible and appeared as a tiny mist that left his lips, as if he were in the winter of a frozen tundra. Without warning, the three scorpions all became encased in ice.

Water began to trickle off the blocks of ice from the sun's pounding heat, but Yuu closed his palm and all of the creatures immediately exploded into tiny bits. The Magus looked at the pieces of ice that were scattered on the ground with pity and then twirled his sword, sliding it back into its sheath.

As the noble was rewinding his bandages, he turned to notice that Zahir had emerged from the tent and was walking towards Yuu, holding a letter that one of the Persian soldiers had given him. "We've got a location on Ahriman's corpse. Luckily for us, it's not far from here. Hopefully we won't run into any more nuisances along the way." His gaze scanned the defeated scorpions but he didn't seem the slightest bit impressed. He simply nodded, as if the massacre was what he expected of his apprentice. "Gather your things. We're leaving."

It didn't take long for the party of Persians to gather their belongings and leave the area; most of the soldiers didn't want to stay anyway after that encounter with the scorpions. They were eager to reach the end of this accursed journey.

Yuu was simply relieved that they wouldn't have to stay in the desert for long before they discovered Ahriman's body. He couldn't imagine spending prolonged months in this hell.

Galloping across the Lost Sands for two hours finally brought Yuu and his fellow comrades to the top of a mountain of sand that overlooked a stretching wasteland, filled with statues of hundreds of creatures like demons, dragons, and phoenixes. These monsters were all from various cultural stories of an amalgam of religions throughout Terrador. All of these statues stood between Yuu's party and the gigantic tear in the earth that seemed to span at least five miles long. Inside of the fault was nothing but darkness for as far as Yuu could see.

The noble had no idea how they were going to get to the bottom of that chasm without dying. Climbing down definitely seemed like an insane option at this point. Yuu turned his head and saw the thousands of other Persians who had already arrived at the site and were waiting at the bottom of the hill, near the statues.

Yuu narrowed his eyes. "Those soldiers should not be so close. They'll awaken the hundreds of Guardians that lay on this wasteland. Should those Guardians awaken, we'll all perish. Did you not say that you would order these Persian warriors to turn back and return to Persepolis?"

"I already gave an order earlier today demanding that a majority of the Persian army return to Persepolis," Zahir said, his arms folded as he stared across the flat desert before him. "The remaining three thousand Persians that are at the bottom of the hill will serve as bait so that you and I will be able to make it through these Guardians and to the chasm."

"That's still a lot of men that you're sacrificing!" Yuu protested.

"A few thousand lives for the power of a god is not a high price to pay by my standards."

"I disagree," Yuu said. "These are men with families and homes to return to. You cannot simply put a price on their head as if…."

"I beg to differ." Zahir turned and glared at the noble with his gleaming purple eyes, causing Yuu to stiffen. A cold sensation surged through the apprentice and he ground his teeth, annoyed that he still felt intimidated by his master. "The lives of ordinary men are nowhere near as precious as magical humans such as you and I. Those soldiers down there volunteered to join the Persian army, knowing very well that on any occasion they might die."

"But this isn't fair! They won't stand a chance against the Guardians out there!" Yuu argued. "The gods have chosen their greatest creations to guard the corpse of Ahriman. Those men down there will be massacred."

"And they will be remembered," Zahir said stubbornly and turned his attention away from Yuu. "If you don't want to watch their gallant sacrifices then look away. When you finally harden your heart and become a man, you're free to follow me into that abyss to claim the power that will make Persia the strongest empire in this world." He extended his hand outward and yelled so that everyone could hear him. "*Forward!*"

Yuu's hands balled into tight fists at his side and he scowled, watching as the thousands of Persian soldiers began to march forward across the Lost Sands. They only knew that their mission was to get to the chasm several miles away. They weren't aware that these statues would be brought to life the moment that they stepped onto that wasteland. The Magus watched as the dauntless warriors marched proudly in the direction of the army of Guardians in the near distance. Zahir was tricking those warriors down there. This wasn't right! Yuu's throat tightened and he found it harder to breathe the closer that the Persian ranks got to the stagnant figurines. Sweat formed on his brow and his hands began to ball up into tightly clenched fists at his side, his knuckles turning a ghostly white.

What would Darien have done? What would Tetsu have done? The two friends he knew from childhood would've stopped this madness immediately. They would've stepped forward and fought for what was right. Power hadn't been everything in the world to them. Yuu remembered that. Darien didn't even want to be king and Tetsu believed that power was what corrupted mankind, which was why he despised slavers.

Yuu cracked a tiny smile. He had become a Magus for the sole purpose of gaining power so that he could make a difference. Yet, here he was, still helpless. He straightened his back and groaned. "Screw this."

Zahir turned to his apprentice and watched as Yuu leapt into the air and clicked his fingers, creating a pipe of ice that streamed down the sand dune to where the Persian soldiers were. The Magus leapt down the pipe, sliding at an incredible speed as he accelerated down the sandy hill. Reaching the bottom, Yuu snapped his fingers again and the pipe dissolved into water as he slid to his feet. The noble sprinted forward, swinging his arms as he lowered his head. He ignored Zahir's disapproving shouting and continued onward to the Persian army. "Stop!" Yuu yelled, realizing that the Persians were getting far too close to the statues. But by the time his voice reached them, it was already too late.

A warrior stepped onto the wasteland, activating a chain reaction of events that scattered across the sandy plains. The ground began to rumble with a minor tremor, then a loud groan echoed through the silence as if a titan were awakening. Yuu watched in awe as the massive statues snapped and crackled to life. Some creatures transformed from stone to flesh, recovering their lost color. Some stayed in their stone form but were still as horrifically intimidating.

Yuu grabbed the hilt of his sword as an army of mythological monsters roared to life, all turning to face the force of the trembling Persian soldiers. The Magus knitted his eyebrows, realizing what he had just gotten himself into. This was most definitely not going to end well.

Becoming a God

"Darien, run!" Yuu's voice echoed.

Darien blinked, realizing that he was staring at his feet. He was wearing his royal garb from before he became Ares. He held out his hands before his face, examining them, but they still looked the same. He looked forward and found that he was standing in the center of the Persian throne room. But he saw death everywhere around him. There were bloody corpses of Persian guards scattered on the marble floor, with streaks of crimson smeared beside their pale bodies. Yuu's unmoving cadaver lay sprawled on the ground with a deep gash ripped across his back. Darien's heart sank as he hesitantly crept towards his old friend. "Y-Yuu…."

The prince's eyes snapped upward and saw that his mother and father were both dead on their thrones, blood splattered across their cheeks. A new throne had been conjured and forcefully inserted in between his father and mother's thrones. Sitting upon the golden seat was Cambyses, who wore a wicked grin as he gazed upon Darien.

Darien began to breathe harder, sweat forming on his brow. He heard a choking sound and spun around to find Zahir squeezing the life out of Tetsu's lungs. The boy was pale and was still fifteen, his legs dangling as he struggled for life. "Tetsu!" the prince yelled but his weak voice did nothing because the Magus crushed the boy's windpipe and dropped the corpse to the ground, where it landed with an unnatural thud. Darien's lips quivered and his eyes widened, his hands trembling at his side.

Zahir smiled fiendishly. "How does it feel knowing that you'll lose everything that you've come to care about and you can't do a thing about it?" He extended his hand and pointed his index finger at Darien's forehead. "How does it feel to be powerless?"

Darien clenched his jaw, frustrated. The entire memory exploded into a puff of black mist that swirled around him, leaving him in a world of darkness. Standing behind him was man with red ancient markings engraved in his skin. It looked as if the tattoos were just recently burned into his flesh, for they glowed the color of lava. The stranger had tussled brown hair and wild orange eyes that looked like they belonged to a beast. He was completely shirtless and wore torn pants that were stained red. His very presence invoked the putrid stink of corpses and blood. The prince turned to look at this man and demanded, "Who are you?"

"I am Ares," the man said.

"As am I."

"No, you are Darien," Ares said with a grin. "You are a betrayed, dying prince who was given my power five years ago. You, however, are not me, no matter what that foolish sun god, Ra, might think. No matter what anyone tells you, I am the true Ares. I am the real God of War. I may be dead, but my consciousness exists within you. It's unfortunate that every day I have to sit inside of your body and watch you pathetically solve your problems like a mere inept human. You have the power of a god, a war god, and you don't even use it to destroy your enemies."

Darien said nothing.

"The memory you saw just now showed the individuals that have torn away everything from you. They hurt your friend, Tetsu. They killed your other friend, Yuu. They assassinated your parents, stole your rightful throne, and assumed control over the empire that was your birthright." Ares touched his hand to his forehead, bursting out laughing. "Meanwhile you're sitting here twiddling your thumbs doing nothing. Do you not care at all for vengeance?"

"Vengeance will bring me nothing."

"It will bring your throne back. It will make you a hero. It will bring justice to those who deserve to be judged," Ares growled. "The victims of Persia suffer drastically every day because of your poor decision not to eradicate the corrupt monarch and his pet magician. You are no longer human. You have joined the supreme race of gods that rule above the humans, making no mortal dream out of your reach. Yet you have no aspirations, Darien.

"Watching you wander the Lost Sands for five years has brought me to the realization that you are nothing but a sojourner that knows nothing of what he wants. You don't know if you want revenge for your deceased parents or if you even want the throne at all. It's almost as if you are relieved that the responsibility of the throne was stolen from you and taken by a hubristic king who simply abuses his power. Even now you seek to stop the revival of Ahriman, but for what purpose? To protect the innocent people of the east? Well, if that was your damned goal from the very beginning, why not just end the life of your accursed uncle and have the whole problem over with? You need to make up your mind, Darien. You don't know what it is you want to do."

"Then what do I do?" Darien demanded. "With this newfound power that I was granted, I am supposed to be responsible. I can't just use this godly strength that was bestowed upon me to bring a whole empire crumbling down to the ground. Every man I've murdered died in an unfair way, for they never stood a chance. It's just unnatural for a deity to live amongst humans and solve their problems."

Ares reached out and drove his fist straight into Darien's nose, sending the boy sprawling onto his back, pain spiking through his face. The god of war scowled, annoyed with the naïve prince. "Responsibility means that you use your power for justice. You use your power to protect the innocent and to make sure that darkness doesn't rise in this world! Our duty as gods is to maintain balance. Is Persia bringing about balance? For five years you've waited patiently, allowing countless people to suffer under your uncle's reign as you hunted for your purpose for existence. You may have never had any intention of murdering Cambyses, but know that in order to bring about balance, his death is required."

Darien rubbed his face and groaned, pushing himself to his feet. Ares was right. For five long years, he had sat in the Lost Sands and done nothing while millions suffered at the hands of the empire that was supposed to be his. His mistake was allowing Cambyses take the throne without a fight. He had to correct that mistake.

"I know what you want me to do, Ares," Darien said. "You want me to go to Persia and obliterate everyone in my path until Cambyses lies dead at my feet. You want me to bring justice to

Dastia so that balance can be achieved. I'll go to Persepolis and I'll stop Cambyses."

"You'll *kill* Cambyses," Ares corrected.

"I'm going to do things my way," Darien said. "I am a different person than you. Killing isn't something that I enjoy, Ares. But for some reason whenever I'm in combat, I feel this growing rage that burns within my chest. All of this time, it's been you, hasn't it? This urge to murder surges through my veins and an unforgettable aura of bloodlust surrounds me when I enter the thrill of battle. But I refuse to be like you. No matter how much you try and take over, no matter how much you hate how I do things, I'm going to do things my way. You're right. I'm not you, I'm Darien. And I won't kill Cambyses, I'm not searching for justice or revenge. I'll eliminate him from his throne of power to protect those that I care about and to ensure the safety of the innocents of Dastia."

Ares cracked a tiny smile. "You've got guts. I'm glad we had this conversation because I was seriously sick and tired of watching you embark on this quest without real resolve. Something to acknowledge, though, is that if you die in battle, so do I. So I'll keep trying to take over this weak child's body of yours until finally I am reborn. Just a head's up."

"Try it," Darien snarled. "I'll never let you massacre hundreds of thousands of people again."

Ares guffawed wickedly. "What can I say? The call of war beckons to me."

***

Ares snapped his eyes open and he found himself looking up at the morning sky. A dream? Or was that truly a confrontation that he had with the original Ares? Either way, he now knew what he had to do. The young god was lying on the sand beside Amon, who sat on the ground with his gigantic legs outstretched. The golem was gazing up at the stretching skies, as he usually did. It was unfortunate that Amon couldn't sleep, because he had to sit here and wait for Ares to wake. However, he definitely enjoyed looking at the sky. Amon claimed that looking to the skies passed the time as swiftly as water in a rushing stream.

Ares leaned forward, brushing some sand off his shoulder, and turned to see that Aleysha was awake. She was sitting and munching on a stick of meat that she had somehow found. The mercenary had been asleep for several days and hadn't eaten the entire time. Ares had forced some water down her throat so that she didn't get dehydrated, but food didn't go down so well. The boy glanced over his shoulder at Amon, who snorted.

Yeah, I caught something for her. So what?

"Figures," Ares murmured. He didn't expect that Aleysha would be able to slay one of the legendary beasts of this desert on her own. He frowned. Then again, after her previous display of strength against the dog-headed Guardian, he could be wrong. His eyes wandered to a huge pile of cooked meat that she had piled up. A smothered fire showed that she had cooked the food herself. Ares winced. "Amon, how big was the monster that you caught?"

It was only a couple tons.

"That's too big!" Ares exclaimed and turned back to Aleysha, who was eying him. "U-Uh … good morning! You must be hungry, I mean, you were unconscious for a couple days so…."

Aleysha picked up a piece of cooked meat and held it out to Ares. "You want some?"

"N-No!" Ares stammered, folding his arms and looking away. His stomach groaned, sounding like a choking cry. His face turned red as he bit his bottom lip hard, feeling Aleysha's grin send waves of heat through his body. "I-I'm not hungry! Honest!" he insisted.

Unfortunately, the god didn't even remember the last time that he had eaten a decent meal, and there was more than enough food to feed him and Aleysha. Temptation bested him and he eventually succumbed to the wafting aroma of succulent meat and walked over to the mercenary and sat down beside her. Ares bit down into the meat that Aleysha offered him and smiled at the delicious taste that swept into his mouth. It tasted as if it had been seasoned somehow. Or maybe it was just that he was that hungry. The meat, however, had an odd slimy texture that made his mouth twitch. Stuffing his face with more of the unknown meat, he talked with a full mouth. "So, what am I eating?"

"A core-digger," Aleysha said, swallowing another piece of the meat as she leaned back.

Ares winced, almost spitting out the food. "You cooked a giant worm?"

"Yeah, surprisingly enough it actually has meat. It's a little slimy tasting but I took what I could get." Aleysha shrugged. "I was starving."

Ares scooted away from the pile of meat, feeling his appetite fading. He had lived in this desert for many years and gotten accustomed to eating many things. But he wasn't quite ready to start eating cooked worm yet. "I'm assuming that you're quite full then."

"Yep." Aleysha smiled. "Thanks for taking care of me after I passed out. I didn't know that I would lose so much energy from calling down the energy beam."

Ares cleared his throat. Now that she was awake he could finally question her about her connection to Ra. He opened his mouth, about to speak, when suddenly the ground began to shake tremendously as if there were an earthquake. The god's eyes widened when he suddenly felt the almighty presence of at least a hundred Guardians. And they were all awakening at once.

Amon grunted. That could only be one place.

"Ahriman's body," Ares said and stood up. Aleysha gathered her materials and suddenly was swept off her feet by the young boy. Ares jumped off of the ground and landed on Amon's shoulder. "Amon, we need to head in that direction!"

Amon nodded and pushed himself to his feet, stomping on the ground a few times. The rock golem responded, its eyes blazing red with gleaming light as it broke into a sprint. Each step covered hundreds of meters, and soon Amon was dashing with haste across the Lost Sands. A powerful breeze blew back against Aleysha's face as the wind grabbed at her cheeks and pulled them back. The mercenary squinted her eyes against the roaring gusts of wind that rushed at her. Soon she found that they were climbing over a massive sand dune. Peering over the peak of the hill, she saw that they had come across a stretching sea of packed sand.

Storming across the desert plain was an army of monstrous

creatures that varied from phoenixes to minotaurs to dragons, and dozens of other species of mythical beasts that Aleysha had only read about in stories. The cluster of monsters was trampling towards a small army of terrified Persian soldiers that were scrambling about, trying desperately to fight back against the brutish creatures that attacked them, to no avail.

Ares gently bit his lower lip as he watched the Persians battle the Guardians. The gods truly had picked a dangerous bunch to defend Ahriman's grave. His eyes flickered across the battlefield to a giant fault that was ripped across the earth. So that was where Ahriman was buried. It seemed that there were still several stagnant Guardians positioned around the fissure. They had yet to be awakened.

"We need to help them!" Aleysha exclaimed, pointing to the dispersing army of Persians. Thousands of men dispersed across the plains, battling their hardest against the relentless monsters that descended upon them. "They're getting massacred out there!"

"Do you see him?" Ares asked Amon, scanning the battlefield for Zahir.

Amon snorted. On the hill, watching from afar.

Ares' gaze followed the rock golem's eyes and he spotted the Magus standing on a sand dune in the distance with his arms folded, watching as his subordinates were slaughtered by the Guardians. "Amon, do you think you're a match for these Guardians?"

Amon pounded his chest in response.

"Alright, good. Throw me onto the battlefield. I'm going to carve my way to Zahir, I'll make sure that he doesn't get to the chasm," Ares said, turning to Aleysha. "You should stay here. It's really chaotic out there."

"I want to help—" Aleysha began.

"And you will. But going out there now will just get you killed. Trust me," Ares said. "Just because you handled one Guardian doesn't mean that you can fight a hundred and expect to survive. This is out of your league. Your strength is impressive, Aleysha, but no human should be out there on that battlefield. Alright, Amon, throw me!"

Amon grabbed Ares off his shoulder and turned his body, hurling the boy at sonic speed into the air in the general direction of the warzone. The rock golem grunted, reaching to pluck Aleysha off his shoulder and put her down on the ground so that the elemental could proceed to the battlefield.

"W-Wait, Amon! Please," Aleysha protested as the rocky hand of Amon approached her. "I can help, you just have to trust me! Just let me stay on your shoulder when you go into the battlefield. I'll explain to you on the way there."

Amon hesitated, unsure of what to do. He didn't want to disobey Ares, but he also didn't like doubting Aleysha.

"Trust me," Aleysha reassured the Guardian. "I can make a difference here, I promise! Together we can defeat more Guardians and save more of those soldiers' lives."

Amon groaned and lowered his arm to his side, beginning to storm towards the battlefield after Ares. *Whatever. Just hold on tight and don't die. Otherwise Ares will be furious.*

***

Ares felt the powerful wind yanking back his cheeks as he descended towards the battlefield from the sky. He grunted as he smashed into the earth, sending waves of dust and sand exploding in all directions. He sank into a gigantic crater in the ground created by his landing. He exhaled, opening his eyes to see that he had sent several Guardians and Persians flying backward from his landing shockwave. He held out his hand, conjuring his legendary golden spear into his palm. Gripping his signature weapon, he whirled the spear and wielded it with both hands, pointing its sharp tip at his first opponent.

A creature known as a manticore, with the head of a human, the body of a red lion and webbed wings, stepped forward. Its scalp was bald and had black horns protruding from the top of its skull. It snarled, its high-pitched voice more of a screech than an intimidating growl, revealing an array of tiny, pointed teeth that looked like they belonged to a shark. The manticore outstretched its large, bat-like wings and stormed forward on its four legs, scampering towards Ares. The abomination made Ares cringe; he'd never seen a manticore first hand before. He had only read about such a creature in Persian tales.

The manticore pounced through the air, crashing down on Ares, but the god hurled his spear into the creature, sending the weapon sliding up into the beast's chest. The Guardian screamed in agony, a shrill cry that pierced the ears of everyone on the battlefield. Ares made a slight movement with his index finger and the spear continued to jam upwards, tearing out of the manticore's back, sending a burst of blood splattering into the air. As the wounded creature fell upon Ares, the god drove a sinking punch into the beast's stomach. There was an explosion of power that ignited between his knuckles and the creature, sending the manticore flying across the warzone and out of sight.

Ares held out his arm, his spear automatically returning to his hand. He turned his head and watched as two Persian soldiers screamed in anguish, grabbing at their eyes. Every vein in their body became outlined and glowed bright red as if fire were coursing through their skin. Suddenly the soldiers disintegrated into ashes, disappearing in a single moment. The god turned his head and saw a lizard-like snake that slithered across the ground, with sharpened fangs and gleaming yellow eyes. The moment that Ares looked into the creature's eyes, he felt a sharp pain erupting through his own. He glanced away, gasping as he felt his energy sapped from his body, dropping to his knees, weakened.

That snake was a basilisk, a creature that could ordinarily kill a human with its glare alone. Its venomous bite was nothing to take lightly either, for even touching the tooth of such a monster could result in death. Luckily, since Ares was a god the creature's stare would only enervate him. However, a direct bite would be dangerous.

Ares winced, rubbing his eyes, looking up to see that the creature was snapping out at him. He felt the ground rumbling and also saw a giant humanoid Guardian rushing at him from behind. The monster had the head of a bull with giant, curved horns poking from the top of its skull. The creature had hooves and roared loudly as it charged Ares from behind, while the basilisk struck from the front. A minotaur — Ares had faced one of these vicious beasts once before in the Lost Sands. They were fierce and enduring, but didn't really have brains.

The god leapt into the air, flipping backward over the charging minotaur, who couldn't slow to a stop. The bull-man snorted in frustration as it charged into the basilisk, slamming its horns deep into the hardened scales of the serpent. Blood spurted from the wound, but the basilisk was still alive, snarling. Ares hurled his spear and the weapon ripped through both Guardians, skewering them together.

The boy held out his hand and the spear retracted from their bodies, sending the beasts crumpling to the ground in unison. Catching his weapon, Ares turned his head to see that Zahir had noticed his entrance. The Magus glared at the god's interference, and suddenly disappeared into a puff of black smoke that began to float over the battlefield, slowly easing its way towards the chasm where Ahriman was located.

"Oh no you don't!" Ares yelled, preparing to break into a sprint after Zahir when suddenly a giant humanoid crashed down on the ground in front of him. The Guardian was about to get up when suddenly a giant icicle spike smashed down into the creature's chest, burying itself deep into the monster's flesh. Ares stumbled backwards, surprised. A stranger landed on the giant's body, wearing a flapping white cloak and flowing hair the color of snow. His eyes, however, were unmistakable. "Yuu?"

The figure turned his attention to Ares and his expression turned to disbelief. A smile spread across his face when he first saw the god, but quickly faded. He held a sword and extended the weapon to Ares, pointing its tip at the god. White bandages dangled from his wrists and his turquoise eyes lacked emotion. "Ares, is it?"

"N-No! It's me, Darien!" Ares exclaimed. "You remember me, right?" He lowered his spear as he smiled. "Come on, Yuu. Remember how Tetsu, you, and I used to hang out every single day at the castle?"

"You're the god of war, Ares," Yuu said, convinced. "But how dare you transform to look like my old friend, Darien? Where is he now? Is he still alive?"

"I'm not transformed!"

"Silence!" Yuu yelled, waving his hand and a volley of needle-like icicles conjured before him, tearing through the air towards Ares. "What have you done to Darien, you cruel god?"

Ares smashed his feet into the ground and took off into the air, leaping above the noble. Yuu was a Magus now? He had obtained direct control over magic and from the looks of it, his element was ice. How unexpected! "I don't want to fight you!" Ares yelled, landing beside Yuu. "Please, just hear me out!"

"I will not listen to a murderous god who preys on the weak," Yuu murmured, his burning gaze making Ares melt. The noble wielded his sword with both hands and ripped the blade through the air in elegant slashes with perfect form. But despite Yuu's perfected strokes, Ares was easily able to maneuver to avoid the blows.

The god smiled. "You really haven't changed. Your form is exactly the same as the royal fighting style of Persia, right from the books. You must've studied a lot, huh? After Tetsu and I were banished, I mean."

Yuu clenched his teeth, refusing to believe that Darien and Ares were the same person. Zahir had distinctly said that Ares would try to trick him. But with every word that left Ares' lips, he was growing more and more convinced that this was Darien. Was it possible that Zahir could've tricked Yuu because he didn't want the two of them reunited?

There was a bark and Yuu suddenly snapped his attention back to the issue at hand. A pack of hounds with black fur and demonic red eyes were charging across the battlefield towards the two boys. The canine creatures had teeth as sharp as the tips of swords, with yellow saliva pooling around their mouths. "Hellhounds!" Yuu grunted, extending his hand to activate magic to fend off the oncoming wave of beasts. But the movement caused him to suddenly lose his balance, and he slipped off the dead giant that he stood upon and fell onto his back, landing hard on the sand. The wind was driven from his lungs and he gasped, trying desperately to regain his breath.

Ares leapt forward, grabbing Yuu and pulling him away as the hellhounds leapt over the giant's carcass, dashing towards their prey. The god grunted, grabbing his spear and jabbing it into the jaw of one of the dogs, sending blood spraying into the air. Pulling his blade from the slain hellhound, Ares gasped as the beasts overwhelmed him and rushed from all sides. He kicked one in the face as it snapped at him while he slashed the stomach of another pouncing hellhound that came from the other side. "Get up, Yuu!" Ares yelled. "It's already hard enough defending myself against these monsters!"

Yuu stared at Ares as the boy defended the noble from harm.

Who else but Darien would risk his life for Yuu like that? The Magus forced himself his feet, stumbling forward as he pushed Ares out of the way, extending both of his hands in front of him, his eyes flashing a bright sapphire color. "*Freeze.*" All of the hounds suddenly became encased in giant blocks of ice, freezing in place. The noble closed his hands into tight fists and the ice detonated into millions of glittering shards of crystal that crumpled to the sand, melting in the baking sun.

"Whoa!" Ares exclaimed, clapping his hands like an excited child. "That's so cool! Where'd you learn to do stuff like that? I didn't even know you were a Magus!"

"Huh." Yuu smirked. "And I didn't even know you were alive, Darien."

"To be honest, I didn't know you were either, Yuu." Ares beamed.

"You've got yourself a new name then? Ares, huh? I like it better than your old one anyway," Yuu teased.

"Joking already, school nerd?" Ares grinned and walked forward, embracing his old friend in a tight hug. "Man, I thought that you were dead after that stupid stunt you pulled in the throne room. You scared Tetsu and me both to death."

"I'm sorry." Yuu laughed, patting Ares' back. "But you haven't aged a day, Darien. You look the same after all of these years."

"I'll explain everything later. Right now we have to stop Zahir from obtaining that godly power of Ahriman. You can't possibly think that it's right, do you? The amount of people that will suffer from his wrath will be countless. Millions will die and hundreds of thousands will be enslaved by the Persian Empire," Ares said, pulling back from the hug. He clamped a firm hand on Yuu's shoulder. "Will you help me fight Zahir?"

Yuu hesitated. A part of him had always despised Zahir for defeating his two lost friends and for always making decisions that disregarded the value of human life. It was as if Zahir regarded the Magi as a separate race from humans. He looked down on all humans as lesser beings. Not to mention that Zahir had proved just how cruel he was when he had sent all of these Persians to sacrifice themselves to distract the Guardians while he headed off to awaken Ahriman's power. Darien was right; once Zahir received the power of Ahriman he would abuse the power and crush human lives. Zahir was the person least qualified for that power. "Yes. But I have to help these soldiers first. Zahir ordered them to storm this wasteland without any idea that these Guardians would awaken."

"So he baited them into becoming human sacrifices so that he could just float across the chaotic battlefield and claim the power on his own, huh?" Ares growled, mashing his teeth in annoyance. "He seriously pisses me off."

Amon roared suddenly, smashing through a line of monsters with his arms raised into the air. *I'm here! I'm here!*

"Amon!" Ares exclaimed, turning to his rock golem. His eyes narrowed when he spotted Aleysha on the giant's shoulder. "Aleysha, I told you to stay back! Amon, why did you let her come?"

The Guardian shrugged.

"The two of us will handle the rest of the Guardians here, Ares. Just go on and head to the fissure!" Aleysha called down. "We saw

Zahir fighting a few of the Guardians that were defending the fault!"

"You better be careful, Aleysha. If you die, I swear … I'll find a way to revive you just so that I can smack you upside the head," Ares grumbled.

"Nice friend you've got there." Yuu whistled, sheathing his sword, examining Amon up and down in awe. "And a rock golem as your companion, Darien. How classy of you."

"I'm glad that you think that a banished prince still has the luxury of pretending he's classy." Ares scoffed and took Yuu by the hand. "Alright! My friends are going to handle the issue here. That means that we can head off to stop Zahir. Come on!" he exclaimed, jumping suddenly into the air, flying thousands of feet, dragging the noble behind him. Yuu screamed the whole way.

Aleysha folded her arms as she sat on Amon's shoulder, watching as Ares and his new friend flew through the air. "He likes doing that, doesn't he? Scaring the crap out of people by taking them on a flight with him." She knew first hand. "Who do you suppose that person is that's with him?"

Amon snorted. *Who knows?*

Aleysha looked at the carnage around her. Before a couple weeks ago, she hadn't even seen a monster before. Now she was witnessing hundreds of unique creatures slaughtering a bunch of Persians. This felt like something straight out of a tale that she had read as a child. "Well," she murmured, pulling her giant shield off of her back and sighing as she unsheathed her sword, her eyes scanning the vast sea of monstrosities before her. "Come on, Amon. We promised Ares that we'd take care of this. So, let's get to work."

***

Yuu yelped, the volume of his voice rising as he descended towards the ground. The sound of the howling wind that rushed into his face drowned out his terrified cries. Just before he hit the ground, Darien turned him sideways and caught him as if he were some type of fair maiden that needed saving. Then again, after falling from that height, anyone would need saving. Yuu gulped, realizing that he was now safe on the ground. His head slowly turned and he saw that they had jumped all the way from the battlefield to the fissure in a single leap. He looked at Darien, trembling. How had his old friend become so strong over the past five years? Yuu had thought that he had become much stronger in comparison to his old self. But compared to Darien, he knew he still didn't stand a chance.

The way that Darien stood, his confident aura could embolden anyone around him. The gleam of hope that beamed from his eyes and his brave smile that reflected liveliness left Yuu in awe before the new god. It was empowering and inspiring.

Yuu rolled out of Darien's arms and stumbled onto his feet, brushing some sand off of his pants. He harrumphed, feeling a slight stinging sensation in his throat from screaming so loud. It was the first time in many years that he had made such a shrill and terrified sound. He turned and found that there was a gigantic collapsed dragon beside the chasm along with a metallic robotic creation that was now in bronze scraps. The noble walked forward slowly to the edge of the fissure and raised an eyebrow, gazing over the edge into the pitch-black abyss below. "That's deep."

"Yeah," Darien said, taking a few steps back.

"What are you doing?" Yuu said, turning to face Darien. He waved his hands in front of himself when the prince started rushing forward. "N-No! No, no, nooo!" The god tackled Yuu and sent the two flying off of the ledge into the gulf, disappearing into the darkness. Yuu's final "no" stretched and echoed in the silence as they vanished into the shadows of the abyss.

Darien caught Yuu in the air and landed hard on the solid ground after falling for what felt like minutes. Cracking the earth beneath his feet, the god slowly exhaled and let Yuu roll back to his feet. "Hey, there's no better way to get down here," he murmured when he saw the annoyed look that Yuu shot him.

It took a minute of constant blinking for Yuu to finally adjust to the thick cloud of darkness that obscured his vision. He looked upward and saw the daylight just barely creeping into the bottom of the abyss. Gritting his teeth, the noble knew that he would have to find Zahir before the Magus reached Ahriman. Once Zahir claimed the power of a god, Yuu wouldn't stand a chance.

Grabbing the hilt of his sword, Yuu unsheathed his magnificently elegant blade, which he whirled through the darkness. "Which way do you expect the body is?" Yuu asked, his back against Darien's. The two gazed down opposite directions of the fissure.

"Only one way to find out. We go opposite directions," Darien offered. "If you spot Zahir or the body then you use whatever magic you can to make as much noise as you can. I'll come quickly. The same goes for me."

"Got it," Yuu said with a nod. Without another word the two friends sprinted off in opposite directions. The noble breathed heavily as his armor clanked loudly in the silence. Even though his eyes had somewhat adjusted to the darkness of the abyss, he still found his vision cloudy. He could only see several feet in front of him. Past that point, his sight ran into a sheet of impenetrable blackness. If he happened to go in the same direction as Zahir then surely the Magus would hear him coming a mile away, but Yuu wouldn't be able to react until Zahir finally came into his line of vision. By then, it would be too late.

Yuu worked his jaw, knowing that he should probably be moving more cautiously. But if he didn't hurry, he didn't know whether he would actually catch up to Zahir, who already had a significant head start. After running for about fifteen minutes, Yuu figured that he had picked the wrong side. He slowed to a stop, debating whether or not he should just turn back and assume that Darien had gone the right way. Suddenly a large purple light illuminated the darkness, flooding the cave walls with its ominous glow.

An evanescent light streaked across the walls once more and then vanished. Yuu slowly began to inch forward, making sure to keep as silent as possible. Pebbles crackled underneath his metal boots and he reached into his cloak, holding his sword between his armpit and his arm. He pulled out two iron gauntlets with open palms specially made for his hand, so that he could cast magic while protecting the majority of his hands from harm. Sliding the gauntlets onto his hands, he clicked them into place on his armor, and wielded his sword with both hands. Steadily creeping forward towards the glowing light, Yuu's heart began to race.

He spotted it now. There was a fallen corpse of a man with long, greasy, black hair that fell over his middle-aged face. He had been wearing a black robe, but it had been incinerated, and it looked like he was topless because most of the cloth had been burned off. Burn wounds and severe slashes covered his body, creating a pool of pure ruby blood beneath the god that glistened brighter than any human blood would. Kneeling at the foot of the deceased god was Zahir.

Zahir reached forward, cupping his hands, about to catch some of the god's blood in his hands.

Yuu extended his palm and released a bolt of ice that tore through the air without warning and smashed against Zahir's shoulder, sending the Magus flying backwards. Splintering ice scattered in all directions as the man smashed hard against the wall of the abyss, breaking off a chunk of rock before he crumpled to the ground. Yuu knew better than to give Zahir a moment to recover and he quickly sprinted forward with his sword brandished, fully prepared to bring an end to the insane mage.

Zahir slowly pushed himself to one knee, wiping some blood off of his lip with a small smile. He glared at Yuu from the corners of his purple, gleaming eyes. "You dare to betray me, Yuu? What's gotten into you?" He flicked his wrist and a surge of fire smashed straight into Yuu's chest, sending dancing flames spraying across his body.

The noble fell onto his back, gasping at the heat that surged through his chest. He smacked his head hard on the rock ground, making his head spin. But he forced himself to get up and stumble to his feet nevertheless. Facing his mentor, his cold gaze never left Zahir's eyes.

Zahir smirked. "You're betraying the Persian Empire by going against me, you know."

"I know."

"And you'd throw away everything that you care about, your family, your home?"

"What you'll use this power for is wrong," Yuu said. "You demonstrated to me today that you are unworthy of wielding Ahriman's strength. The power of a god comes with responsibility. Wreaking havoc upon all of your enemies and utterly obliterating them is not what this power is for! The power of the gods has always been to maintain balance in our world."

"Maintain balance?" Zahir paced back and forth, watching Yuu. He burst out laughing, holding his belly as he did so. "That's a riot! Who cares about balance? This power can set me on the high end of the scale so that I rise above everyone else. All of the puny humans of this pathetic, cruel world will finally see just what it's like to truly feel fear. They'll understand what it's really like to be powerless. And they'll know what it's like to have a powerful deity to protect their worthless, useless lives! I will become a god and I will become the emperor of more than just Dastia! I will rule this accursed world with my power and change it to my liking! Balance? Such a thing will never be achieved. Do you know why? Because as long as there are rulers, as long as there are leaders, some people will be worth *more* than others. That's just how it is and that's how it always will be. There will never be balance, not in this world."

Yuu grunted, sprinting forward as he swung his sword through the air in a sideways slash at Zahir. The Magus ducked the blow and stumbled backward, surprised by Yuu's sudden burst of aggression. The noble then jabbed out at Zahir with rapid thrusts of his blade, unleashing a barrage of fast attacks on the mage. "Darien risked his life, as a prince, to save a foreign boy who was doomed to die. He treasured that young boy's life the same as his own. A prince and an ex-slave. Lives are worth the same, no matter how you look at it. A human life is a damned human life!" he yelled, spinning around as he ripped his blade at Zahir's throat.

Zahir dodged each movement with ease, never wiping the grin from his lips. Ducking Yuu's final swipe, he pulled up his sleeve and revealed his dragon tattoo. He extended his right hand and released tendrils of electricity surging from his fingertips. The energy snapped and crackled, grabbing onto Yuu's metallic armor. The boy screamed in agony as the ends of his hairs stood up, electricity coursing through his body. "And that is why that prince is a fool that must be disposed of."

Yuu dropped his sword, his hand twitching uncontrollably. The electricity broke off his body and dissipated, but he couldn't get the agonizing feeling of the roaring heat snapping through his body out of his mind. Falling onto his side, Yuu convulsed as he curled up into a ball, trying his best to cope with the sharp pain that erupted throughout his body. Tears formed in his eyes as he clenched his jaw, biting back his suffering. Small droplets streaked from his closed eyes, down his cheeks and to his chin.

Zahir didn't waste a moment and sauntered over to the corpse of Ahriman. He reached down, gathering a pool of blood in his cupped hands, and sipped the unholy liquid. His eyes widened and he lowered his hands to his side, the godly blood splattering down at his feet. His veins began to bulge from his skin as he gasped, staggering backwards. He bumped against the wall of the abyss, a fiery heat surging through every inch of his body. Zahir released a bloodcurdling scream that echoed through the abyss, covering every inch of the darkened space with his cry.

Within five seconds, Darien had made his way to the scene. The god tore his way from the misty darkness and flew through the air, driving both of his legs in a solid kick to Zahir's side. The Magus smashed hard against the stone wall, sinking deep into the rock. Several pieces of the wall chipped off from above and collapsed onto the ground around Darien but the god had his attention on Yuu, who was still twitching on the ground in pain. "Yuu!" Darien grunted and reached down to pick up his injured friend. Yuu's eyes were still closed and he was crying from the searing agony that had surged through his body. "Hey, it's going to be okay. I'm here."

There was a crack, and Darien looked over his shoulder to see that Zahir had somehow pulled himself from the hole in the fissure's wall, snapping his broken arm back into place. His lips were a rosy red color from the blood of Ahriman that he had drank. Zahir split a malevolent grin across his face and he burst out laughing, his purple eyes glowing in the darkness. "I … I feel amazing!" He raised both of his hands into the air and laughed hysterically.

***

An upward current of purple energy filled every inch of the

fissure, exploding from the chasm and up into the surface, striking the sky with its enormity. Ares had grabbed Yuri and leapt out of the fissure just a moment before the fault exploded with Zahir's magic. The two rolled onto the sand outside of the fissure, smoke drifting off their bodies from the scorching heat of Zahir's magic.

Ares' eyes bulged and he slowly glanced up to see Zahir leaping from the obliterated abyss and into the air. Zahir extended his arms outward, still laughing. "Wow, Ares! Is this the power that you've been flooded with all this time? You really must hold back, huh? This amount of strength that I have now is more than I ever could've imagined!"

"Zahir, what have you done?" Ares yelled.

"Zahir? Oh, don't call me that anymore. My name is Ahriman now." The god held out his hand before him, pointing his index finger at Ares. "Now that I have this unstoppable power, I can put an end to you, Ares."

Ares' eyes widened as he shoved Yuu away from him. A skinny beam of purple magic shot from Ahriman's fingertip and smashed hard into Ares, sending the boy crashing a mile across the sandy wasteland, leaving a trail of dragged dirt in his path. Ignoring the pain that exploded through his chest, the god of war grinded his teeth, propping himself onto his elbows as he gazed up at the floating Persian. He had never fought against an opponent that could utilize such terrifying power before. The possibility of battling another god had never crossed his mind. The outcome would surely be destructive. No one nearby would be safe.

Ahriman suddenly teleported beside Ares, who gasped in

surprise. *How fast is this guy?* The Persian god grabbed Ares' face and thrust the boy's head backward into the earth, destroying the ground with his unmatchable strength. A swirling cloud of dust whirled around Ares' unmoving body.

Ahriman stood over the injured god and smirked. "If you don't have what it takes to let out your full power, Ares, then you'll never come to defeat another god. You have to be willing to sacrifice everything and destroy the world around you if you want the strength to defeat me. Go on, release all of that hidden strength. Obliterate your friends around us with your power. Show me your bloodlust and awaken your inner-self so that I may face the true god of war."

Ares winced, trying to move. But his body wouldn't respond.

A pillar of light exploded from the sky and crashed down on the earth beside Ahriman, singeing the earth. The Persian god of darkness looked over his shoulder with an apathetic gaze as a man with brown curly hair and golden armor that gleamed as brightly as the sun emerged from the light. The pillar receded back into the heavens and the mysterious new man worked his shoulder, as if he hadn't been active in a while. His irises were the color the sun, glowing so brightly that no ordinary human could stare directly into them. His armor was decorated with a painted symbol of the sun and he gripped a lit torch in one hand and a sword with a golden blade in the other.

Tossing his hair, the man pointed the tip of his sword at Ahriman, who raised an eyebrow in amusement. "Oh? And who might you be?" Ahriman demanded, his eyes narrowing as he gazed upon the golden armored stranger.

"My name is Mithra. I am the Persian god of war and justice," the man declared, his eyes flashing. "I have been sent by the gods to make sure that you were not awakened. Unfortunately, it seems that I am too late. Though that means that I now have a second chance to condemn you to death, Ahriman."

Ahriman scowled and turned suddenly as a beam of light erupted from the heavens once more and smashed down into the ground where he was, creating a gaping hole in the earth. The Persian god had leapt out of the way just in time to emerge unscathed from the abrupt attack. His eyes flickered across the battlefield and saw that a giant rock golem was dashing across the plains with a young girl on its shoulder. He turned to Mithra, who also seemed puzzled. If Mithra wasn't the one who had summoned that powerful beam, then who did it? Ahriman looked back to the elemental and eyed the mysterious girl that mounted the Guardian.

Ahriman sighed, watching as Ares also managed to force himself back to his feet. "A Guardian and a demigod, huh? One by one more bugs keep entering the fray. This is becoming troublesome."

Demigod? Ares turned his head and frowned at Aleysha. *Her?*

A demigod was a person who had one parent that was a god and one parent that was a human. Ares had met her mother and she had definitely been human. He blinked. Could her father be a god? That would explain her abnormal ability to call upon that incredible beam of energy from the heavens.

Ahriman clapped his hands with a wicked grin on his face. There was an outwards pulse that erupted from his hands and a sweeping wave of dust flew out from his position, engulfing everything in a mile radius around the god.

Ares covered his eyes and was blown backwards, tossed around by the relentless power of the new Persian god. Staggering to his feet, the boy brushed some dust out of his eyes and coughed. He turned to look at Amon and Aleysha to see if they were okay. He found that his best friend, the great rock golem, had been petrified into a statue. Ares' eyes began to water and he bit his lower lip hard, trying to hold back the cries that wanted to explode from his lungs.

Amon had pulled his arm over Aleysha to block her from the shockwave and was frozen in his position, rubble crumbling from his solidified body. All around the battlefield in the distance, the Guardians and Persian warriors had all transformed into statues as well, permanently immobile. Aleysha, however, seemed unharmed.

"A-Amon?" Aleysha whispered, reaching out and patting the unmoving golem. "You can't be…."

Ares' hands were quivering at his side. He scowled and glared at Ahriman, who was guffawing maniacally, gaining pleasure from seeing how many lives he had ruined. "You bastard…!" Ares boomed, kicking off the ground, soaring straight at the Persian god.

Ahriman stopped laughing and extended his hand, releasing a surge of black energy that shot forward and exploded into Ares, sending the boy rolling backward across the battlefield. The Magus smirked, impressed with his own strength. A flicker of movement over his shoulder caused the smirk to vanish from his lips in an instant and he grunted, ducking a vicious slash from Mithra. "What a bother," Ahriman murmured, floating out of reach of his opponents.

Having just obtained his new powers, Ahriman was unsure if he would be able to defeat a fully trained god such as Mithra while fending off Ares. One god of war was troublesome enough. "Take your golem's fate as a warning, Ares! If you try and bring judgment upon me, all that you hold dear will perish by my hands. And once they're eradicated I'll end you next." He waved at Mithra cheerfully and chortled, flying away. "Hopefully I won't see you fools again. If I do, it'll be your demise."

Ares pushed himself from a pile of sand and spat the hot dirt out of his mouth. Gritting his teeth, he balled his hands up into tight fists. "Get back here, you coward!" he roared, hurling his spear outward at the fleeing god. But Ahriman had already flown out of range. He punched the ground in frustration, tears beginning to flow down his cheeks. It was the first time that he had cried in five years. "Damn it!"

Mithra looked past the defeated Ares to the solidified Guardian. Aleysha was tapping the petrified rock golem as if doing so would awaken the elemental from its eternal slumber. The Persian god looked at Ares, who was sobbing, a look of agony painted upon his face. Such frustration, such pain, such despair. It had been a long time since he had seen a deity wear those emotions. Gods usually only formed bonds with other gods. It's interesting that Ares befriended one of his Guardians. After all, Guardians were merely tools to battle on a god's behalf, nothing more.

"He thinks that I'm going to heed his little threat?" Ares growled, his eyes beginning to turn red with burning rage. "I'm going to rip that bastard apart. I'll shred him to pieces until there's nothing left for doing this to Amon!" he bellowed, slamming the ground with his fist again. The earth trembled from his frightening strength.

Aleysha stepped away from Amon and looked to Ares with a pitiful gaze. "Ares…."

Ares continued to punch the ground, releasing his fury into the earth. Black markings began to form on his body, curling around his skin as it ate away at his self-control.

"Ares!" Aleysha called, but the boy couldn't hear her. She dashed forward to the rampaging god and wrapped her arms around him from behind, hugging him tightly despite his fit. The god froze, panting heavily, not expecting to feel such warmth. "It's okay, Ares. It's okay," Aleysha whispered, trying to calm him down. She pressed her cheek gently against the boy's back and closed her eyes, trusting that he wouldn't hurt her. "Remember what you promised; you won't transform."

Ares clenched his teeth, biting back all of his burning rage and frustration. "I … I let Amon down. I couldn't protect him like he's protected me all these years." He closed his eyes, more tears streaming down his face as he sniffled. Amon had always been there for him. The rock golem had saved his life countless times in the Lost Sands and had taught him how to survive and fend for himself in the dangerous desert. Amon was the one friend that had never left his side. The god turned and looked at his frozen friend and exhaled. The black, ancient markings began to recede from his skin and his eyes returned to their usual sky-blue color. He was calmer, but his heart felt like it had been torn out, a feeling that had been so distant that he had almost forgotten how agonizing it was to lose someone that he loved so dearly.

Mithra was surprised that Ares showed so much love for a lump of rock. But he said nothing. "It seemed that the magic that he used only affected ordinary organisms without magic." The god nodded his head towards the distant battlefield and Ares saw that several creatures were still moving about. "Some of those Guardians have magic infused into their bodies and therefore were not harmed by Ahriman's twisted spell. All of us also have magic as well so we weren't harmed."

"Neither was I," Yuu called, striding across the sandy desert, clutching his bleeding arm. He gave Ares a weak smile. "I'm still alive somehow." He saw the tears on Ares' face and looked to his old friend's petrified Guardian. He bit his lip and said nothing more.

"I'm glad to see that you're okay." Ares smiled, wiping his wet face.

Mithra looked from Yuu to Ares and assumed that the two were companions. He disregarded the newcomer as a threat. He turned to Ares. "Those words that you spoke earlier — I'm assuming that you meant them."

"Yeah," Ares said, anger still roaring through his veins. The thirst for vengeance was not a feeling that he felt often. After all, he hadn't even felt the need to exact revenge on his parents' murderers, let alone the man who had condemned him to the Lost Sands when he was only fifteen. But now he felt differently. He wanted Ahriman on his knees, apologizing and begging for his life. But Ares would grant him no mercy. The boy wondered if any satisfaction would come from the murder of Ahriman. Would the gaping hole in his heart be filled? Would the pain that he felt from Amon's fate be extinguished?

"If you're fully willing to eradicate Ahriman from this world, then I will join you. He's far too dangerous to roam this continent freely," Mithra said. "I assume that he's returning to the capital of Persia so that he may begin testing his powers and his limits. With every moment, I believe that Ahriman will grow stronger."

"How are we going to get there?" Ares asked. Mounting Amon had always been the fastest way to travel through the Lost Sands. Without his Guardian, Ares feared that it might take months to walk to Persepolis safely. By then, the continent could be wiped out entirely by Ahriman. Time was fleeting, they needed speed. *Should I…?*

Mithra raised his hand and four bulls burst from the sandy earth, appearing at their master's side. These bulls were golden, similar to the color of the gleaming sun, and had curved white horns emerging from the tops of their heads. They trotted forward and snorted, nodding towards Yuu, Ares, and Aleysha. There was one bull for each person. "These will serve as our mounts," Mithra said, stroking one beast on its snout gently. The bull shook its head, closing its eyes, clearly enjoying the massage. "They are reliable, fast, and much tougher than any ordinary steed."

Ares looked over his shoulder at Amon once more and Mithra winced. "Do you need some time to mourn for your … companion?"

"No," Ares said, keeping his hardened gaze on his frozen friend. Lowering his head and sighing, he turned to Yuu and Aleysha. He nodded at the two of them. "We can't waste any time. Ahriman needs to be stopped." He looked to Mithra with an expression filled with determination and resolution. "Let's go."

***

King Alkaios drove his heels deep into his steed's side, storming across the desert sands around the perimeter of the Lost Sands in the direction of Persia. Behind him was the entire army of the United Eastern Nations of Dastia, a vast force of over a hundred thousand soldiers, all mounted on horses that were galloping with all haste for Persia.

"Milord! We must rest!" one of Alkaios's generals warned the King of Luxas. "Our men and horses are both tired. There's a town coming up ahead."

Alkaios rotated his jaw and sighed, squeezing his reins tightly in his hands. He wanted to get to Persepolis as soon as possible to put an end to Cambyses's rule. But it wasn't just that. He had an odd feeling in the pit of his stomach that Kira and Tetsu were both in danger. If both of them were still in Persia, then surely something was churning up in the capital city. But the king knew better than to tire out his men before the battle had even begun. He nodded, slapping his reins down and bolting on ahead.

It was true that there was a town ahead, and as Alkaios slowly approached the small village he was met with silence. The rickety buildings were made of aged wood that looked ancient. Every structure creaked and looked ready to collapse at a moment's notice. The town gave off the ominous impression that no one had lived there for decades. But that wasn't possible. Alkaios had visited this town only two years before. It had been a lively, simple village with many friendly inhabitants that had greeted him when he had first arrived. Now there was nothing but silence. The only sound he heard was the trotting of his soldiers' horses.

"Milord, something is amiss," Alkaios's general said, galloping beside his lord.

Alkaios said nothing and lowered his reins, swiftly dismounting his mount. Landing heavily on the dirt, he looked down and saw that the ground looked scorched as if a raging fire had just incinerated the earth. It wasn't any ordinary fire either. The ash-filled ground made it look like the town had been transformed into a burning inferno the night before. But the buildings were still intact; none of this made any sense.

The king left his horse and walked towards the village. The moment that he stepped onto the village soil, he shivered, stopping in his tracks. He stared at the ground, feeling a menacing aura radiating from the village. It was an odd, chilling feeling that made him tremble in fear. The aura was filled with despair, pain, and misery.

"Milord!"

Alkaios snapped back to his senses and glanced upward, turning to see that there was a pile of skeletons in the center of the village. There was no flesh to be seen. The king swallowed the lump in his throat and slowly trudged forward, staring at the pile of bones. "What is this?"

"It looks like they were killed centuries ago. There's no sign of any creature coming near the village to eat their flesh. If there was, there would be signs of gore and the bones would be scattered, not piled all neatly like this," Alkaios's general observed, scratching his chin. "Everything here looks ancient."

"That's impossible," Alkaios said. "We were here only two years ago."

"*This is the work of Ahriman, the Persian god of darkness. The ancient lord has been awakened,*" a deep, rumbling voice echoed in the heads of all of the humans in the area. Alkaios's men dropped their weapons to the ground and clamped their hands over their ears, trying to block out the mysterious man that spoke in their heads. "*He can awaken thousands of new diseases that could wipe this entire continent clean of life if he wanted. He withered away everything and everyone in this village to test his ability, thus making it so that everyone in the village aged a thousand years in only a second's time.*"

"Such power is possible…?" Alkaios muttered under his breath. He raised his voice to a yell. "Who are you?"

A vortex of whirling sand churned in front of the pile of skeletons, tossing the bones around in the blistering gust. The whipping wind settled down, the sand blowing away, revealing a glowing man standing before Alkaios. He had a hat crafted from the carcass of a dead white falcon. His eyes glowed as powerfully as the sun itself, and none of the humans could look the man in the eye. He was shirtless, his muscular, tanned, body glistening with sweat. The outline of the stranger's body was glowing a golden color, making it rather clear that this man was a deity of some sort. "My name is Ra. I am the god that created Dastia," the man spoke.

Alkaios gulped, unsure if he should be terrified or thankful that this god had presented himself before the King of Luxas and his army. Did he come to curse them? Alkaios didn't want to take any chances. He quickly knelt before the deity, his head tilted down towards the sand. There was a dissonance of clanking as thousands of men followed their leader's example, bowing down before the unknown deity. "Why have you come before us, Great Lord Ra?" Alkaios could feel the burning eyes of Ra upon him. Sweat began to form on his brow.

"I come to give you my blessing," Ra said, turning to gaze upon the massive army that stood outside of the village behind Alkaios. He smiled, impressed with their organization. "You've combined the forces of a dozen kingdoms to amass an army worthy of challenging the infamous ocean of warriors that battle under Persia's banners. Normally, I am not allowed to intervene in your mortal conflicts. But Ahriman's awakening has changed the rules a bit in my eyes. The Persian god of darkness is in Persepolis, your current destination. One of my daughters is also on her way to that city, where her life will be in danger.

"I don't expect your army to defeat Ahriman. But I want you to carve a path for a particular god so that he may march forward to challenge Ahriman. I'm sure you know of him. After all, you all worship him." Ra smiled. "Ares."

Alkaios licked his lower lip, nodding his head slowly. "He is our god of war."

Ra snapped his fingers. In an instant, a bright symbol, a transparent, round, golden sun disk appeared above every single horse in the area. The mounts whinnied in unison, but didn't do much else. The god lowered his hand to his side and cleared his throat. "I've blessed all of your mighty steeds with great speed. They'll move at three times the speed of an ordinary horse and won't need to rest. My blessing will wear off in one week. I expect that you'll reach Persepolis by then."

"M-Milord! Even with such speed we still may not reach—"

"I have also granted all of you safe entrance into the Lost Sands," Ra said. "As long as you are with your steeds none of the creatures of the forsaken desert will attack you. Feel free to cut through the desert to reach Persia if that makes things faster for you," he said. "All I ask is that you get there and challenge Persia's army so that Ares may concentrate on defeating Ahriman. I'm sure that he could use the backup. In addition, might I ask that you keep an eye on my stubborn daughter?"

"W-Who might that be, milord?" Alkaios stammered, glancing up to look at the deity.

Ra grinned, revealing a set of perfectly white teeth that gleamed like starlight. "I believe you're already acquainted. Her name is Aleysha."

Infiltration

Tetsu groaned, his eyes cracking open as daylight shined onto his face. Wetting his dried lips, he leaned forward and turned to see that Kira was cuddling closely with him. Her arms were tightly wound around his forearm and she slept soundlessly. Tetsu sighed. That meant that he wouldn't be able to move without abruptly waking her up.

The man reached over Kira and grabbed her broom, sneakily replacing his forearm with it so that the Magus cuddled with her broom instead. Tetsu slipped away silently, careful not to wake her up. The two of them had spent the night on his carpet while Ramses slept on the cold sand by himself. The Persian didn't really seem to mind at all and was more than willing to let Tetsu and Kira share the carpet together.

Tetsu narrowed his eyes. Why did everyone insist that he and Kira were together?

For two weeks, the trio had traveled across the Lost Sands towards Persepolis. They avoided a majority of the dangers in the desert because they flew on Tetsu's magic carpet and Kira's broom. Overall, they had shot across the wasteland in record time, and made it to the outskirts of the Persian Empire without any trouble at all.

Tetsu clambered over a sand dune that lay stagnant next to where his group had slept. Peering over the peak of the hill of sand, the man finally found himself gazing upon the gigantic metal walls of Persepolis in the distance. Buildings made of clay were scattered along the inside of the city and Tetsu's eyes locked onto the massive castle that towered upon a hill overlooking the rest of Persepolis. That castle was where his life had been torn apart five years ago. He exhaled any rage that had built up in his chest and smiled slightly. "It's been five years, huh? Looks like I'm finally back."

He turned and saw that it hadn't taken Kira long to find out that she had been curled up with a broom. The mage stirred, yawning as she leaned forward. Her eyes squinted slightly, clearly still half-asleep. "Good morning, Kira." Tetsu called down to her.

"Eh? You're up already, Tetsu?" Kira groaned, collapsing back onto the carpet. "I'm exhausted! Let me sleep more."

"That would not be wise," Ramses murmured, leaning forward and rubbing his eyes with the back of his hand. "The morning is the best time to get into the city because the guards won't bombard us with their questions. They're tired too."

"Is that so?" Kira murmured, scratching her head as she rolled over. "Fine, fine. Let's get to saving Ramses' family then."

It took two hours for the trio to pack up their belongings and hike across the remainder of the desert to the entrance of Persepolis. The towering walls of the city were much higher than Tetsu had expected, making him feel like an insignificant ant in comparison. Behind Tetsu, the sun shined its light on his back from the east and he was thankful that he didn't have to walk those two hours in the searing heat.

The group reached the front entrance of Persepolis, a giant, thick, metal gate that looked strong enough to withstand anything. A Persian soldier peeked his head over the top of the wall and yelled down at the three mysterious figures. "State your business in Persia and where you hail from!"

Ramses pulled back his black hood, revealing his face and the soldier winced. "I am Ramses, Magus of King Cambyses. Please allow my companions and me to pass."

"Who are you bringing with you, Lord Ramses?" the soldier asked.

"Does it matter? They are of importance to the king. I will be bringing them to him directly," Ramses spat. "Now open this accursed door. I've had a long journey and I just want to return home to my family. If you have any complaints, take it up with the king."

The soldier nodded and yelled something to another man on the other side of the wall. There was a loud whirring sound and then the door creaked open, groaning as it slowly opened the entrance to the lively city.

Tetsu smiled as he walked through the entrance of the city. It was similar to how he remembered it. Luxurious homes were posted on both sides of the entrance for show, to give newcomers the false impression that Persepolis was a rich city filled with only affluent people. But Tetsu knew that poverty existed elsewhere in this city. There would always be imbalance in the social structure of the empire. That was just how things worked. Following Ramses through the paved streets and the armies of civilians that walked about, Tetsu saw that the architecture had hardly changed in his absence.

The buildings were just as he had left them. Even the

blacksmithing shop where he had bought his original sword was still present. Seeing his old home again brought nostalgic images flowing back into his mind. His memories were still fresh in his mind, as if they had just occurred yesterday. Memories of him, Yuu, and Darien exploring the city with their escorts. Usually Cambyses accompanied them, but on one special occasion the three of them had slipped away from the guards and spent the day alone, playing hide-and-seek with the Persian escorts. In that time, they had explored a large portion of the city. They saw its greatness but also its hidden horrors. How overseers treated their slaves, how there were many homeless and starving civilians, how the disabled were left to die alone. Some of the images that they saw while freely exploring Persepolis were horrific and scarring.

That was when Yuu had adopted the belief that not following the rules would lead to corruption and disorder. He believed that it was better to live in the city blind than to see the terrifying truth of how some lower-class civilians were treated; it helped him sleep easier.

Tetsu lowered his eyes. Maybe that was true, but he hated the idea of having information hidden from him.

Still following Ramses, Tetsu walked past a group of injured slaves who were on their hands and knees, picking up the shattered pieces of a vase that they had dropped. Meanwhile an overseer was relentlessly whipping them, sending screams of agony echoing through the air. Tetsu halted. One thing hadn't changed. The people. Civilians continued to stroll past this spectacle as if it were nothing. They were apathetic, not sympathetic at all to the slaves' situations.

Their ideology was that those slaves were of equal worth to animals. Not a single person would stop and help.

Clenching his teeth, Tetsu turned to the slaves. Kira reached out and touched his shoulder, knowing that he was eager to go and stop the overseer from being so abusive. But there was nothing that he could do about the unfair cruelty of slavery at the moment. Nevertheless, the mercenary shrugged the mage off and began to trudge forward towards the slaves.

The overseer who was whipping them frowned at the one pedestrian who was storming towards the dirty, bleeding, lackeys. The slaves looked like they were just loose skin slapped onto a skeleton. Their tanned skin told of their hard work in the baking sun, and their bony features showed how little they were fed. Their chapped lips and dazed look proved how dehydrated they were, while their bloodshot eyes expressed their exhaustion and lack of sleep. Their bodies looked like canvases that had been painted with swift strokes of slashes from the overseer's cracking whip. They didn't even look human. They looked undead.

Tetsu knew what it was like to be one of them, to be in that situation where they just barely clung onto life. He knew that if he were them, he would wish that someone would come to his aid.

The overseer lowered his whip, watching Tetsu curiously as the foreigner dropped to a knee. He reached into his cloak and pulled out a few loafs of bread that he had been saving for himself. Handing out the individual slices to each slave, the man smiled at the wounded workers. "You've done a good job so far. One day your hard work will be rewarded," he said, rising to his feet.

"What do you think you're doing? Those are my slaves that you're feeding!" the overseer barked angrily.

"*Your* slaves?" Tetsu raised an eyebrow and turned to look the overseer in the eyes. His eyes flickered to an insignia that the slave-driver wore on his belt. The overseer was topless, wearing nothing except for torn shorts and his leather belt. His pudgy belly, clearly from too much eating, slumped over his belt. He looked like an absolute slacker. The fact that he was the one holding the whip enraged Tetsu. "That insignia there belongs to General Shazir, doesn't it? That means that these slaves are actually his."

"And?"

"General Shazir is dead. He was killed at a battle outside of Yuusus, a neutral city very far away," Tetsu said, pointing to the slaves. "That means that these people are free, no?"

"General Shazir … dead?" The overseer gaped, absolutely stunned at the news. "How could you possibly know?" He frowned suddenly, looking into Tetsu's eyes. "Do I know you? I feel like I recognize you from somewhere."

Tetsu gulped, his face paling. How had he not recognized this overseer? It was the same man that Tetsu had gotten into a fight with five years before when he was with Darien and Yuu! This guy was still out here whipping slaves?

"He is dead," Ramses said, intervening. He walked forward with his hands slid deep into the pockets of his black cloak. He sighed as the overseer quickly dropped to his hands and knees, bowing before the Magus. "I can confirm that your master is now deceased."

"L-Lord Ramses! I was not aware that this was your

companion!" the overseer said shakily. "But if it is true that Master Shazir has perished in war, t-then that would only mean that these slaves would be put on the market again to be sold. T-They would not be free."

"Alright, I'll buy them from you then," Ramses murmured, reaching into his cloak and pulling out a golden coin for each slave. He tossed the currency onto the ground at the overseer's feet and nodded towards the slaves. "Alright, I suppose the lot of you are coming with me. Leave the fragments on the ground. I'm sure this man would be more than willing to clean up the mess, isn't that right?" He looked at the overseer, who nodded his head quickly as he scrambled to pluck up the golden coins out of the dirt.

The slaves all looked at each other, perplexed at how quickly their situation had changed. A flash of hope flickered in all of their eyes and their previous distraught looks were wiped from their faces. They stumbled to their feet and limped towards Ramses and Tetsu, bowing their heads and muttering words of thanks.

Ramses simply turned away and continued to walk through the streets, assuming that the slaves would follow them to wherever they were going. He exhaled. "Tch, I thought that was going to get bad. You need to control yourself or you'll end up drawing unnecessary attention."

"Control myself? These slaves were being abused and no one was going to do anything about it unless I stepped in. That overseer could've had these people beaten to death!" Tetsu protested.

"That's my Tetsu for you! Always helping people!" Kira clung to Tetsu's arm affectionately.

"Huh…." Tetsu narrowed his eyes and sighed at Kira. He looked at Ramses' back. "Thanks for helping, though. It's true; things might've gotten chaotic if you weren't there to shut that brute up."

Ramses shrugged. "It's fine. You're one of those types of people who just can't stand it when something unjust is happening, huh? You're different from your friend, Ares."

Tetsu frowned. "What do you mean by that?"

"The banished prince stayed hidden within the Lost Sands while his empire transformed to become a superpower. The lower-class citizens in Persia now bear a much larger burden than before and suffer tremendously, buried so deep in debt that their conditions will never be improved. Some even end up in slavery. Meanwhile, the Persian army went on to conquer dozens of nations to the west, slaughtering thousands of people and pillaging hundreds of villages. And then there's the Hayashi clan genocide." The hairs on Tetsu's arms stood up and his body stiffened. "Innocent people that were born into that clan were judged for a crime that was out of their control, their birth. Something so unjust would make many vigilantes leap for the opportunity to make a change. With Ares' power, surely he is the best one suited to bring about that change. Yet he did nothing."

Tetsu said nothing. It was true. What had Darien been doing all those years when he had been in the Lost Sands? Why hadn't he come out of that desert sooner to help all of the people who were out there suffering?

"At least you have done something," Ramses said. "I've heard from your girlfriend that you actually have spent the past couple years building up relations between nations in the east. You've been pulling together an army, and an enormous alliance of the strongest eastern empires of Dastia has banded together to strike against your enemy, Persia." He smiled. "That's impressive."

Tetsu's face turned red and he looked at Kira, who was still wrapped around his arm. "S-She's not my girlfriend!" he murmured, flustered. "What about you? You don't mind seeing injustice?"

Ramses' expression hardened. "I see terrible things every day and I've done even worse things in order to survive." He sighed, averting his eyes from Tetsu. "But I do have a young daughter, and in order to protect her I had to become a Persian Magus, thus forcing me to fight battles that I did not want to fight. I hate watching unjust things happen, Tetsu. But I am not brave enough to risk my own wellbeing for the sake of others, as you are. I almost feel powerless because correcting the small injustices that occur every day in Dastia is like attempting to tackle minor symptoms while the disease itself rages on. To try and become a vigilante, and judge all the wicked while saving all of the innocent, would be the same as trying to correct a fault of mankind. It's an impossible task."

"But I believe that saving the life of one is better than not saving a life at all," Tetsu said, smiling at the free slaves that followed them. "Wouldn't you think so?"

Ramses gave the slaves a glance and smirked but said nothing.

It took the group several hours to walk through Persepolis and make their way up to the castle. No guards questioned the party once they recognized Ramses and simply allowed the group to pass. Walking on the fragile grass of the yard just outside the large castle of

Persepolis, Tetsu couldn't help but remember a distant memory.

The three friends, Yuu, Tetsu, and Darien had all laid on the grass in the yard outside of Persepolis's castle to gaze upon the stars together. Darien loved to look at the stars when he was thinking. Yuu thought that praying to the stars would allow for the gods to hear him. Tetsu simply thought the night sky was beautiful.

It felt so distant, almost like a dream. Tetsu looked up at the grand castle that towered before him. Somewhere in here was the bastard, Cambyses, who had plotted to overtake the throne to accomplish his own agenda for Persia. After all these years, would the king recognize Tetsu if they crossed paths?

Ramses stopped suddenly and pointed to the slaves. "I am willing to grant all of you freedom. However, in order to earn your freedom, I want you to find the way to my room in this house under my order. Ask nearby guards for directions. Make sure that my family is alright and I will meet you there shortly." He reached up and pulled his skeleton necklace from his neck, tossing it to one of the slaves. "If anyone questions you, show them this and tell them that Magus Ramses has sent you."

One of the slaves caught the medallion and nodded swiftly. The group of laborers scampered off, filled with newfound vigor and motivation, into the castle.

Kira raised her eyebrows. "Um, I thought that we were going to go to save your family first? Shouldn't we be following them?"

"We will," Ramses said. "But we have some business to settle with Persia's king first. After all, it would seem that he stole the throne from the true heir of the empire," he said, beginning to walk forward towards the castle.

Tetsu blinked, walking after the Magus. This guy couldn't possibly be thinking of assassinating the king, could he? That would surely change everything in the Persian Empire. But that didn't necessarily mean that it was the solution to all of Persia's issues either. Not to mention, the king was surely heavily guarded. How was this all going to work out?

Ramses clicked his fingers, sending a tingling sensation shaking through Tetsu and Kira's bodies. "I've placed an invisibility spell on the two of you. Just make sure to stay near me and don't make any noise, otherwise you'll be caught. Follow me closely." They had reached the end of the castle yard and were now walking through the entrance of the castle.

Tetsu could feel beads of sweat forming on his cheeks as he and Kira slipped past two guards, who were simply gazing forward at the courtyard. The soldiers had ignored Ramses' entrance, given his high status. However, without the invisibility spell, Tetsu and Kira would've been deemed suspicious and the entire mission would've immediately gone downhill once they were spotted.

Tiptoeing through the castle, Tetsu found that it was actually quite hard to keep quiet while walking. He couldn't let his footsteps echo otherwise it would sound as if Ramses had two or three pairs of feet. Yet, trying to follow Ramses at his quick pace without making sound at all was rather difficult. The marble floor made it especially hard.

Passing through lines of soldiers and squadrons of Persian guards, Tetsu felt like a ghost. He smiled as he and Kira slipped past dozens of Persians, all of whom didn't even acknowledge their existence. Invisibility was awesome.

Ramses walked through two giant golden doors and into an open throne room. The room was surrounded by a perimeter of treasures as well as a squadron of guards that all observed Ramses' uninvited entrance into the king's room. The Magus presented himself before Cambyses, who stared at the visitor with a surprised look on his face.

"Ramses, is that you?" Cambyses said, leaning his chin against his knuckles as he sat upon his golden throne, looking down at the mage. "Zahir had informed me that you were killed along with Amam and Shazir."

"Well, he was wrong," Ramses said, eying two Magi that were standing at the king's side. The two radiated intimidating auras that made Ramses' back straighten. He stormed through the silent room, his footsteps echoing in the silence. The soldiers and Magi pierced him with their hostile glares, but Ramses kept his face as hard as a stone as he knelt before his king. "I have returned, milord, and I am here to provide whatever service it is that you want me to perform."

One of the Magi got up on his toes and whispered something into the king's ear. Cambyses raised an eyebrow and lowered his eyes, his face paling a bit. Tapping the arm of his throne impatiently, the king smirked. He pointed at Ramses with such assertive authority that the mage flinched at the king's action. "Zahir actually mentioned the possibility that you survived. He said that the only way that you would survive is if you received magical treatment from someone. You were surrounded by foes with not a single magical ally for miles.

The only way that you could be alive right now is if you were saved by the enemy." Cambyses's eyes flashed with victory and a sly smile split across his lips. "Zahir, as a result, proposed a theory that your return would mean that you've conspired with the enemy. Isn't that a funny thought?"

Ramses kept his expression hard, but a bead of sweat raced down the side of his face. He felt extremely hot, as if there was a sun inside of his chest, radiating heat to the rest of his body. Ramses knew that Zahir always thought ahead, but there was no possible way that he could just predict that Ramses would return as a traitor. This was only a theory. But was the king going to rely on such an untrustworthy prediction? "It is funny, milord. Why would I betray the grand empire of Persia?"

"I don't know," Cambyses said, his gaze suddenly reflecting hostility. Ramses gulped at the intensity of the king's terrifying stare. The king continued to tap the arm of his throne rapidly and impatiently, as if he were waiting for something. "Why don't we ask your friends?"

Tetsu's eyes widened and suddenly the two Magi appeared behind him and Kira, flashing across the room with inhuman speed. The two invisible intruders were pinned to the ground before they could even react to the king's trusted mages. Tetsu felt a calloused hand grasp the back of his neck and force his face downward, slamming his cheek hard against the marble floor. He grunted and glared up the king. The cloak of invisibility that shrouded the two invaders slowly vanished. How had Cambyses known that they were there? Was Ramses' magic not potent enough, or was this whole situation just a giant trap?

Tetsu glanced around the room and saw that several of the soldiers had unsheathed their swords. They wore looks of shock upon their faces. It seemed that they definitely hadn't expected for Ramses to secretly sneak two intruders into the throne room.

"You really thought that we wouldn't be able to sniff out a dog from the Hayashi clan?" one of the Magi snarled. He had a scar tearing across his left eye and was completely bald, revealing his oddly circular shaped head. The man wore a full, skinny, black suit that clung tightly to his body. Wrapped around his waist was an iron chain whip with two sharp scythes at each end. He had Tetsu's arms pinned behind his back and laughed. "Is this a joke or something, Ramses? You have no faith in our abilities as Magi, do you?"

Ramses gritted his teeth and said nothing, looking away, defeated.

The other Magus had a head of curly brown hair that wrapped like a bowl around his head. He wore a long white robe made of fine linens with golden sleeves and had leather slippers that revealed his purple painted toenails. Smiling wickedly and widening his crazed, red eyes, the Magus towered over Kira. He sat on her back and took a bundle of the struggling mage's hair in his hand, letting the strands fall through his hands for a moment. "So … silky. Hey, Sahad, you need to touch this!"

"Let go of my hair, you freak!" Kira screamed, struggling against the man's iron grip.

"Whoa!" the creepy Magus yelped in response to Kira's rebelliousness. "We've got a fighter!" He burst out in hysterical laughter, holding his stomach while his other hand gripped Kira's wrists behind her back.

Sahad, the Magus with the chain-whip, sighed. "I don't share your abnormal fetishes, Jafaar."

Jafaar raised an eyebrow at his partner. "Huh? Abnormal? I have no idea what you're talking about!" He grabbed another handful of Kira's hair and held it up to his nostrils, inhaling a deep whiff of her scent. "Ah, so sweet!"

"Let her go, you freak!" Tetsu roared, struggling against Sahad. He thrashed about, trying to break himself free from the Magus's grip. But the man that was restraining him was clearly experienced. He shifted his weight according to which way Tetsu was struggling so that the mercenary couldn't break free.

"Oh, we've got a couple over here!" Sahad scoffed. "I never thought that a girl as beautiful as this one would take a liking to scum from the Hayashi clan." He grabbed the back of Tetsu's head and slammed the man's face hard into the marble floor. There was a hard crack and blood spurt from Tetsu's nose. Pain exploded from the man's face and stars danced before his eyes. "Now shut the hell up before I cut off your tongue and make you choke on it. That's not the cleanest way to die, *trust me*."

Tetsu gasped, wrinkling up his stinging nose. Blood streamed freely from his nostrils and he groaned as he was again bashed into the ground, this time landing hard on his cheek. Squishing the side of his face against the floor, he soon realized that there was no way that he could escape from this precarious situation.

"Your new companions seem to be struggling," Cambyses said,

looking at Tetsu curiously. His eyebrows went up and a sadistic smile stretched across his face. "Oh my. Tetsu, is that you? All of these years and you're still up and kicking? I was wondering why a member of the Hayashi clan was here, still alive. After all, the genocide of your clan seemed to be a success so far. One of my first mandates when I first became king was to increase funding for the extermination squads that were executing the members of the Hayashi clan. As a result, we've cleansed this country of hundreds of your family members!" He laughed. "Isn't that wonderful?"

Tetsu clenched his jaw, glaring up at Cambyses with disgust. "You're a sick man, Cambyses. Just because you murdered the original king and stole the throne for yourself, you believe that you're all powerful now? In reality, you're still just a little man shouting big words and…." He grunted as Sahad smashed his face into the marble ground once more.

"DIDN'T I TELL YOU TO SHUT UP?" Sahad boomed in Tetsu's ear, causing the man to shiver. He brought the heel of his foot down and drove it into Tetsu's spine, sending agony surging through the mercenary's body. "Talk one more damned time, scum. One more time, I DARE YOU!" He reached to his side and unhooked his chain-whip, whirling the iron chain in a circular motion. The blade of the weapon was spinning at such a high speed that it became a mere blur. The Magus glared down at Tetsu with an irritated look. "I have no problem executing one more member of your cursed family."

"Tetsu!" Kira cried as Jafaar gently stroked her cheek, causing her to tremble with rage. But as much as she wanted to strike the

Magus in the face, Kira knew that she couldn't move.

The sinister mage shushed her with a light giggle. "It'll be okay! The two of you just have to shut up. If you do that maybe we won't have to gouge out your eyes. Maybe." He burst out chortling hysterically.

Ramses still held his stone-cold expression, as still as a statue.

"So, Ramses," Cambyses said, extending his hand to the two intruders. "I'll give you a choice. Decapitate Tetsu right now and I'll spare the girl and let her go free. I'll even restore you to your position as one of my Magi, and I'll forget about your betrayal. Your family will still be underneath my protection, and life for you will resume." He smiled. "All you have to do is execute this man that you've only just met."

Ramses stood there looking at Tetsu, who was clearly suffering. Kira was shaking, horrified because she was so close to Jafaar, who was known for being deranged. Everything would be forgotten if he just decapitated this man that he'd only met days ago. That offer did not seem half bad, especially since Tetsu had been antagonistic towards him when they first interacted. Kira had saved his life. Ramses owed it to her to save hers as well, and with the way things were currently going, both Tetsu and Kira would die if Ramses didn't make a decision. He would have to kill Tetsu. That was the best way.

Ramses wasn't just thinking about Kira, but his family as well. Protection. Wasn't that why he had joined Cambyses's side to begin with? He had become a Magus of Persia for the sole purpose of protecting his family from the relentless massacres the Persians had carried out when they invaded foreign lands. Ramses remembered the gentle ashes that blew in the gusting wind as burning ancient buildings that he had seen all his life crumbled to the ground in a heap of destruction.

His home had become a conflagration from hell, an inferno filled with slaughtered corpses and incinerated homes. The Persian soldiers had stormed through Ramses' old city, ransacking everything that they saw. Like savage barbarians, they despoiled his home, pulling him and his defenseless family out into the streets to be executed along with the rest of the victims of the razed city.

That was merely the fate of every nation that stood in Persia's way. If they did not submit, they were mercilessly massacred. The Persians cared little for the lives of anyone but their own. But Ramses had been given a chance to live. Zahir had come just when his family was about to be butchered before him and had offered him a chance to fight at the Persian king's side. In exchange for giving up his life to defend a lord that he didn't really care about, he was given incentive: lifelong protection of his family. The very thought pleased Ramses. He would no longer have to fear that his wife and children would be killed at the hands of a powerful emperor, for now they would now be protected by one.

Ramses reached to his side and slowly unsheathed his sword, revealing its ringing steel as he walked forward towards Tetsu, his boots thumping loudly in the silence. Sahad grabbed the mercenary by his spiky hair and forced his head back. Tetsu looked into Ramses' eyes with fading hope and he gulped, perspiration streaming down the side of his face.

Tetsu closed his eyes. This was not how he had imagined dying.

Betrayal. How blind could he possibly have been? Of course the chances of this Persian Magus going against them were extremely high. Why on earth had they volunteered to help him? It was a Persian Magus for gods' sake! If his hands weren't bound behind his back by Sahad he would crack his head hard on the marble ground for being an absolute fool.

Ramses pressed the cold metal of the side of his blade against Tetsu's throat, watching as the sweat of the trembling mercenary dripped onto the untouched steel. The mage stared into Tetsu's quivering eyes that were somehow still filled with courage, as if he didn't fear his unfortunate fate. Courage. Hope. Ramses smiled. This man had plenty of it.

Clicking his fingers, a spark of light radiated from Ramses' finger, filling the room with its blinding shine. Jafaar and Sahad cringed, staggering backwards as they grabbed at their burning eyes in agony. Cambyses covered his eyes with the sleeve of his robe, grunting. When he glanced back, he saw that Jafaar and Sahad were standing there in the center of the room. Alone.

A vein bulged from the king's temple as his face turned red, swelling with rage. He slammed his fist against the arm of his chair and roared, "FIND THEM! FIND THEM NOW!" His soldiers didn't need another second to process the command; they hastily sprinted out of the room to pursue the fleeing intruders. Cambyses gripped the ends of arms of his throne so hard that his knuckles blanched ghostly white. "That bastard really did betray me then, huh? Jafaar, Sahad! Gather the other Magi and have Ramses' family executed immediately! He's broken our accord."

***

Tetsu stumbled through the narrow hallways of the castle, following Ramses. Slapping her bare feet on the marble floor beside Tetsu was Kira, her eyes trained forward. She had no intention of getting caught again after her encounter with Jafaar. She gripped her staff with two hands, ready to unleash magic at the first sight of any hostile enemy. "You helped us," Tetsu said to Ramses. "I'll be honest, I'm surprised."

"Well, I'm overjoyed at how much faith you've put in me," Ramses murmured, turning right through one of the corridors to find a squad of Persian soldiers rushing at the trio.

Ramses slowed to a stop but Kira quickly leapt in front of him, swiping her staff. A bolt of lightning scintillated from the tip of her weapon, snapping outwards and sizzling the first Persian soldier, causing the other warriors to gape at the magical assault. Kira jabbed outwards once more with her staff and released another surge of electricity that crackled, individual bolts branching out and spreading as bright energy filled the hallway with its dazzling light. The bolts charged straight through the Persian soldiers, making the hairs on their heads prick straight up. Within a second of being struck, the warriors were on the ground convulsing and writhing about until finally they lay still, smoke rising from their unmoving bodies. The miasma of burning corpses filled the hallway, but Ramses didn't seem the slightest bit disturbed and leapt over the Persian bodies, pressing onward. Kira followed closely.

Tetsu winced and inched over the corpses, quite disgusted with their deformed, smoldering bodies. But the shouting of other approaching Persian soldiers prompted the mercenary to sprint after Kira and Ramses with haste. Reaching his two companions, he saw that Kira and Ramses were ruthlessly dispatching any soldiers that they came across without so much as a spoken word.

Bodies of slain soldiers lay sprawled across the ground and Tetsu found himself jumping over dozens of corpses, finding it hard to keep up with how fast the two Magi were dispatching enemies. "Where are we going?" Tetsu shouted over the sound of Kira's snapping energy magic.

Ramses slid to a stop in front of a door and was about to grab its golden handle when he looked down. Soaking into the mat at the bottom of the door was a pool of blood that was seeping from the other side of the door. His heart sank and he gritted his teeth, grasping the handle and throwing the door open.

Kira and Tetsu stumbled into the room behind the Magus and turned to see that the slaves that Ramses had freed were now slain and lying on the ground. They lay in a heap on top of one another, their arms entangled in a cluster of bloodied, unidentifiable flesh. Kira raised a hand to her mouth, ready to throw up.

Tetsu mashed his teeth, tearing his sword from its sheath as he stormed forward through the room. Stepping behind Ramses, he turned and saw that a man was slowly approaching a defenseless woman, who was shielding a young boy from the perpetrator. The man had an eye-patch and was wielding a sickle-like dagger, the blade curved like a crescent moon. "Bator?" Tetsu recognized this man. It was that mercenary from Yuusus, the one who had assaulted him at the bar with his cronies. What on earth was he doing all the way in

Persepolis?

Bator turned his head and recognized Tetsu, grinning and revealing his wicked teeth. "Oh, wow. Aren't I in for a treat? The great mercenary of legends has blessed me with his almighty presence. Oh, except this time he isn't drunk and isn't stealing from women! What a riot!" He chortled, twirling his dagger in his hand with profound expertise. Tetsu was surprised; the man hadn't nearly been this skilled with a weapon the last time they met. "You know, I didn't know that Aleysha was your sibling until I did some research. The wench has been stealing my contracts for months now. But with the power that Zahir has granted me, I don't have to worry about being outshined by weaklings like her anymore."

"Zahir?" Tetsu growled. "He offered you power?"

"Oh, he offered me more than just that!" Bator grinned, holding out his arms as if he were hugging the world in thanks for his great fortune. "He offered me aggrandizement. Wealth, a home, a commanding position, protection, strength, and an opportunity to work for the empire that will dominate all of Dastia."

"You've joined the Persians?"

"Who wouldn't? Why would I stay a part of a neutral community of damned mercenaries that are just scraping by with change earned from dangerous contracts? That lifestyle just isn't worth it. The Persians were going to storm into Yuusus and take all of that anyway, and soon they'll have all of Dastia in the palm of their hand. I'd rather be on the winning side, thank you very much." Bator smirked, pointing the tip of his curved dagger at Tetsu. "But you, you're different, aren't you? You don't mind a challenge. Perfect. I'll give you one and this time the odds won't be in your favor."

"Step away from my family!" Ramses snarled, but suddenly Bator's image flickered and the man appeared right next to the Magus, driving his knee heavily into Ramses' solar plexus. The wind coughed up from Ramses' lungs and he lurched forward, his eyes bulging and his face paling as saliva forcefully spewed from his mouth.

Bator's hand moved with blinding speed as he cracked a hard punch into the back of Ramses' head, slamming the mage into the floor with a swift motion. It had all happened so fast that Tetsu didn't have time to react. "I hate when weaklings make demands. Now I understand why it was that you were so stubborn on that day, Tetsu." Bator looked to Tetsu and smiled slyly. "You wouldn't listen to me because I was insignificant, I was weak. And the weak will always be bullied, they will always be shoved down with no hopes of ever getting back up because it's the strong that dominate this world and take everything. I see that now and I'm glad … I'm glad that I've become strong!" He cackled as he whirled his dagger and brought it tearing down towards Ramses' back with lightning speed.

Kira was about to rush forward and strike Bator, but suddenly stopped and watched as Tetsu practically teleported across the room and halted Bator's movement by grabbing the man's wrist, stopping the blade inches from jamming into Ramses' spine. Kira's eyebrows went up and she smiled. Tetsu had used the Sands of Time to let him move with enough speed to halt Bator's attack. Bator's magic seemed to allow for him to move with supernatural speed, so fast that it was blinding to the ordinary eye. That was most definitely an advantageous form of magic, for Bator could strike down other mages before they could even use their powers. But it wouldn't work on Tetsu if he could slow time.

Bator glanced at Tetsu with utter surprise, his hand shaking as he attempted to drive his dagger into Ramses' defenseless body. But he couldn't overpower Tetsu, who still had his wrist in an iron grip. The one-eyed man looked to Tetsu's left hand, which held a diamond hourglass, one that he recognized from the bar. "You really are a nuisance," he snarled, pulling his blade back and stumbling away from Ramses' body.

Kira had guided Ramses' family across the room and towards the doorway where they stood, waiting to see what happened next. Ramses stirred lightly, clutching his stomach in agony, and began to slowly push himself to his feet. "What a punch…," Ramses choked out.

Tetsu held out his sword. "Alright, the two of you need to get out of here quickly. I'll hold this cyclops off. Just make sure that you get out of the castle. I'll meet you guys somewhere in the lower city."

Ramses hesitated, not sure whether or not leaving Tetsu was actually a good idea. Could the mercenary actually handle one of Cambyses's new Magi? Ramses did not recognize this new mage, but it definitely seemed like he and Tetsu were already acquainted somehow. However, Kira had already led Ramses' family out of the room and was escorting them through the corpse-filled hallways of the castle. It seemed that she was willing to put her faith into her friend. Perhaps Ramses should do the same. "Alright, get out of this in one piece. We'll be waiting for you," Ramses said, limping out of the room to follow Kira.

Tetsu shifted over to the door, blocking the exit for Bator as he whirled his sword. "That's the plan," he muttered as his eyes shifted from dark brown to gleaming red.

Bator laughed as he watched Tetsu. "The Shokugan, how rare. It's no wonder they're off executing the whole lot of you Hayashi scumbags. You're a bunch of freaks!" He pointed his sickle to the doorway behind Tetsu. "Do you really think your friends are going to get far? The other Magi are already on their way. You and all of your friends are doomed and have been from the very beginning."

Tetsu smirked. "Then I suppose I ought to deal with you quickly so I can go and dispatch the rest of your new Persian friends."

There was a flash of movement as Bator completely vanished, bursting at sonic speed straight for Tetsu's body. Tetsu's hand tingled as the Sands of Time activated, the golden sand slowly trickling down the hourglass until barely a grain was falling per minute. As time began to slow, Tetsu saw that Bator was still moving at a normal pace. The Magus was now in front of Tetsu, slashing his crescent sickle through the air at the mercenary's throat.

Tetsu lashed out and chopped Bator's wrist with a fierce blow from his hand. The Magus's hand broke into a spasm before dropping the dagger. The action was so swift that Bator hardly even had any time to react before Tetsu drove a sinking kick straight into the mage's stomach, launching the man backwards. Time resumed at its normal pace and Bator crashed down loudly onto a glass table, shattering the household item with his weight. The mage reached up and grabbed his throbbing head, groaning. His hands were sliced from the sharp glass beneath him. "You filthy mongrel! I can't wait until I peel the skin from your mutilated scalp!"

"Oh, that sounds like so much fun!" a voice called from behind Tetsu. "Can we join?"

Tetsu grunted, jerking around to find Jafaar and Sahad both sauntering in from the hallway to converge on his position. His heart thumped and he bit his lower lip, knowing that there was no way that he could defeat three Magi at once. He had to find some way to escape. Tetsu glanced at the diamond hourglass in his hand. If he used the Sands of Time correctly to mount his magic carpet, he could potentially get out of this situation alive. No, that was risky. Tetsu still didn't know what magic Jafaar and Sahad had. It was best if he outsmarted them somehow. He pointed his sword at Jafaar and Sahad suddenly, causing the two Magi to stop their advance. "Stay back!"

"Oh! You got me! I'm totally scared now! Please, mister, don't cut me with that dull sword of yours!" Jafaar burst out laughing.

"Put that needle down or I'll bash your face so hard that no one will be able to recognize you for the rest of your miserable life," Sahad gnarred.

Tetsu glanced at Bator from the corner of his eye and smiled, jamming his sword into his sheath. He held his hands up into the air and turned back to the shocked faces of Jafaar and Sahad. "Alright, alright! I give up." He stuck out his tongue. "That's what you wanted me to say, right?" Suddenly, the mercenary vanished completely.

Sahad blinked in puzzlement, taking a step backward. "What?

Where the hell did that runt go?"

Jafaar scratched the back of his neck, tilting his head to the side. "I'm pretty sure I just saw him there. Huh."

"You idiots! He's using the Sands of Time so that he can escape!" Bator bellowed, scrambling to his feet. "We've got to get after him, now!" The Magus bolted through the hallways with a surge of speed, rushing after Tetsu, who surely had dashed out of the room to try and get away.

Sahad spun around and grunted. "Jafaar, we should go too! Cambyses will lop off our heads if we don't capture Tetsu."

"Eh? L-Let's go!" Jafaar yelped, scrambling after Bator with Sahad.

Little did those fools know that Tetsu had just hidden himself in the closet in the Ramses' room. The warrior peered through the cracks in the closet door's wood, scanning the room to see if the Magi had really left. It was empty and silent for a moment. Suddenly he heard footsteps echoing in the room. He gulped and slunk back further into the closet, melting into the darkness. A mysterious man strolled into the room and examined the pile of slave corpses in the corner of the room. He then turned his head to look at the broken glass table on the floor, raising an eyebrow.

Tetsu's eyes widened when he recognized the man. Zahir. The Magus then looked straight at the closet door and smiled. Panic exploded through Tetsu's veins and he shivered. *Damn it, he's found me! How?* Tetsu unsheathed his sword swiftly and burst from the closet, charging straight at the mage. Time froze entirely as he activated the Sands of Time. It was much more taxing for him to freeze time completely but he would only need a second to kill the Magus. This was his chance to finally kill Zahir!

Zahir's eyes suddenly flickered to life, making Tetsu's heart leap to his throat. *How? You shouldn't be able to move!* The mage reached out and grabbed Tetsu by the neck, despite the fact time had been completely frozen. The Sands of Time rolled out of Tetsu's twitching hand and clattered loudly to the floor. Zahir's eyes gleamed with malice and he smirked, eying the hourglass curiously. "So you managed to outsmart the other Magi using this magical item. Smart, Hayashi scum. But your tricks won't work on me." He released a burst of black magic into Tetsu's diaphragm, sending the man flying backwards into the closet.

The mercenary smashed straight through the wall and landed hard in the parlor of another noble family. Tetsu rolled on the ground, grabbing his stomach in agony. A burning sensation rippled through his skin and he gasped for air, tears glinting in the corners of his eyes.

"I am a god now. You ought to get on your knees and grovel before me, mortal," The god extended his hand, pointing at Tetsu with his index finger. "That's the least you can do for infiltrating *my* territory."

"A god, huh?" Tetsu grumbled, pressing his palm to the ground as he forced himself onto his knees. This guy claimed Ahriman's power? Did that mean that Darien had failed? Tetsu clenched his jaw and squeezed the hilt of his sword as he sprinted straight at Zahir. "Like hell I'll ever bow to you, bastard!"

Ahriman swung his hand and an invisible force smashed into

Tetsu's side, sending the mercenary crashing into a wall on the far side of the room. Pain erupted through Tetsu's arm as he slid to the ground, coughing. Ahriman walked forward, eying the struggling man with pity. "Without that hourglass of yours, you're weak. You're a simple swordsman just like the rest of the peons in this citadel. There is no difference. You are just a human."

Tetsu's hands balled into tight fists at his side and he turned his head to see that his sword rested on the floor far away from him. There was no way that he could reach for it without Zahir killing him. His eyes flitted to an unbroken expensive vase that was lying on the ground next to him. He snatched the vase and hurled it straight at Zahir.

Ahriman extended a hand toward the pot and it exploded into a thousand pieces. But the pieces did not fall to the ground; instead, they levitated magically in the air. The sharp parts of the vase slowly began to turn towards Tetsu, pointing straight at the injured mercenary.

"There he is!" Bator yelled, staggering into the room with Jafaar and Sahad close behind him. The three Magi stopped and stared in awe at Ahriman as he controlled the pieces of the broken vase with his dark magic.

"This is the result of all of your efforts, valiant warrior. You do not give up no matter what the obstacle and do not succumb to pain, no matter how harsh. Humans like you are able to achieve much in this world, for their persistence allows for them to reach a height above others. But against gods, you will never be victorious. I'm glad that I get to be the one to erase the hope from your eyes, Demon

Mercenary." Ahriman snapped his fingers and the pieces of the vase shot forward and buried themselves into Tetsu. There were dozens of heavy thumps like bullets pounding into his body. Blood splattered onto the wall behind the mercenary and the man's head slumped forward limply, red liquid dribbling down his chin and onto his lap.

Ahriman glanced over his shoulder at the three shocked Magi, lowering his hand. "What of the other infiltrators? I expect that he was not the only one responsible for the incursion on Persepolis."

"R-Ramses has escaped with his family and the female mage," Sahad reported, averting Ahriman's authoritative gaze. "Two Magi were slain by their hand along with two squadrons of Persian soldiers. They're somewhere within the city, though. The gates have been shut and we would be notified immediately if someone tried to flee Persepolis."

"Alright," Ahriman said, beginning to walk out of the room. "Clean up here and begin a search for those fugitives. I won't punish you for your failures here because I'm in a good mood. But the next time a simple human tricks you idiots I will mount your heads on my wall, do you understand?"

"Y-Yes, sir!" the three Magi stammered in unison.

"It's *milord* now." Ahriman glared at the Magi over his shoulder before leaving the room. He opened and closed his palm as he strolled through the silent hallways of Persepolis's castle. Ahriman's power was beyond imagining. Even Sacred Treasures like the Sands of Time were useless against him now. With this power, he could make anything happen! Ahriman smiled. But first he would need to eradicate the two gods that were on his tail, Ares and Mithra. The two gods of war would surely be coming after him. This was good. Ahriman knew that he needed to test the extent of his strength on someone anyway. Why not have it be two foolish deities?

Falling Stars

Cambyses tapped the arm of his throne as he watched Zahir saunter into the room. He was surprised when he saw that the Magus did not bow before him upon entering but he said nothing. "Were you successful then, Zahir?"

The man's lips peeled into a nefarious smile. "My name is Ahriman now."

Cambyses smirked. "Did you run into any trouble?"

"Ares was there along with his friend, a demigod. I do not yet know who her parent is but I doubt that she'll be a real threat. Yuu betrayed the empire to return to Darien's side. I believe that their party will arrive at Persepolis's borders relatively soon."

"Is that so?" Cambyses murmured. "In the past few weeks that you've been absent we've been cut off from some of our fortified units to the east. Do you know anything about that?"

"No," Ahriman said with a casual shrug. He wasn't worried. Whatever it was, it would be crushed by his almighty power. "I'll handle it on my own time."

"I originally believed that it was Ares slowly defeating our Persian units that were sent east to conquer lands on the way to eastern Dastia. But if he was in the Lost Sands combating you, there was no way that he could be in two places at once," Cambyses muttered. "The scouts that we've sent to find out what happened are too slow, and if there were any real threat they surely wouldn't return in one piece. Perhaps you ought to take a look."

Ahriman's face contorted into an annoyed scowl. "I ought to take a look? Have one of the other weakling Magi do it. Don't waste my time." The god turned away from the king, ready to leave the throne room. He was weary after having traveled from the Lost Sands. He'd been testing out his godly powers without much restraint. He felt depleted and wanted to sink into his comfortable bed and fall into a deep slumber.

"Zahir, how dare you turn your back on your king?" Cambyses boomed and Ahriman stopped suddenly. The king gulped, realizing that he might've made a mistake raising his voice to the god. But hadn't this god pledged his allegiance to Cambyses? Then why was he feeling so unbelievably terrified? A chilling sensation shivered through his spine and his mouth became dry as a desert, his hands squeezing the arms of his throne.

Ahriman glanced over his shoulder with a glare that would make armies flee in fear. The intensity of his stare made the king sink back into his throne, his hands quavering nervously as perspiration streaked down his cheeks. The god's violet eyes coruscated and he cracked a tiny smile across his lips. "Cambyses, you're funny. You're a king amongst humans. But now I am a god, a being beyond you. Learn your place, otherwise the next time you try to talk down to me, I will dispatch you. Our vision of a united continent does not need you in it, mortal." He turned away and continued to walk towards the exit of the room.

Cambyses watched as Ahriman left the throne room and

lowered his eyes. The soldiers that stood like statues around the perimeter of the throne room all shifted nervously, not really sure what to make of Zahir's sudden rebellious behavior. Cambyses knew that he could no longer control Zahir. Now that he had become Ahriman, there was no way for the king to physically restrain the god. The king had gone from the player to the pawn. Cambyses bit his quivering lower lip lightly.

The doors of the throne room opened once more and the king glanced up to see Sahad, Jafaar, and Bator all sauntering into the room, dragging Tetsu's bloody, limp body behind them. The mercenary was unconscious, with pieces of a broken vase jammed into his flesh. Streaks of blood trailed behind his body as he was dragged across the throne room and tossed to the ground before the Persian king.

Cambyses watched as the three Magi bowed before him. The king swallowed the rock in his throat and sat up straighter, giving his Magi a nod of approval. At least he still had these subordinate mages. "You've captured him. Good. What of the search for Ramses and his family?"

"Still unsuccessful, milord. We're working as swiftly as we can. The city is massive, and they could be hiding anywhere. We've put out a bounty on their heads to give the citizens an incentive to have them captured. The greedy bastards of the lower cities will find them in no time, milord. I can ensure you that," Sahad said, his head bowed to the ground.

"Make sure you don't disappoint me. Take this broken toy to the jail and schedule him for execution tomorrow. Oh, and bring him a final hearty meal. He was a friend of my nephew. I think he deserves a proper last meal," Cambyses said with a wave of his hand. "Don't bother returning to me until you've found Ramses and his family. Now, leave me. Except for you, Bator."

Bator blinked, staring at the ground, still kneeling before his king. He heard the fading footsteps of Jafaar and Sahad as the two Magi left the room. Saluting his king by striking his fist to his chest, Bator nodded his head nervously. "Yes, milord?"

"I want you to go and scout east of Persepolis along the main roads. We've lost contact with a few of our dominated territories to the east. I believe that a threat is coming and I want to know exactly what it is we're up against," Cambyses explained. "With your speed, you're the best suited to scout ahead and see what threat lies to our east. Just make sure you get there and come back in one piece."

"Yes, milord," Bator said with a swift nod of his head. "I want to ensure you that you shouldn't be concerned, milord. The Persian army has returned from the Lost Sands. If there is a threat, then they'll surely be defeated by our army."

"I am aware of that. Thank you, Bator. I just want to know who has the audacity to challenge the Persian Empire." Cambyses snapped his fingers and closed his eyes, waving Bator off. "You may go." The king watched as the new Magus fled the room hastily, and he exhaled a breath of warm air, tapping the back of his head gently against his throne. Now, what would he do about Ahriman? The god was becoming uncontrollable. At the rate things were going, Ahriman would deem Cambyses useless and would kill him. This could've been Zahir's plan from the very beginning, to use Cambyses to give him the resources he would need to claim Ahriman's power. And now that Cambyses had fulfilled his role, he was no longer needed. The king shut his eyes. Things were not going as planned.

***

Ramses led his wife and child down into the Royal Jail, entering the dark hallway of the prison. Shadows crept along the walls and torches illuminated the corridor of the jail, revealing rows of cells on both sides of the hallway. Kira stumbled down the stairway after Ramses and his family, quite puzzled as to why they were down here. She was pretty sure that the Royal Jail would just lead to a dead end. But the Magus simply followed Ramses, expecting that he knew what he was doing.

The cells were stuffed with starved political dissidents of Cambyses. They didn't even lift their heads when they saw Ramses' family walking in the hallways. Instead, they stared blankly at the ground as if they were all lifeless undead. Their eyes reflected hopelessness and dismay, the life torn from the distraught prisoners.

"Where are we going?" Kira whispered, listening to Persian guards hastily dash by in the corridor above them. "We're sitting ducks here!"

Ramses pressed his index finger to his lips and shushed Kira. The mage frowned for a moment but soon saw that the Persian Magus was making his way to the far end of the hallway of the jail. Ramses extended his hand outward and there was a creaking noise as the bars of one of the cells suddenly forcefully pried apart, revealing a skinny opening. Ramses squeezed himself through the opening and nodded for his family to follow him.

Kira wasn't exactly sure what the man was doing but she followed Ramses' wife and child through the opening and into the only empty cell in the Royal Jail. She watched as Ramses placed his palm to the cold stone wall of the cell. The moment his palm touched the stone, the wall groaned and collapsed in a heap, revealing a small stairway that descended into pitch-black darkness.

"You have a staff, right? Light the way," Ramses said with a nod, indicating that Kira should go first. When he saw that the Luxas mage was hesitant he reassured her that it would be safe. "Only certain Magi are able to unlock this opening. Trust me, there's nothing down there. We need to hurry through."

"Daddy, I'm scared," Ramses' young son whimpered, wiping his face with the sleeve of his golden linen shirt. The child had black hair in a bowl haircut and couldn't have been older than six.

"There's nothing to be scared about, Riza. I am here to protect you no matter what," Ramses promised with a genuine smile. He got down on his knee so that his head was level with his son's. He patted Riza's head gently and smiled. "Just stay close to Mommy. When she tells you to, close your eyes. You can do that, right?"

"Yes," Riza said quietly.

"Alright," Ramses winked at his son and stood up, nodding to his wife. He turned back to Kira. "Let's go."

Kira's wooden staff illuminated the way with a gleaming white light that beamed from the tip of her weapon. Descending the ominous stairway, she found that they were being led into an underground pathway that traveled underneath the castle. She led Ramses and his family through the dark, silent, pathway for an hour without a single occurrence. No one spoke a single word or made any noise besides the tapping sound of their footsteps.

As Kira walked, she wondered whether or not Tetsu had made it out alright. He was already battling one Magus, which was difficult enough. Surely other Persian soldiers and possibly other Magi would end up leaping into the fray. Would he still be able to leave the battle unscathed as he usually did? Kira's heart pounded and she swallowed hard, knowing that she should trust Tetsu. *He said that he was going to meet us in the city. Has he ever broken a promise, Kira? He'll be fine.* Nevertheless, she couldn't stop worrying. Her heart was racing, for some reason she didn't feel positive about leaving him to fend for himself.

Kira's eyes fluttered when she realized that she had bumped into a metal ladder, completely lost in her own thoughts. She glanced up and saw that the ladder led to a wooden hatch. Where did that opening lead to? Well, wherever it was, it was probably better than standing around in this underground tunnel. The mage gripped her glowing staff in one hand and began to climb up the ladder slowly, careful not to make a lot of noise.

The Luxas Magus pressed her palm to the hatch and pushed it gently, silently opening it. She winced as she was suddenly overwhelmed with the acrid scent of manure. She scrunched up her nose and scanned her surroundings, realizing that she was in a small wooden building filled with dozens of horses and tons of hay. Clambering out of the underground tunnel, Kira helped Ramses' wife and Riza up the ladder. "Where are we?" Kira asked as Ramses climbed up behind his wife.

"A stable, obviously."

Kira narrowed her eyes. "I managed to figure that much out."

Ramses turned and groaned when he saw that there was a young man in the stables with a pitchfork, staring incredulously at the intruders. The stranger was wearing ripped, tattered clothing along with a hat knit from red straw. "Wait…!"

The man pointed his pitchfork at the infiltrators, tiny bits of hay clinging to the metal. His hands were shaking and his lips were quivering as his knees rattled against one another. "W-What are you doing here? How'd you get in here?" the man demanded, his teeth chattering as if he had just taken a dip of a lake of ice water. He didn't exactly sound too confident. Clearly he had never threatened another human before.

Ramses took a step towards the boy. "Look—" The man jabbed out with the pitchfork, nearly stabbing the Magus. Riza cried out and Ramses reached up, touching his throat, retreating several steps backward.

"Don't take another step closer!" the young worker yelled.

Kira gently placed her staff on the floor, her eyes never leaving the man. She held her hands in the air as she slowly inched forward towards the stranger. "We mean no harm, I swear. We just escaped from the Persian castle; the Persians are after Ramses and his family. That's the honest truth."

"R-Ramses? The Magus?" The young worker tilted his head to the side and examined the cloaked man before him. "The infamous mage? But why would the guards be after someone like you? Don't you work directly for the king?"

Ramses shrugged. "I guess Kira doesn't know how to keep her mouth shut." He darted a disapproving glare in Kira's direction. The female mage shrugged. "I don't work for the king anymore. Actually, currently Cambyses wants me dead."

"Speaking about keeping their mouth shut." Kira coughed.

The young farmer lowered his pitchfork and smiled. "Wow. So you're going against the government then?"

"Yes. You don't seem particularly fazed, boy."

"No, I'm excited! This is great, I've been trying to support my grandma but the government has been taxing me like crazy. I can hardly afford to feed myself, let alone buy expensive medicine for my sick gran. I believe that she'll pass soon with the way that things are going," the young man said quietly, lowering his eyes. "Something needs to be done. The poor are only getting poorer, if that's even possible. If you're truly against Cambyses then I'll help you."

Ramses smiled. "Hm, I thought that the underground tunnel led to an abandoned warehouse. They've changed this into a stable?" He looked to the young man. "Do you have somewhere we can stay to lay low? The guards will be searching hard for us for the next couple of days. I have money to compensate you and…."

"Yes, of course," the young man said, motioning for the party to follow him. "Just, er, make sure that you aren't seen. We need to make a quick cross through the main road of Persepolis to get to my place. Guards might spot ya if your heads aren't down. Just stay with me."

Kira and her party followed the young man out of the stable and across a patch of dirt towards a road in Persepolis, which was packed with hundreds of people. The civilians were wearing fine silks with an assortment of various colors. There were also many slaves lumbering around on the streets. Her heart skipped a beat when she spotted Bator sprinting down the street with a squadron of guards, barreling their way through the crowds of Persians.

"What's your name again?" Kira asked the young man.

"It's Cassim," the farmer said.

"Right," Kira looked to Bator, who was noticed by practically everyone in the area. "That man is going to recognize us. We need to—"

"I've got it," Ramses said, snapping his fingers. In an instant, the entire party became invisible. To the ordinary eye, Cassim was standing there on the side of the road alone. Ramses dropped his tone to a whisper. "Stay perfectly still until the Magus passes."

Bator was dashing through the road on his way to leave the city, his eyes trained before him. Suddenly, he sniffed the air and came to an abrupt stop, halting right in front of Cassim. The Magus held up his hand and his guards stopped at his side as he eyed the innocent farmer boy for a moment. He caught a slight whiff of magic in the air. "Could that be Ramses?" he murmured aloud. "They're nearby."

Kira felt a bead of sweat forming on her brow and she swallowed lightly, watching Cassim. The young man had a staid look on his face and bowed his head in respect to Bator. The Magus paid the young farmer no attention. He seemed unable to pinpoint where he was sensing the magic.

"Bah! I have other matters to attend to. Guards, start by searching this area for Ramses. I have to make my leave," Bator grumbled and continued to trudge down the street. The guards scattered about, beginning their search for Ramses and his family.

Cassim exhaled, as if he had just been holding his breath. "Alright, let's get out of here. I'm feeling far too nervous. Quickly, follow me." The invisibility spell faded, but guards had already left the area to search nearby homes. It was easy for the group to melt into the massive crowd of Persians that occupied the streets.

Kira weaved through the crowd, keeping her eye on Cassim and his giant pitchfork, afraid that she might get lost in such a populated city. Within five minutes, they had arrived at a small hut that looked like it could house three people, at the most. The rickety old building hardly looked stable, and the wood was moldy. Not to mention that the roof was made of straw. The hut looked like a giant pile of kindling.

"It ain't much, but it's home," Cassim said as he opened the door. The farmer's home had a total of three rooms. There was one bedroom, one living room and one bathroom. The bathroom was a hole in the ground and it stank of excrement, just like the stable. There was a basin filled with water and a couple of leaves next to the hole. The common space was an empty room, with no furniture. The bedroom consisted of a hard bed that looked like it was a plank of wood with multiple blankets to cushion its hardness. A mat was placed on the ground beside the bed where Cassim slept. On the "bed" was Cassim's grandmother, an old, weary, woman who looked as blanched as a ghost.

The decrepit woman's face was wrinkled from old age and she seemed extremely frail. She raised her hand as Cassim entered the house and her entire arm was trembling. Kira thought that she was convulsing, judging by how much she was shaking. Sweat was racing down her face as if she were outside in the baking hot sun, and she wore some ragged clothing that looked like it hadn't been washed in months. Her clothes had apparently once been white, but were so caked in dirt and grime that they looked brown.

Kira rushed to the grandmother's side immediately. "By the gods, you weren't kidding when you said your grandmother was sick." The Magus reached out and touched the elderly woman's forehead. "She's got a raging fever and several other symptoms of illness as well. Ear infection too by the looks of it. She's weak. Very weak."

"I know," Cassim said softly. "I don't have the money to buy medicine to treat her. Eighty percent of my earnings go straight to the government. The rest are spent on food and medicine. But the medicine I can afford can only ease the pain. It won't cure the illness. I don't know what to do…."

"We can help," Kira said. "We can probably afford the medicine your grandma needs. Ramses, you can sell some of that jewelry of yours to get some spare change, right?"

Ramses looked at the gleaming rings on his fingers and sighed. "Yeah."

"Alright. We'll go to the market and grab the medicine once things calm down," Kira said with a smile at Cassim. "Don't worry, we'll help you out. Thanks for letting us hide here."

"No, thank you so much for being willing to help my grandmother," Cassim said with a lively grin.

"Hey Daddy, isn't that the guy who wanted to save us?" Riza said, pointing through the bedroom window.

Ramses looked at where his son was pointing and spotted a piece of paper slapped right onto the window of Cassim's house. It must've been blown off one of the city's buildings. The Magus frowned as he examined the drawing. An execution? His eyes widened as he read the headline. "Tetsu Hayashi … to be executed tomorrow at noon?"

***

Days of riding on the bulls across the Lost Sands had gone by. Ares sat on the ground, watching the night sky silently with Yuu, Mithra, and Aleysha. The god of war sighed, missing Amon's company. The moon shined its glistening light upon the party and the stars glowed brighter than Ares had ever seen them before. But they did not make him smile.

Aleysha noticed that Ares hadn't really shown any expression in days. In fact, he almost seemed in a daze as if his mind was elsewhere.

"You know," Mithra said, breaking the silence. "I haven't met many gods like you, Ares. You're a lot different than your family's last god of war."

"My family?"

"Ah, yes," Mithra said. "You see, gods are categorized into specific families. Each family is worshipped by different civilizations around the world. Your family, Hellas, is worshipped by an eastern country on Dastia as well as another continent somewhere in this world. You're quite spread out, I've heard."

"What was the last god of war like? From my family, I mean."

"Well, the last Ares was quite brutal. He was a sadistic fellow, always wanting to pick fights with others and always out pissing off the other gods. Not to mention he was cocky as hell; that led to his downfall. But he was strong, courageous, and very powerful, much like you, I suppose. Though, I don't think he ever got as close to his Guardians as you have. I don't know many gods who have genuine attachments to their Guardians. After all, you have so many, don't you? Why not just summon another?"

Ares said nothing.

"Wait, you can summon more Guardians? I thought Amon was your only one." Aleysha frowned, tilting her head to the side in puzzlement.

"Guardians are merely pawns of gods that are used and sacrificed. The fact your rock golem has 'died' should not bother you. I mean—"

"*Stop talking about Amon like that,*" Ares growled, shooting Mithra a hostile glare that silenced the god instantly. "He was my friend. Not just some pawn that I could just *use* to accomplish my desires. I don't care about how you gods utilize your Guardians, but I won't abuse mine." He ran a hand through his blonde hair and sighed. "Amon has been there for me from the very beginning. He was my protector. He can't be replaced."

Mithra raised an eyebrow. "That doesn't explain why you won't use your Guardians for other reasons such as travel. The last Ares had a chariot pulled by four flaming horses that can get you anywhere you want within the hour. Why would you rather travel there with my bulls than quickly get there on your chariot? Inefficiency, that's what it is."

Ares lowered his eyes and sighed. "The idea of making something else *subordinate* to me just makes me feel uneasy. It reminds me too much of my life before I became a god. I don't want to use Guardians to complete tasks for me. I'll do them myself."

"Soon you'll have to learn that you can't do everything by yourself, Ares. Your Guardians exist to serve you," Mithra murmured, scoffing. "You're going to live a dangerous life if you don't use your Guardians. After all, gods are mortal on this world. We can be killed just like any other living thing on this planet."

Ares nodded.

"In Heaven, the gods have their maximum amount of power as well as their immortality. There they are able to grant wishes that worshippers pray for and can make miracles happen. However, once they leave Heaven, their powers are suppressed to some extent and they become mortal. Your Guardians exist so that they can help you, in your weakened state, to combat the natural evils of this world. Ahriman will surely use his own Guardians to fight you. You can't hope to simply fight him on your own."

"You're right. I've got you with me." Ares smirked. "I understand what you're saying, Mithra. I'll use my Guardians if things get dire. But for now I don't want to risk anyone else's life. Yuu and Aleysha, the two of you will not be coming with us into Persepolis to confront Ahriman."

"What?" Aleysha exclaimed, leaning forward in disbelief.

"This is my fight as much as it is yours, Darien," Yuu snapped.

"There's no way that I'm going to let you and Mithra go in there alone to fight that bastard! He was my mentor. I need to be there to help you defeat him!"

"I agree with Ares," Mithra said, receiving glares from both Aleysha and Yuu. "Just because you're a demigod, Aleysha, does not mean that you will be able to fight on the level of a god as powerful as Ahriman. You'll be killed nearly instantly. The only reason that you aren't dead now is because Ares' Guardian protected you. So count yourself lucky. As for you," the Persian god of war spoke to Yuu, "you're a human with magical capabilities. But your magic pool is nothing in comparison to Ahriman's. It's like comparing a puddle to an ocean. He'd crush you in an instant. Instead of throwing away your life, you could put it to use doing something else."

"Like what?" Yuu grumbled.

"I don't know, I haven't thought that far yet," Mithra said, scratching his neck.

"You honestly expect for us to just sit back while you are battling a god of darkness! The result of that battle decides the fate of Dastia, and I don't intend to sit back and—" Yuu began but his eyes narrowed when he received a glare from Ares. He lowered his gaze and clenched his jaw.

Ares stood up and began to walk away from the party, climbing a sand dune. His head was pounding as he reached the peak of the hill of sand. The god glanced up at the twinkling stars that flashed their tiny lights across the sea of darkness in the sky. He looked over his shoulder and saw that Yuu was still arguing with Mithra. "I don't want to lose anyone else, Amon," Ares spoke gently to the cool night breeze. "I know they're good friends because they want to help but … I'd never forgive myself if something happened to them. Tomorrow, I know that if Aleysha and Yuu go into Persepolis I won't be able to protect them if I'm against someone like Ahriman." The boy reached up and grabbed a fistful of his hair and squeezed. "What do I do?"

"You need to trust us," Aleysha said, walking from behind Ares. "This isn't just your fight, you know."

Ares glanced at Aleysha over his shoulder and said nothing. He turned back to gazing at the gleaming stars that glittered like diamonds in the sky.

Aleysha reached up and touched her necklace, a tiny cross that rested just above her breast. "You have one too, don't you? A necklace, I mean. Mine is to remind me of the past, even though it's a painful and distant memory. Although I'd love to just forget my painful memories, I know that it's impossible to run from the past. Eventually, it'll just reveal itself again."

Ares tore his gaze from the sky and looked down at the golden necklace that dangled from his neck. He bit his lower lip. His mother had given him this for his fifteenth birthday. She said that whenever he wore the necklace, he would become fearless. The boy reached up and touched the hard metal, his fingers tracing around the medallion's perimeter. *Forget that the past ever happened. I've already tried. But no matter what … I can't convince myself to throw this necklace away. Why is that?* Ares licked his lip and closed his eyes, squeezing the golden necklace in his hand. *I'm not Darien anymore, right? That old life is gone now.*

"Is that why you still have your necklace too?" Aleysha asked.

Ares ignored the question. He exhaled through his nose and slowly opened his eyes. "Why do you want to forget?"

Aleysha's eyebrows went up in surprise, not expecting such a question from Ares. But she smiled and stepped beside the young boy. "My real dad is a god and I've always wanted to meet him, you know. But he's never really been there since I was a little kid. When I was seven, I lived in a village to the east, outside of the Lost Sands. I was living with my mom, my uncle, and my grandma at the time. It was a pretty peaceful lifestyle actually. Until a party of raiders stormed into our village."

Ares' shoulders stiffened and he looked away.

"My uncle died so that my mother and I could escape. My grandma was mercilessly killed before my eyes, for the raiders didn't even think about sparing an old woman's life. You wouldn't really understand how terrible it was that they just butchered her like that; she was the kindest woman that I've ever known. She didn't deserve to die. No one in that village did. My mother and I were lucky to have escaped the burning village alive." Aleysha took a deep breath. "My grandma's fate is the reason that I decided that I would spare those who surrendered themselves to me."

Ares' lower lip quivered and he wiped the moistness that appeared in his sky-blue eyes. He turned to Aleysha, eyeing the cross necklace on her chest. It was the same one that he had seen in her bag weeks ago, in that cave in the Lost Sands. "Why is it that you don't want to forget such a horrific memory?"

Aleysha smiled warmly. "Because I learned important things on that day that changed my life forever. I learned about the cruelty of the world, the meaning of sacrifice, and the importance of mercy. Besides, forgetting all about the past would mean that I would have to forget all the good memories that my uncle, my grandma, and I all shared." She tilted her head to the side. "When I think of my deceased family, I like to remind myself all of the great times we had together before it was their time to pass."

Ares' eyes widened and he stared at Aleysha, his mouth slightly open in surprise. *Think about the good memories?* He touched his necklace once more and suddenly countless, priceless memories rushed through his head. Birthday celebrations, the first time he had learned to ride a horse with his father, the first time his father had taught him to joust, the first book he had read with his mother … the list went on. Ares glanced away from Aleysha, tears gleaming in his eyes.

The boy suddenly turned and began to walk away from Aleysha, heading down the sand dune and back towards the camp. "I'm going to sleep," he said quietly.

***

"That Persian god of war is absolutely right, you know," the original Ares grumbled, sitting in a world of absolute blackness with his arms folded. His legs were crossed over each other as he eyed Darien. "You have an enormous amount of power at your disposal: your Guardians. Yet you completely neglect it just because you're afraid of responsibility. You're afraid of loss. They're *tools*. Stop being an idiot."

"Guardians are not tools," Darien growled at Ares. He looked around and saw that everywhere he looked there was just nothingness. He was stuck in some type of a void. Was this a dream? "No matter what you say you won't change my mind."

Ares scoffed, staring at Darien. "What is it that makes you say that? Is it that you hate getting your friends involved? It makes sense. After all, every time someone's gotten involved in your quarrels they end up hurt, or even killed. Yuu, Tetsu, Amon, Aleysha — nearly all your greatest companions have been severely scarred by your very existence. It would probably be better if you just left them out of your life, huh?" The ancient god of war spun a dagger on the tip of his index finger, the blade red as blood. "Maybe then they'd have some peace in their lives."

Darien said nothing.

"Well, that's not the reason that I've come to talk to you tonight, Darien," Ares said with a sly smirk. He flipped his dagger and caught it by the hilt, pushing himself to his feet so that he towered over the young Persian prince. "I've come to say goodbye."

"What was that?" Darien growled, glaring into Ares' beastly dark orange eyes.

Ares grinned wickedly. "Tomorrow is the day when you confront Cambyses and Ahriman. The very moment that you feel bloodlust you will lose complete control over yourself, and I will take over. You've already lost your mind to me twice and this third time is the last. You're weak, Darien. Do you know why that is? You're too human.

"Humans are weak, spineless, creatures that submit far too easily to fear. I know what your fear is, Darien. Responsibility, isn't that it? You may be an almighty god with all of the power in the world in the palm of his hand, but you're still a coward. You've been running from the very start. Dashing away from the responsibility that you had to the Persian Empire. Why did you not return to Persepolis the moment that you claimed my power in the Lost Sands five years ago? It's obvious! You're afraid that you don't have what it takes to lead this country's people. And you're completely right, you don't."

Darien lowered his eyes, biting his lower lip.

"Ra was a fool to choose you, a soft child, to be the heir to my power. Your compassion and childishness are what will hold you back from being a great god. But it's fine, because I know that starting tomorrow I will take the reins once again as Hellas' God of War!" Ares exclaimed with gleaming eyes and a wide grin, revealing his razor-sharp white teeth. "The moment that you feel even the slightest hint of bloodlust, the very second that you lose yourself in the heat of battle, I will eradicate you, Darien. And you will cease to be Ares."

Darien chuckled softly. What began as a mere giggle then transformed into loud, uncontrollable, laughter. Ares stared at the boy, stunned, his eyebrows going up in confusion.

"Wow, I didn't know that the original barbaric god of war was capable of such great analysis!" Darien held his stomach, still laughing. He sniffed. "Phew, that's a riot! But I already made a promise that I wouldn't transform again. I don't intend to lose myself tomorrow. I'll never murder someone just for the sake of killing them."

"Bloodlust isn't something that you can simply control, Persian," Ares snarled.

"Well, I'll control it," Darien snapped. "You say I can't? I will. And when I gaze at the beautiful sunset at the end of tomorrow with the feeling of victory gleaming in my heart, I'll return to this dark oblivion just to tell you to your face that I've won. Tomorrow, if you want to play tug-of-war for control of my body while I'm fighting, then so be it. After what happened in the Lost Sands five years ago … after I got Tetsu hurt outside Yuusus … I'll never lose sight of who I really am ever again! So sit back down, Ares. I'm your new god of war."

Battle of Gods

The sun shined down on the hot sand of the scorching desert. Ares stood upon a sand dune, gazing across a stretch of flat land that consisted entirely of dirt. In the far-off distance were the great walls of Persepolis. Mithra stood next to the young god, his hands on his hips as he pursed his lips at the sight of the grand city. "It's been centuries since I was last here. I have to tell you, the city has improved greatly from what it originally was," Mithra said, trying to make conversation. When he saw that Ares wasn't going to respond, he sighed. "What's our plan to defeat Ahriman? None of my plans will work if we don't utilize our Guardians to their full potential. Expect that Ahriman knows that we're coming. Our magical auras are much more potent because we're gods. He can sense us from a mile away."

Ares looked over his shoulder at Aleysha and Yuu, who both slept silently on mats at the bottom of the sand dune. He snapped his fingers and a small, black puppy popped its head through the sand. The tiny animal whimpered and clawed its way out of the ground and then jumped up playfully before Ares, who smiled. "Hey there, little guy," he said, squatting down and patting the puppy's head gently, stroking just behind the ears. "I'm going to need you to stay with my two friends, alright? I want you to make sure that they don't come after us. Can you do that, buddy?"

Mithra raised an eyebrow. "I thought that you weren't going to use your Guardians."

"I'm not going to risk their lives," Ares said. "This little guy is just here to make sure that Aleysha and Yuu don't get hurt. As for our plans, I propose that we just head to the front gates and then move from there." Ares gazed out across the desert plains, his eyes lowering. A gentle breeze blew against his face and he sighed. He couldn't get the original god of war's words out of his mind. He was weak, afraid to face the responsibility that he had as Persia's prince. He was afraid to lose others, which was why he had always pushed away Aleysha and refused to use his Guardians. And yet, he knew that he would have to conquer both fears in order to move forward.

Face the responsibility you have to Persia's people. Allow your friends to fight this battle by your side. You don't have to do everything on your own anymore.

Ares looked over his shoulder at Mithra. *Guardians are your greatest weapons and tools to utilize in battle.* Amon had said the same thing five years ago when Ares had first learned how to summon his Guardians during his training in the Lost Sands. *They are forever loyal to you and will do anything to win your approval, Ares.*

Tools. Weapons. Ares didn't want his subordinates to be called *things.* He wanted to consider them as his companions. Was this battle against Ahriman winnable without his Guardians? Probably not. An image of Amon's frozen body flashed through Ares' mind and the god bit his lower lip. *I don't want to lose any more than I already have. But in order to save the lives of many others, I'll have to make the sacrifice! These Guardians can help me save more people than if I was alone.* Ares extended his hand outward to the stretching sands before him. "You know what, I've changed my mind."

Mithra blinked, confused. "Huh? About what?"

"Everything." Suddenly an explosion of fire roared from the heavens and smashed into the ground at the bottom of the sand dune that Ares stood upon. Small fires swept outward, revealing a black chariot pulled by four warhorses that had glowing, red demonic eyes and coats the color of night. Bright flames flickered on the manes of the horses, making these steeds seem like they came straight from the depths of hell. Ares' spear materialized in his hand, and he gripped his weapon as he leapt from the sand dune and landed beside the chariot, glancing up to Mithra. "This isn't the time for me to be thinking about myself and what I want. So let's get this over with and stop Ahriman before any more innocent people die."

***

In the distance, invisible to the eyes of everyone but Darien, was the original God of War, Ares. The middle-aged man smirked, his arms folded as he watched Mithra and Darien mount the flaming chariot and shoot forward across the desert sands with a surge of speed, darting towards Persepolis with haste. A trail of flames exploded behind the hellish chariot.

The old Ares rubbed the back of his neck. "He doesn't intend to give up his body that easily, huh? He's willing to do whatever it takes to defeat Ahriman. Even use his Guardians. Looks like he's learning that it's better to fight with others rather than alone. But that doesn't mean that he'll be victorious against Ahriman. The moment that he's weak and defenseless, just barely grasping onto life, that's when I'll step in and take over. It's nice that you're starting to change your ways after our talk, Darien. You're finally confronting the injustice that plagued your life five years ago. But that doesn't mean that you're strong enough to save this continent from the destruction that is about to ensue. Only I am."

***

Tetsu groaned, his eyes slowly cracking open as he stared blankly at the dark ceiling of an empty cell. He glanced down and saw that there were bloody bandages wrapped around the wounds that he'd received while fighting Ahriman. The young man rolled onto his side and heard a clanking sound, looking down to see that his wrists were bound by cuffs. He tried to move his legs and saw that there were shackles on his ankles as well, keeping his movement drastically limited.

The mercenary's head pounded with a raging headache and he winced as he turned to look at the thick metal bars that confined him in this small, empty room. On the other side of those bars was nothing but darkness, an abyss of blackness. He grunted, pushing himself up into a sitting position when he suddenly heard footsteps echoing from the darkness outside of his cell.

A man in fancy clothing strolled out from the shadows into Tetsu's vision — Cambyses. The king was accompanied by two guards that were standing at his side, their weapons sheathed. "It's been a while, Tetsu! When I look at you it's like looking at a ghost. I was under the impression that both you and Darien were dead. Impressive. You two were lucky to survive the Lost Sands."

Tetsu leaned back against the cold wall of his cell as he glared at the king with his glowing red eyes and scoffed. "Darien will be here soon to reclaim what is truly his, false lord."

"Hold your tongue, slave."

"Slave? It's been years since someone's dared to call me that," Tetsu growled. "You think that you're safe just because I'm chained up and you're behind bars? I'll have your head soon, Cambyses. You'll pay for what you've done to Darien, to Persia, and to the rest of Dastia! I'll make sure of that."

Cambyses smirked. "You don't have many chances left, Tetsu. After all, your execution is today." He snapped his fingers and one of the guards opened the door to the cell and placed a platter of food on the floor of the cell. On the tin plate was a giant, juicy steak, grapes, and a full loaf of bread. "This is your last meal, Hayashi clansman. I figured that a friend of my nephew's at least deserves a full stomach before he's decapitated in public. Don't you think so?"

Tetsu gritted his teeth, lowering his head. Then a small smile cracked across his lips. He sprang forward, swinging his legs outward to sweep the first soldier cleanly off his feet. The man slammed to the ground hard, the wind driven from his lungs. But Tetsu wasn't going to give him a second to get his breath back. The mercenary brought his hands crashing downward on the man's face, breaking the soldier's nose with a heavy crack. Turning to find the second soldier rushing into the cell, Tetsu kicked off the ground and sent himself flying forward like a bullet. He bashed his head into the second guard's gut, sending the Persian staggering backward in pain.

Tetsu held out his hands and caught himself before he struck the ground, shifting his body to a handstand. He clamped his ankles on both sides of the surprised Persian guard's head and swung his body downward, flipping the man to the ground in a fluent motion. The soldier hit the floor hard, reaching for his sheathed sword, but Tetsu was already upon him. The mercenary leapt on the man's back and slung the chain on his handcuffs over the man's head and yanked backward, choking the soldier. The silver metal dug into the Persian's throat and he gasped, clawing at his own neck in a desperate attempt to remove the chain but Tetsu relentlessly pulled back, his eyes filled with bloodlust.

Cambyses watched from outside of the cage, unsurprised. He'd expected this. When his final guard collapsed in a heap at Tetsu's feet, he smiled. "My, my. What an aggressive fellow you are." There was a blur of speed and suddenly Tetsu was thrown across the room, slamming hard into the wall with tremendous force. The mercenary gasped, sliding to the ground, his eyes clamped shut as pain exploded through his back. Cambyses held out the Sands of Time, dangling the hourglass before Tetsu's eyes. "How troublesome."

Tetsu winced and watched helplessly as the king drove a heavy kick into his stomach, doubling the mercenary over in agony. Tears glistened in Tetsu's eyes from the pain and he coughed, saliva splattering on the cell floor. He grabbed his aching gut, listening to the door of the cell slam shut.

"I believe Darien is finally coming, after five years, to stop me," Cambyses said, looking at the unconscious guards in Tetsu's cell. "Thank you for the artifact, Tetsu. I'll use it to silence the god of war that has been giving me so much trouble. Oh, and enjoy your final meal."

***

Ares' flaming chariot slowed to a stop before the gigantic walls of Persepolis. Hundreds of Persian archers had nocked their bows and were pointing arrows down at the two gods halted outside of the gates of Persia's capital. Ares stepped off of the chariot, landing on the burning sand. He looked up at the line of archers above him. "It is I, Darien, your prince. Let me into the city!"

The archers, unconvinced, kept their weapons trained on the god. However, some of them did recognize the prince as Darien. He looked exactly the same as he had five years before. Such an occurrence was not possible. Regardless, some archers began to lower their bows, unsure if they should be threatening the unknown outsiders.

"Do not listen to his lies," Ahriman's seething voice echoed in the minds of everyone on the wall.

The archers yelped, startled and frightened by the mysterious voice that boomed in their minds. Some dropped their bows and clamped their hands over their ears, screaming in a futile attempt to try and drown out Ahriman's voice.

Mithra dismounted the chariot, unsheathing his golden sword, his eyes scanning the walls of Persepolis for any sign of the Persian god of darkness. "Show yourself, Ahriman! We have come here to cleanse this world of your existence."

"Come and get me then, gods of war!" Ahriman's voice roared.

Mithra leapt off of the ground and punched the fortified wall of Persepolis with a frightening crack of his fist. There was a massive explosion as pieces of stone and metal went flying into the air.

Archers fell around Ares and the boy stared, impressed. The Persian god bolted through the gaping opening in the wall that he had created, storming into the city of frightened civilians.

Ares leapt back onto his chariot and yanked the reins on his horses, watching as the flaming war steeds bolted forward and leapt through the opening in Persepolis's wall, dragging the chariot behind them. The boy gripped the railings of the chariot to balance himself, his hands squeezing the metal tightly. The wagon rocked abruptly when it landed harshly on the ground and Ares swallowed hard, realizing that he was racing through the main road of Persepolis. Pedestrians were leaping out of the way in a desperate attempt to escape the flaming horses' path. "Out of the way!" Ares boomed, turning to see that Mithra had summoned a colossal bull that was the size of a mammoth. The creature was trampling over everything in its path and smashing through any Persian buildings in its way, bolting straight for the castle in far distance.

Ares winced. The determined look in Mithra's eyes said that he was willing to do anything to defeat Ahriman. Then again, a lot was at stake here. More than just the few lives that Mithra was trampling over. Though, Ares wished that the Persian god were less destructive in the way he was traveling. "Do you know where he is?"

"He's in the throne room!" Mithra yelled to Ares, smashing through a line of Persian soldiers with his massive bull. "I can feel his aura there," he growled.

Ares suddenly glanced up and saw a beam of purple energy descending on him. He pulled the reins on his chariot, yanking the horses to make a hard right. The wagon skidded as the magical beam struck the earth next to his chariot, creating a huge explosion of magic that swept outward and engulfed the street in destruction. Ares' chariot slowed to a stop and he leapt onto the ground, finding two men standing in the center of the road, blocking the way. Magi. "I'll go on ahead!" Mithra shouted. "You handle those small-fry!" Soon the Persian god was out of view as he barreled through the city straight for the castle. Nothing was going to stop him from getting to Ahriman.

Unfortunately for Ares, he was stuck facing these two intimidating Magi. One was holding two scythes that were connected together by a chain, eying Ares with a determined gleam in his eyes. The other Magus looked quite odd, wielding only an ordinary broadsword as he trudged forward towards the god of war. *These guys look like more than just small fry.*

"Sahad, so this is the god of war! Do you think his squeals of pain sound as amusing as the others?" the man with the sword said, a crazed look in his eyes. He licked his lips as if he were about to devour a delicious meal.

Sahad whipped his chain scythe through the air, ripping the ground around him. He smirked as he slashed a Persian slave across the back by accident. The man screamed and collapsed to the ground, blood gushing from his wound. But Sahad didn't seem the least bit concerned. "I don't know, Jafaar. Let's find out."

Ares winced. This was bad. There were so many civilians around them. There was no doubt that many innocent lives were about to get caught up in this battle. He gripped his spear tightly in his hands and pointed it at the two Magi before him. Heartless. These Magi were heartless warriors that preyed on the weak. It was up to Ares to bring justice upon them. The god of war grunted as he shot forward with a surge of speed, appearing right in front of Sahad in an instant.

The Magus's eyes widened when he witnessed Ares' supernatural speed. He crossed his arms in front of himself, blocking a heavy kick from Ares. The god's blow sent the mage flying backward through an entire building. The structure groaned as it collapsed on top of Sahad, sending a wave of debris and dust sweeping outward.

"Whoa! That's fast!" Jafaar burst out laughing cheerfully. He twirled his sword in an elegant fashion, moving the weapon at such a blinding speed that it was a mere blur to the ordinary eye. He stomped his foot into the ground and suddenly the earth shifted, cracking beneath the Magus's feet. A spike of rock tore from the earth beneath Ares, smashing into his stomach. The god was launched backwards, smashing through several buildings, causing the structures to collapse instantly. Jafaar raised his sword and licked his blade gently, giggling maniacally. "But you aren't fast enough to match the two of us, god."

Ares groaned, his head spinning as he gazed up at the blue sky. He leaned forward and saw that Persian civilians were scattering in all directions, screaming in terror as buildings collapsed around them. This was utter chaos; too many people were getting caught up in their battle! He clutched his spear and pushed himself to his feet, glaring at Jafaar. His eyes then flitted to Sahad, who was walking from the ruins of a collapsed building, brushing some dust off his expensive clothing. He dragged his chain scythe on the ground behind him and smirked as he looked at Ares. "Man, that tickled."

Ares clenched his teeth, knowing how strong Magi were. These guys weren't just some random chumps. They were highly trained and extremely powerful. He wouldn't be able to defeat the two of them if he was holding back. He glanced around him at the scattering civilians were scampered away in all directions. But how was he going to minimize the collateral damage from the battle?

***

"This plan is so dumb," Ramses murmured, paying for the bag of medicine that Kira would need to heal Cassim's grandmother. His hood was pulled tightly over the top of his head so that the cowl covered his facial features. Luckily, the merchant only cared for his coin rather than whose money it was. "Tetsu's execution is going to be heavily guarded. It might be a trap that Cambyses's set up. If we all go there we could be killed."

"We're not going to leave him to die if that's what you mean," Kira snapped, snatching the paper bag from Ramses. The young woman also was wearing a cloak that she had borrowed from Cassim, who was standing next to her in Persepolis's marketplace. The plaza was a flat open area of dirt where merchants set up tables, tents, buildings, and stands and sold their products. "After all, Tetsu is the reason that we got away. He's the reason your family is still alive."

Ramses scoffed but said nothing.

"Do you at least know where the execution will be held?" Kira asked the Persian Magus.

"District Four, the middle class district," Ramses said. "The lower class and upper class gather together to watch executions. It's a pastime for everyone in Persepolis. Except my family and I, that is. I've never really been to one."

"We only have an hour before the execution starts. We need a plan!" Kira exclaimed, handing Cassim the bag of medicine. "Here, take this to your grandma and have her take two of the pills with some water. Make sure that she stays hydrated until I get back." The mage watched as Cassim nodded and left, rushing back in the direction of his home. "It might be difficult, Ramses. But I know that if either of us had switched roles with Tetsu, he'd come and save us. We can't just leave him to die."

Ramses shrugged, beginning to walk in the direction of District Four, strolling down a street that left the marketplace. He slid his hands into his pockets. "Alright, I have an idea. I'll explain it to you on the way."

***

A bag was clamped over Tetsu's head, making the air inside thick and warm. His breath was heavy as he was led through the city streets in a metal cage on a wagon pulled by three horses. His head was lowered as he felt the juices of thrown fruit splatter at his feet. Insults tore through the air, ripping at his ears. He licked his chapped lips and swallowed hard, rubbing his thumbs against each other as he sat in the wagon, enduring the waves of verbal abuse that were thrown at him.

"Die along with the rest of your accursed clan!"

"Filthy demonic blood, I can't wait to see your head roll!"

"Death to the Hayashi!"

Tetsu clenched his jaw. How had things become like this? Why did these people hate him so? The chains on his handcuffs jingled as the cart slowed to a stop and suddenly the bag on his head was torn off, revealing the blinding light of the afternoon sun. He squinted as he was pulled to his feet and thrown out of the cage and onto the dirt street. The prisoner grunted, glancing upward to see mobs of angry people, suppressed by guards, surrounding him. Their insults kept coming. Their rage radiated like an aura and Tetsu's heart raced as he was shoved forward.

Three Persian soldiers, fully armed, were right in front of him, leading him through the crowds of people to a stage where an executioner stood. The executioner had a heavy, bloodied axe, and wore a red mask that was painted with the face of a demon, indicating that everyone that he executed went straight to hell. He was heavily built and extremely stout, his chest puffed out as he showed off his rippling muscles to the crowd.

Tetsu looked around him at the endless sea of Persians that had come to witness his death. All of these people had come to see him die? He watched as a child raced through the lines of Persian guards and rushed forward to Tetsu, driving a kick straight into his shin. The Hayashi clansman winced, leaning forward and grunting, before the guards quickly yanked the young child back. The kid couldn't have been older than seven.

"Burn in hell!" the child screamed.

Tetsu stared at the youth, his hands balling into fists that trembled with uncontrollable rage. But he did nothing. *Cambyses … how much have you brainwashed your people?* He grunted as he was shoved forward once more towards the stage.

Slowly climbing up the steps that led up to the stage, Tetsu felt chills tingling through his skin. He didn't want to die. This was too soon! His heart pounded and his mouth was dry. His eyes darted around in a desperate attempt to find something that could save him. A weapon, something to break these chains, Ares, something! Someone! His eyes lowered as he stood wearily next to the executioner. *Anyone....*

"This man, Tetsu Hayashi, has been condemned to death for attempting to assassinate King Cambyses and High Magus Zahir. He is also a member of the Hayashi clan and according to the Demonic Cleansing Act enacted by Cambyses, the Persian government, and the Heaven's Court, all members of the Hayashi clan are to be exterminated immediately for they are a plague to society and to all mankind. Prepare to return to hell, demon."

Tetsu was forced onto his knees and he gasped, breathing faster as sweat raced down his face. The executioner tapped the cold steel of his axe against the back of Tetsu's neck, ready to wind up and decapitate the prisoner. *So this is it, huh.* He scanned the crowd and blinked when he saw sudden movement shoving through the sea of people. It was Kira! She smiled and put her hands over her eyes as she held her staff high into the air.

Tetsu acted immediately, shutting his eyes as a bright light radiated from the staff, expanding outward and filling the entire crowd with a blinding flash. Small blots of light were still flashing before Tetsu's eyes despite the fact he had closed his eyes and he turned to find the executioner lying dead beside him in a pool of his own blood. He glanced up and saw that Ramses was standing next to him, helping the prisoner to his feet. "We've got you just in time, huh?" Ramses said with a small smile, unsheathing his sword at his side. "Let me break those chains—"

Suddenly, a horn boomed through the area, and hundreds of Persian soldiers flooded into the plaza from the surrounding buildings. Archers took their positions on the rooftops, nocking their arrows and aiming them straight at Ramses and Tetsu. Meanwhile, dozens of armed foot soldiers advanced towards the stage while the crowd of Persian spectators scattered, fleeing at the sight of brandished weapons.

"Well, damn," Ramses said with a nervous chuckle, unsure of what to do. "I can't say that I didn't see this one coming. A trap."

Cambyses was standing on top of a building in the distance with several archers and soldiers surrounding him. He burst out laughing at the sight of Ramses and Tetsu. "Do you have a plan to escape this one, Ramses? I've got thousands of Persian soldiers watching every inch of the surrounding streets. No matter what you do, no matter what you try, your fate is sealed. There is no escape this time." The king tossed the Sands of Time into the air and caught it, wearing a sly smirk on his face. "Kill them both," he said, pointing to Kira, who was amongst the fleeing crowd. "Oh, and dispatch the girl too. No matter what it takes. You're free to fire into crowd if you like."

"You bastard!" Tetsu barked, tugging at his cuffs as if he could break them. They didn't budge, as expected. "Don't you care for your own people's lives?"

"Care for them? Of course, I do. They're the reason I'm so affluent, aren't they? They're the reason that this kingdom is thriving with wealth. They're the ones that drive this empire," Cambyses said with a sly smile. "But a few sacrifices here and there are fine. Unlike me, everyone here is expendable."

Tetsu's face turned red with rage. "I can't wait until I get my hands around your throat, you wretched old man!"

"Throw all the insults you want," Cambyses called. "That won't change your fate. Fire when—" He was interrupted when he suddenly saw Bator at his side. The man seemed frantic, his hands jittering and his face pale. "Bator? What is it? Have you returned from your mission already? I expected you to at least be a couple days…."

"They're here already!" Bator screamed. "Thousands of them! An army that could easily topple the city!"

Cambyses frowned. "Who is?"

"Some king from the east has assembled an army using all of the soldiers of the eastern nations of Dastia! They've come to destroy Persia, milord. B-But … they're already a few miles away from the capital! They've destroyed the outside patrolling units and are advancing on the city!"

"How is that possible? We would've been notified…."

"Milord, they came from the Lost Sands. All of them, unscathed!" Bator exclaimed.

Cambyses swore under his breath. "How is that possible? Assemble my military generals and make sure that there is a secured perimeter around Persepolis's walls. We will not let those barbarians from the east take our city. Gather the other Magi as well. I'm heading back to the castle." He turned to one of the archers at his side. "Execute these fools immediately. We have other enemies to attend to."

***

Aleysha's eyes fluttered open and she blinked a few times, turning to find that Ares and Mithra had already left. She glanced up and saw that Yuu was standing on a sand dune, gazing at Persepolis in the distance. The noble then knelt down and began to pet a small puppy that was panting at his side.

Aleysha rubbed her eyes as she climbed up the mountain of sand and stopped at Yuu's side. She smiled at the adorable puppy that was at Yuu's side. "Aw! He's so cute! Where did this little guy come from?"

"He's one of Ares' Guardians," Yuu said with a chuckle. "That idiot just went on babbling last night how he wouldn't use his Guardians. Yet, here he is using one to subdue the two of us. A waste of resources, isn't it?"

"Wait, so this puppy is supposed to keep us from going to help?"

The puppy nodded its little head.

Aleysha frowned, folding her arms. "And he can understand me."

"Yep," Yuu said, sighing. He could see that smoke was rising from Persepolis in the distance. There was a battle raging within those walls and he wanted to help. Sitting here and doing nothing while Ares and Mithra were fighting to save the continent was degrading. "Well, little guy," he said to the puppy. "I hope you know that we aren't going to stay here. We're going to go and help."

The small dog growled, its fangs elongating into the size of sharp swords. Its eyes morphed from an adorable blue into a demonic red as its body began to shape shift. Its bones cracked and stretched as the tiny puppy transformed into a massive hound, one that was the size of a horse. Saliva dribbled down its chin and the beast snarled, making Aleysha take a step backward.

Yuu smiled fearlessly at Ares' Guardian. "Look, I understand that you're following orders. But your master is in trouble, you know that, right?"

The beast was silent.

"We want to help him. If we don't, he could die. You know that, right? Your job is to protect your master. So by preventing us from going to aid Ares you're going to put him at even greater risk," Yuu explained. He reached out to the hound and gently patted the creature's wet nose. "There, there. Don't you want to help Ares too?"

Aleysha winced, expecting the monster to bite Yuu's hand off at any moment. Fortunately, the creature didn't.

The beast whimpered, nodding its head gently.

"Alright, because I'm standing here feeling as useless as a doll. Do you feel that way too?" Yuu moved closer, scratching the beast behind the ears and beneath the chin. The Guardian snorted and nodded once more, closing its eyes as it enjoyed Yuu's gentle massage. "So you'll be willing to help us save Ares, right?"

The Guardian pulled away and stuck out its tongue, panting excitedly. *Yes!*

Aleysha exhaled. "Wow, you're pretty good with animals, aren't you?"

Yuu patted the Guardian on the top of the head with a laugh. "Yeah, I spent a lot of time with them as a child. Hey, little guy, you're going to need a name, aren't you?"

Aleysha raised an eyebrow. *Little guy?*

"You've got some pretty sharp teeth, huh? How about Fang?" Yuu said, hugging the hound's neck while smiling broadly. "That seems to fit you."

Aleysha narrowed her eyes and stuck out her lower lip. *What a way to pick a name….*

Fang suddenly turned his attention to the distance and growled, baring his pointy teeth. Aleysha turned to see what the Guardian was looking at and spotted an army of horsemen storming from the Lost Sands in the direction of Persepolis. Her eyes widened when she saw how fast these horsemen were riding. They were galloping at triple, if not quadruple, the speed of any ordinary riders. The hoofs of their horses glowed with a gleaming yellow light that matched the shining color of the sun, and a giant cloud of swirling dust streamed behind the thousands of galloping horsemen.

The leading horseman was upon them within minutes and slowed to a stop as his mount trotted up the sand dune slowly. When the steed refused to climb any higher, the rider dismounted and continued forward on foot. Clearly his mount was frightened of Fang, who snarled at the newcomers. The man was wearing golden plated armor and had a helmet with bronze horns poking from the top. His greaves clanked as he stopped before Yuu, Aleysha, and Fang. He was wearing a blue mask of some demon entity that wore a creepy smile. The stranger reached up and pried off his mask, revealing that he was Alkaios, the king of Luxas. He smiled when he saw Aleysha. "Glad to see that you're still in one piece, Aleysha. Where's Ares?"

"In Persepolis, wreaking havoc," Aleysha said, pointing to the city over her shoulder. "He's with Mithras, another god of war, confronting Ahriman right now. We were actually just about to go and back him up."

"Ah," Alkaios said with a nod to Yuu and Fang. "These are your friends?"

"Yeah! This is Yuu, he's one of Ares' old friends. And this big fella is Fang, he's one of Ares' Guardians," Aleysha introduced, tilting her head slightly. "How did you guys get here so fast? It's only been a week!" She pointed to the vast army of horsemen that were galloping from the Lost Sands. "How did you get all these men across the Lost Sands safely?"

"We received a blessing from a particular god, your father, Ra," Alkaios said. "At least, he claims to be your parent. He said that we were to come and make sure that you're alright because he knew that you were about to dive into some deep trouble. Looks like he was right." He nodded towards the walls of Persepolis, where thousands of Persian soldiers were gathering. Foot soldiers piled through a gaping hole in the wall and archers took positions on top of the walls, preparing to launch a volley at the oncoming army. "Ra allowed us to pass safely through the Lost Sands without any dangerous encounters. He also granted our horses swiftness, allowing us to move at increased speed. These mounts have never needed a moment's rest. My men, on the other hand, are quite exhausted after racing here with haste. But we knew that we had to get here quickly. Otherwise the fate of the continent would've already been decided before we arrived. Have you seen Tetsu or Kira?"

"Not yet, why? Are they in Persepolis?"

"Yes," Alkaios said. "I'm worried about them. They went into the city alone, and from the looks of it, Persepolis's main army is in there. If they weren't careful, they could've easily gotten caught. Those soldiers out there are going to prevent you from getting inside. But we'll get you in so that you can help Ares out. Just make sure to go and find Tetsu and Kira to ensure that the lot of them are alright. Can you do that for me?"

"Of course," Aleysha said with a resolute nod. She looked over her shoulder at the assembling Persian warriors. They must've begun bolstering their defensives after Ares and Mithra dove into Persepolis. "You intend to conquer the city?"

"If we manage to take the capital and overthrow the king, then Persia will collapse," Alkaios said. "But we will need to defeat Ahriman if we want to fully eliminate Persia as a threat to Dastia. You need to get to Ares' side and help him." The king glanced over his shoulder at the thousands of horsemen that waited patiently behind him, their steeds bathing in golden light from Ra's blessing.

Yuu and Aleysha mounted Fang, the beast growling as it turned its head towards Persepolis. The sea of warriors that were gathering outside of the walls seemed to be growing by the second. Just how many soldiers did they have?

"Forward!" Alkaios boomed, his voice filled with authority as he mounted his steed. The king drove the heels of his boots into the sides of his mount and the ground rumbled like a furious earthquake as the thousands of armed horsemen charged towards the walls of Persepolis, ready to strike the city with everything they had.

***

Cambyses walked through the empty hallways of Persepolis's castle, making his way to the throne room. Bator had already informed the generals of the current situation. There was no doubt that the Persian warriors were already forming ranks and fortifying their defenses against the oncoming invaders. A raiding army from the east, huh? Surely, the Persians would not fall to such unsophisticated barbarians. The ground trembled suddenly and Cambyses halted, turning his head. The two guards that were standing at his side also stopped. What was that? An earthquake?

Suddenly a wall in the castle was torn apart as a gargantuan red bull barreled through the stone, sending debris scattering in all directions. The beast trampled over one of Cambyses's soldiers and continued onward, smashing into yet another wall as it charged towards Cambyses's throne room. The king was on the ground, dust covering his face, his heart caught tight in his throat. He choked on his own words as he stared in shock at the obliterated walls of his castle and the deformed, squashed corpse of his guard. How on earth had a creature as large as that gotten into Persepolis? How was it even in the castle? Was it from the Lost Sands?

Cambyses slowly pushed himself to his feet, brushing the dirt off his expensive clothing with an annoyed look on his face. Where was Zahir? That bastard ought to take care of this beast. He began to inch forward slowly and his eyes went wide, his face blanching of color, upon spotting upon a powerful man with curly brown hair, wearing golden armor. He stood with such authoritative posture that he had to be either a god or a king. Beside the stranger stood the monstrous bull that Cambyses had seen only moments before. A familiar that could only be summoned by gods. So that had to be the intruder's Guardian.

"Zahir, your selfish claiming of the unholy powers of the Persian god of darkness has been brought to the attention of all of the gods," the man shouted, wielding a golden sword in one hand and a flaming torch of white fire in the other. "I, Mithra, of the Persian pantheon, have been sent forth to bring about your destruction. Surrender yourself and we will make sure your powers are stripped properly without taking your life."

Cambyses peered cautiously around the corner of the hole in the wall and saw that Mithra was standing in the throne room, and Ahriman was sitting upon the golden throne that belonged to Cambyses. The Persian king winced. What was Ahriman doing in his throne? Only those of royal blood were allowed to sit there, surely he knew that! Breaking that rule was punishable by death.

Ahriman eyed Mithra as if he were a bug, easily squashable. He slammed both hands down on the golden arms of his throne and stood, rising to his full height. His eyes flashed a glowing shade of violet and a wicked smile cracked across his lips as he held out his hand, his golden scepter materializing in it. The weapon gleamed with the colors of all of the gems in the world. "Surrender myself? Why would I surrender to a lapdog that the gods are sending to subdue me? I'll make an example of you, Mithra. Destroying you will prove to the gods that I am not afraid of them. And I'm not afraid to do what it takes to make my dream of a united continent come true!"

Mithra raised his hand, his eyes coruscating bright orange as they reflected the radiating color of the sun. The white flames that blazed upon his torch suddenly leapt outwards and curled around his body, licking at his gleaming armor. Soon the bright flames filled the room, transforming the throne room into an inferno as howling fires snarled around Ahriman. "In that case, I'll dispatch you myself."

Cambyses's heart pounded when suddenly a gust of black magic swept through the room and sent both Mithra and his bull flying backward. The god and his gigantic companion tumbled through multiple walls, quaking the Persian castle. The king threw himself to the ground as Mithra's body smashed through the wall right next to Cambyses. The Persian lord turned shakily to find that the god of war was buried under a pile of debris, which shook slightly. Tiny pebbles began to roll off the heap of debris, clattering to the floor.

Mithra burst from the pile of detritus, sending stone and marble spraying in all directions as he rose to his feet. He didn't look the slightest bit injured after receiving such a dangerously powerful blow from Ahriman. Mithra looked past Cambyses, hardly even noticing the cowering Persian king, and sprinted forward at his enemy.

Cambyses clung to the floor, his body shaking uncontrollably. There was no way that he could stay here, not with these barbaric gods battling it out in his castle! He was about to turn to his guard to ask him to escort Cambyses out but he found that the soldier had been crushed underneath a collapsed wall, a bloodied hand sticking out from underneath the cracked stone. How useless. The king clawed at the ground, dirt and dust clinging to his expensive clothing as he began to crawl across the battleground in the direction of the exit. With gods battling within Persepolis and an unfamiliar invading force just outside Persepolis's walls, Cambyses wasn't sure if they would still be victorious. Then again, in lore, it was said that Ahriman was one of, if not the strongest god from the Persian pantheon. Surely, he wouldn't fall to Mithra. But would he be able to fend off the foreign attackers as well? Was he even willing to? Cambyses winced, realizing that Ahriman was no longer under his control. Cambyses hadn't realized until now that his throne had been usurped by the Persian god of darkness.

***

Ares staggered backward, sweat pouring down his face. There were several cuts across his arms and legs from slash wounds and his face was slightly bruised. The two Magi, Sahad and Jafaar, were definitely formidable opponents. The entire area around their battle had been reduced to rubble. The broken corpses of several bystanders who had been caught in the fight lay sprawled out in the open. The god exhaled and was about to lunge forward at his enemies once more when he suddenly felt the ground rumbling and heard a loud cry that sounded like a resounding roar from a ravenous beast. He turned in the direction of the sound and realized that it was coming from outside of Persepolis.

"What's that?" Jafaar said with a frown, tilting his head to the side.

"Sounds like some kind of a monster to me," Sahad murmured, lowering his chain scythe to the ground. "It's coming from the Lost

Sands."

"An army," Ares said aloud. He could feel the vibrations in the ground from thousands of horses dashing across the Lost Sands. But whose army was it? He lowered his head. That old man from the mansion in Yuusus. The king of Luxas. He'd offered to let Ares lead an army to storm Persia. Could that be his men attacking Persepolis?

A flash of movement shot from Ares' peripheral vision and one of the blades from Sahad's chain scythe ripped through the air just past his face. The tip of the weapon grazed Ares' cheek, slicing his skin slightly. The god winced, staggering backward at the sudden attack and saw that Jafaar was already sprinting at him with his sword swiping through the air. "You're dead!"

Ares' eyes widened as a shadow suddenly loomed over him. He glanced up and saw an enormous hound leaping over him, descending on Jafaar. The beast smashed into the Magus, sending the man flipping wildly through the air. The man struck the ground with a heavy thud, his arm snapping unnaturally as he landed. He rolled several feet in the dirt before he went limp.

"Jafaar!" Sahad screamed, his hands shaking at his side at the sight of his injured friend. "You bastards are going to pay for this!"

Ares blinked, turning to see that the giant hound was his Guardian that he had summoned to protect Aleysha and Yuu. He narrowed his eyes when he saw his two friends dismounting the Guardian. "What are you guys doing here? I told you that you were to stay back!"

"Stay back and watch as the eastern nations battle the Persians only a mile away? Do you know anyone who would sit there and watch their comrades die?" Aleysha snapped, patting the Guardian. "Besides, you were in trouble and we came here to save you. Fang got us here pretty quick, didn't ya?" The mercenary nuzzled the hound's cheek and the Guardian panted, content.

Fang? Ares sighed and looked at a wrinkled piece of paper that was lying at his feet. It showed a drawing of Tetsu, all beaten up. *His execution … at noon?* His heart began to race and he glanced upward. *Tetsu is here in Persepolis? That idiot, I left him back in Yuusus for a reason!*

Do you know anyone who would sit there and watch their comrades die?

A bead of sweat trickled down the side of Ares' face and he lowered his head, chuckling. Man, I guess I really don't know anyone who's willing to just sit back and stay safe, do I?

"Yuu … you're with these guys?" Sahad growled, tightening his grip on his chain scythe. "You're committing treason! What the hell is wrong with you?"

Yuu stared at Sahad with a cold gaze that sent chills through the enemy Magus. He unsheathed his sword and twirled it through the air perfectly, his turquoise eyes gleaming, taking a step forward. "I don't like being lied to. The boy that you're fighting is the true heir to the Persian throne. Not that hubristic fool, Cambyses. I will see to it that Darien claims what is truly his."

"Cambyses is making Persia more prosperous than ever before. Even the previous Persian king didn't build an empire as grand as this!" Sahad snarled, whirling his chain over his head, making the blade move at such blinding speeds that it was no longer visible. "He's a great king!"

"But at what cost?" Yuu said, pointing the tip of his sword at Sahad. "He's destroyed the lives of hundreds of thousands by taking over their homes. Entire countries have been burned to ashes and countless families have been torn apart. I know what it's like to lose family. After all, you're fighting someone that's a brother to me. A few weeks ago, I thought he was dead. I'm sure you know what it's like to lose someone important to you, Sahad. Imagine millions of people feeling that same agony. Persia has been nothing but an aggressor to the other nations of Dastia, led by a greedy king with a nefarious plan to conquer every inch of this continent. How many people will have to die for that dream to become reality? How many people will have to suffer?"

Sahad didn't speak.

"Man, stop babbling on and on about peace and all that junk," Jafaar murmured, a sliver of blood streaking from his mouth down to his chin. He slowly rose to his feet, his left arm cracked in a twisted position. The Magus dragged his sword across the ground weakly as he slowly began to limp towards Yuu. "Peace, peace, peace. That's all the king wants! Who cares how many people have to die to maintain peace. Even if you try to stop Cambyses from achieving his dream you'll have to kill even more people! Isn't that what you and your army are doing right now? *People are going to die regardless. You can't change that!*"

Yuu's eyes widened as Jafaar suddenly bolted forward, swiping his sword up at the noble mage. The white-haired man took a step backward, planting his feet firmly. He held his sword out in front of him as Jafaar engaged him, the emotion sucked out of his unwavering glare.

"Jafaar, you idiot, stop!" Sahad yelled. "There's no way you can handle Yuu! Not in your current state!"

"*Shut up!*" Jafaar boomed, tearing his blade through the air at Yuu's face. The Magus grunted when he realized that the noble had ducked the blow easily, calmly seeing straight through the attack. Yuu clamped his other hand on the hilt of his sword and rotated his body, swiping his blade in a diagonal slash up from Jafaar's torso to his upper chest. Blood spurt into the air like a fountain and Jafaar's face paled as he stared at Yuu. The noble struck with such perfect speed, accuracy, and force that his skill was easily unrivaled by any ordinary swordsman. Everything he did was perfect, straight from the books. So why was someone like him rebelling against his superiors?

Jafaar slammed his foot into the ground, his legs quivering weakly and screaming for him to collapse. But the Magus clenched his bloodstained teeth and launched himself once more at Yuu, unwilling to surrender. "How dare you go against the lord who gave you everything? You selfish brat, you'll pay for going against Cambyses!"

Ares stared at Jafaar. This man was so loyal to Cambyses, very different from Ramses. The god was about to step forward to help Yuu but saw that the noble was already prepared for the assault.

Yuu stepped backwards, allowing Jafaar to strike out into open air. The noble swiftly ripped his weapon downward, cutting straight down Jafaar's body. The crazed Magus collapsed in a heap, blood pooling around his body. Yuu squeezed the hilt of his sword as he eyed the unmoving body of his old comrade, but said nothing. He turned to Sahad. "You don't have to do this, Sahad."

Sahad was quavering with rage, stricken by the death of Jafaar. He rushed forward, whipping his chain scythe downward at Yuu. The blade cut a downward arc straight at Yuu's body. "You'll pay, you spoiled brat!"

Yuu was about to take a step backward when he suddenly felt someone grabbing his ankle. He glanced downward with horror and saw that Jafaar had grabbed him. The man was just barely alive and was gasping, blood hemorrhaging from his fatal wounds. Yuu tried to tear himself from Jafaar's grip so that he could avoid Sahad's whipping scythes but grunted, realizing that Jafaar wouldn't let go.

Aleysha stepped in front of Yuu, raising her sun shield to the air. One of the scythes smashed into it, glancing off harmlessly. The noble sighed with relief, glad that Aleysha had come to his rescue. Suddenly a spear shot straight past Yuu's face, blowing his hair slightly, and buried itself straight into Sahad's chest. The Persian Magus was forced off his feet and smashed into a building made of clay. The structure collapsed in an instant on top of Sahad, sending a wave of dust dispersing outward.

The spear tore itself from the wreckage and returned to the hand of its owner, Ares. The god walked forward and nodded to Aleysha and Yuu. "Thanks for the help." He looked down and saw that Jafaar had loosened his grip on Yuu's leg. The Magus had already died from blood loss. "Tetsu's in trouble. He's in District Four, scheduled to be executed. I need you two to go there and help him as soon as possible."

"What are you going to do?"

"Mithra is off fighting Ahriman right now and I have to help him. I trust that you guys can save Tetsu," Ares said with a smile. "And you, Fang, make sure these idiots don't get killed, alright?"

Fang stuck out his tongue playfully, panting excitedly.

Ares smiled and snapped his fingers. His flaming chariot, pulled by the four black warhorses, leapt into view and drifted to the god of war's side. The young boy mounted his chariot, grabbing the black reins, turning to look at his friends. "Good luck on your side. Once you've got Tetsu to safety, go and help Alkaios and his forces with taking the city. Make sure that there are as few casualties as possible." He snapped the reins down and his horses bolted forward, pulling his chariot through the chaotic city of Persepolis.

People are going to die regardless. You can't change that! Jafaar's voice echoed through the boy's head. So what could he do? Was facilitating the downfall of Persia and the elimination of Ahriman really the best course of action? The number of civilians that would perish in this battle would be enormous. Ares' expression softened as he raced through the streets. But it was either that or allow Ahriman to slay millions. *The world is unfair. The world is cruel.* Darien had learned that firsthand five years ago.

In order to save lives, he was going to need to take them. What a barbaric cycle.

***

Tetsu analyzed his situation, beads of sweat racing down his face. He was surrounded by hundreds of fleeing civilians while thousands of Persian foot soldiers were closing on his position. Kira was stuck amongst the panicking crowd and had melted in with the civilians, meaning that it was difficult for the archers to pinpoint her exact location. Persian rangers were positioned on every rooftop around the plaza. Their arrows were nocked, and with a single command, both Tetsu and Ramses would be pumped full of bronze pricks. On the bright side, Bator had left the scene earlier to go and warn the Persian generals of some incoming threat. That was one less enemy to worry about.

Tetsu looked down at his hands, which were still cuffed together. He narrowed his eyes. *Damn, this bites.* The mercenary closed his eyes and exhaled, calming himself. His heart rate slowed and his shoulders relaxed as all of the panic left with the air he expelled through his nose. His eyes opened, glowing bright red like two perfect rubies. "Alright, let's do this."

Ramses looked at him and smirked, reaching up and pulling his cowl over his head. "I'll follow your lead then, big guy."

Tetsu leapt off of the stage, hitting the ground and rolling swiftly as he broke into a mad sprint towards the crowds of fleeing civilians that were rushing for the plaza's exit. If he managed to get close to the civilians, it would halt the archers from firing. After all, they didn't want to hit their own people, right? Even if Cambyses gave them the order that they were allowed to fire into the crowds, Tetsu knew that those archers were still human. Humans with families, and they could potentially be firing at people that they knew.

Ramses extended both of his hands out in opposite directions and released bright beams of light from his palms that matched the evanescent flashing color of the sun. The beams cut through the air for only a swift second but smashed into the rooftops of buildings, obliterating entire structures. Archers screamed in terror as the roofs beneath them collapsed. In only a moment, Ramses eradicated a majority of the surrounding buildings, leaving nothing but sweeping clouds of dust and rubble.

Archers who were positioned on buildings that hadn't been decimated were firing rapidly at Ramses, but soon realized that the Magus had melted into a cloud of dust that came from a nearby building that had fallen right next to the stage. "He's getting away!"

Meanwhile, arrows were smacking into the ground behind Tetsu. He scrambled forward, his heart racing as he dove into the crowd of fleeing Persians, fully ready to use anyone as a shield against the arrows that rained down on him. But the projectiles stopped coming, as he expected, and Tetsu sighed with relief, realizing that amongst these civilians he was safe. That was until he saw the Persian foot soldiers converging on his position. He grunted, the chain on his handcuffs jingling as he turned to try and find Kira. Unfortunately, she was nowhere in sight. *Damn it! I need to get these cuffs off or I'm screwed!*

A soldier rushed through the crowd towards him, his scimitar brandished freely in the air. The crowd scattered around Tetsu, and the Persian sprinted forward, bringing his blade cutting downward towards Tetsu.

Tetsu rolled to the side and leapt towards his opponent, driving both of his legs into the Persian's chest. The soldier grunted as he staggered backward, stunned from the blow, as Tetsu slammed hard onto his side, unable to catch himself with his hands. He groaned and swung back onto his feet, realizing that dozens more Persian soldiers were shoving themselves through the crowds of people, closing in quickly on Tetsu's position. Soon he would be completely surrounded if he didn't do something. His eyes darted around, but all that he could see were Persian soldiers rushing at him. *Where the hell is Kira? Where did Ramses go? Damn it, guys!*

Tetsu sensed a flicker of movement from behind him and swung around to the side as a sword jab punctured the air where he had been only a moment earlier. He jammed his elbow back into a man's throat, causing the soldier to collapse in an instant. But he didn't have time to rest. More slashes and blows came raining down on him and he gracefully avoided them. His eyes could see the tension of his opponents' muscles and the direction at which they would strike far before they actually attacked. This was the power of the Hayashi clan's infamous demonic eyes. But Tetsu knew that he couldn't dodge forever. He hardly had any opportunities to take the offensive. If things kept up like this, eventually he'd make a mistake and would get cut down.

Suddenly there was a frightening roar as a gigantic beast smashed through a wall of one of the plaza's buildings, smashing out into the execution area. It was a ferocious hound with black fur and beastly red eyes. It bared its sharp fangs and snarled loudly as it dashed in the direction of Tetsu.

The Persians around Tetsu had lowered their swords and were now scattering at the sight of the charging monstrosity. Tetsu cringed as the beast rushed towards him. *What the hell is a beast from the Lost Sands doing here?*

"Fang, stop! Tetsu, are you okay?" Aleysha's voice called.

Tetsu frowned and looked up to see that Aleysha was on top of the beast with another man who had flowing white hair. His turquoise eyes were unmistakable. "Yuu?" Tetsu's eyes widened and twinkled with excitement as he exclaimed, "It's you, isn't it?"

Yuu brushed some of his hair from his eyes and he smirked. "It's been a while, Tetsu."

"Hell yeah it's been a while! I thought you were dead all these years!" Tetsu exclaimed with a broad grin. Then he lowered his eyes, remembering that Yuu had sacrificed himself for Tetsu's sake five years ago in the throne room. "Look, man…."

"You don't have to say it," Yuu said. "Just get on Fang and let's get out of here."

"Wait, Kira and Ramses are here as well—" Tetsu began when suddenly he heard an explosion. He turned his head and saw Ramses burst from a cloud of dust and slam hard to the ground, his face heavily bruised. "Ramses!"

Emerging from the smokescreen of dust behind Ramses was Bator, who wielded his crescent-shaped weapon. "Ah, there you are, Tetsu! I was beginning to think that you had already escaped!" He sauntered forward casually and brought his boot down on Ramses' cheek, smashing the Magus's face hard into the ground. Blood spurted from the man's lips into the dirt. "But you always put your friends first, don't you?"

Tetsu gritted his teeth. "Take your boot off of him or you'll regret it!"

"Oh? I'll regret it? And what are you going to do to me? You don't have the Sands of Time anymore, infamous mercenary. Do you know what that makes you? *Nothing.* You're no one special. You're just an idiot bound by chains just like when you were a child. I know your story, Hayashi clansman," Bator said, pressing his boot harder into Ramses' face. "But do you know what pisses me off the most? That you have the audacity to even think that you can still beat me even without that Sacred Treasure. Look around you! You're finished."

Tetsu looked over his shoulder from the corner of his eye and saw that Persian soldiers had completely surrounded their position. He worked his jaw, digging his nails into the palms of his hands in frustration.

"R-Run…!" Ramses let out through clenched teeth. He pressed his palms into the dirt ground, trying to pick himself up.

Bator smirked at the Magus's persistence and smirked wickedly. "Great Tetsu Hayashi, I want to see you suffer. Watch, powerlessly, as your friend is sent to the afterlife. Realize the reality, Tetsu. You're too weak to protect anyone. Even yourself." The Magus whirled his crescent dagger and jammed it down into Ramses' back, twisting the blade. Blood soaked Ramses' cloak and he cried out in agony, tears gleaming in the corners of his eyes.

Tetsu scowled and his hands balled up into tight fists as he quavered with rage. He yanked on his chains, wishing that he could just shatter these cuffs, fly outward, and bash Bator's face in. He wished that he had Ares' power. *Powerless. What am I without the Sands of Time? Just an ordinary man fighting amongst gods.* He continued to pull on the chains in futile attempts to shatter his shackles.

Bator watched him pitifully with a sadistic grin on his face.

"Bring out the other one," he ordered. Emerging from the dispersing cloud of dust were two other Magi that were holding Kira. The Luxas Magus was covered in bruises, and was barely conscious as they forced her onto her knees. Her staff fell from her limp hands and clattered to the ground. Bator tore his blade from Ramses' unmoving body and began to saunter towards Kira. "She's next."

"*Don't you dare touch her!*" Tetsu screamed, sprinting forward with his bound hands swaying in front of him. Suddenly there was a flash of movement and he saw that Bator had practically teleported from his original position to Tetsu in an instant. His speed was too fast for even his eyes to follow without the Sands of Time.

Bator ripped his dagger downward at Tetsu's face, perfectly prepared to kill the Hayashi clansman. Suddenly there was a crackling sound, and Bator's eyes bulged when he saw that his hand had been completely frozen in ice, stopping his motion mid-air. An orange shield suddenly came crashing down on his hand, shattering the ice into a million pieces. Bator didn't feel the pain, but he screamed in agony when he realized that he could no longer see his hand. All that was there was a bloody stub covered in frost. "*AGH!*"

Tetsu glanced to his left and smiled at Aleysha and Yuu, who had come to his aid.

"You'll regret hurting Tetsu's friends, Magus," Yuu said, dismounting Fang. He snapped his fingers and Tetsu's shackles chilled to such a freezing temperature that the metal snapped, and the chains clanked loudly to the ground. The noble reached to his side and unsheathed his sword. "I'll make sure of that."

Tetsu shook his hands, satisfied that he had been freed. He

turned around and walked to the body of the soldier that he had knocked unconscious and picked up his sword. He tested the weapon's balance as he tossed it from hand to hand and kept his eyes trained on Ramses. He walked forward and stepped past Aleysha and Yuu. "You guys handle the two Magi who have Kira. Make sure she doesn't get hurt. I'll handle the one-eyed freak."

"Are you sure?" Yuu asked. "He's got magic. He isn't just an ordinary…."

"I know," Tetsu said with a smile. "I'll handle it. You know, Yuu, you're a lot different than I remember. Though I can't quite place why. Maybe it's the lack of wimpiness."

"Oh shut up," Yuu murmured with a snicker. "Just don't get yourself killed. Aleysha, let's take care of these guys."

Aleysha nodded and clapped Tetsu on the back and shot her brother a wink as she unsheathed her sword. "We'll save Kira. Give this guy hell." She turned her head to Fang. "Fang, get rid of the rest of these soldiers, will you?"

Fang nodded his head and bared his fangs as he pounced into the army of soldiers, his claws shredding through dozens of warriors at a time with ease. Their screams of anguish echoed through the plaza.

Bator watched as Yuu and Aleysha rushed past him and engaged the two Magi that were holding Kira. He was clutching the stub of his arm, shocked by the fact he had just lost his hand. The Persian Magus glared angrily at Aleysha and Yuu, rage coursing through his veins. "You wretched mongrels! I'll eviscerate all of you!" he screamed, snatching his dagger off the ground with his other hand as he turned to help his fellow Magi.

“Looks like I can call you one-handed Bator instead of cyclops now, huh?” Tetsu called, halting Bator in his tracks. The Magus whipped around and glared at the mercenary, squeezing the hilt of his weapon. Tetsu whirled his scimitar and pointed it at his opponent, his gaze resolute with hatred. “You’re going to pay for what you’ve done to Ramses, I swear by that.”

Final Words

Aleysha felt sweat rushing down her face as she engaged the two Magi that were holding Kira. The mages dropped Kira in unison and leapt away, scattering in opposite directions. Clearly this was a tactic to try and split Yuu and Aleysha up. The two looked at each other.

"Just hold your guy off. I'll handle my opponent and come over to help you as soon as I can," Yuu promised and quickly rushed to the left to battle his Magus.

Aleysha's eyes flitted to Kira, who was lying on the ground, unmoving. Was she unconscious or dead? Her heart raced as she realized that flying straight at her face was a surge of roaring flames. She raised her shield, which dispersed the fire as soon as it touched the orange metal. The girl whirled her sword, peeking over her shield to observe her opponent.

The enemy Persian Magus was a woman with long, red hair, the color of a tomato. She wore very loose red silks the same color as her hair. The clothing curled around her breasts and her lower body, exposing her shoulders, stomach, and knees. Like Kira, she didn't wear shoes. Two expensive ruby earrings dangled from each lobe and she wielded a skinny long sword. Her lips pursed together, covered by a thick layer of rosy red lipstick. "My, my. What have we here? A female warrior with no magic coming to challenge me?" The Magus smirked until she locked her dark eyes onto Aleysha's shield. "But you have a Sacred Treasure. Ra's Shield, I'd recognize a prized possession like that anywhere. Where did a damsel such as you manage to pick up such a rarity?"

"Doesn't matter to you, does it?" Aleysha retorted, lunging outward. She slashed downward but the Magus easily maneuvered away, stumbling backward.

"Oh well," the Persian Magus said, pointing the tip of her sword at Aleysha. "I suppose I'll just pry it from your corpse then. Spoils of war and all that. Goodbye, wench." The tip of her blade coruscated bright red as flames began to burn on the metal of her sword. Suddenly, a beam of concentrated fire shot as fast as an arrow from the tip of her sword, piercing the air towards Aleysha.

Aleysha reacted instantly, raising her shield into the air. The beam gently smacked into her shield, thumping as lightly as a pebble. Upon impact, the beam expanded into a wall of fire that smashed against her. But Aleysha kept her head down, perspiration streaking down her face from the astounding heat that radiated from the flames. Despite the incredible attack, the magical fire was not able to penetrate Aleysha's shield.

The female mage raised her eyebrows in surprise, impressed that Aleysha had survived. But the fact that Ra's Shield managed to absorb all of that magical power without even a scratch was even more incredible. Instead, the shield glowed as if it were getting stronger. "Not bad," she said and then slashed her sword left and right. Flames shot from her blade and rushed at Aleysha from both right and left sides. "But you can't block both!"

Aleysha swung her shield to the left side and smashed it against the flames just as another beam of concentrated fire was about to strike her from the other side. The moment the fire struck her shield, it expanded into a wall of roaring flames just like before. Her eyes flickered to the right, seeing that the other flames were still approaching. She grunted, pulling her shield around to her right before the wall of flame subsided. A cold sensation rushed through her arm and she winced as she smashed her shield against the second attack coming from her right. The fire on the left licked at her arm, eating away at her skin for a moment before vanishing.

The Persian Magus stared incredulously as her fires died out and she smirked, intrigued by Aleysha's tactic. She had endured a small percentage of the fire in order to fend off both attacks. This woman did not fear pain. The mage reached out and touched her red tattoo of a snake, inscribed into the top of her breast. "You're gutsy! I like that." She extended her hand outward. "It's a shame I have to kill you, isn't it? Oh well, *turn to ash*."

A surge of snarling fire howled as it launched forward from the Persian Magus's fingertips, smashing into Aleysha. The fire, however, didn't strike Aleysha as the mage expected it to. Instead, it swirled around the girl, creating a vortex of fire that spiraled upwards towards the very heavens in a brilliant display. The mage stared at her rogue flames, perplexed. "What's going on?" she demanded. The Magus stared into Aleysha's eyes and suddenly her eyes widened.

Aleysha's pupils had transformed to tiny slits, like that of a hawk, while her irises had turned from blue to a bright orange. It was almost as if her eyes were glowing. Aleysha held out her shield, which glowed as brightly as the sun, filling the plaza with its dazzling light.

Yuu and his opponent paused in their battle and turned to look at Aleysha, who was vibrating the ground with her arcane power. The noble stared at Aleysha. He hadn't realized that she was this powerful. Originally, he had sensed no magic from her. But now, he could feel it. Magic equivalent to a god.

"W-What are you?" the Persian fire-mage choked out, her eyes wide with terror as she took several steps backward. A glowing symbol of a sun disk materialized above Aleysha, shining as brightly as the sun. The Magus winced. "Ra? It can't be…!"

Ramses turned his head, cracking open an eye weakly as he looked at Aleysha. A weary smile split across his face before he closed his eyes.

"I'm not Ra," Aleysha declared, holding her shield out before her. She'd never used this much power at once but she knew that without this strength, she'd never be able to defeat this Magus. "He's my father." She held her shield up to the sky, the ground rumbling beneath her feet. "Looks like you're the one turning to ash."

There was a loud boom that echoed as a beam of light tore from the heavens and smashed into the plaza, obliterating the ground where the Persian fire-mage stood. The earth exploded and dirt flew in all directions. Nearby buildings collapsed from the massive shockwave that rippled outward.

Aleysha found herself surrounded in dust and she suddenly felt sapped of energy, collapsing to her knees, gasping for breath. She looked around and saw that the entire Persian force that had been around them was now reduced to nothing. A majority of the soldiers were lying on the ground unconscious while some were crushed underneath the debris of fallen buildings. She turned and saw Yuu approaching her. Aleysha saw that Yuu's opponent had also been knocked unconscious by the shockwave. "Sorry about that," Aleysha panted. "I probably should've held back a little more."

"No, you did good," Yuu said, kneeling down beside Aleysha. He looked at the nasty burn wound that wrapped around her left arm. "Does it hurt?"

Aleysha shook her head. "No, it's just a little tender. Ow!" She screeched when Yuu wrapped a bandage around the burn. The mercenary winced and sighed. "Thanks."

"So, daughter of Ra, huh?"

"Oh, shut up. I don't like to tell people about that."

"Huh. I figured that you were the daughter of some lesser god when Ahriman pointed you out as a demigod. But daughter of Ra, now that's really something. Legend has it that this entire continent was created by him. No one knows if that's actually true, though," Yuu said as he stood up, extending his hand to Aleysha with a weary smile. "Alright, we need to go check on your friends. Then we'll go and help Tetsu."

***

Tetsu lay on the ground in a complete daze after the explosion. The plaza had practically been reduced to ruin from the stunt that Aleysha pulled. Her opponent must've really been strong if she'd used her demigod powers. He groaned, a headache pounding in his head as he slowly leaned forward. Tetsu hadn't really been winning his fight. Actually, if anything he was getting his butt handed to him. Bator's speed was just too much for Tetsu to handle. As a result, he was covered in cuts and bruises. He managed to avoid any serious wounds but at the rate that things were going, eventually Bator would land a fatal blow.

The Hayashi clansman rolled over onto his hands and knees, groaning. Pain erupted through his back and his shoulders. His face was caked in dirt mixed with blood and the metal cuffs that were still clamped to his wrists were biting into his chaffed skin. Tetsu turned and saw that Bator was already stumbling to his feet, barely conscious. "Why don't you ever just stay down?" Tetsu complained, his arms trembling as he pushed himself to his feet. Gods, his muscles were aching.

"Shut up, only the weak stay in the dirt," Bator gnarred, spitting blood onto the ground as he twirled his dagger in his hand. "The strong will always emerge from the battle victorious, no matter what the obstacle."

"Keep telling yourself that, princess," Tetsu said and bolted forward at Bator, but the Magus moved with lightning speed and struck Tetsu straight in the jaw. The metallic taste of blood filled his mouth as Tetsu's head snapped back abruptly and he slammed hard onto his aching back, the wind knocked clean from his lungs. The man rolled onto his side, coughing painfully. *This really isn't working out.*

Bator panted, also out of breath. His face was pale and he shuddered, staring at the stump where his hand had been. It was hemorrhaging blood now and it sure didn't look like it was going to stop soon. "I'm going to make you and all your friends regret what they've done to me, I swear!"

"Yeah, yeah…." Tetsu groaned, spitting out the metallic taste of blood as he got onto his hands and knees, prepared to get up. There was no way that he could beat Bator by fighting him fairly. Charging him head-on in a fight would result in defeat. "Whatever helps you sleep, cyclops."

"*SHUT YOUR MONGREL MOUTH!*" Bator boomed, swinging a hard kick at Tetsu's ribs.

Tetsu acted accordingly, grabbing Bator by his ankle and yanking hard. The Magus was pulled downward, unable to use his magic while he fell. Tetsu cracked a smile, snatching his sword off the ground with his opposite hand. "Looks like you fell into a trap, Bator," He ripped his blade upward and jammed it straight into Bator's stomach, tearing the weapon straight out the Magus's back. "That was for Ramses," Tetsu growled into Bator's ear, tearing his sword from the body of the dying mage. He allowed Bator to collapse at his side, his heart racing.

Wiping sweat from his brow, Tetsu turned and looked at the obliterated plaza and the countless number of unmoving Persian bodies that lay broken and unconscious on the ground of District Four. How many people had died today? How many more would need to die before Cambyses's reign was finally brought to an end? Tetsu released his sword, letting the bloody weapon clatter to the ground beside Bator's corpse. His hand was shaking, a tingling sensation that felt like needles were pricking into his flesh spiked through his palm. *We still need to deal with Ahriman. That's going to be a problem.*

Tetsu walked back to the center of the plaza where he saw Yuu and Aleysha tending to Ramses. Kira was awake, her face slightly bruised and cut. But she was okay. Meanwhile, it looked like Ramses was just barely clinging onto life. He was gasping and blood was pouring from the wound in his back.

"He's lost too much blood," Kira said quietly.

Tetsu stopped beside Ramses and knelt down beside the Magus. He bit his lower lip in frustration at the sight of the dying mage. "This is my fault. You guys came to save me. And now…."

"Don't blame yourself, idiot," Ramses said with a scoff. "This was because I was careless and let that one-eyed Magus beat me. Tetsu," he said, "you're a good guy, you know. I judged you back then when you tried to save those slaves. But I want you to know that what you're doing is the right thing. Protect your friends, save them. Make sure that they all get out of this mess in one piece, alright?"

Tetsu hardened his expression, trying not to show how distraught he was. He bit his lower lip, holding back the tears that wanted to stream down his cheeks. "I'll do that. Thank you, Ramses, for everything."

"Make sure my family is safe, alright?" Ramses said with a strained smile. "And tell little Riza that I'm sorry. Having to grow up without a father … I know firsthand what that was like. I … was hoping that I would live long enough to be there for him. But…." Tears began to slowly creep down his cheeks and his lips trembled. He leaned his head back and his eyes fixed on the clear sky, his hands going limp at his side. His eyes never closed.

A shadow loomed over Tetsu's face and he slowly stood up,

reaching up and running his hand slowly through his black spiky hair. "Sacrifices are a part of war," Tetsu said, "and I absolutely hate that."

Aleysha wiped some tears from her eyes. "What do we do now?"

"I need to check on Ramses' family to make sure they're okay," Kira said. "And … let them know the news." She gave her staff a tight squeeze, looking to Fang. "I'll take this fella with me."

Fang panted with excitement.

Tetsu nodded. "Yuu, Aleysha, and I will go and find Cambyses and put an end to his reign," he said, turning to Aleysha. "Is Ares here?"

"Yeah, he's fighting Ahriman I believe. He sent us here to help you out," Aleysha said.

"Then after we deal with Cambyses, we'll head after Ahriman," Tetsu said, ignoring the pangs of pain that screamed from the dozens of wounds and cuts that covered his body. "But first, I have a few words I want to say to the king of Persia."

***

Ares walked on the flat rooftop of one of the large clay buildings that overlooked the rest of the city. He could see that Alkaios's forces were shoveling themselves through the opening in Persepolis's wall and were beginning their incursion on the city. He could also see waves of Persian soldiers flooding through the streets, converging on Alkaios's men. The god turned his head and saw that the civilians were fleeing to the western side of the city, probably escaping through the western entrance of Persepolis. He sighed with relief. At least a majority of the innocent civilians were getting out of the city instead of getting caught up in this brutal war.

Ares glanced up at the castle, on a hill that towered over the rest of the city. The noble section was practically destroyed. A majority of the castle was already crumbling to the ground, and dozens of odd-looking creatures were flitting around the castle grounds. Ares squinted, taking a good look at the deformities.

These undead creatures had decaying flesh and were lumbering about, their arms swaying. Their rotted yellow teeth chattered together as their bloodstained hands clawed outward at the corpses of Persian soldiers. Ghouls. Ares had read stories about the undead abominations that feasted on the dead. But what were ghouls doing in Persepolis? They couldn't have come here on their own, they must've been summoned. *Ahriman.*

The god of war leapt from his spot on the rooftop, launching himself thousands of feet into the air as he soared towards the castle. He descended on the castle grounds, smashing down into the lawn with a massive explosion, creating a deep crater in the dirt. Ares brushed dust off his shoulders, and turned to find that all the ghouls had turned their attention to him. The ghouls didn't have eyes; they only had empty sockets of blackness, and they used their sense of smell to locate their next meal. They snarled hungrily and sprinted at Ares in a frenzy, their shrill screeches piercing the god's ears as they clawed at the air.

Ares, however, knew that ghouls were weak Guardians to summon. He snapped his fingers and his spear automatically sprang to life and darted forward, smashing through each individual undead creature. Ripping through their bodies, the weapon returned to Ares' hand once it was finished eradicating all of the ghouls. The undead lay sprawled on the ground with giant puncture wounds in their bodies. Meanwhile, Ares began to storm towards the castle of Persepolis.

One of the walls of the castle erupted, sending bits of debris flying out into the air. Mithra burst from a cloud of dust that had formed from the explosion. The god slammed into the ground and rolled several hundred meters before he went still on the ground. He was quavering, his body clearly in pain.

Ares turned and saw Ahriman stepping through the hole in the wall, gently landing on the grass of the castle's lawn. The god of darkness raised an eyebrow when he spotted Ares and smiled. "So you've come, Ares. I was beginning to think that you were still drowning in tears over the death of your best friend, a craggy rock. Pitiful, really." He turned and spotted the dead ghouls that lay sprawled around the lawn. "You don't see me crying over a few lost Guardians. After all, there are thousands more where they came from. I have an army at my disposal, Ares. But I don't want to use them to bring you to your knees. I want to use my own power to make you grovel at my feet." He twirled his scepter in his hand and pointed the tip of it at Ares. "Even Mithra didn't stand a chance."

Ares took a fighting stance, both of his hands wrapped tightly around the handle of his spear as he pointed the golden tip straight at Ahriman. He dug both of his feet into the ground, his heart beginning to beat faster. He shot a glance to Mithra, who had his eyes closed. But he was still breathing. *At least Ahriman didn't kill him.* "That power that you wield is not meant to be abused, Ahriman.

Why do you think the gods locked it away? Does it even matter if you defeat both Mithra and I today? Tomorrow Heaven will send down more gods that will seek your execution. No one wants a rogue deity roaming the planet freely."

"You're right," Ahriman said with a smile. "The other gods will see me as a threat after I kill the two of you. But by murdering two gods of war I am setting an example. Anyone, even gods, who crosses me will be doomed to perish. No matter how strong they are, no matter how many enemies are before me, I will lay them all to waste. My power is unlimited." He held out his quivering hand before his eyes, which glowed with dark-purple arcane energy. The god held out his palm and the magic was expelled in the form of a bolt that rocketed through the air towards Ares, causing the air to shimmer with glittering purple light.

Ares rolled out of the way, the bolt of magic shattering the earth beside him. Dirt geysered upward into the air and rained down, splattering on the grass. The god of war spun his spear and then jammed it into the ground, cracking his knuckles.

Ahriman observed the god, unsure of what the boy was doing. Suddenly Ares' clothing began to glitter brightly, as if it were made of the stars that filled the sky at night. The Persian god glanced away, unable to look directly at Ares' flashing attire. When the evanescent glow faded away, Ahriman turned to find that Ares was now clad in perfectly fitted golden armor with rubies embedded all over it. Flames danced on his spiked pauldrons, flickering and snapping. Giant gauntlets were clamped over his hands, and his plated armor glinted in the sunlight. "I'm glad that you're taking this seriously, infamous Guardian of the Lost Sands. But note that your impressive armor will not protect you from my magic. No matter how impenetrable you claim it is, I'll tear straight through it."

Ares snatched his spear out of the ground, whirling it in his hands. "We'll see about that, won't we?" He burst forward with a surge of speed, cracking the earth beneath his feet as he appeared right in front of Ahriman. The god of war gripped his spear tightly and jabbed outward with a fast and fluent motion, stabbing his weapon through the air straight for Ahriman's face.

But the lord of darkness tilted his side with perfect reaction, the tip of the spear piercing the air inches from Ahriman's cheek. The Magus swatted the spear away from his face and slammed his fist straight into Ares' face. A spurt of blood streamed from the boy's nose and Ahriman spun around and drove a solid back-kick into the young god's stomach. The blow sank, releasing a burst of energy straight into Ares' diaphragm. The god of war was launched backwards, rolling into the ground with smoldering smoke rising from his golden armor.

Ares landed hard on his back, gasping for breath and coughing the dust from his lungs. The world was spinning and he gripped his roiling, aching stomach. He was surprised; the ancient armor of Ares should've been able to withstand blows even from other gods. But he could still feel the agonizing pain from Ahriman's strike. Slowly leaning forward, Ares winced. *Inhuman reactions, incredible strength, and absolute control over magic … so this is what it's like to fight another god.*

"You feel it, don't you?" Ahriman called with a wicked smile, sauntering forward towards Ares. "The fear. Oh, but you don't even look scared, little boy. Dear prince Darien, perhaps I ought to make you feel true fear. Fear that will make you tremble and cry out for your lost parents. Yes, that's what I'll do." The Persian god snapped his fingers and suddenly a cloud of swirling black mist curled around his body and began to drift towards Ares. "I'll bring you despair."

Ares' eyes widened as the dark fog swept outward and swallowed him, locking him in a world of swirling darkness. His heart was pounding and he gulped, his eyes darting around, as the fog began to construct a setting around him. Giant walls rose up to a grand ceiling and two thrones materialized before the young god. He soon realized that he was in his throne room, standing before his live parents. His father was sitting in his throne with perfect posture. He was expressionless as he looked at his son, Darien. Tapping the arm of his throne impatiently he sighed, as if disappointed. "How many times have I told you and Tetsu not to go on pestering Hassan, Darien?"

Darien stared at his father, tears pooling in his eyes. His hands were shaking at his side and his lips quivered. "D-Dad?" he choked out. "Is that really you?" He looked to his beautiful mother, who stood up from her chair.

"Darien? What's wrong?" his mother asked, ready to run forward and give him a hug.

His father held up his hand, stopping the queen. She reluctantly sat back down in her throne. "You cannot baby him, my Queen. After all, he'll be a man before you know it." The old king of Persia turned his attention back to Darien. "It is okay to cry, my son. But you must know when the opportune time to cry is. Shedding tears can be seen as a sign of weakness. But it can also be a sign of compassion. It is not okay for you to be weak. But I will be proud of you if you are compassionate to others."

Treat others with respect and with time they'll come to respect you. In the future, when it is finally your time to become king, the people will greet your ascension to the throne with acceptance. Darien, I'm sure that you'll be a great king. You just have to have more faith in yourself. His father's words from many years ago echoed through his head.

Darien took a step forward, reaching outward. "Dad! I—" He never had the chance to finish his sentence. The scene exploded into a gigantic puff of black fog, swirling around the young prince. Darien watched as the darkness fabricated another setting and he was placed back in the throne room. On the thrones were his murdered father and mother. His mother was face-first on the floor with a pool of blood forming under her body. The crimson liquid trickled down the stairs that led to the throne and crawled slowly towards Darien's feet.

The prince looked to his father, who was staring at Darien with widened eyes. His face was pale but he was alive, just barely. "Why didn't you save us?" *Why was the most useless member of the royal family chosen to survive on that day?* The life faded from his father's eyes and the king's body went limp in his golden throne, his arm swaying loosely at his side.

Aren't you angry? Don't you want to make them pay for your parents' deaths? You aren't even the slightest bit furious with what happened five years ago? Tetsu's words, from their reunion in Yuusus, rebounded off of the walls of the throne room, echoing in

Darien's ears. Revenge.

Darien's hands trembled at his side, burning rage coursing through his veins. He glanced up and stared at the corpses of his parents. *They're dead. They're gone forever … and I didn't do anything about it. I was powerless then. But right now I have the power to make anything that I want happen!*

The old Ares was standing behind Darien with a sly smile spreading across his black lips. His long, messy hair came down over his face and his wild orange eyes gleamed brightly as he gazed at the Persian prince's back. "So what do you want to do?"

"I want justice," Darien growled, still staring at his parents' corpses.

"How can you achieve justice? How can you avenge your parents? There is only one way. *Murder the ones responsible for your misery.*"

Darien grinded his teeth, rage usurping his mind. Every other thought besides hatred was cast aside and he shook with fury, ready to unleash his wrath upon the world. He was frustrated. Frustrated that he hadn't done anything to avenge his parents' deaths. Frustrated that he had been powerless to do anything to prevent their assassination. Even now, as he faced Ahriman in reality he knew that he was too weak to defeat such an opponent on his own.

"You're afraid of responsibility and losing those that you love. But I know, Darien, the one fear that dominates above all others. The fear that haunts your mind with every day. Powerlessness. It's ironic, isn't it?" Ares said with a nefarious laugh. "You, one of the new gods of war is afraid of being too weak. Too weak to protect your friends. Too weak to uphold your responsibilities. Too weak to do anything but grovel in the sand at the mercy of your first *real* opponent, Ahriman."

Darien felt tears streaming down his cheek, his head lowered.

"Too weak to avenge your parents' deaths. I'm sure that they are watching from the Heavens and they are disappointed that you did *nothing* to account for their deaths. After all, I'm sure their souls cannot move on if their murderer is not brought to justice. There he is, right there in front of you," Ares said, an image of Zahir materializing in front of Darien. "But you don't have what it takes to bring about justice. You don't have the strength. I do."

Darien looked up, staring at Zahir, the tears in his eyes glistening. His gaze hardened and his nose crinkled as untamable hatred burned in his eyes.

Let me in. It's over. I know what you want.

"Kill him," Darien whispered, the colors of his irises morphing from sky-blue to a coruscating orange. An aura of bloodlust radiated around the young prince and his knuckles turned ghostly white as he clenched his fists. "*I want Zahir dead for what he's done.*"

***

Yuu was panting as they raced through the silent city streets, advancing towards the castle. The ground rumbled like an earthquake, and the Magus knew that the shaking was coming from the castle. That was surely where Ares and Mithra were fighting Ahriman. Why were they heading in that direction? Surely Cambyses wasn't anywhere near such a dangerous battle.

But where else could Cambyses be? The eastern half of

Persepolis had been turned into a battleground, with Alkaios's soldiers massacring the unprepared Persian warriors by the hundreds. Perhaps he was on the western side of Persepolis trying to escape with the rest of the civilians.

"There!" Tetsu shouted, pointing to the sky. "He's on my carpet!"

Yuu glanced up to the afternoon sky and saw a flying carpet, with the Persian king sitting on it. Accompanying him were two other Magi, standing beside the lord, overlooking the city. They were flying west, eager to escape the city that was doomed to destruction.

Aleysha whipped out her shield, wincing as a chilling sensation bit through her arm. Her burn wounds were still hurting through her bandages. "I'll take him straight out of the sky."

"Don't," Yuu said, holding out his hand to stop the female mercenary. "Your power is very destructive and there are still civilians in the area. You could accidently take them out with collateral damage. Leave it to me."

"How are you—"

Yuu rushed into an alleyway between two buildings, leaving Tetsu and Aleysha alone in the empty street. He leapt off of the ground, kicking off of one wall and leaping to the next. He continued to hop from wall to wall until he was high enough to lash out and grab the ledge of the rooftop. His arms cried out in aching pain as he hauled himself onto the roof, rolling onto the flat, sandy platform. The Magus held out both of his hands, the markings on his palms beginning to glow a chilling blue color. He rushed forward to the edge of the rooftop and aimed his hands at Cambyses. A gigantic spike of ice was suddenly conjured in front of him and it shot forward, ripping through the air in the direction of Cambyses and his carpet.

Both of the Magi on the carpet noticed the incoming projectile and turned to the flying icicle. A surge of purple lightning scintillated through the air, smashing into the massive icicle. The projectile smashed into a million pieces of sharp ice, floating in the air.

Cambyses turned his head, tilting it when he saw that the ice wasn't falling as it should've.

Yuu relaxed his shoulders calmly and snapped his fingers. The pieces of ices shot forward faster than before, and now thousands of projectiles raced at Cambyses and his Magi. The two Magi released bolts of crackling lightning that pierced the air, attempting to destroy all of the incoming icicles, but there was no way they could stop it all.

One of the Magi leapt in front of Cambyses as the daggers of ice bit deep into his back. Blood soaked the mage's clothing as his body went limp and he slid from the carpet, falling to the city below. Pieces of ice had torn through the carpet, forcing the Sacred Treasure to plummet to the ground as well.

"I've got him," Yuu exclaimed, pointing towards the area where Cambyses's carpet had fallen. "Let's get—" He was about to finish but he saw that Aleysha and Tetsu were already racing through the streets towards Cambyses. The noble sighed and shrugged, leaping off the roof of his building to join his friends, to finally confront the king.

***

The world was a whirling blur and there was a terrible ringing in the king's ears. Cambyses lay on the ground, his left arm completely shattered at his side. Tears were springing to his eyes, and he couldn't remember the last time he had felt such unbearable pain. It was like someone had taken a hammer and crushed every bone in his arm all at once. Beside him was his last Magus, who was barely conscious. The mage was on the ground, a bloody splotch on his forehead where he had cracked his skull.

The other Magus lay several hundred meters away, his corpse broken from the fall.

Cambyses reached into his robe, pulling out the Sands of Time with his free hand as he crawled backward, pressing his back to the wall of a building. His heart was racing, knowing that soon his enemies would be upon him. He grimaced, putting the Sands of Time down on his lap as he reached out and snatched a dagger from the belt of his unconscious Magus. Twirling the weapon in his hand, he put it in his mouth, clamping his teeth down on the hilt of the dagger. The king grasped his diamond hourglass once more and slowly staggered to his feet as he saw Tetsu and an unfamiliar girl sliding around the corner of the street. *Tetsu, huh? You're still alive.*

Cambyses remembered how Yuu had been the one who was slashed in order to save Tetsu in the throne room five years ago. He recalled tossing Tetsu into the Lost Sands afterward. The bastard still survived and had the guts to come back to Persia. And even when Cambyses had sent thousands of Persian warriors and three Magi to ensure that Tetsu and his friends were executed, he still came out alive. The king bit harder into the hilt of his dagger, his nose crinkling as he glared at the Hayashi clansman. It must've taken dozens of miracles for this fool to still be standing. Cambyses raised his eyebrows when he saw that Tetsu was gushing blood from dozens of wounds all over his body. It was a wonder the mercenary hadn't passed out from blood loss yet. Judging from the weary look in his eyes, he was already about to collapse.

Cambyses snorted. And you still have the audacity to come before me with those fatal wounds, Tetsu?

The king froze time using his ancient hourglass, darting forward past the unfamiliar female warrior towards Tetsu. He felt as if he were moving through layers of thick pudding, his movement becoming more restricted the longer he froze time. Finally reaching Tetsu, he swung his head to the side, slashing the blade of the dagger across the man's chest. *Fall like the weakling you are, plebeian.*

Time reverted back to normal and Tetsu's blood spilled onto the ground. The young man's eyes were wide and he gasped tautly, falling to his knees before slamming hard into the dirt.

"Tetsu!" the girl screamed, rushing to his aid.

"*Cambyses!*" a familiar voice roared.

The king glanced up and saw that Yuu was descending upon him. The noble drove a heavy kick straight into his stomach, sending him rolling uncontrollably across the ground. Cambyses felt the Sands of Time slipping from his hands, and the dagger in his mouth flipped through the air and buried itself in the dirt several meters away. The king grunted, the metallic taste of blood filling his mouth. His stomach spun like a churning maelstrom and he groaned, grasping his diaphragm, watching as Yuu stormed towards him.

"For five years, I stood by you blindly thinking that you were just doing what you thought was right for the empire," Yuu snarled, grabbing the king by the collar of his robe. "Even with this incredible power that Zahir offered me, I was still powerless before you. I never spoke out against your nefarious plan to dominate the rest of Dastia and expand Persia's borders. I never saw through your insane plot to eradicate your brother, sister-in-law, and nephew. I was a fool to follow you, mindlessly fulfilling whatever excursion you set out for me without even questioning what I was doing. You told me that Darien murdered his own parents. *You lied to me.*"

The noble's fist sank hard into Cambyses's face, drawing out more pain as the king's legs buckled and he crashed onto his back. The corners of his vision were blackening, and he sputtered blood onto the dark beard on his unrecognizable face. His nose was cracked to the side and his eyes were puffy and swollen, barely even cracked open. The king's quivering hands went limp at his side, his bruised face pulsing as quickly as his heart was beating. Cambyses watched Yuu powerlessly, accepting his defeat, and waited for the man's next move.

Yuu grabbed a handful of Cambyses's hair and yanked hard, forcing the king onto his hands and knees like a dog. The Magus grabbed the king's face and forced him to look at Tetsu's unmoving body. "You've hurt my friends far too much, Cambyses!" Yuu growled, cracking his knee into Cambyses's chin.

The king slammed onto his back once more, warm tears streaking down his cheeks. Memories of watching Tetsu, Darien, and Yuu play together around the castle flashed through his head. He remembered stopping them constantly from upsetting Hassan, the head royal chef. And now here he was, trying to murder the young boys that he had watched grow up over the years. "Just kill me…," Cambyses choked out through his set of broken, bloodied teeth.

"No," Yuu said, turning his head to Cambyses's final Magus. The mage was slowly pushing himself to his feet after waking up. He seemed quite groggy and dazed, for he swayed slightly but Yuu knew the man could still fight. That was how Magi were. He extended his hand to the Persian Magus and watched as the man solidified into a giant block of gleaming ice. Yuu closed his hand into a tight fist and the statue suddenly detonated, sending shards of shattered ice clattering to the ground in a heap. "Killing you is far too easy."

***

Kira staggered forward with Fang padding by her side, snarling at the dozens of battling soldiers that filled the streets of Persepolis. But the female mage was leaning against Fang's furry body, preventing the hound from lashing out and brutally massacring the Persian warriors.

Kira's head was pounding but she trudged onward anyways, making her way through the side streets of the city to try and avoid the main roads where a majority of the chaos took place. She dug her staff into the ground and used it as a walking-cane as she neared Cassim's home. But as she turned the corner of the home she found a Persian man jamming a broadsword through Ramses' wife. The mage's eyes widened and her lips quivered as a mist of blood sprayed into the air and onto the face of young Riza.

The little boy screamed, every inch of his face drenched in his mother's blood. Tears mixed with the crimson liquid as he collapsed to his knees, falling alongside his mother. He clutched at her bloodstained attire, squeezing the cloth tightly between his small fists.

Kira gripped her wooden staff tightly and was about to rush forward to the boy's aid when suddenly two warriors leapt in front of her, blocking her from reaching Riza's side. She swung her staff forward, a burning sensation searing through her wrists as she attempted to let magic flow through her weapon. But to no avail. There was a sizzle and nothing happened. The mage's eyes widened with disbelief as she stared at her trembling hands. *I'm out of juice already? N-no…! This can't be happening! Riza and Cassim need me right now! Damn it, come o—*

A club smashed into her cheek, sending Kira spinning abruptly through the air. The Magus crashed onto her side, warm blood beginning to seep onto her tongue. Her head felt like a bomb had detonated inside, jumbling up all her thoughts. She tried to move but her hands only twitched as she lay on her side, staring blankly at the dirt. The ground was shifting before her blurry eyes and the corners of her vision were blacked out. *Am I going to pass out? Now of all times? Please … get up!*

Fang roared and pounced forward, rending the two soldiers in half with a single swipe of his claws. The deformed bodies of the Persians crumpled to the ground and the beast slowly began to nudge Kira's unmoving body.

Riza was screaming but soon his voice became muffled until there was silence.

"S-Stop! Don't you touch her, you damned bastards! She's a Persian, I'm telling you!" Cassim's voice yelled.

"Hiding criminals doesn't make you a Persian, scum!"

Kira pressed her palms to the dirt, shakily pushing herself onto her knees. Her head turned and she found herself watching as two Persian soldiers rammed Cassim's grandmother through with blades just as they had Ramses' wife. The elderly woman died instantly and collapsed to the ground beside Riza and Ramses' wife. Both were also deceased. Kira tried to push herself onto her feet but her arms trembled, still not fully responding. *Move…!*

"*You damned barbaric monsters!*" Cassim howled, frantically snatching his pitchfork off the ground. He jammed the metallic prongs of his weapon straight into a Persian soldier's chest, driving one of his grandmother's murderers into the ground. "How dare you?" he boomed, tears streaking down his cheeks. "S-She … she never did anything wrong…."

Kira bit her lower lip, shaking her head as she reached out and grabbed her wooden staff from the ground at her side. She looked over her shoulder and saw that Fang was protecting her from dozens of other soldiers that were rushing forward to try and finish off the Luxas Magus. She squeezed her staff until her knuckles blanched. *You're right, Cassim. She was innocent … and so were many people who died today.*

"How could you bring yourself to kill someone who's defenseless like that?" Cassim roared, rage conquering his mind. He stabbed downward once more into the corpse of the Persian soldier, drawing more blood into the air as he entered a frenzy. "How can you live with yourse—" His words were choked off as a second Persian soldier slashed his throat with a fluent cut. The farmer stared at his murderer for a long moment before collapsing onto his back, grasping at his hemorrhaging neck.

Kira began to sob, her hands shaking as she pointed her staff straight at the lone Persian soldier, who stood right in front of Cassim's small house. *It wasn't anyone's fault that this happened.* Kira's gaze suddenly blazed with determination, tears brimming in the corners of her eyes. *The world is just cruel.*

Adrenaline burst through her veins. The mage let out a shrill yell as electricity exploded from the end of her staff, scintillating forward and smashing straight into Cassim's house. The energy swallowed the Persian soldier, releasing tendrils of snapping energy extending in all directions. The house groaned as it burst into flames, collapsing several seconds later. The Persian warrior that had slain Cassim and his grandmother was now lying on the ground, his flesh crisped black.

Kira panted, slowly lowering her staff. She felt sapped of energy, as if everything had been drained out of her in that last magical release. Her eyes gazed over the corpses of Ramses' family and then upon Cassim's. The Magus weakly pressed her staff into the ground, gripping the wood with both hands, easing herself to her feet.

Fang was gnawing on the body of one of the Persian soldiers that had attempted to flank Kira. The beast tossed the corpse away and rushed over to Kira's side, whimpering at the sight of the feeble mage.

"I'm alright," Kira assured Fang as she slumped her body over the gigantic hound. The soft fur felt like a pillow and she closed her eyes with a deep sigh, wiping the moisture from her eyes. "There's nothing more we can do here. Can you take me back to Aleysha?"

Fang nodded, looking at Kira with his big gleaming eyes. The Guardian turned to see that a squadron of Persian warriors was advancing on their position from the main road. The hound barked and burst forward, sprinting through the side streets of Persepolis back in the direction of Aleysha.

***

King Alkaios charged through the thick mist of blood that plagued the battlefield of Persepolis's streets, drenching himself with the crimson liquid. The lord swung his broadsword left and right, rapidly dispatching Persian warriors all around him. The incursion was going as planned. The Persian Magi were difficult to deal with but the great force of the United Eastern Nations easily overwhelmed them. The only real problem now was pushing through the waves of Persians that kept flooding through the streets.

Every time Alkaios cut down a Persian soldier, two rushed forward to claim their fallen comrade's place. It was a never-ending cycle. The United Eastern Nations still hadn't even forced their way through the eastern quarter of Persepolis yet. Then there was the issue of Ahriman.

Alkaios didn't even want to think of facing such a formidable foe. After witnessing the destruction of that random village, the king knew that Ahriman was an enemy that could only be defeated by another god. But would Ares prevail?

Warriors plowed into Alkaios and the king frowned, realizing that there were too many enemies for him to deal with. He glanced around him, searching desperately for reinforcements. The comrades that had been fighting beside him only moments before were now lying dead on the ground. Even his Head General was sprawled across the ground with the shaft of a spear protruding from his bloodied chest.

Alkaios blanched when suddenly he felt a thump on his body. A chilling sensation swept over him and he glanced down to see that there was a bloodstained blade poking out of his chest, straight through his mail armor. He winced, sputtering warm blood onto his chin as the weapon was torn from his body. The king collapsed onto his knees, pain detonating in his body. Hope faded from the lord's eyes as he groaned and fell forward, smacking his face hard against the dirt ground.

How could Ares prevail? The army of the United Eastern Nations is falling beneath the stampede of Persia's endless ranks and such a young, inexperienced god can't possibly match Ahriman's immeasurable strength. To win this battle, we need more than just luck. We need a miracle.

***

Ahriman watched as the black cloud of mist disappeared around Ares, smiling sadistically. After using his illusionary magic, the young god should've lived through an unforgettable nightmare. But suddenly the ground around Ares began to rumble, and the wind began to churn as if there was a hurricane swirling right where the god of war stood. Ahriman's eyebrows rose slowly in puzzlement and he retreated a step as he felt a dramatic increase in the level of power that Ares wielded. The aura that he felt in the air was filled with murderous intent, something he had never expected from the young boy. Ahriman clutched his scepter tightly with his clammy hands, his stringy hair blowing about in the blistering wind. He recognized this ominous aura. It was the same one that Ares had released when he had lost control of himself at the Battle of Yuusus. *The old Ares has awakened once more.*

The tip of Ahriman's scepter began to glow an ominous purple color. Seven surges of black flame howled to life before the god of darkness, revealing seven demons that rose from the dark fires. Their skin was a hellish red and ebony horns protruded from the top of their heads, each curving to create an arc. "*Awaken, arch demons of my Daeva! Aesma Daeva, Aka Manah, Indra, Nanghaithya, Saurva, Tawrich, and Zarich! Come, protect your master!*"

The demons grinned wickedly and took formation in front of Ahriman, eying their new enemy curiously. The Guardians each produced a different weapon, spanning from daggers to tridents to spears and much more.

Ares opened his eyes, revealing that his irises were a gleaming orange color. A satisfied smile stretched across his lips and he burst out laughing. "*Man, it's good to be back! And a fresh body too. How perfect, the power of youth never ceases to amaze me!*" The god of war turned to face the demons that stood before him, taking a whiff of the air. His nose twitched and the smile vanished from his face. "*I remember that stench. You needed to summon your lackeys to fight me in your stead, Ahriman? Do you honestly think that you can hold me back with weaklings like that?*"

One of the demons gnarred, baring its sharp fangs, as he scampered forward on all fours with a gleaming sword clutched in one of his hands. He approached Ares and slid across the dirt, clutching the hilt of his weapon with both of his hands, tearing the weapon through the air towards the god's throat with a yelping cry.

Ares yawned, not even bothering to react to the attack. The Daeva laughed sadistically as he slashed the god's throat. The demon expected the blade to sink straight into the boy's throat, but instead the weapon shattered on impact, sending pieces of metal thumping to the ground. The arch demon stared in disbelief at Ares. Ahriman's hands trembled. *How is his skin so hard?*

"*That tickles.*" Ares swatted the demon across the face with the back of his hand. The creature's entire head snapped around with a sickening crack. The Daeva instantly collapsed in a heap. "*The last time we faced each other, Persian god, you killed me. I believe it's my turn to pay you back in full, don't you think?*"

"Aesma!" one of the demons cried out.

"You'll pay for this, God of War!" another snarled.

All of the Daevas suddenly sprinted forward, rushing directly at Ares in frenzy, their eyes crazed with their thirst for vengeance.

Ares scoffed, irritated that Ahriman's Guardians were still fighting the battle for him. "*Get these demons out of my face.*" Ancient markings began to appear on his skin, crawling around the god of war's body until he was covered in the black tattoos. He snapped his fingers and, without warning, a thousand arrows were pumped straight into the Guardians' bodies, making them look like prickly porcupines. The earth was blanketed in iron arrows, the tips buried deep into the dirt.

Ahriman's heart leapt to his throat and he glanced upward, spotting two identical female archers with flowing brunette hair, standing on the rooftops of the castle beside Ares. They had golden bows in their hands and quivers filled with an endless supply of arrows. *Those are Ares' Guardians … twin archers!*

"*That should even the playing field*," Ares said, waving to his Guardians. "*Don't worry, you needn't interfere in this quarrel*." He clapped his hands twice and suddenly the ground behind him exploded. Entire racks filled with thousands of different gleaming armors and weapons burst from the earth behind the god, filling the area with a cloud of swirling dust. Ares extended his hands outwards, showing off his collection. "This is my armory. Since this is the last battle you'll ever have, Persian god of darkness, I'll give you the luxury of choosing which weapon I get to kill you with."

Warlord of Terrador

Ahriman gritted his teeth, facing the ancient Hellas god of war. Such incredible power, he was being humiliated! Mithra was nothing in comparison to this god. The original Ares must've had an unmatched amount of battle experience. He clutched his scepter tightly, trying to swallow the lump in his throat. He would have to tread carefully and look for Ares' weak points. Summoning more Guardians to his aid would do nothing. Those twin archers that Ares had called upon seemed to be able to unleash thousands of arrows in a single instant. There was no telling what other Guardians the god of war might have hidden as well.

"*No preference?*" Ares smirked and shrugged. He reached out and a gigantic hammer the size of his entire body flew straight into his hand. There were two runes that were embedded into both sides of the hammer. The infused stones glowed like sapphires. The weapon weighed over ten tons but the god wielded the weapon as if it were as light as a feather. "*I might switch around, who knows. Sometimes I get bored if I use the same weapon for too long.*"

Ahriman grunted as the god of war burst forward, sprinting with blinding speed straight for him. He swept his hand outward, creating a wall of black magic that exploded from the ground. But the barrier did not halt the god's charge, for Ares simply leapt into the air, jumping a hundred meters over the magic wall. Ahriman kicked off of the ground, retreating backward as Ares descended upon him.

Ares smashed his hammer hard into the ground, shattering the earth with his omnipotent strength. The castle groaned as it was blown away, the debris raining around him. Dirt sprayed everywhere as the entire noble district was leveled out to nothing; every structure in sight was reduced to rubble. A whirlwind of dust swept around the area and Ahriman stared in shock at Ares' frightening power. A single downward swing of his hammer was enough to destroy everything in a mile radius. The grass, which had once been lush and freshly cut, was now burned to a crisp from the shockwave that had pulsed outward from Ares' strike.

The god of war stood in a deep crater, slowly heaving his hammer over his shoulder as he looked up at Ahriman, quite disappointed that he had missed. Ares turned to see Mithra still unconscious several hundred meters away. Some debris had fallen on top of him but that definitely wasn't enough to hurt a god. "*You know, Darien had one final wish before he passed control to me,*" Ares called up to Ahriman, squinting as the sunlight shined on his face. "*He wanted me to kill you more than anything.*"

Ahriman said nothing, his face deprived of emotion.

"If I were him, I would want the same thing," Ares said with a hearty laugh. "Oh well, he isn't going to be around anymore so don't get your hopes up that I'll revert back to that weakling. He doesn't know how to use my strength. He constantly holds back because he's afraid that he'll hurt the people around him. You might be wondering how I'm so much stronger than him. I'm really not, we have the same powers. It's just that I don't give a crap about mortals," Ares suddenly teleported in the air, appearing right next to Ahriman. "And that makes all the difference."

Ahriman didn't have any time to react before Ares swatted him straight out of the sky with his legendary hammer. The Persian god gasped, unexplainable pain detonating through his chest as he smashed into the lower city, crashing through entire rows of buildings. Structures of wood, stone, mud, marble, and steel all collapsed around him as he tumbled across the earth. *Darien was holding back? He had this much power all along?*

The Persian god of darkness groaned, slowly pushing himself into a sitting position. He was lying in the middle of the street and turned to see that there were dozens of civilians around him fleeing for their lives. His eyes narrowed. He was in the western side of Persepolis, where all of the civilians were evacuating. This area was currently highly populated. He worked his jaw. *Ugh, who cares? I need to figure out how I'm going to kill Ares. I haven't had enough time to practice using my powers to battle an opponent of this stature.*

A flaming chariot pulled by four warhorses soared across the sky and Ahriman saw that Ares was standing on the flying wagon, nocking an arrow on a diamond bow. The archer fired a projectile that looked like an orange beam that streaked through the air, bolting like a bullet straight for Ahriman.

Ahriman held up his hand and grunted as a shield of black magic formed around him, shimmering as the arrow smashed into it. There was an explosion as orange energy from Ares' projectile exploded around the Persian god and swallowed the entire street in destruction. Hundreds of innocent Persians were vaporized instantly, incinerated by the radiating heat from the magical explosion of Ares' arrow. However, Ahriman was still sitting in his shield, watching Ares. "You're powerful, I'll give you that," Ahriman said, the shield collapsing around him. "Finally, a worthy opponent so that I may test my abilities!" The god of darkness began to cackle with mirth. "This is perfect!"

Ares looked at the hundreds of injured civilians that were screaming out in agony in the lower city. Those were the lucky ones that had survived the explosion. He raised an eyebrow, rather surprised that Ahriman didn't care even the slightest about the deaths of other humans. After all, hadn't he been mortal once? The god shrugged. It didn't matter. This Persian was about to meet death soon anyway.

***

Darien sat alone in a universe of darkness, sitting with his legs crossed before him. A tranquil pool of water was set before him, showing him all of the events unfolding in the real world through Ares' eyes. The boy stared at the serene pool mindlessly, watching as hundreds of people died. The color from his eyes had faded and he looked much like a soulless doll, sitting there with purposeless existence.

"You're going to just let Ares wreak havoc like that?" Suddenly an image of young Tetsu from five years before appeared right next to Darien. The young boy squatted down next to the young Persian prince, peering into the pool of water, witnessing the destruction of Persepolis. "He's going wild. He cares nothing for the people."

Darien said nothing.

"H-he has no restraint!" Young Yuu sat down on the black floor on the other side of Darien. "I-I mean, he's just so b-barbaric! He's scary, don't you think? Is that how you want to be, Darien? Scary?"

"He's irresponsible," Darien's father said, standing on the other side of the pool with his queen at his side. "He strikes with no regard for the consequences that come with his actions. As a god, he should control his own strength."

"He shows no mercy," Aleysha said, appearing beside Darien's father. She folded her arms and watched as Ares punched Ahriman through a building, murderous intent coursing through the god's veins. "He's not like you, Darien."

"You're right," Darien said, still staring at the pool of water blankly. "He's not like me. He's stronger than me. He's not afraid and won't let anything hold him back from achieving what it is he really wants, for he doesn't care about any of these mortals around him. He's the only one who can carry out my wish for vengeance."

"But is that what you really want?" Kira asked, standing beside Aleysha.

Darien didn't reply.

Or is that what you think you want? Amon's voice echoed in Darien's head. The prince pried his eyes away from the pool of water and he glanced up to find the massive rock golem standing behind his father, mother, Aleysha, and Kira. The Guardian stood tall and snorted with a slight nod of his head. *You think that it was your duty to go back to Persepolis, avenge your family, and reclaim your throne?*

"That is my responsibility as prince!" Darien barked.

Not as a prince. Your duty as a prince is to lead your people.

Darien gritted his teeth, lowering his head. "Then it is my responsibility as my parents' son."

Your duty as their son is to move on from their deaths.

"Move on?" Darien glared upward at Amon, rage rising in his heart. "How is it possible to move on from the brutal deaths of the two people who raised me since I was a child? They gave me *everything*! I was so lucky to have someone as caring as my mother and someone as hardworking as my father in my life. But I never thanked them for being there. Not once! All I ever did was pester them about how I thought I was too irresponsible for the throne and how I would never live up to my father's legacy. I spent five years in the Lost Sands trying to *forget* my life as Prince Darien. And so I became Ares, someone that I'm not, in a futile attempt to leave behind the life I once had. But I'm not a barbaric god of war who loves fighting. I'm not a dauntless warrior who fears nothing and is fierce in the face of danger. I'm just a grieving prince who has locked up his suffering deep inside. I can't move on, Amon. I've tried."

Amon tilted his head to the side and grunted. Do you think your parents honestly care at all if you slay their murderer? My young master, you are misled. Ares may have told you that they aren't able to move on without Zahir and Cambyses's deaths but do you think that is true? Ares doesn't know your parents. You do.

Darien lowered his eyes. His father wouldn't condone violence as a solution to the issue. There was no doubt about that. His mother wouldn't either. In fact … now that he thought deeply about it, he realized that neither of his parents would really care for redemption.

You don't have to be a fierce warrior. You don't have to be dauntless, fearless, barbaric, careless, or wild as the old god of war once was. Darien, you are not him. You're you. I remember the last request that you made of me, young master. You told me to stop you if you ever started to lose yourself. Well, here I am, Darien. I'm here to tell you that it's okay for you to be human and be a god at the same time. It's okay for you to suffer, to feel pain, to cry. It's okay for you to be yourself.

Darien felt tears beginning to rush to his eyes and he felt two reassuring hands touching his shoulders. He turned and saw Tetsu and Yuu both there at his side. The young prince sniffed, turning to see that Alkaios had appeared in the world of darkness along with his gigantic army of the United Eastern Nations of Dastia, creating a sea of supporters around the boy.

Ramses was standing beside Alkaios and gave the young prince a slight nod of his head.

Mithra appeared sitting on Amon's left shoulder. The Persian god of war and justice smiled at Darien and winked. "You're a lot different than the other gods, Darien. You care for your friends, you care for your Guardians, and you restrain your power to protect those around you. I think that's remarkable, to have that much control. You once told me that you were an irresponsible person. But you use your godly powers more responsibly than any other deity I've met."

Darien smiled and saw that Ra was sitting on Amon's other shoulder, taking the form of a young man with tanned skin. He wore a cap made of the carcass of a falcon and he wore strips of tattered clothing that curled around his waist and dangled down to his knees. "You're here too, Ra?"

Ra nodded. "This world is your heart. Everyone in here is a companion that you hold dear. They're people that support you, are willing to fight for you, and they're willing to die for you. Five years ago, I chose you to become the next god of war for the Hellas pantheon. Do you remember why that was?"

"Something about being courageous, brave, and persistent?" Darien said, slightly unsure. "I had traits that the old Ares had."

"Ah, you did have qualities that the old Ares had. But you also had many that he didn't. I acknowledged kindness, selflessness, and determination as a few examples back then. Your willingness to sacrifice yourself to help others is a trait that we need amongst our gods these days. We need heroes, deities who are willing to put themselves on the line. Because you were once human, you are compassionate and understanding of other mortals. That is a unique quality that none of the other gods have," Ra said. "Before I put Ares' corpse in Zerzura five years ago, I had a discussion with Zeus, the leader of the Hellas pantheon, *your* god family. Zeus was worried that an irresponsible mortal would claim Ares' strength, one that wasn't worthy. One that would abuse his almighty strength as Zahir is now.

"I can honestly tell you, Darien, that you are the best choice that I ever could've made for picking an heir to Ares' legacy. As Mithra said only moments ago, you are the one god who uses his powers sparingly. Do you see Ares as he is now?" Ra said, indicating to the pool before Darien. "He's using his strength to destroy all of

Persepolis, killing thousands of innocent people. All without a care in the world for their wellbeing."

Darien closed his eyes. "My friends are there as well."

"Then you must save them," Ra said with a gentle smile. "Along with the other mortals that suffer under the wrath of both Ahriman and Ares."

"How?"

"You fight back and claim what is rightfully yours: your body, your mind, your godly power, and finally, your throne."

***

Darien's eyes slowly opened and he found himself standing inside of a gigantic temple made of stone and gold. Giant pillars supported a transparent ceiling that stretched hundreds of meters high. The young prince could see that it was nighttime in this alternate universe. He looked around and saw that the temple was located on a giant slab of land that floated in the middle of space where they were surrounded by billions of glowing stars. Braziers lit with golden flames illuminated the dark temple, revealing a gigantic statue of Ares that towered dozens of meters high. At the foot of the giant figure was a throne made of smelted steel that was tinted orange. Sitting upon the throne was the original Ares.

The god had long, stringy hair that came down over his face. His lips creaked into a sly smile, revealing his white teeth. He was shirtless, revealing rippling muscles that were honed to perfection after centuries of training. He wore torn, brown shorts that looked like they belonged to a commoner. Ares tapped his bare feet on the stone floor of the temple, the sound echoing, and began to chuckle.

"To think that you'd come here to my realm to challenge my place as the true god of war, Darien." Ares placed both of his coarse hands on the arms of his throne and stood up, tossing his dark hair from his face, revealing his orange, gleaming eyes. "I didn't think you had the guts, pampered prince."

Darien said nothing, rubbing his fingers against his clammy palms. His heart was racing but he knew that this was no time to be afraid. He was the true god of war. This power was his to control. The old Ares was dead, and it was time to cast away the ancient god once and for all.

"This is my temple, placed upon an island in a private universe. Only a being's soul may come here. If you die in this universe, Darien, your soul will forever be locked away and sealed within your own body. So, a duel, a challenge of skill. That's how we'll settle this. One soul against another. The winner will get to keep your body, how does that sound?" Ares said, snapping his fingers. His massive armory materialized beside his throne, thousands of weapons and armors filling racks upon racks. "No magic, no special skills, nothing. Just an honorable battle between warriors. Go on, pick a weapon."

Darien extended his hand to his spear and watched as the weapon flew from the rack and landed perfectly in his hands. He twirled the spear in his hand and slammed the butt against the ground, sending a bang ringing through the temple.

Ares smirked. "How expected of you, Darien. You always pick the same weapon no matter what, don't you? You don't like to experiment and you don't like to have fun! What a shame. The art of war is a skill that you should embrace and enjoy. After all, war is what we're best at, isn't it?" A two-handed sword that had a bright red blade raced straight into his right hand. The god gripped the hilt, wielding the gigantic sword with only one hand. Veins bulged from his muscular arms but he simply smiled as if the weapon wasn't even heavy.

Darien watched in disbelief as a second two-handed sword with a blade made of sapphires flew into Ares' left hand and the god wielded both weapons with ease, slamming the blades against one another, sending blue and red sparks flying into the air. The prince spun his spear and took a defensive position, gulping hard. *If this is all based on skill, I've only been training for five years. Ares has centuries of combat experience. I'll have to find some sort of weakness if I want to best him.*

Ares sprinted forward, rushing across the temple with his blades trailing behind him. His eyes went wide, reflecting a crazed look, and he whipped both of his blades in a downward slash towards Darien. The prince sidestepped the blows, watching as the weapons cracked the stone floor of the temple. Darien's eyes spotted the muscles in Ares' arms still tense and watched as the god scraped his blades across the ground and tore them through the air towards Darien in a futile attempt to catch the boy off-guard.

Darien ducked the speedy slash with ease and jabbed outward with his spear, smacking Ares straight in the gut with the butt of his weapon. There was a heavy thud as the god staggered backward, his eyes burning with rage. Darien spun his spear, spinning the weapon around himself and stabbing outwards from around his back. The positioning was so unexpected that Ares was barely able to dodge the jab. The prince whirled around and gripped the shaft of his weapon tightly, unleashing a relentless barrage of fast strikes that jabbed straight for Ares' head. Hoping to pop the god's head like a balloon, Darien continued to stab with incredible, blinding speed.

Ares weaved around Darien's speedy strikes, his teeth clenched. He was rather surprised that Darien had such expertise with the spear. The god grunted as the prince's spear sliced his cheek, drawing a slight sliver of blood that streamed down his cheek. He'd gotten hit? By this fool? Ares' eyebrows went up suddenly as he saw Darien's spear racing straight for his face. The man crossed his swords in front of him, blocking Darien's jab with a swift motion. "About time I took you seriously," Ares growled, breathing fog onto his crossed blades.

Darien winced as Ares' swords swooped outward, nearly rending him in half. The boy staggered backward, sweat racing down his face. If he wasn't careful, one mistake could be fatal. Ares rained down countless, fierce, blows that numbed Darien's arms as he attempted to block the attacks with the long shaft of his spear. *He's too strong…!*

"Gah!" Darien grunted as a final slash sent the boy flying backward through the air and slamming hard onto his back. The overwhelming power of Ares' strikes was far too much for Darien to handle. The boy was nimble, able to deliver attacks quickly and dodge. But when it came to enduring the vicious strikes that Ares unleashed he was at a loss. The boy was about to get up when suddenly Ares smashed his boot down on the prince's stomach, driving the wind straight from his lungs. He gasped, trying to get his breath back.

Ares tapped one of his blades to Darien's throat, the cold steel sending a chilling sensation shivering through Darien's body. "Oh, don't tell me that it was that easy," Ares said with a sadistic grin. He tossed one of his blades away, the weapon clattering to the ground loudly. He reached down and grabbed Darien by the collar of his shirt, lifting the defenseless boy up into the air as if he weighed only a pound. "Surely the gods could've chosen a stronger *replacement* than you."

Darien clutched the hilt of his spear tightly, his feet dangling a foot from the ground. He jabbed towards Ares' torso but the god saw the strike coming and brought his sword slashing downward, severing the boy's hand in a swift motion. The prince's spear clattered to the ground and he stared in shock at the bloody stump where his hand had been only moments ago. His face paled and Ares released his collar, allowing the boy to collapse to the ground and cry out in anguish. Darien was surprised to find that losing his hand didn't hurt. Instead, everything was numb. All that he felt was a warm sensation in the stump of his wrist where his left hand had been only moments ago. Blood hemorrhaged from the wound and splattered onto the stone ground, creating a thick pool beneath Darien. Salty tears spilled down his cheeks and he sniffed up the mucus that was about to stream out his nostrils. Darien could see it, the pale, unmoving slab of flesh that was lying right next to Ares' foot. The pungent miasma of metallic blood filled his nostrils, causing his stomach to heave. He reached to his mouth with his right hand, about to vomit.

"Are you that afraid of pain, Darien? So much that you'll retch at the sickening sight of your own blood? Well, trust me. You'll be seeing a lot more of it spilt," Ares said with a bellowing laugh. He paced forward slowly, dragging his bloodstained sword across the ground. There was a scraping sound that pierced Ares' ears, making him tingle. "It bothers me, Darien, that they chose a wimpy little child like you to be my successor. Did they honestly think someone as feeble as you would be able to control my power? Why didn't they pick some legendary hero known for slaying thousands? Instead they chose a spoiled prince that was surrounded by nothing but wealth since birth. Never once did you experience hardship before your betrayal in Persepolis five years ago. And even after surviving for five years in the Lost Sands, you're still the same craven that you were when you entered that forsaken desert." Ares stopped before the prince, raising his sword into the air. "With this final strike, your soul will be severed and you'll be locked away forever. Your body will be mine. This is goodbye, little boy."

Darien clutched the forearm of his bleeding arm, gasping. His head was lowered, his curly blonde hair falling before his eyes. How on earth was he going to muster the strength to defeat Ares? Was this really the end? The prince reached up and wiped the tears that soaked his face with the sleeve of his shirt, his heart rate slowing down. Could he somehow defeat someone who feared nothing? Someone who didn't feel pain and had thousands of years of more experience than he?

It's okay for you to be human and be a god at the same time. It's okay for you to suffer, to feel pain, to cry. It's okay for you to be yourself. Amon's words echoed in the boy's head.

Darien clenched his teeth, biting hard. His body trembled as he cast the pain out of his mind. He reached up with his free hand and gently touched the golden medallion that dangled from his neck. *You fight back and claim what is rightfully yours.* Ra's words bounced around in his head. "It's not over yet, Ares," Darien growled, glaring up at the surprised god. "Out there I have friends that you're endangering. I have an army that's depending on *me* to defeat Ahriman, not you. In the real world, I have people who I care about and I refuse to leave them behind!" He lashed out with his hand and snatched his spear off the ground, swinging the weapon around in a sudden sweeping motion.

Ares' legs were swept out from underneath him and the god's eyes widened as he fell backwards. Crashing hard onto his back, Ares grunted before feeling a surge of pain spike through his leg. He turned and saw that Darien had jammed his spear deep into the god's leg, drawing a massive amount of blood. "Y-you bastard!"

Darien tore his spear from the bleeding god, spinning his weapon with blinding speed, using one hand. "This is my body, Ares! Get the hell out." He jabbed outward with quick stabs that plunged deep into the god's body. Ares, who was still on the ground, was not even able to react to such speed and precision. "Someone who disregards the lives of mortals and undermines others as lesser beings doesn't deserve the power of a god!" Darien spun the spear, the shaft swinging around his neck, and he grabbed the weapon tightly as he jammed the sharpened tip of his spear deep into Ares' chest.

Ares' furious eyes narrowed as he sputtered blood from his mouth, his face paling. "T-This is my body…! This is my power! You can't—"

"It's not yours anymore," Darien panted, digging the spear deeper into the god's body. A choking gasp escaped the lips of the dying deity. "Don't worry; I'll use your power to make things right in the world. I'll be the Guardian who will protect the lives of the innocent, unlike you." He released his spear and staggered backward, his heart pounding. "I've wasted plenty of years in the Lost Sands, unsure of what I'd use my godly strength for. But now I know. I'll be a god who protects the lives of the innocent in Dastia."

"A hero, huh?" Ares scoffed, leaning his head back against the cold temple floor. "That's hysterical. A god of war … using his power to save the lives. What a joke…."

Darien limped past Ares' unmoving body and hobbled over to the steel throne of Ares. He winced as he plopped himself down in the seat, leaning back into the chair. "I might be a god of war, but I plan on doing things much differently than you. I won't be a barbaric warlord that instigates conflict." A swirling fire engulfed the colossal statue of the old Ares, burning it to ashes. As the ashes faded, it was replaced with a fresh stone statue of Darien. The new god of war leaned back in his throne, folding one leg over the other. "I'll be myself."

***

Ahriman was on the ground, gasping for air. He was exhausted, and his arm was broken cleanly at his side. Blood streamed down his forearm from a nasty gash on his shoulder and a small river of blood also trickled down from his forehead down his cheek to his chin. Panting, he staggered backward as he eyed Ares. The boy had abruptly stopped attacking and was now standing there, motionless as a statue. As the Persian god of darkness watched, the ancient markings on the boy's skin began to fade away.

Ares' eyes slowly opened but his irises were no longer the wild orange they had once been. Instead, they had returned to their natural hue of sky-blue. He dropped the short sword that he had been wielding, letting it clatter loudly to the ground. The boy looked at both of his unscathed hands and smiled, sighing with relief. Ares scanned his surroundings and saw that they were battling in the southern part of the city. The entire area had been leveled; all buildings for a mile in all directions had been reduced to rubble and debris. He reached up and scratched the back of his neck. "Huh, the old Ares must've really been going all-out," he said, his gaze softening when he saw several corpses of innocent civilians buried underneath piles of detritus. His attention turned to Ahriman. "Have you had enough?"

Ahriman cracked a tiny smile, which then turned into hysterical laughter. The Persian god held his belly as he burst out guffawing uncontrollably. "You mean, you're Darien? Oh, this is rich! Just when I thought—" His mouth was left gaping open when he saw that Ares had completely vanished from where he stood. Instead, the boy had reappeared right behind Ahriman.

Ares clenched his fist into a tight ball, his knuckles popping. He rotated his body and sank a heavy blow straight into Ahriman's back, a sickening snap echoing through the city. The Persian god rocketed forward and smashed like a skipping stone across the ground, slamming over piles of destroyed buildings. The Hellas god of war cracked his knuckles, glaring at Ahriman. "You sure you want to go ahead and underestimate me, Zahir? I'm more than ready to pound your face in."

Ahriman wiped a bit of blood from his lips and scoffed, pushing himself to his feet. His broken arm was hanging loosely at his side and his body was covered in cuts and bruises from his battle against the original Ares. He twirled his scepter in his hand, gripping it tightly. "Underestimate? How could a tiny prince ever come to defeat me?" he roared, releasing multiple bolts of dark energy that shot through the air towards Ares.

The young god of war burst forward with a ridiculous amount of speed, shocking Ahriman. Darien was just as fast as the original Ares, maybe even faster! The deity weaved his way around the magical bolts, charging like a bull towards Ahriman. The projectiles struck the ground behind Ares, exploding into gigantic domes of black energy that incinerated the scorched earth. But the boy outran even those magical explosions, converging rapidly on Ahriman's position.

Ahriman took a hesitant step backward, grunting as he realized that Ares was already upon him. The god was about to cast another magical spell to try and force him backward, but Ares acted far too quickly. The boy held his hand outward and sparkling golden light flashed into his palm. Within a second he was grasping the legendary Spear of Ares, a renowned Sacred Treasure.

The war deity gripped the shaft of the weapon with both hands and rent the air towards Ahriman's throat. The Persian deity dropped low, feeling the air shimmer above him from the ferocity of the blow.

But Ares wasn't nearly finished. He began to spin his spear with tremendous speed, practically creating a whirlwind around himself. He made a full rotation and swept his weapon across the ground, this time aiming directly for Ahriman's legs.

Ahriman grunted, swinging his legs backward so that he was temporarily airborne. The spear missed his feet, but now Ahriman was floating mid-air, completely parallel with the ground. He knew that he was completely vulnerable, at least for a second. And a second was all it would take.

Ares spun around a third time, rotating his body in a perfect spinning kick that cracked across Ahriman's cheek, sending blood spurting from the god's mouth. The Persian deity spiraled through the air and crashed onto the desolate earth, rolling several hundred meters away. Dust swept around him, clouding his vision as he attempted to get back up.

Panting, Ahriman looked at his bleeding arm. His sleeve had been torn cleanly off, revealing a tender wound that had been opened by his prolonged battle with Ares. The injured deity gritted his teeth, opening and closing his fists. Darien's skill in battle, prior to his banishment, had been abysmal, if Ahriman recalled correctly. After only five years of training, how was it possible for Darien to become so skilled with his spear? His godly strength wasn't the only issue; his proficiency with the spear was unlike anything Ahriman had seen before. *What style is that?* Ahriman narrowed his eyes as he watched Ares trudge forward in his direction. *It's barbaric and lacks proper grace. Yet ... it's working!*

Ares dashed forward, tossing his spear up into the air. He

brought back his right hand and smashed the butt of the spear with the heel of his palm. There was an explosion of energy that rocketed through the Sacred Treasure as the spear launched itself like a bullet straight at Ahriman.

The deity of darkness stared, incredulous. He threw himself to the side, the spear bashing into the earth where he had been only a moment before. The ground erupted like an active volcano, spewing dirt and debris up into the air. Ahriman staggered away, his eyes wide. *No one attacks like this! I can barely keep up!*

The legendary Spear of Ares leapt to life and began to follow Ahriman, jabbing and slashing at him wildly. The Persian god of darkness ducked and weaved around the barrage of strikes from the weapon, shocked that the weapon was battling on its own. His eyes flickered to Ares and saw that the boy was now upon him. The spear halted its assault and retreated back to its master, returning back to Ares' hand as the boy leapt through the air and descended upon Ahriman. *This can't be…!*

The boy slammed his palm straight into Ahriman's face and drove the Persian deity back into the earth. But Ares didn't stop there. He rushed forward at sonic speed, dragging Ahriman across the earth by his face, leaving behind a deep trench of dirt in his trail.

Ares released Ahriman, sending the god rolling across the ground and bashing into a building made of wood. The structure groaned as it collapsed upon the Persian god, sending a wave of dust sweeping out in all directions. Ares exhaled, placing his sweaty palms on his knees as he panted.

Ahriman burst from the debris, sending wood scattering in all directions. The ireful god held out both his hands, his fingers each an inch apart. The tips of his fingers began to glow with an arcane purple magic, the ground beginning to rumble as if a Core-Digger were right beneath them. The Persian god's purple irises faded, and his eyes were replaced with blackness. It was as if Ares were staring into the void itself. "I've had enough of you, prince!" Ahriman bellowed, his voice echoing in different pitches all in unison, creating a dissonance that sounded similar to a banshee speaking. "Prepare to be sent to the depths of oblivion! *Khæra!*"

Gravity seemed to reverse as bits of tiny pebbles and wreckage began to levitate around Ahriman, floating around the deity. Suddenly bolts of purple, swirling, energy discharged from the tips of the god's fingers, fusing together to create a beam that rushed straight at Ares. There was a spark and the beam turned black just as it was about to swallow Ares in darkness.

The young god of war held out his right palm to the oncoming beam of magic, his eyes void of fear. "Lend me your strength, *Aegis*."

A gigantic, ovoid shield the size of a castle suddenly materialized in front of Ares, forming a barrier between the boy and Ahriman's destructive projectile. The magical shield was sky-blue and slightly translucent so that Ares could see through it.

"Do you think a spell like that will be able to stop me from destroying you?" Ahriman boomed, his crazed eyes wide with bloodlust. He thrust his hands out further, intensifying the strength of his magical beam.

The Persian god's magic bashed against Ares' shield, sprouting around the gargantuan barrier. However, the beam didn't penetrate it.

Ahriman's eyes knitted together, sweat beginning to pour down his face. "What … how is this possible? *Khæra* has the power to reduce entire nations into naught but dust! But you…," he growled, his eyes widening with fear, "you're blocking it!"

Ares smiled. "That's because *Aegis* isn't a spell. It isn't even a physical shield. It's a Guardian, forged and wielded by my family of gods. Not even you can penetrate it with your spells, Zahir."

Ahriman's eyes widened with terror. "A-A Guardian? N-No! That can't be. Guardians are living monsters that are summoned by…."

"Are you citing your definition of a Guardian from a textbook?" Ares called, snapping his fingers. "Or from experience? Strike out, *Aegis*."

The massive shield spurred to life, flashing radiating shades of blue that filled the air. There was a loud rumble as Aegis burst forward with such speed that it looked like the shield had teleported. Aegis smashed into Ahriman with tremendous force, sending the god flipping backward uncontrollably, smashing into a building a mile away. The structure groaned loudly before collapsing onto Ahriman, sending wreckage and dust splashing outward. Ares watched the still pile of rubble for a moment and was about to go and check to see if Ahriman was actually unconscious when he heard someone call his name. "Darien!" Yuu yelled, sprinting down an abandoned street in the direction of the god. He pointed back in the direction that he was coming. "It's Tetsu! He's injured bad, I'm not sure if he's going to make it!" The noble glanced to his left and saw that District Nine of Persepolis had been completely reduced to nothing but wreckage as a result of the vicious battle between Ares and Ahriman. He swallowed hard.

Tetsu? Ares was about to rush forward to Yuu when suddenly he sensed a flicker of movement behind him. The god glanced quickly over his shoulder and saw that Ahriman had burst from the debris and was about to skewer his scepter straight through the boy's body. A direct blow like that could easily kill him.

"This is what happens when you take your eyes off your opponent!" Ahriman roared, jabbing forward with his pointed scepter towards Ares' exposed back.

A pillar of fire detonated between Ares and Ahriman, swallowing the Persian god of darkness in the snarling flames. Ares squinted and retreated from Ahriman, unable to stay so close to the searing heat of the fire. The ground was scorched black, and ashes drifted into the air as the flames vanished just as quickly as they had appeared. Smoke wafted through the air towards the afternoon sky and Ares turned to see Mithra standing on a rooftop of one of the nearby buildings, wisps of smoke drifting from his fingertips. "Looks like you took your eyes off me first, Ahriman," Mithra joked with a weary sigh. He leapt off of the building and landed on the ground with a heavy thud. The Persian deity shot Ares a grin. "You gave him quite the beating, didn't you?"

Ares looked to Ahriman, who was lying face-first in the ground in a pile of blackened ashes. His body was completely still and it was hard to tell if he was alive or dead. The boy reached up and rubbed the back of his neck, grinning. "I suppose so, yeah. Though it looks like a huge part of the city got destroyed in the process," Ares said, looking over his shoulder at the annihilated southern district of the city. The ancient Ares really didn't hold back at all, did he? "There're hundreds, if not, thousands of innocents dead because of me."

"Don't worry about something like that now. By defeating Ahriman you've saved more than just a few thousand lives," Mithra said and nodded towards Yuu, who was waiting for Darien. "Go on, Ares. Your friends require your company. I'll make sure Ahriman stays put until you get back."

"Thanks," Ares said with a thankful smile and turned to jog after Yuu.

After several minutes of running down an abandoned road in the city, Ares saw Aleysha and Kira kneeling beside Tetsu, who was lying on his back, his eyes closed. Blood pooled around his body and he was paler than Ares had ever seen him before. The boy's heart thumped and he slowed to a stop, walking slowly towards his fallen friend.

Fang was in his tiny puppy form, nuzzling Tetsu's cheek gently as he whimpered.

Aleysha stood up from Tetsu's side and walked over to Yuu and Ares. "I found Kira and brought her to Tetsu as soon as I could, but she says that he's already lost too much blood. He's hemorrhaging from too many opened wounds." She was trembling, looking at the ground. "Even Kira's not sure if he's going to make it."

Ares watched as Yuu began to storm towards one of the buildings. The god saw that Cambyses was tied up, leaning against a wall of one of the street's structures. Yuu lashed out, infuriated, and grabbed the fallen king by the throat, pinning Cambyses against the building with a loud thud. "If Tetsu dies it's on you!" he roared, smashing a heavy punch into the clay wall inches from Cambyses's face, sending shivers through the lord's body. The wall cracked and pieces of clay crumbled off the knuckles of Yuu's metal gauntlet. The noble took a step back and let the king slump onto the ground, tears streaming down his swollen face.

Ares looked at Tetsu's broken body, a tingling sensation running through his fingers. "What happened?" he asked Aleysha softly.

"Cambyses used the Sands of Time to freeze time. Tetsu had already suffered a major amount of injuries before we went to save him from his execution. It looked like he was wounded before we even arrived. But when Cambyses stabbed him … his body couldn't take anymore. He's barely clinging on to life as it is. If I just had seen it coming…."

"Don't blame yourself," Ares said, watching as Kira cast healing magic over Tetsu. "Tetsu always liked to push his limits."

"D-Darien…." a weak voice called out.

"He's awake!" Kira exclaimed, her eyes wide.

Ares quickly rushed to Tetsu's side, kneeling beside his friend. He grasped one of Tetsu's cold, bloody hands and squeezed it tightly. The dying man looked up at Ares with a drained smile, his eyes barely even cracked open. "How'd you do on your end, buddy?"

"I stopped Ahriman," Ares whispered.

Tetsu grinned. "And we got Cambyses, didn't we, guys?" He coughed suddenly, sputtering blood onto his shirt. Wincing, clearly in pain, Tetsu tapped his head back against the ground and sighed. "Man, look at me. I'm a mess."

Ares cracked a half-smile. "Yeah, you are."

"I wish I could say that I've been through worse," Tetsu chuckled weakly. "Unfortunately, I haven't."

"You'll get through this," Ares said, looking right into his friend's eyes, two glimmering lights that were beginning to fade.

"Don't give me that false hope, Darien. No human could survive something like this. I really pushed myself too far this time. Yuu," Tetsu said quietly, looking to the noble. "Make sure to help Darien and his building of a new nation. Persia cannot fall to the hands of a tyrant. You're powerful now, Yuu. Keep an eye on Darien. The idiot tends to act a lot on his own."

Yuu nodded lightly, turning away, unable to look at Tetsu anymore.

Tetsu smiled weakly and closed his eyes. "My body feels like it's made of ice and fragile glass. But your hand, Darien, is so warm. I want to thank you for everything that you've done for me. I've never heard of a highborn prince that would stand up for a lowly warrior. Five years ago, you risked your own life to help me. You *believed* in me when no one else would…."

"That's what friends are for, right?" Ares said, tears glistening in his eyes.

Tetsu grinned and nodded slightly. "Yeah, we're always there for each other … I love you guys," he said, sniffing back tears. "Thank you everyone … for everything." He gave Ares' hand one final squeeze before his whole body went limp, the lights in his eyes dimmed and darkened.

Ares gripped Tetsu's freezing hand once more, hoping that his friend would squeeze back but nothing happened. The god bit his lower lip gently as his vision became blurred by moist tears. He lowered his head, releasing Tetsu's hand, and rose to his feet. Kira had fallen forward and was crying into Tetsu's chest, her cries of anguish muffled by his bloodstained clothes. Aleysha put her hand to her mouth, sobbing quietly as she fell to her knees, staring at the lifeless body of her adopted brother.

Yuu clenched his jaw, mashing his teeth together. He balled his hands into tight fists, his knuckles turning a ghostly white. Spinning around, Yuu began to stomp towards Cambyses, his turquoise eyes wide with burning rage. "This is your fault!" he boomed, reaching for the hilt of his sword.

"Yuu, stop," Ares said softly, raising his head. "What will killing him do? Will it bring back Tetsu?"

Yuu squeezed the hilt of his sword, his hand quavering for a moment. He scowled and slapped the golden pommel of his sword in frustration, lowering his arm to his side in defeat. He tilted his head down, his snow-white hair coming down over his eyes as tears began to trickle down his cheek.

Ares touched Yuu's shoulder as he ambled to the noble's side. The god of war then stepped before Cambyses, pitifully gazing down at the fallen Persian king. "You've made countless people suffer because of your actions, Uncle, including me," he said, brushing some of his blonde hair from his eyes. "And no matter what you say, I will not forgive you for what you've done. You not only took my parents away from me, you also are responsible for the death of my best friend and the destruction of dozens of countries. The suffering of millions is on your head."

Cambyses lowered his head. "I understand. You're angry and I would do the same in your position…."

"I'm not going to kill you."

Cambyses glanced up, staring at Ares in shock.

"Darien…," Yuu said, eying Ares with confusion. "This scum deserves to die for what he's done!"

"I don't think murder will do anything," Ares said, watching Cambyses. "I refuse to murder just for the sake of killing. He'll be jailed and someone else will take his throne. Though it won't be me."

Yuu blinked, puzzled. "What?"

"I have made a commitment. I plan on using my powers to safeguard all of the innocents on this continent. I'll make sure that no tyrants rise up as Cambyses did and that no unfairness comes upon the guiltless. I'll use this power to bring justice upon those who prey upon the weak. I can't spend time leading an entire empire. My duty as a god should be more than just protecting an empire. It should be to help all of those in Dastia. Maybe in other continents too," Ares said. "Though, Persia cannot be without a king. I think you should be its new ruler, Yuu."

Yuu raised an eyebrow. "M-Me?"

Ares turned to his friend, beaming. "You studied politics for many years. You once said that you would be my advisor when I grew up, no? You'd do lots of good on that throne, Yuu. Trust me."

"I just never expected for you to choose me as the successor of the throne. I mean … I don't really deserve it. For five years I followed Cambyses blindly and fulfilled all of his twisted desires without even so much as questioning my own morals. I murdered hundreds, tortured innocents, and caused countless more to suffer. A person like me becoming king?" Yuu shook his head, licking his lower lip.

"Think of this as a second chance, Yuu," Ares said, clamping his hand on the noble's shoulder in reassurance. "I believe in you. I'm sure that you'll do a great job as King of Persia. Besides, I'll be there to make sure that you don't step out of line. You won't be alone, don't worry."

Yuu nodded and suddenly looked up when he saw a pillar of bright white light ripping from the heavens and smashing down into the area where Mithra and Ahriman were. He raised his hand and shielded his eyes from the dazzling light. "What is that?"

"I'll go and check it out. Keep an eye on Cambyses," Ares said, leaping from the ground. He flew thousands of feet into the air and landed hard on the ground besides Mithra, who was staring at something. Ares' eyes followed Mithra's line of vision to a group of three male gods who stood tall, with Ahriman kneeling before them.

One of the men was wearing a gigantic helmet of glimmering golden metal that had two curved red horns protruding from its top. He was wearing an impressive, glittering suit of mail armor with the white fur of an ancient frost wolf covering his shoulders. The warrior wore heavy boots, and was gripping a massive spear with a three-pronged tip that looked like a golden trident. The weapon gleamed brilliantly in the light, mesmerizing Ares with its magnificence. The man had a giant black eye patch clamped over his right eye, and he snorted when he saw Ares. He had a grizzly beard that was as white as snow and a face of deep wrinkles, proof of his age and experience.

Another man was wearing long white drapes that curled around his body and exposed one breast while covering the other. A belt made of smelted bronze was clamped around his waist, fastening the robe tightly to his bare flesh. Golden bands were clamped to his wrists and blue electricity crackled about in the palm of his coarse hands. The man also had white hair and a wizened face. His beard was fluffy, like clouds in the sky, and stretched all the way down to his stomach. The wavy hair on his head was long and flowed down to the back of his neck. He eyed Ares curiously and gave the boy a small nod.

The other figure was Ra, who looked the same as when Ares had seen him in that alternate universe prior to his battle to reclaim his body. The god smiled at Ares and winked slyly. "Ah, Ares! I was just asking Mithra where you were. You've done the world a great service by helping to defeat Ahriman."

The man with the spear grunted. "My name is Odin and I am the leader of the Aesir family of gods." He bowed his head lightly. "Mithra and Ares, we intend to reward the two of you for your remarkable achievement in bringing down this god of darkness."

"Ah," Mithra said with a hearty laugh. He pointed to Ares. "Ahriman actually defeated me earlier on. It was Ares and Ares alone who brought the lord of darkness to his knees. It should be him that you're thanking, not so much me." He grinned at Ares and nudged the boy playfully. "He's a powerful deity, one of the strongest I've seen."

The god with the white robe raised an eyebrow and folded his arms as he examined Ares. "I am Zeus, leader of the Hellas pantheon. You're much different than our previous god of war, Ares," he observed.

Ares gulped. *This is the leader of my family of gods, Zeus?* He averted his eyes from the deity, licking his upper lip nervously, expecting to be scolded for not acting like a proper god of war.

"It's refreshing," Zeus said, reaching out and patting Ares lightly on the head. "The gods of Hellas have been watching you, Ares. Your compassionate nature and selflessness are something that we never expected to see from our barbaric god of war. The other gods are eager to meet you after your accomplishment." He turned and looked to Ahriman, who was groveling in the sand before the three powerful deities. "Now, what do we do with you?"

"Have Ahura Mazda, the leader of the Persian pantheon, decide what Ahriman's punishment should be," Ra said, folding his arms over his chest. "After all, I believe that the Persian family should be the ones to decide what to do with this problematic one." He shot a glare at Ahriman.

"I'll take him to Heaven," Odin said. "Mithra, accompany me and bring this pathetic dung bag. We'll present him before your leader together."

Mithra nodded and bumped Ares' shoulder with his fist lightly. "Good job, Ares. I'm hoping to see you around, yeah?" He walked forward and grabbed Ahriman by the back of his neck, and forced the Persian god of darkness to stagger to his feet and stumble towards Odin.

Ahriman's stringy black hair came over his face and he glared at

Ares over his shoulder as he was forced towards Odin. "This isn't over, Darien. I'll be back for you, Persian prince. I swear by it! Every person you ever loved, all of your filthy friends that you have hiding back there in that street behind you … I'll make them all suffer to the point where they'll wish I just killed them all off! I'll—"

"Enough!" Odin boomed, grabbing Ahriman by the skull. The warrior's grip was tight as he squeezed the god of darkness's skull with frightening force. There was a crack and Ahriman screamed in agony, his voice rising several decibels as his shrill cry of pain split the silence. "Boy, pay no attention to this fool's empty threats. He won't be seeing the mortal world anytime soon. Let's go, Mithra."

A beam of white energy ripped from the sky and smashed down on Odin, Mithra, and Ahriman, bathing the three gods in bright light. Within a few seconds, the beam receded back to the heavens and the three deities were gone. A wisp of smoke drifted from the vaporized earth where they once stood.

"I believe that you have the right to be granted one wish, Ares," Zeus said. "As long as it is within our power, we will grant it to you. That is the least that we can do after what you've done here."

Ares' eyebrows went up in surprise. A wish? Well, what would he wish for? What was it that he wanted? He was about to open his mouth but frowned, realizing that he didn't know what it was that he wanted. Wealth? Power? No, he didn't care for any of that. He didn't need much. All he really needed was his friends. "I wish that everyone who died here at Persepolis would be brought back to life," Ares said, with a slight smile. *You pick to revive all of these people but not your parents? You only have one wish, Darien!* He exhaled. It was either choose his parents or the thousands of people that died today. Even though he knew he would love to bring his parents back from the dead, Ares knew that the lives of two were not worth the lives of tens of thousands. He was responsible for the deaths of many of these innocent civilians. He had lost control, and their fates were on him. Now he had to fix his mistake.

Zeus's eyes widened, stunned at Ares' selfless request. "What?"

Ra simpered.

Zeus looked at Ra and frowned. "He's serious?"

"He is," Ra said.

The god of lightning scoffed and smacked his forehead. "Fulfilling such a request is out of my reach. Perhaps I ought to go to Hades—"

"It's okay," Ra assured Zeus, snapping his fingers. "I've already fulfilled his wish."

A surge of glowing green energy pulsed outward from Ra's position in the form of a wave. The magical wave swept over Persepolis, enveloping the damaged city in healing magic. Those who were injured were mended instantly. Meanwhile, all of the corpses in the city began to glow brightly as their wounds were sealed and their blood mystically soaked back into their bodies. Broken bones cracked back into place and the crushed cadavers of those buried underneath debris levitated out of the destruction, their bodies mended. As Ares had requested, the dead were given a second chance.

***

Alkaios's eyes slowly opened and he found himself looking up at the gleaming sky, his heart racing. He was alive? How was such a miracle possible? He remembered that a Persian warrior had stabbed him right through the chest. The King of Luxas turned and saw that the streets were filled with soldiers from the east as well as Persian warriors. The two armies stared at each other with confusion, everyone was surprised to see that they were alive. Something miraculous had happened. There was not a single dead person in the street. Alkaios dropped his sword, his weapon clattering loudly to the ground, shattering the silence. He was done fighting. He would not die a second time. The gods had granted him a second chance; he would not throw this life away.

The king's subordinates followed suit, tossing their weapons to the ground. They, too, were done fighting.

The Persian soldiers all looked at each other, puzzled by their current situation. It began with one man who decided to throw down his scimitar. Then his friends followed. Then his squadron. Soon all of the soldiers in Persepolis were laying down their arms, refusing to continue the war. The battle was done with. No one was willing to die a second time.

Alkaios saw that a Persian soldier was lying on the ground, staring at the sky blankly. The pallor on the stranger's face reflected his confusion. The King of Luxas ambled over to the soldier and offered his hand to the puzzled man. "It's alright, the fighting is over," he said with a reassuring smile.

"W-Who won?" the Persian asked shakily, accepting the hand reluctantly.

Alkaios shrugged. "Your guess is as good as mine. But I know for a fact that I don't want to fight anymore. Do you?"

"N-No. I could've sworn that I was killed!" the Persian choked out as he was pulled to his feet.

"Me too!" another Persian exclaimed.

"I was dead as well!" one of Alkaios's men shouted.

"The gods have bestowed a miracle upon us all, bringing us all back to life! They didn't do this because they wanted us to continue fighting. They returned us to the world of the living to grant us a second chance!" Alkaios shouted, his voice heard by all of those around him. "I believe that we shouldn't waste the lives that the gods have returned to us! Let's work together and help the civilians. We shouldn't waste our second chance fighting amongst each other. I, personally, do not want to return to the world of the dead. Persians, you are no longer our enemy."

***

Ramses stumbled outside of Cassim's house, which had been burned to the ground. Staring at the ashes of the home, his heart sank. But when he suddenly heard his son's cry, his hopes soared. The Magus turned around and saw his wife and child rushing towards him with open arms. He embraced his family tightly, tears gleaming in his eyes. He squeezed them tight, burying his face into his wife's shoulder as he cried. "I-I'm here…! I'm back. I love you both. I love you both so much!" He kissed his wife's cheek and pulled his family closer to him, never wanting to let them go.

"Daddy, how are we alive?" Ramses' son asked. "I thought that I got my head banged by some stranger! Was that a dream?"

"It must've been a dream," Ramses exclaimed, kneeling down and kissing his son's forehead. Tears were spilling down his cheeks.

They killed my son and my wife. They even killed me. But we're alive. How is that possible? Is this the world of the dead?

Ramses turned and saw Cassim hugging his grandmother, who had been miraculously cured of her illness. The elderly woman was standing up and embracing her grandson tightly, tears glinting in the corners of her eyes. Ramses smiled. *Does our revival have anything to do with Ares?*

Ramses turned and looked over his shoulder into the gleaming cerulean sky. He smirked. After all, you're probably the only god who's selfless enough to revive all of these humans. You're the only one who understands our constant fear of death, our unshakable love for our families, and our struggle for survival. A god who was once a human. Huh, maybe that wasn't the worst idea after all.

***

Aleysha heard Kira abruptly scream with delight and turned to see that the young mage had her arms wrapped around Tetsu's neck, hugging the man tightly. Tetsu's eyes had fluttered open and he was smiling broadly, patting Kira's back as tears raced down her cheeks. Aleysha's eyes went wide and she rushed forward and wrapped her arms around Kira and her brother, embracing the two of them tightly. "Y-you're alive!" she exclaimed, her eyes moistening. "We all thought you were gone…."

Tetsu turned his head to Yuu, who was standing on a roof looking off into the distance. "Hey, Yuu!" he called. "What happened?"

"Darien is standing with a bunch of other gods over where Ahriman was defeated," Yuu called, not taking his eyes off of Ares.

He smirked, looking all around the city to see that thousands of people were being healed by Ra's incredible magic. "Looks like everyone was brought back to life."

"Everyone?" Tetsu said. "Even the Magi?"

"I don't expect that anyone will start fighting again," Yuu said. "The city is in a state of confusion. No one knows who won the battle and who lost. Not to mention, I'm sure those who died don't want to waste their miracle by rushing back into battle." He leapt off of the roof of the building and landed next to Cambyses, who was still tied up. Yuu reached into his pocket and pulled out the Sands of Time, tossing the hourglass through the air to Tetsu.

Tetsu caught it with one hand, frowning.

"That belongs to you. Oh, also Darien named me the King of Persia in your temporary absence. I hope you're ready to help me out with that position."

Tetsu leaned forward, his eyes wide. He burst out laughing. "Really? Amazing! Congratulations, Yuu! Wow, how long have I been out for?"

"You were dead for about twenty minutes," Kira said.

Aleysha laughed. "That's not exactly a long time."

"What was it like?" Yuu asked, leaning back against a wall. "Death, I mean."

Tetsu twirled the Sands of Time in his hands. "It was dark and cold. Really, that's all I remember. That and the constant feeling of falling, as if I were eternally descending into a pitch-black abyss."

"Sounds outstandingly fun."

"I'm not exactly excited to return there so hopefully this miracle of me returning to life is a permanent deal, yeah?" Tetsu said, curling his arms around Kira and Aleysha and pulling the two girls close to him. "Hey, Yuu! Get over here, I need some love right now."

Yuu rolled his eyes as he pushed off the wall and began to walk towards his old friend and the two giggling girls. He couldn't help but grin. "You're such an idiot."

***

Ares stood on the roof of an extremely tall building, which gave him a breathtaking view of the city. Gazing over Persepolis, he saw that people were crying with happiness after their return to the world of the living. The god could see Yuu, Aleysha, and Kira all hugging Tetsu in the distance. He grinned, glad to see that Tetsu was okay. Ares turned to look at the eastern section of Persepolis and spotted Alkaios helping some of the Persians who had been revived but were stuck under rubble of collapsed buildings. Meanwhile, Ramses was leading his family through the city with a broad smile on his face, something Ares didn't expect to see from the staid man. Everything seemed to be going well.

"Satisfied?" Ra called from behind Ares, standing on the rooftop behind the god.

Ares turned to the sun deity and smiled. "Yes. Thank you, Ra, for the opportunity to save the people and correct my mistake. During my battle with Ahriman, I lost control and there was a lot of collateral damage."

"Ah, yes. I know," Ra said with a chuckle. "I saw."

"You see a lot of things, don't you?" Ares smirked.

"I do, yes." Ra winked. "You know, Ares, the other gods are

quite impressed with you. You could've wished for anything. Unlimited wealth, incredible power, a title, recognition … but you chose to save humans. The gods don't value human life as highly as you do." Ra walked forward and patted Ares on the shoulder. "However, I am very proud of you, Darien. You have grown to become a better god than I ever could've imagined. Sometimes being a good god isn't just about having the most power. It's about making the best decisions with the power that you already have."

Ares nodded and smiled. "I'll carry those words with me forever, Ra. I never really got the chance to properly thank you for the power and opportunity that you bestowed upon me in the Lost Sands five years ago. You saved my life and helped me meet a great friend of mine."

"Amon, right?" Ra said and reached out, poking his index finger to Ares' heart. "I can feel your sorrow. You think that Amon's gone? Being petrified does not mean that he has perished, Ares. Come, take my hand," he said, holding his hand out to Ares. "I'll show you."

Show me what? Ares hesitated for a moment before reaching out and taking Ra's hand. There was a flash of light that detonated before eyes and he felt himself being lifted upward. A fast gust of wind rushed into his face and Ares suddenly found himself standing on a lush meadow of green grass. His heart was pounding and he looked up to see that it was nighttime. His eyes widened when he saw that there were three massive moons in the night sky. And the sky wasn't black as it was back in Terrador. Instead, it was a mixture of purple, dark blue, and white, creating an amalgam of brilliant lights that streamed across the sky. In the far distance there were mountains that stretched upward with peaks that were blanketed entirely in snow, something that Ares had only read about in books.

A brisk breeze gusted through the valley and Ares closed his eyes, letting the wind blow back his blonde hair. He inhaled the fresh air, smiling. "Where are we?" Ares turned to Ra.

"This is Heaven, the world of the gods," Ra said, folding his arms. "This is where all of the gods live." He pointed to one mountain in particular that was much taller than the rest, its peak vanishing into the clouds. "That is Mount Olympus, where your pantheon of gods gathers. Come, I will escort you there. I know that your new family is waiting to meet you," he said, turning to begin walking across the verdant field of grass towards the mountain in the distance.

Gods? Meeting me? Ares' body stiffened and he exhaled, shaking his head slowly. "This is a lot, you know. For the past couple of years, I've just been living in the desert. I didn't even thinking about meeting other humans and now I'm going off to go and meet legendary gods. I don't know, I'm just a little nervous."

Ra stopped and raised an eyebrow at Ares. "You're the Hellas god of war, what do you have to be nervous about? Besides … you have a great Guardian to protect you if anything goes wrong."

Ares blinked, confused for a moment. Suddenly he was flicked in the back of the head, and went flipping through the air. He crashed down on the dirt several feet away. The boy's head popped up from the ground, sputtering blades of grass from his mouth. He turned angrily at whoever had assaulted him and his eyes widened when he saw that Amon was standing there, snorting air from the two holes in his face that were supposed to be his nostrils.

Miss me, Ares? Amon grumbled, reaching up and pounding his chest with a heavy thump.

Ares' eyes lit up with elation and he raced forward, tears gleaming in the corners of his eyes as he wrapped his arms around the gigantic rock golem's tough leg. He squeezed the rock tightly, never wanting to let go. "It's never the same without you, big guy. Of course, I missed you."

Amon got down on one knee and wrapped his giant rocky arms around the god and embraced him lightly. *I missed you too, friend. Mithra freed me from my petrified stone form. I am quite grateful to him.*

Ares grinned as he pulled back from the hug. "I'll be sure to thank that old bastard the next time I see him then! Oh, and did he tell you that I beat up Ahriman? You wouldn't believe how hard I knocked him down!" The boy simulated swift punches in the air. He lowered his hands to his side and chuckled. "I want to thank you, Amon."

Amon tilted his head to the side. *For what?*

Ares held out his fist. "For always being there for me. Even when you're a frozen statue, I know you're still there with me."

Amon grunted and reached out, lightly tapping his fist to Ares' knuckles. You're acting awfully soft right now, Ares. You're scaring me. But of course I'll always be there for you. You're my best friend, after all.

The god of war put his hands on his hips and beamed. "That's never going to change." He held out his fist, smiling up at his friend.

Amon snorted and bumped his giant, rocky fist against Ares'.

It's good to be back.

"Now that the two of you have been reunited, I believe that it's time for us to get going, no?" Ra said, motioning for Ares and Amon to follow him towards Olympus. "There are many gods that are awaiting your arrival."

Ares and Amon exchanged quick glances before trudging after Ra. Ares exhaled, feeling his heart rate beginning to pick up pace as he walked across the green meadow, crushing grass underneath his boots. *Things are going to change after this, aren't they? I'm not going to be just a hermit deity that hides out in the Lost Sands. I'm going to be a part of a pantheon of gods that are just like me! Maybe they're even stronger. The journey that I just endured surely was nothing compared to what's ahead because I have the weirdest feeling that this just the beginning.*

My name is Ares and I am Hellas' new god of war.

***

Bator leaned forward, his heart pounding. He stared at the stub where his hand had been only hours before. It was healed and the blood had stopped hemorrhaging from the wound, but his hand was permanently gone. The irritating cheers of thousands of elated men filled his ears, but Bator's head was lowered as he trudged through the streets of Persepolis.

He staggered into a dark alleyway, allowing the shadows to swallow him in blackness. The man's face contorted into a furious scowl as he breathed heavily from his nose. Pressing one palm against a dirty wall, Bator limped through the alleyway alone. However, he spotted a flicker of movement above him and watched as a graceful man descended from the sky and landed in the center of the alley in front of the weary mercenary.

The mysterious figure had lengthy black hair with spiked golden earrings that hung from both lobes of his ears. He had a dark robe that was thrown over a red shirt the color of a burning flame. The man smiled slightly as he looked at Bator with his flashy emerald eyes. "Oh, look. A one-eyed man. You remind me a bit of another god that I know, Odin. Have you heard of him?"

"I haven't heard of such a deity before," Bator growled.

"Such rage radiates from you," the man said with a light chuckle filled with glee as he slowly paced around Bator. "Hatred forged clearly from an event that has scarred you, no? Something that cannot be undone. I recognize that look in your eye. You're suffering."

"What do you know of suffering?" Bator grumbled, keeping his eye trained on the stranger. His hand went to his sheathed sickle and he clenched his jaw. "Who are you?"

"My name is Loki. I am a god from the Aesir pantheon," the man said with a gentle bow. A slow, mischievous smile cracked across his lips. "I have come with a particular proposition for you, mortal."

"A proposition?"

"Your thirst for vengeance is far too clear. I can see the bloodlust in the reflection of your eye. You hate someone, right? After all, they're the one who did this to you." Loki waved to Bator's stump of an arm. The mercenary lowered his head. "But I can grant you strength beyond any ordinary human. Strength to do anything you want. What do you want?"

Bator's eye lit up and he gaped at the god, his arms trembling. "I desire power. Power to destroy my enemies. Power to bring me wealth. *Power to destroy … Tetsu Hayashi!*" He grinded his teeth, his single hand balling up into a fist that was clutched so tightly that his knuckles were pure white.

Loki grinned wickedly and reached down to his belt, unsheathing a tiny knife that looked like it was used to spread butter. He twirled it and jabbed the glistening blade into his wrist. The weapon bit into his skin, causing dark-red blood to ooze from the self-inflicted wound. The twinkling fluid trickled down the god's arm and Loki thrust the injury close to Bator, who flinched. "Then drink. Become mine. I will grant you the power that you seek. But in exchange … you will become my *God Slayer*."

About the Author

Brandon Chen is a freshman at New York University and a self-published author. He has been writing stories since about the age of twelve. His two current novels consist of the first two installments of the Age of Darkness series. He intends on continuing writing books in the young adult fantasy genre for his readers to enjoy.

Made in the USA
Las Vegas, NV
20 February 2021

18194410R00223